Jester
(revised 2nd ed.)
by Geoff Hart

Diskeuasis
Publishing

Copyright

Diaskeuasis Publishing
112 Chestnut Ave.
Pointe-Claire, Quebec
H9R 3B1 Canada
http://www.geoff-hart.com/fiction/

Dedications and thanks

Always and forever, to Shoshanna, for giving me time and encouragement to write, and joy in writing and so much else. To Mom and Dad, for giving me the courage to make my own path through life, the ability to speak my piece without fear, and only good reasons to write this story. To Matthew and Alison, for teaching me things about myself I'd never have learned otherwise—and in the hope I've given you reason to write your own stories, but never this one. To Mark Baker, Brent Buckner, Andy Fraser, Phil Jones, Charles Kellen, Rob Perry, and Guy Shimwell, for many shared tales and lessons in their telling. To Beth Friedman for editorial assistance and encouragement—but long ago and for an early draft, so don't blame her. To John Renish for a thorough and patient review. To Jody Negley, for a lesson in courage. Last but not least, to Thelma Mariano for helping me to find the soul of this story.

ACHARAN DESERT

Amelior

Kardmin

Borderkeep

Kelfan   PASS   Arden

THE SOUTHWOOD (SIDHE)

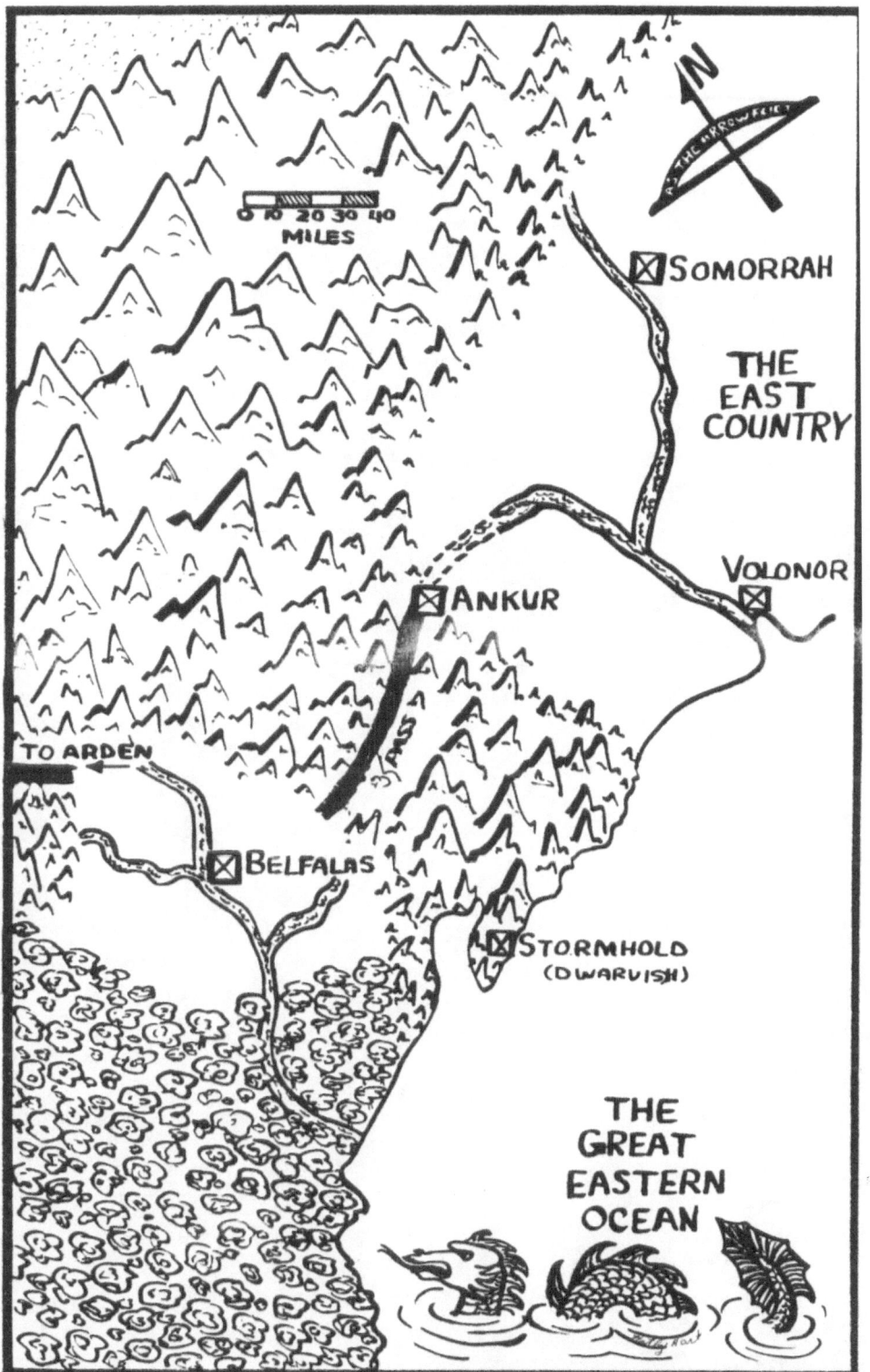

Chapter 1: A walk in the woods

Ankur's not so foul as some cities, and provides my livelihood at Court. Yet it's still a city, with foul air and far too many people. When my distaste grows too much, I'm forced to leave for a time and seek my peace in the woodlands of my youth. Far from those who, appearances notwithstanding, are more my kin than the beasts of the woods. To most, the forest's uncomfortable at best, when it ignores them and their sojourn's brief; when it doesn't ignore them, it's cruel and unforgiving. Yet it's the only place where what I *appear* to be means naught—where what lies within is all that matters. There's an acceptance here, entirely nonverbal, that renews me and grants me for a time the reserves of strength I need to face those who judge me solely by my veneer. Such escapes help me endure my lot.

So it was that I wandered along a game trail, following fresh spoor— purely for the joy of tracking, for my pack was heavy with the best the royal kitchen could provide and there was no need to feed myself. My spirit was already lightening and my breath came easily in the clean air. Easily for the first time in weeks.

The deer I'd been following and hoped to see veered from the trail, as if it were avoiding something. Kneeling to investigate, the reason became obvious: a blood trail, and the deep, forked impressions of a boar's feet in the spongy, fragrant earth. Boars were unpleasant company at the best of times; wounded, they were best avoided. I gritted my teeth and paid closer heed to my surroundings, for someone was hunting here illegally; no forester would have let a wounded animal escape to die alone and in agony in these woods. Yet I saw no human footprints paralleling the wounded beast's path. If not the hunter's responsibility, then it became mine. Though no longer a forester, years of training weren't something lightly set aside.

A boar, even wounded, was nothing to face lightly, and I had only a short spear and my belt knife, more suitable for discouraging brigands than facing the fiercest animal in these woods. Casting about, I found a solid branch perhaps two hands-span long and an inch thick to serve as a cross-hilt, and grubbing in the rich loam beneath a nearby spruce, found the tree's roots. I cut loose a couple feet of root, and stripped the bark and rootlets and soil until naught remained but the slick, elastic root surface. Exerting my strength, I lashed the homemade crosspiece to my spear, and leaned on it to test its strength. It sagged, but didn't slide down the shaft under my weight. With time, the roots would dry and tighten; in the meantime, I hoped their grip would suffice.

Without further delay, lest my courage fail, I followed the boar's trail. Of the emotions that warred in my breast, anger predominated: this wasn't what I'd come here to seek, yet it had found me, and there was no hope of peace until I fulfilled my responsibility to the animal.

I forced the anger away, for I needed all my concentration to avoid stumbling across the beast, and the blood trail weakened as the wound scabbed over. There was little wind, and what there was gusted unpredictably from several directions. After perhaps an hour, spear cradled in both hands, ready to ground and brace against a charge, I found the boar resting on his side deep within a pine thicket. He snorted as a stray breeze carried my scent, and staggered to his feet, defiance glowing in bloodshot, piggy eyes. Bristly, coarse grey hair grew in irregular patches across his body. He was larger than a hunting dog and brawnier, his head level with my own. A chest wound had stained and splashed him with gore, and that wound reopened as I watched. Bright blood trickled, falling to glue together the browning pine needles. His breathing came raggedly, pierced with a gurgling whistle; he'd been hit in a lung. I hurt in sympathy. Warm pig smell mingled with the tang of blood, and we stood there, he and I, uncomfortably alike in certain ways, watching each other warily.

This boar was a giant of his kind, and outweighed me by a hundred pounds or more. My spear seemed unequal to the contest against curved tusks long as my hand and the unconquerable will that drives a boar down the shaft of an impaling spear and still leaves enough fury to savage the man handling it. It was no encounter I anticipated with any glee; indeed, had he been unwounded, I'd have fled up the nearest tree without a second thought and waited for him to leave. But he was wounded enough to miss a step as he gathered his legs beneath him, and I'd faced a wounded boar before. The whole matter became moot as he broke the standoff with his charge.

Even wounded as he was, I had to be quick. As he came at me, I dropped my pack, then grounded and braced the spear. For the second time that day, the boar ran himself onto sharp steel, burying it a good dozen inches in his chest before the broad crosspiece behind the blade brought him up short, spear bending under the impact and trying to spring from my grip. A gout of blood washed over my hands and streamed onto the forest floor, and his agonized squeal echoed in the still air. His breath blew hot on my face, and it took all my strength to hold that spear firm against his last desperate lunge to free himself. If he'd not been weakened by that first wound, I'd never have held him, but he'd lost too much blood, and sagged to his knees after one last abortive effort to wrench himself free. I withdrew the spear from his wound with difficulty, violated muscle spasming and gripping the blade, and watched him warily. Even this near death, he glared, trying to toss his head and gore me.

I changed my grip on the spear's shaft and plunged the blade into his throat, severing the great artery that pulsed there beneath layers of corded muscle. More blood rushed from the wound to soak the ground, but this wound was mortal. With a quiver and a last plaintive squeal, the massive body subsided.

I took a deep breath, forcing the tightness in my chest to subside. An edge of the blade had embedded itself in the bones of his spine, and it took considerable effort to free it. That done, I wiped the blade on his ugly pelt, then did my best to wipe the blood from my hands with the clean litter that covered the forest floor. I hesitated before leaving, and cast one last look back at my vanquished opponent. But the day was waning, and I had one more task before returning to my own concerns.

I followed the boar's back trail, easy enough given how quickly the blood increased as I neared the site of the original confrontation. My path took me towards the village that lay at the forest's edge, and led me to a clearing. The greenlit afternoon silence stole my breath, and the pale sunlight that shone through the spring's new leaves was magical, so despite my caution, it took a moment before I noticed the clearing's occupants. When I did, my reverie vanished and I crouched under cover of some bushes.

Through the leaves, I saw an attractive women of middle years, long brown hair flowing unbound around her shoulders. She knelt across the clearing from me, eyes warily scanning the walls of early-spring growth that enclosed the glade. I remained still, and escaped her notice. She wore a man's leather breeches and jerkin, but the undershirt that spilled from beneath the jerkin was finely embroidered. On the ground by her knees, a somewhat older man lay beside a shattered spear, legs splashed with blood and serviceable woodsman's clothing stained with leaf mould. He had black hair, sun-lightened or beginning to grey, and worn shorter than the current fashion; his weather-beaten complexion spoke of someone who'd spent more time outdoors than in, but the quality of his sword's sheath and hilt told me he was no mere woodsman. The pallor underlying his tan confirmed he was wounded, had any doubt remained.

My anger faded. These were no poachers—rather, unfortunates who'd blundered across the boar's path and been attacked before they could climb a tree. Yet bitterness replaced my anger, washing over me like a green and spiteful wave, for it was spring and I knew why these two had sought out such a sheltered spot—had intruded on my woods and ruined my solitude. I wallowed a moment in the feeling, a grimace twisting my face and bitter tears starting from my eyes. But self-pity's a poor path for one such as me, for it leads to self-murder—or worse, for at least self-murder brings a clean end. I fought that mood down before it could take hold, my instincts for self-preservation reasserting themselves. Envy was replaced by revulsion that I could behave as my foes at Court accused, and revulsion was replaced by a cleansing anger at my own weakness. Finally, concern replaced all else, and once more in control, I stepped from behind the concealing bushes, leaving the spear.

These woods had been nurtured for the King's pleasure, and were well stocked with game animals of all sorts, including the boars so beloved of huntsmen. The woman feared the worst, for as I rose from concealment, she seized the broken spear and made ready to defend herself. Her eyes widened in shock at the sight of me, and I found myself pleasantly surprised she had the wit to avoid fainting—most of the women at Court are too well-trained in that reflex—but I held back a smile, knowing what effect that had on those who didn't know me. Yet even now that she recognized I wasn't what she'd feared, she remained wary. I strode into the glade, my steps silent upon the grass that had sprung up here where the light was stronger, my arms open and empty-handed, hoping she'd accept me as an ally if not a friend.

The man moaned and her gaze went straight to him. I froze, not wanting to startle her with a sudden movement. As I waited, sunlight warm on my back, the man's eyes opened. I was close enough to see the blankness give way to shock as he focused on me. Callused as I was, that awakened a familiar pain in my chest, and it was faint consolation that he'd been expecting far worse. He made a tentative move for his weapon but subsided with an agonized expression as his wound made itself felt. His lady made as if to interpose herself, but halted when he placed a hand upon her arm. He forced himself up onto one elbow and reappraised me, his initial shock replaced by something more like confidence.

When you're born a dwarf in a world of normal men and women, you soon learn to abandon any hope of the trappings of normalcy: friendship, apprenticeship to a suitable guild, and a place to live free of mockery and the torment of being different in a world that doesn't forgive differences. Most certainly, you abandon any hope of the abiding attachments that might sustain you through your life. That's not to say you abandon the available substitutes—in a kingdom as depraved as ours can be, such things can be bought, and there are always those who want something "unique" to brag of. And while my flesh is strong and (despite appearances) healthy, my spirit weakens often, and at times I've sacrificed my self-respect in the face of a greater need, knowing as I did that the fulfillment I sought remained ever out of reach.

What you never achieve is acceptance. I admit that in my more honest moments.

I made my first words light and reassuring, though the tightness in my chest diminished the intended effect. "Fear not, good folk, I'm Morley, the King's jester. I'm here to aid you." Though deficient in so many other ways, I'd been born with a fine voice. The man relaxed further, though his lady remained wary. The couple looked familiar, though I was sure I'd not seen them here at the King's home away from Court; it must have been an overheard description that evoked that recognition. But I had more important things to concern me.

His voice was steady. "The boar?"

"Dead, Sir, by my hand. They're tough beasts, but your aim was very nearly true."

"Truer than the spear's shaft. It surprised us, and I had no time to brace properly." His face grew ashen as he struggled to rise and failed. "It wounded me when the spear gave way. Mercifully, my lady was spared any wound." One hand relinquished the spear to caress the back of his neck. There was something more than formal devotion in that gesture. Though it was something forever denied to me, it was no less pleasant to watch now that I'd pushed away my envy.

"If you'll lie still, I can help." Then, apologetically. "It will hurt." I knelt beside him and appraised the long slash wound that curved tusks had opened along the length of his thigh. There was blood aplenty, but the wound appeared shallow. Most importantly, I saw no bone; rather, there was surface muscle laved by a slow welling of fresh blood. The boar had touched neither artery nor tendon, and despite the blood loss, it looked more the sort of wound to provide a fine scar than something that would lame him in his old age. If the boar had surprised them, he must have been fast indeed to have escaped with so little harm. His eyes narrowed as I drew my knife, but he forced calm upon his face again. The woman watched me narrowly, hands once again tight upon the spear's shaft.

"Trust me," I soothed. "Despite my fearsome visage, I mean no harm." My choice of words startled them into an exchange of guilty looks, but they relaxed as I continued talking. "Modesty notwithstanding, I'll have to bare the wound and cut a bandage." I did this, setting aside what remained of the cloth, and he stoically bore the pain. Once I'd removed enough clothing to reveal bare flesh, the old scars that lay there told me the source of his courage—this one had fought before, many times, and was no stranger to wounds and surgery.

I spoke reassuringly to the woman. "If you'd help him, bring fresh water. There's a stream perhaps twenty yards that way. Mind that the water is fresh, and bears no scum or debris." I pointed without taking my eyes off the wound, and handed her my spare water skin. She left, and from the corner of my eye, I saw his obvious concern. "Fear not. The boar's dead, and I saw no sign of others."

"My thanks for killing him. A slow death when the wound goes bad is no fate even for such as he." He grimaced as I pressed on the flesh on either side of the wound, exploring until I was satisfied there was no deeper damage or debris embedded in the wound. "Would that my first thrust had slain him and spared you the effort!"

By now, the woman was out of sight. I took a skin of fortified wine from my pack. "This will hurt, as you well know, but it's necessary."

He grinned, lips tight but appreciation replacing apprehension in his eyes. "Aye, but better that by far than river water."

We shared a smile, then I washed the wound thoroughly, careful to ensure that I'd missed nothing and watchful for any new bleeding. This time, I saw a suspicious puckering of the flesh. Looking closer, I found and removed a long splinter that had come to rest in flesh after being expelled from the spear's shattered shaft. Then I debrided the edges of the cut with a fine pair of scissors I'd purchased long ago. He bore the pain stoically, even though I'd distanced the woman to protect his dignity should he cry out.

By the time she returned, I'd cleaned the wound as best as possible under the circumstances and begun stitching it closed with some fine thread I carried in my kit. She watched, unflinching, and my respect for her grew. As I worked, she spoke in a soft, pleasant voice.

"What brings the King's jester alone to these woods?"

"My feet," I replied, more brusquely than I'd intended, avoiding her question. I hadn't intended to give offense, but bitterness was always close to hand for me. From the corner of my eye, I saw them exchange glances while I used the river water to bathe the skin around the wound, careful not to contaminate the wound itself as I cleared away the clotted blood. With the wound now stanched, I covered it with peat moss from my kit and applied a bandage. It wasn't as fine a job as one of the King's surgeons could have done, but under the circumstances, I was proud of my handiwork.

"You'll need a proper surgeon to tend to the wound when you return to town, but your leg ought to hold you 'til then. I've packed the wound with peat moss to keep it from festering, but you'll need to change the dressing soon." I verified that the bandage was tight, then rose and washed my hands with what was left of the water. Then I dried my hands on my jerkin and turned to go.

"Wait," he called as I moved to leave the clearing. "Can we not reward you for your help?"

Our eyes met, and I read the expected pity in his gaze, but heard honest gratitude in his voice. "The King cares for me well enough. I'd stay and see you home, but..." I shrugged awkwardly. Once again he looked surprised, then grave as he replied.

"Know then, Morley, that you have the gratitude of Bram of Ankur for what you have done. Should you ever have need, seek me out." He offered his hand, and after a moment's hesitation, I took it. There were calluses there, and old scars across the back, and though he didn't exert his full swordsman's strength, neither did he draw back in revulsion nor grasp my hand limply as he might have with a child.

Now I remembered why he'd seemed so familiar. He was one of the King's advisors, and as ambassador for Ankur, he'd traveled widely. The lady, of course, would be his wife Margrethe. Their return after an absence of more than a year had been the talk of the Court, and I'd looked forward to meeting him, taking his measure, and learning where he fit within the network of alliances and counter-alliances that was life in Ankur.

What little I knew said he'd come from Amelior in the far West, acquiring a measure of infamy to equal the respect in which he was widely held. The infamy was natural for one who'd broken the bloodoath and survived; the respect was equally natural for one who'd played a key role in the war against his former countrymen these nine years past. The couple had been married since the war ended, and—spiteful rumors notwithstanding—I'd heard no reliable evidence either had been unfaithful. In Ankur, there'd have been no want of opportunity.

Our eyes met again, and I was warmed by what I saw. The pity was gone, and in its place lay respect, something I'd rarely seen directed at me. Uncomfortable with the emotions that raised and at the length of the silence that had fallen between us, I turned to go.

"I thank you, Bram. Rest assured I shall."

"And thank you for meeting my responsibility to the animal." I grunted assent, and left to reclaim my spear, for I had much to think on and much to resolve. Without looking back, I turned and moved off. I'd told my liege I'd return that day, but now found I needed more time to think. It was likely this would be my last visit to these woods for some time, and scant time remained to restore the peace I so desperately needed before the King's entourage returned to Ankur.

Chapter 2: Another twist of the dagger

When I'd chosen to leave the woodland life and seek my fortune in the city, my foster father shook his head in incomprehension. It was beyond him why I'd leave the safety of the forest and secure employment as one of the King's foresters. Though my father was learned in his own way, and knew the songs the minstrels had taught him and the histories that lay behind them, he could never understand my need to learn more of our land and seek the same acceptance in Ankur I'd gained in these woods. I wasn't sure of my own reasons, save that the other foresters had not so much loved me as accepted me, and despite having earned their respect, I felt driven to find something more. What that was I couldn't say, but if I could find it anywhere, I felt sure it would be in Ankur.

"And how will you provide for yourself?" my father demanded. "How will you protect yourself from those who will torment you because of what you are?"

I'd spent long nights pondering this, and had an answer ready. "I'll earn my living by my wits and by the music you've taught me. Perhaps I'll even find employ at the King's Court, for he has no jester to mock him and teach him wisdom, and who better to fill such a role than one who has been mocked his whole life and learned wisdom thereby?"

Gaining employment had been a near thing, for though it was easy enough to play for my dinner and a warm, dry place to sleep in the many taverns of Ankur, I acquired more than a few bruises and had once or twice been in peril of my life from those who hated and feared me based solely on my appearance. But I'd fought down what rose within me and I'd persevered, enduring the city's stench and foulness and trying not to remember how clean and pleasing the forests had been by comparison, until I earned an audience with the King. The quality of my music and the gentle mockery with which I'd reminded him of his own flaws had gained me a room in the palace and the King's protection, if not yet his love.

It hadn't gained me the acceptance I'd fooled myself I could achieve, and even the protection wasn't always as efficacious as one might wish.

"Come now, little man. Surely even you can leap this high?" The taunting emerged from amidst a greasy mass of jowls. Because I kept my expression neutral and failed to furnish the response he'd sought, he grew more angry than mocking and waved a large fist beneath my nose. Arms akimbo, face calm but chest aching, I waited patiently for him to tire of his sport.

Another voice chimed in. "Jump, dwarf, or we'll teach you some respect for your betters."

I kept my voice calm, in part by imagining my hand drawing the long dagger belted at my side and cutting him a second mouth. A week in Ankur had done much to erode the calm I'd won in my brief sojourn in the woods. "Sir, I'm the King's Fool by occupation, not by wit." Then, noticing a familiar tall figure striding towards me, I couldn't resist adding a taunt of my own. "But do enlighten me, Sir, how it is that you should have the wit of a Fool and not the profession?"

He made as if to strike me and I stood my ground, daring him with my smile. Then Bram's hand fell on Fatty's shoulder, spinning him around to face the King's Advisor. "Surely you haven't forgotten the penalties for striking the Fool, Osric?" The fat man hesitated, then glared at my savior. "I thought not. Now unless I'm mistaken, that Lady yonder—your wife, is she not?—beckons for your attention."

I smiled gratefully as Osric dropped my motley hat to the floor with a clash of bells, spurned it with his heel, and strutted away among his friends, without looking back. But beneath that smile, my anger seethed, and it was several breaths before the pain in my chest eased and the pounding of my heart slowed. I tucked my hands in my belt to hide their trembling, as Bram bent to retrieve my headgear, not meeting my eyes and granting me time to collect myself. But his strong hand fell on my shoulder and squeezed as he set the hat back in place. From anyone else, I might have mistaken this for pity, but from Bram, I'd learned to accept the gesture for what it was: understanding and commiseration. That lifted my mood more than anything I could have done.

"I suppose I should be thankful, Bram, that he torments me only briefly. His wife must endure him constantly." We shared a smile and parted, he rejoining his wife Margrethe, a faint limp evident in his gait, and me continuing on my rounds, sprinkling a witticism here and a song there, and keeping an ear open for words I'd report later to the King—and humiliating myself as the situation required, of course, for my job was to play the fool, not to leave that responsibility to others.

I passed the evening that way, uneventfully, though as always, much was said—and left unsaid—that I would report to my King or keep in mind for the future. As always, more of my countrymen laughed at me than with me. But that was something I'd long since learned to deal with, soothing its gall with enough ale to dull the pain's edge without dulling my mind's edge. Indeed, with that aid, I could believe my lot was better than it might have been. For instance, had I stayed with my birth parents rather than fleeing into the woods, I'd surely be dead now or crippled from their incessant beatings. Instead, my foster father had helped me earn the self-esteem that sustained me against the worst these people could inflict. Now, deep within, I had strength on which

I could draw when times grew bad—strength that let me laugh at them even as they laughed at me. It made the evening tolerable.

As the night grew older and the revelers drifted away, alone or in pairs, I bent my path nearer the high table and watched for signs the King would soon be seeking his chambers. So it was that when he rose to leave, I was positioned to watch the few who still remained at table and note their expression or carefully affected lack of expression as their Lord left.

John had been a warrior before claiming his throne, and given the times we lived in, had been given ample opportunity to keep his skills sharp; that fitness, my delayed departure, and my inadequate legs conspired to keep me some distance behind him. I arrived at his chambers in time to see his squire struggling to remove a new pair of boots, not yet broken in well enough to slip easily from the King's feet. At the jingle of bells, my liege looked up in distaste from his strivings, his look slowly easing into tired affection. "So, my short spy. What heard you that passed beneath my notice?"

"The musing of the mice, my liege, and the ruminations of those more nearly my height—your hounds, that is." He snorted, and encouraged by his mood, I continued. "And—happily—little else to distract you from matters of such gravity." I swept him a bow that ended with my hat tucked beneath one arm, the other arm indicating his boots, with which the squire still struggled.

The first boot, not without some reluctance, conceded the field to the perspiring squire, and the King's sigh was loud in the quiet room. "By such small joys are my days lightened, Morley. Yet surely there was something of wisdom in the musings of the mice?"

I returned his smile, pleased to have my words and my self thus welcomed. "Aye. There were those, Osric included, who made their usual halfhearted mutterings against you." I named their names, and his face darkened, but he said nothing. "Your counselor Raphael defended you, of course, sufficiently strongly that Osric and company sought their diversion elsewhere."

The King spat on the rushes. "And another loyal counselor defended you against that diversion. Morley, I counsel you to exercise your considerable wit more judiciously lest you find yourself again in need of aid."

I fought down the outrage that arose at that warning, for I'd done nothing to justify his censure, and the accusation's injustice stung me. "Sire, I—"

"Peace, Morley." The tone was quiet, but the command was clear enough to stop my protest before it escaped my throat, where it caught, tangled and blocking my breath for a moment. In the silence, the second boot yielded with a suddenness that propelled the squire backwards onto his rump, and the King shot him an annoyed glance. "I wasn't accusing you, but rather warning you. Were I you, I'd watch my steps upon returning to my chamber."

I bowed, bells jingling, to conceal the sudden flush in my cheeks, and made sure to swallow the lump in my throat before I spoke. "A wise suggestion, Sire."

"And one whose wisdom I shall ensure by seeing you home in good company." He gestured at the squire, who had picked himself up and set the boots against the wall by the bed. Bowing, that worthy clapped a hand upon my shoulder and steered me towards the door.

"Good night, my Fool."

I stopped at the door. "Good night, my liege." I bowed again, bells jingling, and the squire and I sought my chamber in companionable silence. He left me at the door, with a slight nod that might have passed for a bow if one were feeling charitable.

My room was a tiny afterthought left behind when the architect mismeasured that part of the palace. As I set my key in the lock, I heard a heavy footfall from behind me. Fatty again? I spun on my heel to face the sound, preparing wearily to defend myself, but instead, faced an old man, unkempt grey hair spilling over sloping shoulders draped in stained, threadbare robes. The cautionary hand he held open towards me gave me pause, and I put aside the blade I'd drawn without thinking, watching his seamed face. There was evidence of long study in the lines graven about his eyes by years of squinting under inadequate light, and traces of soot from cheap candles deepened those lines in the weak lamplight; the deep set of those wide-spaced eyes hinted at wisdom. In contrast to the rest of his appearance, those eyes were sharp and hard as tempered steel, and I forced alertness despite my fatigue.

"I would speak with thee, Morley." His voice was rich and self-assured, but pitched low and holding none of the condescension of most who addressed me. He had an odd, antique sort of accent, with a richness that warmed my musician's ears after the dull sameness of Court speech. Though we'd just met, I found myself liking him, and the voice of caution spoke more faintly at the back of my mind.

"I'm afraid you have the advantage, m'lord. You are...?"

"Merely a simple scholar, Orgrim by name, with an offer that should interest you. Is there somewhere we might talk?"

I indicated my chamber with a wave, and he accepted with a nod. Humble though the tiny room was, it was home and I showed him in with all the misplaced pride of a host. I urged him to make himself com-

11

fortable in my one chair, too large for me by half, and sat on my bed. A child's bed, but large enough and a comfortable enough nest when my life's burdens grew too much to bear. I turned my gaze upon the scholar. "Well, Milord Orgrim. What brings you in search of the King's Fool?"

Those sharp eyes focused with surprising intensity, seeking something, then the intensity subsided as swiftly as it had appeared. Orgrim's voice was soothing, erasing my momentary apprehension at this appraisal. "Perhaps 'tis I who am the fool, Morley, but I feel certain we can aid each other."

I allowed myself a look of polite interest, stifling a yawn that nearly escaped me. "How so?"

Again, that disturbing intensity crossed his face before vanishing into the depths of those eyes. Those unpredictable flashes of inner fire made it seem as if Orgrim had spent so long with his dusty scrolls that he'd forgotten how to mask his emotions against the scrutiny of those accustomed to courtly life, but it might only have been that I was so tired, and sought shadows where there were none. "You see," he went on, ignoring my yawn, "it may be within my power to help you achieve normal size and appearance."

I blinked in shock, now very much awake, torn between the need to hear him out and the rage that arose at the thought this was just some new and particularly cruel joke at my expense. I'm sure in that moment that despite what I'd learned in my year at Court, my emotions stood as clear on my face as Orgrim's had so recently done. I took a deep breath and mastered myself well enough there was no trace of anger when I spoke. "If I heard you right, then you mock me, and I have no taste for such humor." My hand clenched on my dagger's hilt until my knuckles hurt, but he ignored that provocation and his voice was calm in reply.

"You do me an injustice, friend jester. I am quite serious. I believe I can help you in this manner, else I should never have been so cruel as to mention the possibility. Are you willing to explore this possibility?"

The sincerity in his voice was so real, and I so badly wanted to believe, that I almost missed his last words. There were tears in my eyes at the vision he dangled before me, and a knot of uncertainty the size of a mace head formed in my gut as I strove for a reply. My teeth had clenched so tight I could do naught but nod. And again, lest he'd missed it.

A satisfied look descended, erasing that intensity I'd noted before, and rising, he moved the few steps necessary to cross the room and kneel at my feet. He placed a firm yet gentle hand on my shoulder, and the compassion in his eyes was such that all my tension fled from me in a great gasp and all wariness vanished. I began weeping, great racking sobs torn from the depths of my being. He knelt and pulled me to him, holding my head on his shoulder until I regained control. Then, squeezing my shoulder as he turned away, he left me with the promise he'd return the next day and urged me to be patient until then. I vowed I would be, lying through my teeth.

Later, I lay in bed, too tired to think straight, yet too anxious to sleep. Fighting off a cloying sense of unreality, a fear began to grow in me, for only powerful magic could bring about the change Orgrim had proposed, and magic had been gone from our lands for generations. Indeed, the dark tales from the past that informed the bleaker of my songs made it clear why our ancestors had bloodily cleansed themselves of any taint of magic before undertaking the Exodus. But the dread in those songs warred with the cynical pragmatism that had kept me alive for so long. At last, it was my bladder that dominated and forced me to seek the castle privies, for I'd long since learned that the size of my room opposed the use of a chamber pot. I wrapped my robes about me, slid into my boots, and left the room. So lost in thought was I that I ran full into the tall figure that slid from the shadows to block my way.

Distractedly, I looked up to see who confronted me, framing an apology. I never succeeded, for before I'd completed that chain of thought, a second man seized me from behind and a third forced a gag between my teeth. The first man clutched a rag over my nose and held it there until I inhaled, smelling the sting of some drug and tasting its bitterness at the back of my throat. It was as if something heavy had crashed down upon my skull. As the corridor reeled about me, I felt the strength draining from my limbs and collapsed forward, striking the floor hard enough to feel the pain wash over me despite the drug's numbing effects. As my mind fled somewhere far away, I heard words echoing in the expanding, pain-shot void that was my head.

"We'll show the little rat, won't..."

***

I awoke, supine and wrapped in a darkness so thick my first thoughts were of blindness caused by the drug or by striking my head on the floor. Despite the pain, I brought a hand to my eyes and probed at the blood that had caked there. I hadn't imagined falling, and the blackness crowded even closer, a tangible pressure on my skull. I felt icy fear run down my spine and loosen my bowels, but I fought it hard, squeezing my eyes shut for what little comfort that gave and forcing my breathing to slow. I was increasingly aware of my bladder's fullness.

The gag was no longer in my mouth, so I inhaled, not without some difficulty. Stale incense and a residue of torch smoke clung to the air, slowly dispersing in a sluggish draft. Thick silence hung about me, silence so intense I feared for my hearing. But the sound of my gasping breath reassured me, and the darkness pressed less heavily. I began mustering my resources, the same ones I'd learned as a child sleeping in the forest, burdened with the sure knowledge there were wolves and perhaps other, more horrible things, beyond the fire's light where I couldn't see them. Nonetheless, a scuttling sound in the dark brought the fear back stronger than before, for here there was no fire, and no foster father to reassure and protect me. It was several moments before I could force another breath.

The scuttling noise ceased, which was in some ways worse than had it continued. After all, something I couldn't see was now watching me. I cleared my throat and swallowed hard to return my heart to its accustomed place, and the sound echoed. A small, enclosed space? As the thick atmosphere swallowed the first echoes, the scuttling noise came again, now moving away. Sweat sprang out on my brow and trickled in a clammy stream across my temples, for I still lay upon my back.

Once more I slowed my breathing, and my thoughts began to clear. There was a near-physical tearing sensation as I forced away the last of the drug's grasp, and a calmness descended. Someone had intended to "fix me", but since I still breathed, the fix had obviously stopped short of murder. Some twisted idea of humor? The thought comforted me. I lay still, hoping my awakening senses could offer some clue as to my whereabouts. I shivered, realizing belatedly I was cold.

A distant gong sounded, muffled by a depth of intervening stone; that changed the atmosphere from stifling to merely enveloping, for it meant I was near or perhaps even in the palace. The gong rang twice more before stopping—three bells in the morning if it was the same night. From the direction of the gong, overhead as best as I could tell, I was somewhere in the lower reaches of the castle. The crypt perhaps? Or mayhap the dungeon?

Despite my bladder's urging, I lay still a little longer, cold seeping into my bones and beckoning darkness to follow. It was stone that supported me, probably a long, low slab if I was correct as to my location. I still couldn't see, but my thoughts were clearer, despite a buzzing in my ears and a warm fuzziness that had taken root behind my forehead. I'd been rendered unconscious often enough in my youth to recognize the after-effects, and it felt much like that but with a difference I couldn't place. That slight movement of the heavy air returned, reminding me there was at least one exit to this room. I only had to bestir myself and seek it. That took more effort than I'd expected, and I was scarcely able to roll onto my side before a sweeping dizziness took hold of and carried the world beyond my grasp for a time. I rested, waiting for it to return.

I continued trying to move once the world returned, resting each time the vertigo tore at me, and at last managed to sit up, shivering, my legs dangling over the edge of my resting place. I sat there until the spinning faded and left me lightheaded but able to remain upright. Then I encountered another problem.

When I tried to slip from my perch, I found myself unable to do so. My feet swung against the slick sides of the stone, an unknowable distance above a hypothetical floor, while some instinct of self-preservation screamed its adamant refusal to proceed. I couldn't force myself to step blindly into space, though chill sweat streamed down my sides from the force of my efforts. No matter how I tried to convince myself otherwise, nausea clutched at me and told me I was poised at the brink of some bottomless abyss.

The dark can do strange things to one's mind.

I have no notion of how long I sat there, sick, dizzy, sore, my world narrowed to that part of my world that was within the length of my dangling feet; I can remember no sounding of the bells, which tells me in hindsight that I sat there for less than an hour. But a solution came at last when the increasingly desperate pressure of my bladder could no longer be denied. That gave me an unorthodox but effective tool for gauging my height above the floor, and the surge of amusement at the solution's inelegance restored my morale. I parted my robes, aimed at the floor that lay somewhere below me and to the side, and pissed into the darkness.

Had there been any appreciable delay before the echo, my nerve would have broken and I would no doubt have remained there to this day. As it was, the time between the urge and the splashing on the stone was so short I couldn't have been more than my own height above the floor. Perhaps a slab in the crypt? Thus relieved—and reassured enough to contemplate such wordplay—I seized firm hold of my courage and slid off the opposite side of the stone, dropping to the floor but going to my knees as the lightness rose once more in my head. On hands and knees, I made my way in the opposite direction from the puddle I'd created until I encountered a wall. Cold and slimy though it was, it was welcome. With the wall as my guide, I groped my way to an opening that gave onto a steep flight of stairs.

I crawled up those stairs, so eager to escape my prison that I ignored the damage I did to my knees in the process. My mind dimmed and my head began to buzz again, but I kept on doggedly, shoulder brushing against the wall to keep to my path. At last, my hand encountered a fresh rush mat instead of cold stone, and I raised my head a great distance to meet the faint but welcoming light of a distant torch.

Relief at my returned sight combined with joy at my return to the world of the living. It so overwhelmed me, I swooned like any Court lady at the sight of a mouse.

Chapter 3: Orgrim

In my youth, I'd often been ill, for though long days of work in the forest's clean air had left me stronger and more robust than I'd ever expected to become, I still had a child's body and the associated vulnerabilities. One of my fondest memories was of lying in bed, shaking with a fever's chill, while my father heaped woolen sheets atop me, fed the fire until the sweat sprang out upon his forehead, and softly sang until his voice grew hoarse. I suppose it says much that I look back upon such a thing with fondness.

When consciousness returned, I lay swaddled in a soft, warm bed, though with no fire burning nearby and no quiet song to soothe me. Nonetheless, even though the rough woolens that swaddled me and held in the warmth made my bare skin itch, I was so comfortable in all other ways that I couldn't make myself care. I wiggled my toes for the joy of the sensation and savored the luxury of a child in bed in the morning, the house still asleep and no chores that couldn't be ignored for a time. I opened an eye, and found myself in an unpeopled room with rows of cots lining the walls. The infirmary.

I lay there a time, watching a spider weaving its web high up in the raftered ceiling as I listened to the muted sounds of a castle functioning smoothly in the midst of its daily routine. The ache in my head was still there, imperceptible for so long as I moved cautiously and kept my gaze from roaming; but if I forgot and moved my eyes swiftly, pain surged as if my head were being split with a hatchet. Empty as the room was, there was little to engage my attention, and even the spider moved beyond my sight. After a while, the simple pleasures of warmth, light, and a lack of pain eased me into sleep. I have dim memories of dreaming, but I rarely remember my dreams, and these were no different, hidden at depths where my conscious mind couldn't retrieve them.

The touch of a cool hand on my brow woke me, and I raised my hands to clear the sleep from my eyes. My arms were weak and light in the way they'd always felt after childhood fevers, but they responded willingly enough. The man sitting beside my bed was Orgrim, his seamed face as kind as his eyes were hard. "I trust you're well, friend Morley? It seems you had an accident, and I worried for your sake."

I tried to talk, realized with a performer's instinct that my voice would break, and cleared my throat instead. The pain that answered in my head was enough to blind me. "No accident," I replied when my vision returned and my throat felt clear enough for talk. "Someone took exception to my behavior at dinner last night and chose to teach me a lesson."

His finger pressed my lips shut. "Later, Morley. Console yourself with the thought that the malefactor shall regret having interfered with my plans." He noticed my reaction at his vengeful look, and changed the topic. "There's little time remaining. I've consulted certain auguries, and we must act tonight." He paused in thought. "Listen carefully. We must meet some hours before midnight that I may invoke the change we spoke of. The crypt should be sufficiently private."

I fought down my instinctive reaction, for I'd no desire to return there so soon; nonetheless, excitement at his promise helped me master myself, as did fear of the pain any sudden movement might awaken in my head. I'd recovered enough to attempt a jest. "Midnight in the crypt? Should I bring a virgin to sacrifice? You've left me little enough time to find one." The jest would have been better spoken in a concerned voice, but that was beyond me, so I let the words carry the irony.

He pursed his lips, displeased, and I fell silent. "This is no time to be facetious, Morley. The timing is more important than you could understand, and the location, mere convenience; if you know anywhere else as private, we can go there instead." I remained silent. "But, no, you need bring no virgin, merely yourself. Be glad that the practice of my kind of magic requires no such inconveniences." I felt a sudden cold at his tone, myths and scare-tales of dark magics conjuring themselves for my mind to dwell upon. I hesitated, and he frowned at my obvious doubt.

"Come now. Despite appearances, you're no child, and should place no stock in tales told to scare children. My profession is less distasteful than the mercenary's, who kills for a handful of coins, for I shall end no lives to earn my pay." He reached within his cloak, withdrew a small crystal vial, uncorked it, and thrust it between my lips. Assurances notwithstanding, the stained ivory ring, pallid on his hand, was ominous given the proposed location of our meeting.

"Drink this. It will hasten your recovery enough for you to be a conscious and willing participant tonight." I drank with only a slight hesitation, gagging at the oily feel and the mustiness on my tongue. Then I brightened and sat up, the pain instantly gone and vigor creeping back into my limbs.

He anticipated my question. "Fear not. You'd have no objection to any ingredient. But let it be proof that magic can produce more than ill, whatever you've heard. Now listen, for someone comes and I must be gone before she arrives." He whispered further directions concerning our rendezvous, made me repeat them, then rose in a single swift movement. I heard a door opening nearby and my eyes were drawn in that direction, mercifully without the pain that had greeted such a drastic motion scant moments earlier. I saw movement at the corner of my vision, and though I turned my gaze in that direction, I was too late. The old man was gone without a trace, the crystal flask with him, leaving no evidence he'd ever been here, apart from the clarity still spreading through my head. As I puzzled over his disappearance, a soft hand fell upon my shoulder and the voice of Bram's wife, Lady Margrethe, sounded in my ear.

"It's good to see you conscious again, Morley." Her voice was cheerful and light, but there was concern in her eyes as she hooked a stool with one foot and drew it to my bedside. "How are you feeling?"

I watched her a moment, repressing a smile of welcome until I could manage one that wouldn't look quite so appalling. I shook my head. "No pain," I replied, marveling. "My... doctor... has done a most excellent job. In fact, I think I could leave this bed right now." I started to rise, then fell back, realizing in that instant I was naked as a babe.

"Or could," I added, "were I alone. A pair of trousers, among other things, would make me more confident of my ability to depart with dignity."

A look of puzzlement crossed her face, then she laughed delightedly—and delightfully—when she caught my meaning. "I'll see to that at once. When you're dressed, if you feel well enough, come visit. Milord Husband commanded me to fetch you so you can meet our family."

"*Commanded?*"

"Yes." She smiled charmingly. "He labors under the burden of belief that he has some control over matters domestic. Let's keep the truth a secret between us."

"He wouldn't be the first husband to be disabused of that notion," I replied, smiling. "Very well: you have my word on it." We laughed, enjoying our shared secret, and it was a warm feeling indeed. She left before that warmth faded, leaving me with a parting wave of her delicate hand. I lay back, contentedly smiling. For a moment, I let thoughts of Orgrim fade before the sweet memory of her laughter. Then I pondered my incredible luck, that soon I'd be normal, that my health had returned so rapidly, and that perhaps this would mark a truly new beginning.

When my clothes arrived, borne by a skeptical court physician, I dressed hurriedly, ignoring his distaste and ill-concealed surprise at my recovery. I thanked him for his help, and left the room before he could think to question me further. In the near-empty streets outside the palace, I strode along to meet my new friends. It wasn't an opportunity I could afford to miss, whatever the remainder of that day held.

Bram was one of the King's senior advisors and ambassador to the West. Though foreign born, he could still have claimed a mansion as a reward for his part in the recent war. He hadn't done so. Instead, he'd turned down that lavish reward in favor of a smaller building, less ostentatious and farther from the palace. After our encounter with the boar, I'd researched the man and found much to my liking. For one, he was well liked by the commoners for his role in the increasingly legendary defeat of Amelior. His charity and defense of the commoners hadn't hurt his standing either. But things balance, for he was not well liked by the old nobility, who resented his example more than his origins. Nonetheless, one could take the measure of a man by the enemies he'd made and the friends he kept. Both spoke well of Bram.

Despite the house's distance from the palace, it lay in a pleasant part of the lower city. Smaller than a mansion, it was nonetheless a larger home than any I'd lived in before coming to Ankur. It was nondescript but attractive, with the main building crouched behind a low wall and a small stable nestled up against one side. There was no armed guard outside the gate, but the jagged barrier atop the wall suggested none was necessary. From what I could see, looking over the top of that wall as I descended the gentle slope towards the house, I suspected the presence of an atrium. The home was an appropriate metaphor for the man given the delicate political dance Bram played with Ankur's many unfriends, both inside and beyond the city's walls: formidable barriers without, but a warm welcome within. Bram himself had initially struck me as soft, but it was the softness of a dancer, concealing surprising strength.

I approached the gatehouse and knocked, preparing for a short wait, but my approach had been expected and the small viewport slid aside. Eyebrows furrowed when no one was visible, then those eyes narrowed and he looked down at me. Before I could give my name, the port slammed shut, echoed by the rasp of heavy bolts being drawn. The door opened, and a plainly dressed youth still in his late teens swept me a courtly bow, though without taking his eyes from me for an instant, and bade me enter. The gate shut behind me and he shot the bolts before the echoes had faded.

The gravel path leading to the door was neatly raked, and stones rolled beneath my feet, but even on the gravel, my escort moved almost too smoothly. My eyes were drawn to telltale bulges beneath his attire that suggested the presence of light armor. Moreover, a long scabbard swung against one hip, a sword's worn leather grip protruding, and a matching dagger hung on the other. Weaponry held so near to hand, even at home, confirmed my sense of enemies—significant ones—at Court. In this light, I reappraised my guide and was no longer surprised at the smoothness and economy of his motion. He was neither a youth nor a household servant, and it wasn't hard to guess his true profession.

"Lord Bram has interesting taste in... butlers." I hesitated on the last word, but if he caught my emphasis, he gave no sign.

"Thank you. This way, Sir." The floor inside the house's main door was carpeted in woolen rugs, an interesting concession to luxury. He led me through several sparse but tastefully decorated rooms, past a few closed doors, and on into the atrium whose existence I'd suspected. What I hadn't expected was the beauty of the small garden it concealed. Well tended trees and bushes drew the eye to a small pond, the ground around which was covered by moss and other low-growing plants. On the far side of this miniature forest, still vibrant with the pale green of spring and unobtrusively unnatural, there was a flat stretch of grass upon which a small blanket had been spread. Bram and Margrethe sat on the blanket, hands clasped and enjoying the peace of the moment. My guide cleared his throat, drawing their attention from each other to us.

"Ah! Morley. Welcome to our humble home." Bram rose and came to meet me, proffering a hand to be shaken. His grip was firm but not ostentatiously so, and though I'd not yet seen him bearing a sword, the suggestive calluses were still hard, the product of considerable work.

"Thank you, Milord. But I confess surprise at your invitation." I kept my voice neutral, but I didn't meet his eyes lest he note my eagerness. Diplomats, like witches, are skilled at reading one's thoughts.

"Not *milord*, merely Bram. At least, as long as we're here among friends." I cocked my head at the silent servant, and Bram grinned. "Consider us alone. James is one of the family, right James?"

"Right." James sounded proud, though perhaps a little embarrassed. I suspected the pride was justified. "Drinks, Bram?"

"And food. Our friend is sadly underfed, which is understandable considering his condition."

"My condition?" I blurted out.

"Yes," he replied quietly, placing a hand on my shoulder and guiding me along the garden path. "A hungry, recent patient. I've spent enough time at the profession of arms to prefer even field rations to hospital food, and I can offer better than field rations." Now that he mentioned it, I'd not been hungry since Orgrim's draught had done its work. But I could feel a certain hollowness beneath my ribs, and his words made it grow hollower still. We sat together on the blanket, Bram settling companionably beside his wife. Margrethe cast a brief, warm smile at her husband, and I felt a twinge of jealousy.

Bram spoke again before the brief silence could grow awkward. "Well, Morley. As you may suspect, I've called you here for more than social reasons. "You see, Margrethe told me that you'd been surprised and beaten last night."

"I did no such thing," she interrupted. "It was your spy network that said so. I did nothing more than goad your conscience." They frowned at each other, with well-practiced mock irritation.

"I sit corrected," Bram chuckled. "In either event, I was informed of your 'accident' and I have chosen to do something about it, if you're not averse to my intervention."

A response seemed indicated, but I was unsure what to say. "I'm not sure I follow you, Milord."

"*Bram*".

"Bram. Last night's incident was just one of a long series of such events. A little harsher than usual, but nothing extraordinary."

From the corner of my eye, I caught a momentary flash of pity from Margrethe before she mastered herself. Bram went on. "True though that may be, it was unacceptable, and I'd halt this behavior. If you accept, I shall have it known that you're under my protection henceforth."

He paused, waiting and watching my face, and I resettled my weight, testing his words for condescension. An old reflex. "Out of pity, perhaps?" I asked in a low voice, regretting the bitterness that had crept into the words.

His reply was gentle but firm. "Before I knew you, I confess that might have been my sole motive. But as my wife so indiscreetly mentioned, I am nothing if not careful in staying informed. You're skilled and brave, and unless I've misjudged you badly, as quick with a blade as with your wit. What I offer is a place outside my household, yet one that will inform your tormentors where you stand." A pause, but he held my gaze with no telltale deflection of his eyes. "Should that explanation prove insufficient, consider that you provide an important source of information on the inner doings of the Court, and one I would be wise to benefit from."

Margrethe elbowed her husband in the ribs, and her voice was sweetly mocking. "Make no mistake, though, you'll be out on your backside the moment you misbehave. My husband is a beast at times!"

"But a fair one," Bram added ruefully, and we laughed together.

As the laughter waned, James reappeared bearing a wooden tray of bread and cheese, glasses balanced amongst the food and a sweating bottle of wine clutched under one arm. Bram allowed his offer to rest for a time while we ate. Conversation was sparse, for the food was good and our attention was devoted to eating. When the last crusts had been consumed, James rose with a grin and collected the debris. He departed, leaving the remainder of the wine.

"Well then," said Margrethe, brushing the last crumbs from Bram's clothing. "Shall we consider you one of us, Morley?"

Perhaps it was the wine, but tears blurred my vision at the sweetness of the offer, and I fought hard to keep them from showing. It *must* have been the wine, a strong western vintage. "How can I say no?" I said around the lump in my throat, watching her face light up and Bram's watchfulness ease. "But I must say no, nonetheless," I continued before I could take the words back.

"Why's that?" Bram's reply was deceptively mild.

My face twisted as I fought to word an answer that wouldn't offend them. "It's not so simple as being unable to accept charity. Not, you understand, because I think you're condescending, because I know you're not... it's just..."

"That you've depended on yourself for so long that you're not yet ready to lean on another. That you've never been given cause to trust, and you have no reason to do so yet." Margrethe's face showed an understanding born of memory, giving the truth to her words.

"In part," I replied. "Then there's the matter of acquiring a dual loyalty that might come into conflict some day." Bram's eyes narrowed. All her reasons were correct, and my replies were not precisely lies, but they only touched on the real reason—the night that lay ahead and the different freedom it promised. "That, and I'm loath to bring any trouble upon you. There would be questions asked at Court about why someone other than His Highness had taken responsibility for protecting the King's Fool." I added the last to cover the brief pause after my answer.

"That's not a consideration," replied Bram. "My position at Court is secure."

"So I see," I nodded, my gesture taking in the broad-shouldered gardener who'd just emerged from a side passage. A sword hilt projected from a cart full of litter he was trundling across the garden. The man's eyes were never still, flitting from his path to take in those buildings which overlooked the house.

"Touché!" chuckled Bram. "But I can accept your other reasons even if we quibble over the last one. Let me rephrase our offer. The position shall be yours should you request it. Until then, let us make the arrangement informal, on the basis of your accepting rewards commensurate with value tendered."

"An arrangement I'm given to understand you have some experience with. Very well. *That* I can accept."

I gathered myself to leave, but he hadn't finished yet. "I thought you might also be interested to learn that Sir Osric disappeared from the Court some time after you were found half-dead in the halls near the crypt. Your incapacity has been accepted as clearing you of any taint of guilt in the matter. But it appears you have friends at Court you were unaware of." His eyes narrowed, and I turned away lest he see the thoughts trying to surface. Thoughts of Orgrim's words as he knelt by my bedside, and the fierce gleam in his eyes as he mentioned payments for deeds done to my person. I shuddered, not trying to hide it from my hosts.

Chapter 4: A bargain fulfilled

My one experience with real, tangible magic—the mystical, dangerous kind, not the poetical stuff that has to do with love and other metaphors—came during my youth. It was my first deer hunt, and to be honest, I was scared spitless, my mouth so dry I could hardly swallow. I'd seen several of the other foresters kill deer, I'd helped butcher the carcasses for our larder, and I'd drunk the still-steaming blood along with the others, so it wasn't the blood itself that bothered me. No, it was the fact that I'd be taking a life. I'm not sure why that concerned me, for there were many people, my real parents among them, who I was quite convinced I could destroy without a moment's hesitation. And aren't we humans somehow more important than animals, though we live and die the same way they do? Looking back, I'm no longer sure what weighed upon my thoughts, other than perhaps the fact my companions would expect me to cause pain to a poor, dumb beast that had never done me harm nor was ever likely to, and to deprive said beast of the only thing it owned in all the wide woods.

My foster father, sensing as always what I was thinking, was sympathetic but firm: if I were going to live here with the other men, I was going to be blooded. And blooded I was. The older men surrounded me, laughing as they did, and from a flask of half-congealed blood, painted my face in vivid patterns, muttering half-heard phrases under their breath. The blood stank, and made my skin itch, but they assured me it was part of the ritual. Much of what happened afterward is a blur, save for two things. The first was the *snap!* of my crossbow and the moment of frozen time as the bolt sped across the clearing and sank into the deer's chest, those long legs buckling beneath it before its panicky start could carry it more than a body length farther. A perfect shot—something magical in the mundane sense of the word.

The second thing—the literally magical one—was what happened as we stood over the corpse. As in the past, one of the men sliced open the big artery in the beast's neck and let the blood flow into a small cup that would be passed from man to man to celebrate my achievement. This time, though, as slayer, I was to be first to drink. As I raised the cup to my lips, trembling with relief that this rite was nearly over and that there'd never again be a first time, my father's hand fell upon my arm and restrained me.

"Wait, Morley. For a first time, there must be something special."

The men linked arms to form a circle around me, then closed their eyes and began chanting something. I learned the words much later, but I shan't repeat them, for they're older than our time in these new lands and only for the ears of those who hunt together in the King's service. The chant paused a moment, thick with the tension of hesitation, and my father nodded. I took a deep sip from the cup, the salty, metallic tang of the blood making me gag as it had always done. But as I lowered the cup, the chant resumed, and this time, I felt a burning in my throat. My first thought was that someone had slipped strong liquor into the cup as a joke, knowing my inability to withstand strong drink, but this was like nothing I'd ever experienced before. The fire spread from my throat to my chest, and thence to every smallest part of my body, as if I'd fallen into a campfire and couldn't rise. Yet despite that great warmth, there was no pain, just a tremendous sense of energy coursing through me. Gradually, the sensation faded, and when my gaze turned to the men who surrounded me, all trace of mirth was gone; now, all that remained were smiles—some even gentle.

"Welcome to our brotherhood, Morley. You're now part of this forest as we are, and as much a part of its cycle of life and death. Some of the strength that courses in the blood and sap of all the living things that surround us now lives in you, and you'll return that strength to the forest the day you die."

Never since, in all my years, have I encountered something I could truly call magic. Today, I was chilled by the realization that I would soon participate in a second magical rite, and one such as had been unknown to my kind since the time of the Exodus. The dampness of the air this far below the earth accentuated that feeling, and in the crypt's torchlit darkness, the cold sought gaps in my clothing like a thing alive and wrapped its fingers about my skin. My nose itched from the dust deposited in that chamber by as many lifetimes' use as I had fingers on one hand, and raised again by our footsteps. The torch smoke that eddied along the ceiling before beginning its gradual descent to the floor didn't help. I shivered in anticipation, certain now this whole thing was somehow wrong and hating myself for wanting it too much to do the wise thing and flee.

Orgrim was intent on his own preparations and oblivious to my struggle. The learnèd kindness on his face was gone, and the iron concentration that replaced it contained elements of a harshness that had been absent before—or that I'd failed to note because of my preoccupation with his promise. Seen askance, side-lit by the torches, that face seemed less and less human with every passing moment, though there was naught but human he could be. The mage knelt, using a long ivory wand to trace a circle in the dust and hedge the drawing with contorted symbols and glyphs that writhed beneath my gaze if I concentrated on them too long. That done, he rose and turned an appraising eye on me.

The cold objectivity in that appraisal, like a vivisectionist teaching a class of surgeons over the squirming body of some malefactor, made the chamber's chill seem warm by comparison. I stepped back a pace, turning to flee, but those eyes seized me and transfixed me, held me to that spot as if I'd sunk to my knees in clay. I watched, helpless as a beetle trapped in amber, while he turned once more to the circle; with a sweep of one hand and a flash of ruby light from his wand, he swept the dust from the circle as if it had never existed, leaving a clean-traced outline in the center of the floor. Once again, those eyes turned to me.

"Come." The flatness of his tone contrasted with the sharpness of my response. Involuntarily, my hindmost foot traced an arc through the dust and turned me towards the circle. Terror rose in me, trembling in my hands and heart, but I moved helplessly until my other foot stepped into the center of the cleared space. Marshaling what strength of will remained, I turned to face my captor—for such he now was—with what defiance I could muster. In the amber glow of the torchlight, the blade of the obsidian dagger that had appeared in one hand took on a lurid gleam, and I felt my eyes drawn to the blade.

"Calm yourself," he intoned, and a drugged calm fell across my heart, easing my fear. But it was an imposed peace, and sat uneasily.

"The dagger?" I gasped, voice small and unrecognizable in my ears.

Orgrim laughed, an unpleasant, sharp bark. "Blood," he replied, voice and gaze steady. "For all life magics, the sorcerer needs something of life to work with. You won't miss what little I need." He stepped forward, careful to remain outside the cleared circle, and I felt panic rise and struggle against the bonds he'd laid on my mind. The bonds won. "Your hand," he demanded.

I raised my hand and with a firm grip, he took it in his own. I had time to note the strength of his grip before the blade sliced into my palm. I tried to draw away, but his grip was too strong, and the imposed calm dulled the pain; the wound should have been agonizing, but it felt no worse than removing an old, blood-encrusted bandage. Blood sprang up in the wake of the blade's passage, and he nodded, satisfied. A wave of dizziness assaulted me, though I'd sustained many worse wounds with no ill effect. From out of nowhere, Orgrim conjured a small crystal flask into which he squeezed perhaps an ounce of my blood. Then, releasing my arm, he slashed the dagger across his own palm. Before I could wonder at that, he clasped his hand to mine and pronounced words that echoed in the beat of my heart even as they rang in my ears. Though I'd steeled myself to make no more unbidden comments, I found myself speaking words I half recognized. A cold burning awoke in my hand, and a roseate glow sprang up, visible through the skin and bone and gristle, and when he released me, the wound was gone, leaving a fading scar.

From within his robes, Orgrim produced a small, fine-tipped brush and knelt once more by the edge of the circle. With sure, quick strokes, he began a meticulous tracing of the circle's boundary and the several runes by its side, using my blood for paint. He finished by adding a five-pointed star that walled in my feet, and began tracing yet another series of odd symbols where each point of the star met the line that marked the circle. As the brush lifted from each figure, he spoke a word with a strange sibilance to it and the figure twined upon itself and vanished. The design now complete, Orgrim finished by encircling the star once again before flinging the flask and the last of the blood into the air. There was no sound from their fall, but my attention had been caught up by the small pouch that replaced them in his hands. From this he dusted small amounts of a glittering powder onto the circle, scattering pinches symmetrically in four directions around its perimeter to complete the process. There was a sharp metallic tang to the air as he flung the pouch after the earlier implements.

"Prepare yourself," he said, voice deep and resonant with the same sense of gathering power that precedes a thunderstorm.

I needed to hear my own voice for what courage that would lend me. "For what?" My lips were dry, my voice drier.

"For what is to come. There will be pain, but it will not last." Again panic clawed at the bonds on my mind, but a lassitude growing within me defeated it. The mage's eyes closed and he relaxed into the placidity I had come to associate with the old man. Under the circumstances, that illusion of normality scared me more than anything that had come before. But as I watched, things grew worse.

The old sage's calm, patient face had scarcely reappeared when it began to change. The wrinkles smoothed and vanished like clay being polished flat by the hands of a master potter, and the grey washed from his hair like a fresh painting caught in the rain. Glossy black, the tight curls of his full beard grew dark as night itself. Paler and paler became the tone of his skin until it was somewhere between alabaster and the dull belly of a fresh-caught trout. Straighter and straighter he stood until the last traces of his stoop vanished.

The change complete, his eyes snapped open once more and though a new man stood in the room, there was no mistaking whose eyes blazed at me. Slowly—excruciatingly so—he spread his arms wide, as if struggling against some mighty weight, the wand lifting to the left, the bone ring to the right. A sharp exhalation escaped his taut lips, whether grunt of exertion or exclamation of pain. The torches flickered and died, and in their place sprang up a somber red glow, the color of fresh blood, licking around my feet from its origin in the geometrical figure encircling me.

"We begin."

Orgrim stood silhouetted by the glow, his face limned by the sullen light at my feet, and as I watched, his arms clenched inexorably towards the center of his body, as if he were bending an iron bar between them. The glow brightened in response until a bright orange tinged with cherry red, like new-forged iron, seethed at our feet. An answering glow came from the ring and wand.

"When it comes, open yourself to it, make it welcome. Do you understand?" I tried to speak a denial, but that part which was bound nodded its acceptance. Without another word, he turned the power of those eyes inward. As if of its own volition, his mouth opened and began forming tortuously pronounced words that fell upon my ears like shadows upon my eyes. Slowly at first, then in an ever-increasing rush, the words beat at my mind, at the walls around me, at the very world itself. I bit my lip to hold back a scream of terror, for the drugged calm now abandoned me, and blood from my bitten lip began to trickle down my chin, noticed only later when I examined my face in a mirror. There was a seething within me, the panic beating against the clenching of my jaw, until at last it grew too much and I released it in a cathartic scream. That scream masked, but failed to hide, a ripping sensation, half-heard, half-felt, in the air around me.

I reeled forward a half step in the sudden silence, bringing up against an invisible barrier that stung the hands I'd flung out to stop my fall.

I turned my head numbly towards Orgrim, my mind empty of all emotion in that anticlimactic moment. But even as my heartbeat slowed somewhat from its crazed pace, the mage's intent gaze told me this peace was to be fleeting. A bead of sweat rolled across his forehead, down his nose, and off into space, but his eyes were for me alone. It was then, as a rabbit cowering beneath the stoop of a hawk, that I felt another presence in the room.

Walk some night, late and after a few drinks, into a darkened room. In the envelope of lightlessness, your eyes are of no use, so you extend your hands before you to protect your face from an unseen obstacle. Imagine how your whole world contracts to but two points, your foot sliding across the floor to seek out any obstacle that might trip you, your groping fingers outstretched at chest level. Feel the palpable resistance of the dark, teasing at your fingers with half-real hints of what lies ahead. Then feel a strand of cobweb, downy, immaterial, but heavier than lead as it misses your outstretched arm and brushes your face, avoiding your questing fingertips...

Something touched me then, something nauseating that settled upon my exquisitely sensitive flesh, caressed my body in a grip soft as moonlight yet firm as a hangman's noose. The sense I was no longer alone grew, became a haze before my eyes, shot with a light I cannot describe even though it recurs in the rare dreams—the nightmares—I remember. My skin flinched away from that contact, hairs erecting across my whole body, and my muscles tensed as a warmth began to permeate me again. With that warmth, offensively intimate, came the sense of a sickening hunger that made me turn and try to run, gibbering with fear like a child fleeing unseen bogeymen, held captive by twisted sheets and the bonds of sleep. There was laughter, there was pursuit, and in the end, there was capture.

Backed into a corner of my mind, unable to flee farther, I hid from what approached, unable to confront my stalker. There came a gentle touch at that symbolic arm covering my eyes, a touch that became a prying, firm and demanding. I screamed, flailing out with the hand, echoes of my scream rebounding from the walls of my skull to torment my ears and feeding back into more screams.

"Open!" cracked the voice of the mage, penetrating through all the other signals vying for my attention.

"Yes, open," echoed another voice, sinister with promise.

My last defense was to draw into a ball, fetal, the child brought to bay and hiding in a garderobe, unable to face what lurks just outside the opening door, knowing it's nothing so comforting as the arms of a parent—not even the one who beat you senseless more nights than not. Those final walls crumbled and were as naught. Surrounded in my own mind, I recoiled but was unable to retreat further. A hand caught my jaw, lifted my face upwards, held my eyes to meet those of my assailant. And the face that looked down was my own, distorted with that unclean hunger.

The pain began then, as that face faded and I felt the walls of my body melting, yielding to an intense pressure. It was as I imagined being broken on the rack must feel, though the stretching came from within, not without. An all-consuming wave of pain contorted me, the agony mounting higher and higher while the child crouched in the ruins of the garderobe, shrieking in fear.

Then something snapped, and I soared free into welcoming darkness.

***

There were voices, those of Orgrim and another whose voice was familiar but whose identity I couldn't ascertain. As my eyes opened, both voices ceased, leaving me in silence.

I lay on my side in a tiny room, supported above a bare stone floor by a rough, sturdy bed that was far too small. I was buried beneath a layer of blankets, knees half drawn up to my chest. Every inch of my body ached as if I'd been overexerting myself for days, but the pain was comforting because it meant I was no longer dreaming. My vision cleared. I was alone save for the grey-haired sage who'd become the dark wizard of my nightmare, for such it had obviously been; as I've mentioned, the only dreams I remember are nightmares. My mind followed my vision, clearing, and panic rose in my breast as the elements of the nightmare returned.

A firm hand pushed me back against the pillows, and I realized I'd tried to sit up. Orgrim appraised me a moment, guardedly, then relaxed and let that familiar warmth return to his face. "Welcome, Morley. You'll be glad to know that the transformation worked."

"Worked?" My voice sounded odd, fuller and deeper than I remembered.

"Yes. You're a man as normal as any other, as you desired." Stiffly, the old man rose from the stool he'd occupied and limped across the room to where a mirror leaned, face to the wall. Holding the frame close against his body, fingers clasping its carved edges, Orgrim returned to sit by my side, then turned the mirror. "See?"

Someone calm but weary stared back, handsome, intelligent, but wearing a shocked look and dark bruises beneath his eyes. It was a stranger, familiar only in the eyes that greeted me every time I'd looked in a mirror. *My* mirror, though smaller than before! In wonder, I lifted a hand to "my" face, wincing at the pain such a simple motion evoked, seeing the stranger wince in time with the pain that surged in my abused muscles and bones. Long, graceful fingers stroked that face, even as I felt their caress. Awestricken, I lifted my gaze to Orgrim.

"Is this *real*? Is it *forever*?"

"Aye, it's both." The kindly face creased in a grin as tears sprang up in my eyes, tears of joy and gratitude. Even though a part of me struggled to reconcile the gentle smile with the masterful stranger of my nightmare, I felt elation surge in my breast and used that energy to clamp down on my tears. Tears, as I've already mentioned, can be dangerous for one such as I, for they wash away the self-discipline that protects me. I dabbed at my eyes, hurting them momentarily before my new hands responded to my urging and applied proper pressure. I looked again at the mirror, just as my benefactor moved to take it away. The mirror tilted away, and I caught a glimpse of something disturbing before Orgrim's words recaptured my attention.

"... of course, you'll be weak for days yet. What we did to your body was ungentle. Sleep, and when you've recovered enough, we'll discuss what I require of you."

There was something in his voice that compelled, some part of me that answered, and I felt a wave of weariness sweep over me. I sank back into the sheets, wondering as I did whether I'd imagined that Orgrim's reflection had been absent from the mirror.

Chapter 5: Walking for the first time

When I was a child, I'd once done something that upset my parents. What that something was is long lost, a loss I would never have expected given the intensity of my memories of what followed. I'd been beaten before, to the point of leaving bruises that lasted for more than a week, but this was the first time they'd broken bones.

You never forget your first time.

A broken bone's a strange thing. As it happens, the intensity of the pain is unlike anything you've ever felt—at least if you're like most, and lucky enough never to have been hurt that badly. The pain ebbs, replaced by something less pleasant: a nausea comes in the wake of that pain, and a curious disorientation or unreality. The surgeons tell me it's your mind providing the detachment you need to ignore the damage and escape whatever broke your bone—a simple survival reflex. Of course, some things you can escape more easily than others. The pain returns, and it lingers.

Now, many miles and years away from that memory, I felt many of the same sensations. The pain was a bright but fading memory, but the nausea still lingered and the disorientation wasn't helped by the fact that none of my body parts occupied the positions I'd grown to expect. It was another day before my aches and pains faded enough I could rise unassisted from my bed; I'll spare you the unpleasant and embarrassing details of trying to cope with daily necessities.

Orgrim brought me food, and new clothing, and helped with those other necessities before leaving me to lie in peace. I was in my own room, and for the first time, I noticed how small and cluttered it was. The new me must have been almost six feet tall, a giant among men, and my chamber hadn't been over-large even for the dwarf I'd once been. I was weak from my ordeal, and my memories of the nightmare were growing fainter. All that remained clear was a lurking feeling that something more than passing strange had happened, something both horrible and wonderful.

Yet I couldn't place my finger on what disturbed me so much more than any other nightmare.

More immediately important was the absence of the hard-won grace and coordination that had been mine before the transformation, replaced with an adolescent's awkwardness. This worried me out of all proportion to its significance, and Orgrim was hard put to convince me I'd adjust to my new body in time. While my mentor was away, I stayed closeted in my room, pushing past the pain, moving and stretching until at last the pain waned, the stiffness faded, and I became confident in my movements. My absence from Court had surely been noted, yet this bothered me less than you'd expect. Clearly, I couldn't simply return and pick up my life where I'd left off.

My lute helped me learn the ways of my new body, for I'd acquired some small skill with it in my earlier incarnation, and this skill returned with satisfying speed. In fact, with my longer fingers, I was finally able to play chords that had been painful or impossible to reach. My playing had acquired a wild note, but I attributed this to my excitement and the tension of awaiting Orgrim's return. Those times he visited, bearing food and wash water and carrying away the chamber pot, he complimented my progress and suggested I'd improve faster if I relaxed conscious control and let my body care for itself. He was right, of course, though there was awkwardness in doing so, as if someone else was pulling the strings that moved my limbs. But that feeling faded once I no longer concentrated so hard on what my body was doing, and I soon gloried in the return of deftness to my movements. On the third day, I was confident enough to go out on my own.

Entering the hallway outside my door without looking, I ran into a serving maid hurrying on her business. I reached out to grasp her arm and keep her from falling, pleased at my success and the ease with which

I held her up until she got her feet beneath her again. She was one of the women who'd taunted me before, but I felt too good now to bear a grudge. Indeed, her smile became open and appreciative, and held a hint of promise as her eyes passed over my new body.

I decided I was going to like my new life.

I was preparing to start an innocent little conversation with her, when her eyes widened and she pulled from my grip and fled. Orgrim had appeared as if from nowhere, frowning as had become his wont of late. "I thought I instructed you to keep to your room?"

I smiled warmly, willing to forego promised pleasures for the moment; after all, I had a lifetime of such things ahead. "Not exactly. You said to remain there until I felt well enough to leave. I do, and there are things I'd rather try than remain confined in that cell. I've a fancy..."

"I imagine you do," he interrupted, raising a skeptical eyebrow and thrusting his chin in the direction of the departed woman. "But I think you'd be wise to remember a few things first. For one, there's the matter of your name."

"My name? What of it?"

"Surely you haven't failed to notice that you're no longer the man you once were? Should you go about naming yourself Morley, people will begin to ask unpleasant questions about the disappearance of a certain dwarf. Questions neither of us would be pleased to answer."

"You said *a few things*." My smile faded as some of the sober realities of my new life intruded on my euphoria. "What else must I be wary of?"

"Familiarity with those who knew you before." His distaste deepened. "Such as that woman, for instance. Those you knew before may recognize you from certain habits, including how you express yourself, and the more so should you behave as if you know them. And let us not forget the ancient proscription against letting a witch live; you'd be doing me a grave discourtesy if you made others suspect my existence." As dwarves did not suddenly become normal solely by thinking virtuous thoughts, this was a serious risk. "Finally, there's payment for my services."

"Ask, and if it's within my power to give, I shall." At the back of my mind, there was only a slight hesitation, swiftly erased by gratitude.

"Indeed you shall," he said. Then, with a visible effort, the patient wisdom returned. "Morley, please don't misunderstand. I don't own you despite the great favor I did you. But there are many tasks I must accomplish in coming months, some of which I can't perform myself. I'll need your assistance, and as you're without employment, we can come to some accommodation."

"Aye, there's that," I mused. "More importantly, I wouldn't have you feel I'm ungrateful. Truly, you've helped more than I can express with words alone. In return, I'll help as best I can."

He smiled. Reaching inside his robes, he produced a small but weighty leathern bag that clinked as he dropped it into my palm. "For living expenses. I have a task for you, though it'll be an hour before you can begin. Meet me in front of the library, and I'll instruct you in what's needed."

We shook hands to seal our partnership, and I noted with pleasure the strength of my grip, more than the equal of his firm handshake. Afterwards, I set off down the corridor. I wasn't sure at first where I was headed, but as I walked, I decided to pay a visit to Bram. His offer of a formal bond had been attractive, and now that I'd no longer burden him, I could more easily accept his offer. The notion of treating Bram as an equal—and believing it—and the chance of someday attaining the stature and peace he'd found warmed me. That easily, I cast aside Orgrim's warnings about familiar patterns, certain my friend and protector could pose no danger.

I nodded at the guards on my way out of the building, and they nodded back, politely but with no sign of recognition. That amused me, but I had little time if I was to visit my friend and still reach the library at the appointed hour. I arrived at Bram's house much sooner than I'd expected, so distracted by my newfound speed and the alacrity with which people moved out of my path that I little heeded the walk itself. A knock on the barred gate produced no immediate response, so I settled down to wait. Shortly, there came a grating as the viewing slit slid open, and a pair of wary eyes appeared.

James' voice came from behind the thick wood. "Good day, Sir. How may I help you?"

I cleared my throat, suddenly awkward. James' eyes narrowed when I hesitated. "I'm here to see Bram, James."

He was plainly trying to place me, for his brow furrowed in concentration and once more his eyes swept over me. "I'm afraid I wasn't told to expect your visit, Sir...?"

"Mor... Modred," I improvised.

"... Modred," he continued. "Are you perhaps an old friend of the master's?"

"Not exactly," I sidestepped the question. "More... a friend of a friend. Is your master in?"

James seemed caught between the urge to invite me in and natural caution at the arrival of an unanticipated stranger. He was a good man, his youth notwithstanding. "Umm. No, Modred—Milord and Milady have gone for a walk. If you tell me where you're staying, I can send a runner when he returns." Caution won out over hospitality.

I repressed a grin. "No, that won't be necessary. He doesn't know me, so you'd just confuse him. I'll return some other time to visit."

"Very good, Sir. Have a pleasant day." I nodded, feeling trepidation at his obvious concern and his poorly concealed efforts to memorize my face. Orgrim's advice seemed more sensible now I'd come up hard against the realities of my changed circumstances. I'd avoided thinking things through, and that luxury couldn't last much longer. Heaving a sigh so heavy that a passing merchant shot me a sharp look, I turned my steps towards the library. I estimated I had some moments remaining before meeting Orgrim, but would not risk arriving late and raising his wrath. He'd placed considerable importance on the task he would set me, and that made it important for me as well.

Ankur's library was an imposing building made from piled blocks of neutral-brown stone fitted together seamlessly without the aid of mortar. It was unornamented to the point of drabness—to the point you'd pass by without a second thought were you not seeking it. I waited by the main entrance, noting as I did how most Ankurites ignored it. Not surprising, given that most people couldn't read more than the few words or signs necessary for their livelihood. Even I, who'd learned to read each winter with the other foresters and who'd read every scrap of paper or parchment that came within reach, had never spent any time here, and I was looking forward to learning what the building held now that I—however temporarily—had no formal responsibilities to occupy my days. It was as I pondered these thoughts that Orgrim arrived, as silently as on each previous occasion.

"To business," he exclaimed, the sudden sound of his voice making me startle. "The task I've set you is a simple one, Morley... or should I say Modred?" He smiled coldly at the surprise on my face. "Ah, have you forgotten so soon that I'm a wizard, and that wizards have ways of knowing that are denied common men?" He smiled his gentle smile, removing some of the sting. "I need you to enter the library and retrieve two items." He handed me a scrap of parchment with two titles upon it. "Take this," he continued, handing me my lute, which I'd not noticed he was carrying, "and inform the librarian that you're a traveling minstrel who must consult certain ancient texts so you may more accurately compose a ballad on the days before the Exodus."

"Before we came to the new lands?" A good excuse, for ballads of those days have been popular ever since the King took such an interest in them after the war with Amelior. "But there's one small flaw in your plan."

"And what might that be?" His gaze hardened, though the smile never faded.

"You said you'd need me to retrieve the texts, which I assume means that you want them removed from the library. Were I the librarian, I'd see no reason to let a stranger carry away treasures that may be older than Ankur itself."

"Your wit does you credit, but I wasn't yet done explaining." From within his cloak he removed a medium-sized hemp sack. "In here you will find two scrolls. Spend some time consulting the ones I have sent you for, then exchange them for the ones in the sack when no one's watching."

"That should be simple enough. But I find myself full of questions today. Why do you need me for such a simple task? Couldn't you simply conjure the books out of the library, with none the wiser?"

Orgrim sighed, assuming a look of exasperated patience. "Modred, as you now understand, my existence in Ankur must remain unsuspected. There are certain intricacies involved in any magic, and while it's simple enough to scry the location of the books, removing them through those thick stone walls poses a challenge. One well within my means to surmount, but there are more important things to spend my energies on. Moreover, any such magic would leave my signature behind for all to see."

"Maybe to another wizard, but to a librarian?" I paused in thought. "Ah. I hadn't considered the possibility you might have a... rival." The thought was both exciting and somewhat alarming.

"Quite so. There are certain signs that suggest I'm not alone in this town. Now enough questions. I've set you a simple task, and it's time you proceeded. Cross the librarian's palms with a few coins should she prove obstinate—*there's* a spell even you should be able to manage! Just one thing: under no circumstances make a fuss or do aught to attract attention and cause your visit to be remembered. If you can't obtain the scrolls without making yourself memorable to everyone in the library, leave. There are other mundane ways to obtain the scrolls should the open approach fail."

I quirked a grin, and bowed deeply enough for my still-developing balance to come into question and turn the bow half-mocking before I recovered. Ignoring his amusement, I turned on my heel and entered the library. I half-expected to be stopped by guards or at least to encounter some physical barrier to entry, but evidently there was insufficient interest in old books among Ankurites to make these treasures worthy of theft. In fact, the only obstacle was the thick rug that caught my oversized feet and sent me sprawling. I managed the fall well enough to avoid crushing my lute, but the old woman dusting the shelves and the two scholars conferring at a low table couldn't fail to notice. When I met the eyes of the scholars, challenge in my eyes, their amused contempt changed to solicitous looks. I paused to re-examine my instrument for damage, then got to my feet as the woman came to join me.

"I trust you're undamaged, young man?" she inquired, failing to hide her amusement.

I smiled. "Aye, apart from my dignity, though it appears I've come seeking forbidden knowledge your library's loath to yield." Her smile broadened. "Thanks for your concern." I swung my lute around to my back, careful to not misjudge distances and cause another disaster, then dusted off my knees. As I did, I took the opportunity to look around. The inside of the library was as plain as its exterior suggested: a high, vaulted ceiling crisscrossed by stone arches and illuminated by a combination of slim, thickly glazed windows at the ceiling and man-tall, arm-thick candles in wrought-iron stands in recesses all about the walls. Deep stone shelves rose to the ceiling, and there were ladders here and there against the wall to facilitate access to upper shelves. Two long tables occupied the center of the room, each piled high with scrolls and surprising numbers of the bound books that had begun to appear with increasing frequency. The two scholars had gone back to their discussion, poking at various scrolls now and then as if using them to prove some obscure point.

"Can I help you?" The librarian flipped her feather duster, impatient to get back to work.

I returned my attention to her. "Certainly. I'm in the process of preparing a ballad of the old days in honor of the King. Unlike my colleagues, I believe in first learning about my subject, and that's why I'm here. I was advised that the library contained two old scrolls." I'd palmed Orgrim's scrap of paper while we talked, and presented it with a flourish.

"You're sure we have these?" Her brows knit in puzzlement. "If we do, they're old indeed. I can't remember a request for them."

"I have it on excellent authority they're here." I spoke those words glibly, then realized I had no response ready if she asked the name of that authority; mentioning Orgrim's name would've been unwise, and I knew no other name I could invoke without requiring the construction of a dangerous chain of lies.

But she was more interested in my choices than in learning who'd recommended them. "Bide a while. I'll go seek them."

I watched as the librarian wandered, preoccupied, from one row of shelves to the next, lips moving as if thinking aloud. I'd always assumed there'd be some simple method of finding and retrieving texts, but my assumption proved unjustified; this was still a profession in which masters passed obscure lore to apprentices, such as the location of prize texts, rather than making the information available to anyone. I swung my lute off my shoulder, sat at one of the low chairs, and began tuning, falling into the calm that simple activity always evoked. A glare from the two scholars, who I'd been watching with some interest as my fingers followed familiar paths without my guidance, interrupted me.

"Is there a problem, wise Sirs?"

"This is a library, not the King's audience chamber. Be silent. If you must practice your trade, do it elsewhere."

Surprised by his vehemence, I leaned the lute against the table, not wanting to dislodge the scrolls, and turned to examine the contents of my sack. Orgrim had told me there'd be two scrolls inside, and it was as he'd promised. Each one had an old, musty smell to it and felt dry and brittle to my probing fingers. Opening the mouth of the sack just enough to admit some light, I craned my neck in a vain attempt to see the titles on the scrolls. This occupied me briefly, and when I looked up from my efforts, the librarian was perched atop one ladder, several scrolls tucked under her arm as she craned her neck to read the titles of others. As I watched, she pursed her lips in disapproval and replaced the scrolls under her arm on the shelf.

Having done so, she descended cautiously and crossed the room to my table. "I must apologize, but my search is taking longer than I'd anticipated. I've unearthed several treasures whose existence I'd forgotten, but not the particular ones you sought. I'm afraid that the task may take some time, particularly given that those two gentlemen have provided me an afternoon's work replacing the scrolls they've already consulted."

I nodded sympathetically, and eased a coin from my pouch. "Most inconsiderate of them. Nonetheless, my patron was most insistent that I create the best song that was within my resources." I grasped her wrinkled hand and slipped the coin into it. "I would be more than grateful if you could spare the time." I maintained a gentle pressure on her hand, smiled as warmly as I could at her, and watched with pleasure as she blushed and looked away.

"I'll see what I can do, Sir. Return tomorrow and I'll have the scrolls for you." She pulled her hand from my grasp, and I let her, enjoying the opportunity to play this game.

Outside, Orgrim waited impatiently by the door. "You have the scrolls?"

"No. The librarian couldn't find them, though she promised she'd have them by tomorrow morning." His look hardened. "You seem to feel some urgency about... *borrowing* these old texts. I'm curious why they're so important."

He frowned, and I wasn't sure whether the displeasure was at my impudence or my failure in this first task. "Let me say only that the scrolls speak of events around the time of the Exodus. They provide important clues to the nature of the magical cataclysm that set us to fleeing the old lands. Because the practice of magic has been proscribed since before our departure, honing one's mystical skills is next to impossible without a free exchange of knowledge. For a scholar like me, the information in those old scrolls provides precious clues about the nature of magic."

I pursed my lips, realizing the depth of my ignorance. "Is it wise to pry into such matters? What destroyed our old lands would also threaten the new."

Orgrim's frown deepened. "Don't presume to provide guidance on something you don't understand. Some of us have learned the lessons of the past."

I averted my eyes, not liking the power in his eyes any better despite increasing practice, and wondering about the sense of something left unsaid. Changing the subject seemed wisest. "Point taken. In the meantime, what's our course of action?"

"Obtaining the scrolls tomorrow won't delay my plans, and I must accomplish other things today. Very well. Spend the remainder of the day however you please, though I caution you to stay far from those who once knew you. I shall wake you early tomorrow so we can return to the library."

"Done."

He strode away into the crowd, brisk strides belying his aged, careworn appearance and reminding me of the youthful black-haired man he'd become in the nightmare that preceded my transformation. Those memories still bothered me, though in the clear light of day, they seemed a trivial thing. Surely such an experience as I'd undergone would leave any man with bad dreams for a few nights? I was enjoying my new body far too much to question my fortune, but that didn't stop me from reflecting upon what Orgrim had said—and left unsaid—as well as upon his reaction to my questions. Perhaps some reading of my own would be in order. No one who knew me would be in the library, and there was the enticing prospect of feeding my curiosity and easing my ignorance.

The more I thought of the past few days, the more I felt sure I could no longer afford that ignorance.

Chapter 6: A session in the library

While I still lived with my true parents, there'd been neither scrolls nor books nor anything else literary; indeed, once it became clear what I was, even bedtime stories lay beyond my expectations. I've no idea whether the spoiled children of the nobility find themselves enriched by access to scrolls and books—though a year spent at Court leads me to doubt it—but it was only after I'd fled my home and been adopted by a real father that I discovered what I'd been missing.

The men who patrolled the King's forest had little money and few luxuries; indeed, had they not been given the right to hunt and provision themselves, some would have starved. Yet my father, for all his responsibilities and impoverished means, had acquired a love of the written word, and had spent as much of his paltry wages as he could retain on scrolls and other written materials. Surprisingly many were simply forgotten and left behind at hunting lodges by visiting nobility, becoming the communal property of the foresters. Father was a musician, so much of what he purchased involved music, whether moth-eaten scrolls of musical notation or recent copies of popular ballads, and that fed my musical talents. But many abandoned texts fed my curiosity and vocabulary, eventually providing skills I'd later use to earn employment at Court. Some were rare treasures, collections of tales from the old days, and I'd cherished them and learned to read from them. Indeed, I'd read them so often I could recite most in their entirety from memory.

Today, enticed by access to more written information than I'd ever conceived existed, I returned to the library, this time somewhat less dramatically. The sages continued their quiet discussion, and the librarian stood in the center of the room, lost in thought, hand on her chin and gazing at the shelves. I shuffled my feet and cleared my throat as I drew closer, not wanting to startle her.

"Ah. You're back. I'm sorry, Sir, but I've had little luck. I've found only a single scroll so far."

"Far better than I'd expected, and I congratulate you on your efforts. Actually, I've not returned to pester you. I thought you might know of other, more familiar works that provide useful information while I await your discovery of the two works I seek. But now..."

She smiled, pleased. "An interest in my treasures is rare enough that I don't begrudge you the time I spent searching." She cast a glance over her shoulder to where the two sages sat engaged in battle. "If you wish to begin your studies, you'll find the scroll on my desk." She pointed to a well-lit corner of the room where sat a small, oaken table with a clean surface and one scroll.

"I thank you for your kindness. I'd be honored to make use of your desk." I bowed and made my way to the desk.

She called out as I turned away. "Mind you: that scroll's ancient. Handle it with more care than were you holding a newborn babe."

I placed my sack upon the table, then leaned my lute against the wall. The desk turned out to be—oh pleasant surprise!—almost too small to fit my legs beneath, but I managed. I had the remainder of the day to find an opportune time to steal the scroll, so I decided first to examine it and see whether I could find hints of what Orgrim sought. Apart from my own curiosity, I was beginning to feel I couldn't go too heavily armed into my dealings with the mage. My nightmare may have planted a seed, or it may have just been some overactive survival instinct, but his furtive behavior was beginning to raise alarms. I set aside for the moment the question of why those alarms might be silent in his presence.

The scroll bore a single word for its title, *Exodus*, but it was the subtitle that caught my attention: *Our Doom and How We Fled It*. Every child, even an orphan like me, knew the general outline of the Exodus story, though knowing the details was quite another matter. In those long nights spent with my foster father, alone in the woods after repairing our tools and after the necessary chores of living were done, we'd had little else to entertain us beyond reading, sharing what we'd learned through the telling of stories and the singing of old ballads as a means of passing the time. In consequence, I'd learned more of the story than most; indeed, memories of those tales and songs, acquired through frequent repetition, had been enough to gain me a chance to serve the King as bard and jester.

All versions of the story, however else they differed, agreed upon two things: first, that some great doom had fallen upon mankind's original lands as a result of dire magic, and second, that those who survived fled across a great ocean to land here in the west. Records of that time were scarce, for writing materials and time to use them had been low priorities, and few scrolls or books had survived from that time. The ensuing colonization of the new lands was little better understood, for our ancestors had lacked sufficient time to record any but the most important things while struggling to secure a foothold; mostly what remained were songs and other things that could be preserved orally, and these had changed enough in the singing and telling that the truth of those times was lost. The few writing supplies that had been available during the voyage, the one period during which there'd been time to record things, had been put to use on more urgent matters, such as planning our new home.

If the tales were to be believed, one of the puzzles of the Exodus was that we'd found a new home at all. In those days, the Dwarves—not my kin, popular superstitions notwithstanding—had been a sparse but prolifically combative race, and the magic of the Elves had been such they should have defeated the feeble armies of mankind, undefended as we were against anything magical; together or separately, the two should have cast us back into the seas from whence we came once our intentions became clear. Fortunately, the third race said to have inhabited these lands, the Goblins, had hated us less than they hated their two more ancient enemies. Evidently, they were familiar with the old adage that "the enemy of my enemy is my friend", and had seized upon the opportunity to present the Elves and the Dwarves with a war on two fronts. Apparently, that diversion had been enough to buy us time and—eventually—peace.

The result, these many years later, was that none of these three elder races remained a presence within our lands. Their absence made it increasingly likely that each race was nothing more than a fable, or perhaps a cautionary metaphor intended to keep us united. If the latter, they'd failed in their role, for with no other enemies to fight, we'd repeatedly turned our efforts upon ourselves.

I had my doubts the tales were as mythical as some claimed. It was no great feat of imagination to believe in the Dwarves, for though not one had been seen outside their mountains in living memory, a few traders still regularly made the sea journey to Stormhold to trade for rare metals and skillfully wrought weapons. I'd seen enough signs during my life in the woods to want to believe in the existence of the Elves, though I'd never actually seen one and knew of no woodsman who claimed to have done so. As for the Goblins, there were persistent rumors of bitter warfare against them in the lands west of Amelior, and for some years now, Ankur and the other eastern powers had been sending military aid to Amelior in the form of supplies and observers. Yet neither was there any direct evidence of the Goblins, and I'd met nobody who claimed to have fought one. This lack of evidence was difficult to reconcile with the unmistakable payments of some form of tribute to Amelior even though we'd won that war.

In short, there was much about the Exodus to occupy an inquisitive mind, and I was eager to feed that curiosity now I had both time and opportunity.

I unrolled the fragile scroll carefully, using two flat stones, each the size of my fist and polished smooth, to hold it open to the section I was reading. I shan't bore you with a literal recounting of what I read, for a summary does the matter better justice. The language was antique and verbose, written in an ornate and cramped hand on parchment scraped into near transparency, with a flowery style that made comprehension difficult. But what I'd not expected was the presence of frequent passages that appeared to have been written in some foreign tongue.

No... Not a *foreign* tongue, though that's as close as I can come to describing what was wrong with the words. I studied those sections with considerable care, until my head ached, and grew increasingly perplexed by my inability to comprehend. It wasn't the writing itself, for my careful examination convinced me the lettering was identical to that used in the rest of the scroll, the work of the same scribe; it was obvious they weren't later annotations, for the words were an integral part of the main text rather than subsequent commentary scrawled in the margins or overlying the original words. Besides, the only foreign languages I could imagine were those of the Dwarves, Elves, or Goblins, and how could they have contributed to the scroll?

So the words had been written at the same time as the rest of the text, that was clear. Moreover, the shape and the construction of the words followed the familiar patterns for our language, and it was easy to break the words into their component letters once I'd mastered the peculiarities of the scribe's hand. I tried copying some of the words on a scrap of parchment the librarian had left beside her plume and ink, and it was easy enough to make those copies. Yet these parts of the text had no meaning, even when copied onto my own parchment or when the mystery amounted to a single word whose meaning should have been clear from context.

My association with Orgrim suggested the obvious answer: some powerful magic had been applied to the scroll to make key portions incomprehensible. Certain elements of what I subsequently read provided tantalizing hints of why that might have been, but left me with no answers. Let me tell you what I found—and what I was unable to learn—so that you may judge.

I can say with confidence that our ancestors were a great race, far more prosperous than we are today. Much of their prosperity came from prodigious works of magic, the like of which had never been performed in the new lands. Let me clarify that: Given my transformation by Orgrim and his hints he wasn't alone, it would be more appropriate to say that no such feats of magic were *spoken of* in the tales of our early years in the new lands, nor were there frightened rumors of any such in recent memory. Nonetheless, Orgrim's veiled comments led me to wonder how much magic still existed, entirely unsuspected.

According to the scroll's unnamed author, the magic of our ancestors had tempted sorcerers into feats that wiser men and women would have shunned. As in any cautionary tale, there'd been disastrous consequences for those whose desires outstripped their skills. Indeed, the notion that great magics always had a price was familiar, almost a cliché to those who learned old ballads, and my pondering had led me to conclude this was nothing more than remnants of the moralizing typical of those who preserved ancient lore. Other times, I'd suspected the fearmongering was dramatic embellishment intended to discourage commoners from pursuing dangerous knowledge and threatening their betters. However, my recent experience forced me to reassess my beliefs and suspect that perhaps the old tales contained some truth.

Despite the oft-repeated risks of delving in magic, there were many in those days who became powerful through its study. The scroll painted a brief, but fascinating picture of life before the Exodus. There'd been many luxuries: the ability to produce books in copious quantities to facilitate the spread of knowledge, the ability to heal diseases and wounds that were now fatal, and strange and wonderful contrivances of various sorts. Yet there were also obscure aspects I couldn't puzzle out, things that skirted around our origins and our eventual destiny as a people. Some related to what came after death, a matter that no modern man claimed any knowledge of, and I wasted considerable effort trying to understand these aspects; it had always disturbed me, not to mention far wiser philosophers, that we had no knowledge of where life came from and what happened after death. For such a fundamental matter, this was surpassing strange, and I began to suspect the same magic that baffled my comprehension of the scroll was working on a far vaster scale. That left a deep unease in my heart, for it revealed depths whose existence I'd never suspected.

I was drawn deeper into the story, now eager to look for hints that would support my suspicions. The scroll told of the world-ending events that precipitated the Exodus. I've mentioned that great magics always carried a personal cost, but in this case, they carried a greater cost to the race that permitted them. It was obvious the author was speculating, because much of what he'd written was metaphorical and contained subtle contradictions. What eventually emerged was the image of one or more mages, supreme over all others in skill, who'd attempted something nobody should ever have been foolish enough to attempt. The consequences had destroyed them and nearly mankind too. As a result of their folly, our people had been forced to flee the lands they'd inhabited since the beginning of time. They had time to do three things before fleeing, of which only one made sense.

The first was predictable, and a reassuring testament to how little humanity has changed over the centuries: everyone who fled found time to pack things both prudent and foolish, and carry them onto the ships, and they fought, betrayed, bribed, or sacrificed themselves to determine who would be granted life in a new land, and who would remain behind to die. Many tales of courage and heroism have come to us from those days, mostly as songs and familiar, often-told legends. The scroll told of equally many dark and shameful wrongs men did in the name of survival, including finding room on ships for possessions at the expense of lives.

The second, far more disturbing thing was a terrible massacre and an equally terrible destruction of priceless knowledge before anyone boarded the boats. This sequence of events took much of my time in the library to puzzle out, for although most of the description of these events was clear, these parts of the scroll also contained the highest proportion of obscured text I'd yet encountered. It was clear that anything smacking of wizardry had been destroyed: the spell caster, the books and scrolls that stored the victim's knowledge, and the tools of magic or powerful implements created thereby. This destruction was cold, ruthless, and efficient, and seemed a pragmatic if horrific attempt to rid themselves of what had destroyed the old world in the hope of preventing it from coming to the new world.

The puzzling part was that once that first burst of destruction was complete, a whole new class of victims had been slain and their property and possessions destroyed. The quantity of the obscured words made it impossible to understand what these people had done to merit their deaths; as nearly as I could understand from context, they'd been akin to and yet wholly unlike wizards and witches, and had occupied a more important and accepted role in daily life. What that role had been remained maddeningly unclear, yet our ancestors had felt so deeply and wholly betrayed by these individuals that their betrayal inspired a murderous hatred far beyond that which led to the elimination of magic from our lives. This second slaughter was described in such a manner that the appalling cruelty of the murders and the indiscriminate destruction of property that followed couldn't be doubted. Like all men, I've hated others at times, and with more cause than most, but even so, I couldn't imagine a hatred sufficient to birth what happened to these mysterious people.

The third thing, which appeared contradictory given that it ostensibly followed the destruction of anything that resembled magic, was the casting of a great spell of protection to seal humanity away from the ruin of the old world. This spell was related in some way obscured by the passage of time to the ancient bloodoath that had served to unite mankind in the absence of any other security amidst those chaotic times;

indeed, I now suspected the massive and lovingly described shedding of blood that preceded the Exodus may have played an important part in that final spell. All at once, I understood why Orgrim's blood magic had been so familiar: I'd unwittingly participated in the rite of bloodoath, and thereby bound myself to Orgrim in a manner I'd not suspected at the time. Though Orgrim had played me fair thus far, and had allowed a measure of freedom in my actions, I'd a suspicion it wasn't a necessary freedom. I made a note to test that freedom at the first opportunity, establishing my new limits and thereby confirming or denying my suspicion.

The remainder of the scroll told of the hardships of the journey across the great ocean. I'd never seen an ocean before, but knew that the ocean to our east was said to be much like a lake, only salty enough to choke any man foolish enough to drink its water and so much larger that words were inadequate. From the descriptions in the scroll, it was obvious I'd missed the point in choosing the word *larger* to describe an ocean. The journey westward, into the prevailing winds, had taken many weeks and perhaps even months; as always in old scrolls, estimates of time were unreliable, often chosen more for dramatic effect than to capture the reality.

But the scale of that ocean was even greater than those numbers at first suggested. When I encountered them, I paused in my reading to put them in perspective. In good country, a strong man with long legs could travel perhaps twenty miles along a good road, walking a full eight hours. The ships of our ancestors had traveled at least twice that fast, even upwind and even in bad weather, and they'd traveled throughout the day and night without stopping. The numbers had by now grown far beyond my rudimentary abilities to calculate, but it was likely the ships had crossed a hundred miles or more in a single day. A week of such voyaging would amount to nearly a thousand miles, a span several times greater than the distance from Amelior to Volonor, which distance covered the entire expanse of human habitation in our new lands. If the journey had taken months...

As I say, calling the eastern ocean a large lake did it a gross injustice. Even allowing for the inevitable exaggeration, it was a marvel they'd had sufficient water and food to finish their journey.

The distance alone says much of the desperation of those who undertook such a plunge into the unknown. If, as the scroll suggested, they hadn't possessed certain knowledge of what awaited them beyond the horizon, then the calamity that drove them to such desperate measures must have been more terrible than words can tell. Even if they'd known for a certainty that safety lay beyond the horizon—or at least safety of a sort—the courage necessary to leave would have been enormous, fully the equal of that possessed by any hero of myth or legend. I dwelt on that image, and on the joy that must have sprung up in their hearts when the first lookouts of the mighty fleet bearing all that remained of mankind saw land—land that initially revealed no sign whatsoever of any other inhabitants.

I can also imagine their shock when they learned they weren't alone. The settlers must have soon encountered the Elves, for in those days, the Southwood would have stretched across what was now farmland to the ocean. In no time, of course, the settlers had begun clearing trees for shelter and to make room for farming. They'd had no choice, for their provisions had likely been exhausted long since, and a diet of fish alone had begun to make them ill. There must have been war as soon as the Elves understood what was happening, though there are few tales of these beings and of their conflicts with mankind. Later, as soon as Men entered the mountains to seek the metal ores necessary to forge weapons and other tools, our ancestors would have encountered the Dwarves, and likely begun yet another conflict.

The scroll ended at this point, hinting at the conflict that was soon to begin, and I would have given much for the chance to learn more of those times. Fortunately, the rest of the story is better known, as it deals with the founding of Volonor by the Gordon lineage, the secession and subjugation of Somorrah, and the blood feuds that led to a second exodus westward to found what was now the empire of Amelior.

To me, with no knowledge of magic beyond what the old songs revealed, this scroll lacked any evidence of something that would expand Orgrim's mystical knowledge. Admittedly, I wouldn't recognize most things that would help a mage, but the lack struck me as curious. Of course, it was possible that the information Orgrim sought lay in the obscured portions of the text that were beyond my comprehension, but that explanation rang false given the words that surrounded the incomprehensible material. So neither explanation satisfied me, leaving me much to puzzle over.

As I rubbed my eyes, which had gone dry from that unaccustomed length of reading, I felt something brush against my leg, and looked down to see a charcoal-grey cat rubbing against my boots. I began to push it away, but before I'd done much more than form the intention, it sprang into my lap and commenced a tremendous purring that I fancied would shake the dust from the shelves. "You seem to like me," I commented, reaching out to stroke the cat. In the manner of its folk, the slim sybarite immediately went into convulsions of ecstasy.

The librarian, who'd approached unnoticed while my attention was elsewhere, laughed, startling both of us. "I see that Grey's found a new friend."

I looked up, not stopping my stroking. "Your cat?"

"No, just a stray who wandered in one day and stayed to keep the library clear of mice and other things that might damage my treasures. I call him Grey, though surely he has a real name. Not very imaginative, I'm afraid, but when you've read as much as I have, you start to feel that there's nothing new under the sun."

"I think I may opt for the unimaginative, given that I've acquired a new appendage. Would you mind if I took him?" Acquiring a pet had been the last thing on my mind, and I wasn't all that fond of animals to begin with, but the cat had gone to sleep in my lap, the purring grown intermittent, its powerful claws hooked into the tight weave of my cloak. There was something surprisingly relaxing about its warmth and weight, and its purr was soothing. I sighed, and without disturbing the cat, I palmed another coin.

"Well, I've no claim on the cat, but he does keep the library clear of pests. If you take him, I shall have to find a replacement."

I slid the coin onto the table. Grey stirred, butted my hand with his head, then returned to his nap. "Would this help?"

"It would. You're more than generous, Sir; that amount of money would purchase a dozen cats in the bazaar."

I shrugged. Money wasn't a problem so long as I stuck with Orgrim. "Consider it a bonus for having helped so well in my search."

"Given your generosity, I regret to inform you that it's time to close the library. I still haven't found the second scroll you're seeking, but I feel certain I'm getting close."

"I'll pack up at once, then." As I said that, I realized that in my fascination with reading the scroll, I'd neglected to find time to steal it. A guilty voice at the back of my mind reminded me Orgrim hadn't intended me to read the scroll—just to steal it. That I could do tomorrow, when Orgrim returned to obtain the scroll and its missing cousin. I gathered my possessions, with Grey tucked into the crook of an arm and patently unwilling to leave that shelter. As I left, the librarian began to argue with the two sages. I hesitated a moment, wondering whether I could snatch the scroll, then thought the better of it; if I were caught, there was scant chance the woman would continue seeking the second scroll.

I left. The day had given me much to ponder, and I was grateful for an evening alone in which to do so.

Chapter 7: Transitions

Home is that place where, when you run away from it, you still want them to take you back again when you return. I was almost ten before I learned the cruel truth of that glib phrase. My understanding arrived one night, after a mild beating accompanied by the promise of something far worse later. I'd fled the house, leaving my parents to drink themselves into a stupor sufficiently profound they'd be unable to finish what they'd started. The pattern was familiar, but this time, I found the courage to try to break it. So I fled, taking nothing but the stained clothes on my back and the scars they concealed.

Just then, anything would have been better than staying another night in that place, yet I soon found that escape wouldn't be so easy. The world has little love for a dwarf with neither money to purchase acceptance nor an employable skill to barter for food and a place to sleep. I spent my first night, cold and hungry, on the streets, and it was enough to cast my home in a different light. That first night, I escaped being murdered for my clothing solely because it would fit no one but me. I was too sore and too scared to sleep, and I eluded a different class of thief largely because when he'd drawn close enough, he soon saw there were more lucrative prey elsewhere.

Shortly after, I escaped a rapist because I was able to punch him in the belly when he reached for me; he was too drunk to avoid my blow. As I ran, I wished I'd had the courage to take his money, but I was new at this, and too scared of this new form of abuse to risk staying within reach. Later, I escaped the feral dog that cornered me because he'd recognized the desperation in my eyes and slunk off seeking easier prey.

The next day I discovered that although there was no shortage of work for those with strong backs, nobody wanted a weak young dwarf when normal men could be hired for the same price. Moreover, none dared risk bringing some of my curse down upon their household by making me a part of it. One innkeeper reluctantly fed me after I fainted from hunger on his doorstep, but that courtesy arose from guilt; the meal was hearty, but it was one meal, and my benefactor made it clear there was little likelihood of more.

With nowhere else to turn, I headed home, sick to my stomach with fear and certain I'd be beaten senseless for my act of rebellion, yet for all that, somehow comforted to be somewhere familiar again, with familiar and survivable challenges. But when I returned home, I found the door barred against me, and when I knocked, my mother flung a stone hard enough to draw blood. Before I could knock again, my father came out after me with his favorite cudgel, but his bad leg saved me and I outdistanced him, though it was a near thing. I fled again, this time to the country, for I'd heard of country charity and had hopes farmers would be more hospitable. They weren't, and for the same reason as the inn-keepers: enough runts were born to their livestock already that they had no wish to bring an additional curse upon themselves.

All this time I'd kept the deepening pain locked within, years of prac-tice letting me keep it from ever showing; enduring pain without protest was simple survival, I'd learned. But now, despairing, I wandered into the nearby woods, the fresh air and clear daylight making it a pleasant place, and figuring there'd be nuts and berries and other things to gnaw upon. And at the back of my mind, there was the certainty that should a wolf chance upon me... Well, at least it would be over, and no more pain-ful than what I'd already learned to endure. Instead, I was found by the man who eventually raised me and taught me faith in myself. With few exceptions, that first foray into the woods also marked the last time I let self-pity rule my actions.

Many years later, older and somewhat wiser, I made my way back through the darkening streets towards the palace, where I'd found considerable—albeit grudging—acceptance and where they'd never yet turned me away. Arriving at this new home, I was stricken with a sense I'd returned to the home of my earliest years, and an old fear woke in my belly.

Old habits led me to stride towards the guards, readying a ribald comment or two to purchase my passage, confident this would suffice, for I was well known to the guards. But their wariness as I approached warned me, and I belatedly recalled that "Modred" was a stranger to the Court. Though I'd left the palace easily enough earlier that day, there was scant chance the guards would let a stranger enter and avail himself of its facilities. Leaving had been easy because there'd been no reason for the guards to keep anyone within, absent an alarm. Getting in would prove more difficult.

Instead of provoking a confrontation, I bent my path so I passed just in front of the guards. I nodded politely enough, but kept on walking past the palace, hoping I'd avoided creating any suspicion, which I'd surely have done had I withdrawn as soon as the guards first noticed me. I felt their eyes on my back while I crossed to a small fountain across the open square fronting the palace's massive stone structure. Sitting beside the fountain as the colors of the day took on that softer tone they achieve around sunset, I turned my thoughts towards finding an excuse that would get me back into the palace. I never thought to ask myself wheth-er this was necessary, and whether anything in my small room called to me; I could have been far more comfortable at any of the expensive inns at my back that faced the palace across the square.

I found no solution until Grey woke and grew bored with my inactivity. He freed himself from my arm, yawned, then dropped to the packed dirt beneath the fountain, and began playing with the hardy weeds that grew where cracks in the fountain permitted water to escape. I watched him, amused, enjoying the simple pleasure of companionship with something wild enough to need no care from me yet tame and sufficiently "human" to seek my company. I was less amused when a small insect leapt upon my lute, and the cat pounced upon it, turning it into a small stain on the polished wood.

Angered, I made as if to sweep the cat from my lute, but halted my arm before I came near the cat. Grey rewarded my mercy with a nip at my hand that drew blood. I withdrew my hand and sucked at the wound, frowning. I raised my hand to strike at the cat again, then fought down my anger; I wouldn't let it master me. Grey watched without cringing, as if knowing I'd forbear the second time. I raised my hand higher, then thought the better of it.

"Enough. You're distracting me from finding us lodging in the palace tonight." The cat cocked his head as if listening, then all at once swept one paw, claws sheathed, across the lute's strings. The instrument emitted an awkward sound, and I glared at the cat. "Have a care, beast. I don't want that scratched."

Then I blinked in surprise at the superior look on that small triangular face. All at once, it became clear my companion had provided a means of entry. "Good cat," I said, ruffling his fur. I picked him up, shouldered my lute, and headed back across the courtyard more confidently. The guards watched my approach with interest, for none of the others who shared the streets, still bustling about their business in the fading light, seemed at all interested in the palace. Two crossed their halberds as I approached, barring entry, and their leader stepped forward to intercept me.

"Good evening, Sir. Might I inquire as to your business at the palace?"

Keeping a careful grip on Grey, I swept out a deep bow. "As you can see, I'm a minstrel." Reflecting upon how clean my clothes were, I hastened to elaborate. "I've spent some time in your fine town, but I'm finding it an expensive place to live and not nearly so lucrative as I'd hoped. I was hoping your king still followed the old practice of bed and board, and perhaps a few coins, in exchange for a performance and news of the land."

The guard nodded. "Yes, he does, but you won't be performing for the King this night. He already has a visitor to sing for him, freshly arrived out of the west, which is the only place he's likely to want more gossip from. You don't sound much like a westerner, so..."

I frowned, not liking where this conversation was headed. "Would that be your polite way of telling me I'll be sleeping on the streets tonight?"

The guard started to nod agreement, then changed his mind. "Not necessarily. If you'll accept less in the way of accommodations and food, we can find you space in the servants' quarters. Would that suit you?"

"Far better than cold stone for my bed and water from a fountain to break my fast. Lead on, sir guard."

He laughed. "You want an escort, do you? No, you'll have to find your own way. Head down that corridor," he gestured, "until you come to the servants' quarters. Someone there will get you straightened away. And mind you don't stray from the path. There are guards and patrols, and they've got a poor sense of humor where trespassers are concerned."

I bowed again and proceeded down the corridor he'd indicated. Once out of sight of the gate, I took the first passage that led me to my own quarters; I knew the locations of the guards and the general schedule of their patrols, and had no fears I'd have any difficulty avoiding them. I did encounter one patrol, but I was walking with such certainty they gave me no second glance on their way to more important things. I suspect the cat helped; thieves and assassins rarely carry cats.

When I reached my room, I was alone in the passageway, so I entered without incident and closed and locked my door. Then I lay curled upon the bed so I'd fit, to think and to rest my eyes after the day's hard work of reading. The bed that had been large for Morley was far too short for Modred, and the room felt stuffy. Grey was displeased too, and stalked about poking into things, sniffing, and peering at me in evident disappointment before moving on. I had little experience with cats, and no idea whether such behavior was natural.

Later, my stomach began making its needs felt. I gathered the few possessions I felt I could call my own—a very small bundle indeed—then unbarred the door and left the room, realizing I had no intention of ever returning. Though this home had neither scarred me nor chased me away, it was something I'd outgrown. I made my way to the larder, where I felt confident I could procure sustenance and something for my new charge before seeking new quarters.

The larder and kitchen were tucked away in a large area at the rear of the palace, with unshuttered windows installed high on the walls for ventilation. Despite this, the smell of stale smoke and old grease grew stronger and stronger as I neared the chimneys that had replaced the old hearth. My mouth began to water, reminding me of how distracted I'd been until that moment. After sniffing the air, Grey clambered from the crook of my arm to my shoulders, where he settled down and purred his contentment.

The kitchen was nearly empty, as most of the kitchen staff had made their way to bed to snatch a short night's sleep before an early morning's awakening and another long day. Of the people I saw there, the one I recognized was the burly lad tending the fires, a fellow orphan named Brand who'd beaten me once or twice before I'd come under the King's protection, and later Bram's. Today, he watched as I entered and made my way towards the larder, and I reminded myself he'd never seen the new me before. I nodded to him, and put down my bag and lute next to the wall. As I placed a hand on the larder's wrought-iron door handle, his voice came from behind me.

"I wouldn't be doing that if I were you, stranger." Brand spoke loudly, for the benefit of the few others still in the kitchen.

"I beg your pardon?" I turned towards him.

"I said I wouldn't be doing that if I were you. I don't recognize you, and we're not in the business of charity here. Go beg your meals elsewhere." He smiled insolently, one scarred hand toying with a heavy earthenware rolling pin. Grey hissed at him and dropped from my shoulders to the floor.

I decided to ignore Brand and proceed anyway, but wasn't foolish enough to turn my back on him. A wise choice, for he came after me, weapon swinging by his side, and aimed a vicious kick at the cat. Enough was enough. "Leave my cat alone." I towered over him, hand on my dagger and making the most of my new height.

His eyes widened, and he took a step back. Confident in my new ability to impress, I turned half away to open the pantry door. But it takes more to intimidate a bully than size and a brave front. Even as I turned, he darted forward and swung. I had neither time nor room to dodge, so instead, I brought up my right arm to block the blow, cringing as the heavy rolling pin caught me on the side of my biceps, numbing the arm. He drew back for another blow, his smile broadening, but I closed with him, my greater weight bearing him backwards, off balance, both of us crashing to the ground. I landed on my good arm, rolled away from him, and came to my feet, shaking but turning to face him. But he'd stopped where he fell, and to my astonishment, lay there, pale and rigid.

Grey crouched before him, all coiled energy, like the bow on a ballista, his very lack of motion an unmistakable threat. The cat had puffed up until he looked twice his normal size. But it was the way his eyes held my antagonist that kept that unfortunate pinned to the floor. Brand had the look of a condemned man staring into his executioner's eyes, knowing there'd be no reprieve—or like a warrior meeting the eyes of an opponent he knows outclasses him. Then the tableau dissolved as I approached, right arm still dangling numb, and the tension went out of Grey like water from a tipped pot.

The cat relaxed and padded contemptuously past the fallen man, shot me a too-human look of disappointment, and vaulted to my shoulders, startling me so much I almost tipped him back onto the floor. Behind him, Brand lay still, face pale and lips trembling. I smiled as coldly at him as I could, but the effect was wasted; his eyes were only for the cat whose claws dug into my shoulder whenever my body swayed. From the downed man came the unmistakable odor of loosened bowels.

I couldn't bring myself to stay and gloat over his downfall, for the rest of the kitchen staff had fled the kitchen while we sparred, no doubt gone to summon a guard, and my arm had begun tingling. I began dusting myself off, but changed my mind as Grey growled a warning, and instead gathered my belongings. Then I hastened towards the back of the kitchen, where a large window was open to catch the evening coolness and provide the workers with breathable air.

I reached the window just as Brand's plaintive voice sounded from the kitchen behind me. Without pausing to listen, I climbed atop a crate so I could reach the window sill, then pulled myself up, swung outward, and eased downward until I hung suspended at arm's length. My right arm now ached, and Grey dug bloody furrows in my shoulder, but the size of my new muscles had protected me and I'd sustained no serious damage from the blow. As I hung there, Grey climbed down my body, drawing blood the whole way down, then sprang onto the cobbles.

The drop was short, so I took a breath, then let go. I landed easily, relishing how my powerful new legs absorbed the impact. Then I glanced around, realizing just how tempting a target I made for any sneak thief lurking about. The alley was empty save for a large brown rat that bared its fangs at Grey before slinking into a shadow behind a pile of moldering garbage and vanishing. I walked the other way, breathing through my mouth to minimize the smell.

Once out on the street, I reconsidered my options. Rather than trying again to find a place in the palace, it seemed wiser to choose someplace nearby where I could spend the night in safety. I had a momentary qualm about leaving the palace before Orgrim returned, but suppressed it; the mage clearly had no problem finding me. His money jingled at my hip, promising a warm, clean bed in any of the expensive inns adjoining the palace. A half-formed plan of visiting Bram the next day tantalized me, but I'd have to think hard first if I wanted him to greet me with anything more than polite curiosity—or outright fear if I revealed my identity and what had happened.

I made for the Golden Kettle, a few hundred paces down a side street that gave out onto the square fronting the palace. Grey's purring preceded me, drawing strange looks from the townsfolk I passed. The inn's common room was empty, but the chiming of the door's bells as I entered attracted the serving maid's attention. It was still early, so I had my pick of tables. I chose one near the bar, and when the woman approached, I ordered a meal without paying much attention; Grey, I was certain, would fend for himself. My meal soon arrived, a thick loaf of brown bread and a healthy slab of beef, with delicious, salty brown gravy.

The woman sat across from me behind the bar, leaning forward to display her bosom to greatest advantage, letting me know that more than the meal was for sale, but I was no longer in any mood for company. I'd grown weary all of a sudden, and my body still ached at night from the transformation and now, from the blow I'd received. It was all I could do to concentrate on my meal. Once she'd determined I wasn't interested, she concentrated instead on the cat, who'd sprung up onto the bar and begun disporting himself to attract her attention; soon, Grey had the barmaid absorbed in tearing off strips of greasy meat from a joint sitting on a tray and dangling them before him. Grey rolled over on his back to paw at the proffered prizes before dragging them to his mouth and bolting them. In between feedings, he wormed his way up to the woman, rubbed himself full length against her, and purred until he'd coaxed another morsel from her.

When I was done satisfying my hunger, I arranged for my room. The coins I produced disappeared with remarkable speed, and I was led upstairs. After a last hopeful but fruitless sway of her hips, she left me alone for the night. I made for the bed in sudden urgency, for my day's activities had fatigued me more than I'd expected, and I fell asleep instantly despite the throbbing in my biceps and the dull ache from the rest of my body. Grey stretched out across the top of my pillow. I remember thinking with considerable pleasure as I fell asleep about returning and thrashing Brand.

Chapter 8: Further literary endeavors

Early in my stay with the foresters, I'd been no more popular than I'd been with the residents of my village. The foresters had firsthand experience with blood magic, and told tales of the things they'd seen by night or in some part of the woods formerly unknown to Man, so they had better reason than most to distrust me. The respect they had for my father was all that earned me a space in the bunkhouse and the chance to earn my keep. It did not earn me the respect of his companions, their women, or their brats; that would come later, once I'd proven myself to them and proven that I'd bring no harm down upon them.

The desire to prove myself and bring no harm upon them wasn't always mutual.

I've heard the joke about waking from a dream of suffocation and discovering one's packsack was missing, but as I rarely remember any dreams, it never struck me as funny—and especially not after it happened to me. One morning, soon after my arrival, I awoke with that sensation of smothering. Shaking off the last vapors of sleep, I reached out with both hands and found my breathlessness to be more than a dream; in that instant of awakening, my hands found and wrapped around the wrists that held the blanket being forced over my mouth and nose. Around its edges, I heard the muffled laughter of the youths who'd decided to have some fun at my expense, and though I struggled, given strength by panic, whoever held the pillow was older and stronger. Just as I'd begun to grow desperate, my blood roaring in my ears like distant thunder and feet thrashing, one of my knees made contact with his head, and all at once the pressure eased and I could tear the blanket from my face.

They'd surrounded my bed, vying for the best position from which to enjoy the show, and their faces filled with shame when they saw my wide-eyed terror and mottled face. The one who'd been holding me down lay beside my bed, clutching a smashed nose and moaning, blood seeping between his fingers.

I was still gasping, and an anger such as I'd never before felt swept away the panic. I looked down at my former tormentor, and found it as difficult to draw breath as it had been through the pillow, and for a brief moment, that anger found focus. It must have shown, for the onlookers drew back, even as I turned towards the bleeding youth, my hands crooking as if I'd strangle him where he lay helpless. A part of me I prefer not to show the world, buried nowadays, urged just that: kill him, and let the others know what they could expect should they try again to demean me so. I took a deep breath, savoring those thoughts, then exhaled, the anger leaving with my breath. Instead, I removed the pillowcase that had held the straw ticking of my pillow, and kneeling by the injured youth, pried away his hands.

His nose was badly broken, and he howled when I caught it between my fingers and pulled it straight, as I'd once seen a smith do to himself after being struck a glancing blow by a horse's hoof. Then I pressed the bloody cloth on both sides of the nose until the bleeding slowed to a trickle. There came a sigh of relief from my audience, who'd been holding their breath since I'd emerged from the blanket scant moments earlier. My attacker's eyes were dull with pain, but the fear that haunted them was fading. I remembered the smith, cursing, a fist the size of a water sack poised to fell the horse with the incongruously small shoeing hammer he held in a white-knuckled grip—and I remember him dropping the hammer, a smile growing as the blood streamed down into his mustache and beard, and reaching out to caress the horse's flank. So I smiled at my former attacker, and watched as, bewildered, he returned that smile.

A long journey still lay ahead, but I'd taken a man-sized stride along the path.

Years later, alone in my room, I woke to find Grey sitting on my face, the sensation of smothering indistinguishable from what I'd felt that night in the cabin in the forest. It was an effective way to banish any trace of sleep, but there are far more pleasant ways to rise.

No sooner had I sat up, spitting cat hairs and fighting a tremendous urge to sneeze, then the wretched beast leapt from the bed and raced to the door. I hesitated, thinking wistful thoughts about shoeing hammers, but the cat had set up a desperate yowling that alarmed me. Given the condition of my own bladder, I suspected I knew what Grey wanted, and I got up with some alacrity to set my companion free, navigating towards him by the dim light that passed beneath the door. I assumed he'd find his way back if that was his desire, but having spat the last cat hairs from my mouth, I confess I wasn't in any state of mind to miss him should he choose not to return.

I set about answering my own needs, and when I'd done, set the chamber pot outside the door for the servants. No sooner had I done so than the feeling I was being watched crept over me. And sure enough, when I turned from the door, a candle flared and I found Orgrim sitting on my bed. I jerked, startled, for though I was growing accustomed to his comings and goings, I'd not been expecting him.

"Good morning, Modred. I trust you slept well?" Those stern eyes belied the kindly tone in his voice.

"Well enough." I yawned. "Is it morning already?" It by no means felt that way.

He paused, and the clock on the palace tolled the hour: one in the morning. "So it would seem," he replied. "Prepare to accompany me to the library."

"I'll be sure to remember that the next time you say *early*, you mean it." I gave him a wry smile, but he failed to respond. "Very well, I'm ready. Is there aught I should bring?"

"Only yourself and the bag with the replacement scrolls." Orgrim rose with no further comment and led me to the door. Without listening, he opened it and stepped into the hallway, which was, as I expected, deserted. The light from the low-burning oil lamps was just adequate for us to find our way down the hall without incident. The inn wasn't the most expensive in Ankur, but its business appeared so lucrative the landlord could waste money on nightlights and on securing loosened boards so they wouldn't wake his guests. The common room was empty as the hallway had been, and the banked fire burned in the hearth. When we reached the door, the old mage made an exaggerated clenching gesture with his right fist and exhaled before drawing the bolt. When he swung the door open, the motion was silent, with neither clang of bells nor squeak of hinges.

Outside, we made good time, slipping through the chilly, deserted streets. It was a clear night, and the oil lamps that lit the main street, vying with the nearly full moon to illuminate our path, spread pools of light that made our progress obvious to any observer. Despite this, Orgrim made no effort to seek the shadows, striding in plain sight towards our destination; I suppose that was wise, for had we met the watch while skulking through the shadows, we would have had much to explain. It wasn't long before we reached the library, and though I drew to a halt by the front, he moved past the building, so I held back the obvious question and followed. We entered a narrow alleyway that ran behind the building, the mage vanishing into it without glancing back to see whether I followed. The alley was in near-complete darkness, lit only by what little moonlight filtered through the narrow gap between buildings that revealed the night sky. I'd taken my eyes off the alleyway long enough to lose my night vision, and I bumped into Orgrim.

Orgrim grunted and pressed a rope into my hands. "Have a care, Modred. If you climb as clumsily as you walk, I'll need a new assistant this same morning, and I'll tell you now, I won't be pleased to have that chore. Now pay attention! At the top of this wall lies a ventilation opening you should be able to squeeze through. Use the rope to descend on the other side if there's no ladder within easy reach." My eyes had adapted again to the darkness, so I saw him withdraw a small forked branch from within his cloak. He tucked it into my belt, and went on. "When you're in, use this to locate the scrolls. Hold it with one hand on each tine of the fork, and turn it slowly; the tip will glow more brightly as you approach the correct direction."

I looked up the smooth expanse of wall, unbroken by so much as a crack. I was no thief to climb a sheer, dressed-stone wall unaided. "And how do I get there in the first place?"

"Like this." Orgrim placed his hands together at waist height, palms upward, and spat a word into the night. Then he raised his palms, and as he did, I rose into the night sky. Though I'd braced for something magical, I'd expected something more mundane, like launching the rope through the window and leaving me to climb it. I shivered, for despite my transformation, I was by no means familiar enough with the workings of magic to have grown sanguine about such things.

As I neared the top of the building and my head rose out of the alley's deep shadow, the moonlight illuminated the vent at the top of the wall. The opening was capacious, large enough for my former self to stand in, and adequate even now to pass through with little difficulty. A light wooden screen covered it, but it was a moment's work to remove it; the screen had never been designed to keep out anyone more determined than a bat. As I set the screen aside, leaning it against its frame, and threw one leg over the lip of the opening, Orgrim's spell ceased, and I settled, pinching my thigh. I would have cursed, save that I'd gasped as I felt my balance waver and begin to tip me into the darkness within the library. I clutched at the window sill, avoiding a nasty fall, then set about fastening the rope he'd given me to one of the iron fixtures that had supported the screen.

My right arm ached, but I was confident it would support me. Sure enough, I was able to climb down the rope, hand over hand, until I reached the bottom. I savored my new body's strength for a moment, grinning like a fool in the darkness, then forced my mind back to the business at hand. The library was pitch dark, enough so I feared at first to move. But I was confident Orgrim knew what he was doing, and I took the stick from my belt—not without some trepidation—and held it before me. No sooner had I grasped it as he'd instructed than a faint greenish-white glow sprung up from the end of the stick. My hands shook, casting trembling shadows, but I was relieved to feel nothing more than the stick's dry wood; if I'd felt anything resembling magic, I'd have dropped the stick and lost it in the gloom.

With my eyes grown accustomed to the night, the stick's glow was sufficient to help me find my place in the big room. As a test, I pointed the stick towards the librarian's desk, and as I did, the glow waxed in intensity. When the stick pointed directly at the scroll I'd left there earlier, the illumination was about as bright as a candle. I strode to the desk and exchanged the scroll for the replacement Orgrim had provided, eager to be out of there. Once the real scroll was safely within my sack, I swung the stick in a slow arc until the light brightened once more. By moving the stick back and forth in the direction that caused the brightening, it was easy to find the correct direction, and in no time at all, I had the second scroll in my sack and the stick back in my belt.

Unfortunately, with the stick no longer pointing at the scrolls, the magical illumination vanished, and I was left in near-total darkness save for a shaft of moonlight that fell upon the far side of the room. Fortunately, my problem was easily resolved: I held the sack in front in one hand, and the stick behind it. With the stick pointing again at the scrolls, its glow returned, strong enough to light my path. By proceeding in this manner, I made my way across the room to the rope. At the rope, I replaced the stick in my belt, slung the sack back over my shoulder, and set about pulling myself up through the darkness until I reached the opening. Morley would never have succeeded, but Modred had been gifted with a fine body. I reached the top with naught more than a few twinges from my right arm. Now, a new problem arose.

"Orgrim, how will I get down?" My whisper sounded loud amidst the night's silence. "If I climb down the rope, I'll have to leave it attached." Orgrim declined to answer, but he grunted something and immediately I was floating in midair beside the rope and the wall. I untied the rope, replaced the screen, and as it settled into place, began descending rather more rapidly than was comfortable.

My feet touched down hard and my stomach caught up. I shook like a dog emerging from a pond to free myself of the sensation, then handed Orgrim the sack and his magic stick. He placed the stick in one of his voluminous sleeves, then opened the sack and examined the scrolls; as we'd remained in the shadow of the building, I have no idea how he saw anything, but he gave a satisfied grunt. "Well done, Modred. You can return home now to a well-deserved night's rest. I'll contact you when I need you again. Find some safe way to occupy yourself until then." He must have sensed my hesitation, for he chuckled. "The door at the inn will remain safe for you to open for another half hour; you have only to close the door behind you to banish the spell."

"Thanks..." I began, but I was speaking to an empty alleyway. I shivered again, partially from the night's chill, and returned briskly to my temporary home. I arrived well within the allotted time, and as the mage had promised, I had no difficulties gaining entry. I closed the door behind me, looked for but saw no obvious changes to it, and shrugged and returned to my room, stifling a yawn. Grey waited by the door, gazing in my direction as if he'd been expecting me. I bent down to pat him, and he recoiled until he'd had a chance to sniff my fingers. Whatever he was trying to smell must have satisfied him, for he shot inside the room as soon as I'd opened the door. With the door once more closed and bolted, I was the most attractive thing in the universe: the cat was all over me, begging to be rubbed and purring fit to wake the neighbors. It was some time until he quietened enough I could return to sleep.

Not long after dawn, Grey woke me again, in much the same way. Spitting cat hair for the second time that morning, I reflected that if this kept up, the foul beast would soon be seeking another master, or would be too dead to be seeking anything much at all. This time, however, he was clawing at the door as if a nearsighted wolfhound had gotten into the room and was blundering after him. I hastened to release him, then bolted the door with particular vehemence. When I turned, half-remembering what had followed the cat's first departure, I wasn't at all surprised to find Orgrim seated upon my bed.

"Have you had a visitor?" His voice was demanding, and I felt sure I'd never get away with misleading him outright. On the other hand, I was beginning to feel a need to test the limits of my freedom, just so I'd know for sure. So I bent the truth.

"Just some cat that found its way into my room. It's gone now, and good riddance." A cat hair I'd managed to miss worked its way to the front of my mouth, and I removed it and spat upon the floor.

Orgrim smiled his gentle smile, but again, his eyes gave it the lie. "Stay away from cats. They're untrustworthy companions, and will cause you more grief than their friendship's worth."

I wiped my fingers on my shirt. "I'd have to agree."

"I'm rarely wrong, you'll find." He paused a moment as if gathering his thoughts, and the smile vanished. His entire face was serious now, eyes and mouth both narrowed. "I have another task for you, and one that will be considerably more difficult. In fact, were it not for your background as a forester, I'd hesitate to consider it."

"Should I take that to mean you'll be sending me out of town?"

Orgrim went on as if he hadn't heard. "I have two messages that must be delivered to places our kind are not welcome. I'd be lying to you if I said that your task will be easy. Indeed, a normal man would neither find those to whom I want to send the message, nor have the tact to survive that meeting. You, on the other hand, possess what's necessary to do both, and I trust you'll succeed after I've provided suitable aids."

My muscles tensed at his tone, which suggested that despite my value, I was more expendable than I'd hoped and that he mightn't shed many tears if I were expended. "You're not inspiring much confidence."

"Nor did I intend to. False confidence would be the death of you. For you to survive to serve me again, you must be on your guard."

"Against?"

"First, against the Elves; next, against the Goblins." There was a certain malicious cruelty in the way he savored my reaction.

"I think I'd prefer not to take on those particular challenges. Could I perhaps just fetch you some of the King's private stock of wine from the palace instead?"

Orgrim laughed openly for the first time since I'd met him. Under other circumstances, it might have been a reassuring sound, but now it chilled me. "Your sense of humor will serve you well in coming months. Treasure it." The laughter died away as if it had been smothered with a blanket, or perhaps a cat. From within his cloak, he removed two scrolls and tossed them to me in rapid sequence. I caught them both, expecting some kind of magical shock, but there was none. They were, however, heavier than I'd expected.

"The one with the green seal is for the leader of the Elves." He watched my eyes widen, and smiled with evident relish. "And the black seal is for the leader of the Goblins."

I gathered my courage as best I could. "I assume you're going to give me more help than that. No man's seen an Elf since we first arrived in the new lands, and I'd have said the same of the Goblins had I not kept my ears active during my stay at Court. But though I now believe the Goblins exist, what I've heard suggests no lone man would survive meeting them. So how shall I find them, and more importantly, how will I survive the finding?"

"To seek the Elves, travel west to Belfalas, then directly south to the Southwood. They'll know you're coming and will find you." Though that was meant to be reassuring, his next words ensured I didn't take it that way. "That alone won't guarantee your survival; as I mentioned, surviving after you have delivered my message will be up to you."

"That's reassuring."

"Your sarcasm will serve you less well than your tact, so I advise you to unlearn the more literally foolish aspects of your former profession. You leave today, as soon as you break your fast. A horse awaits you in the inn's stables, and it's equipped with everything you'll need for your journey."

I clutched at what comfort I could find. "You mentioned you'd provide various aids to my survival?"

From his hand, Orgrim removed the ivory ring I remembered from my nightmare. "This ring will provide a contact of sorts between us. Should you need to contact me, close your eyes and imagine yourself sinking into it. If I'm not otherwise occupied, I'll respond." I put the ring on my hand, and was surprised at how well it fit; it burned a moment where it touched my skin, but then subsided to a pleasant warmth, which slowly faded.

Orgrim withdrew a small, broad-necked ceramic jug from his cloak and removed the stopper. "You'll need to be able to communicate with the elder races." As he spoke, he dipped a finger into the jug, and began anointing my forehead with its contents. When he was done, he spoke a brief phrase in some harsh foreign language and pressed hard against my forehead, forcing my head backwards with surprising strength while continuing to chant in that harsh language. My forehead burned as if I'd stepped, hatless, from a warm cottage into one of those winter days so cold the snow squeaks beneath your feet. Then he anointed my head once again and repeated the procedure, this time in a far more musical, pleasant tongue.

Orgrim replaced the flask within his cloak and wiped his hand on the coarse cloth. "I've given you what you need to get by in both languages; that should buy you enough time to charm them into letting you live." The mage reached within his cloak, and withdrew another cloak I would have sworn could never fit there.

"A cloak as full of fascinating items as yours?"

"This cloak will take you to the Goblins once you've delivered my message to the Elves. When you're ready to leave, wrap it about you; pull the hood well down over you until you can no longer see out, then close your eyes. When you open your eyes again, you'll be near your destination. Do you have any questions?"

"No magic swords?"

"I warned you about sarcasm, and you'd be ill-advised to ignore my advice. No, I've provided no magic swords. They'd prove a temptation to fight your way out of problems instead of relying on your wits, and you have considerably greater wits than martial prowess."

I remembered my brief encounter with Brand in the kitchen, and reflected he was right—backhanded compliment notwithstanding. "Thanks for the reminder."

"There's one more thing I've given you: that which lies within and that shall provide you with resources you can draw on in time of need. Should it become necessary, rely on your inner voice for advice and strength."

I pondered what he'd said for a moment. "Once I've delivered my message to the Goblins, how will I return to Ankur?"

"It's unlikely you'll return immediately to Ankur. When you've delivered your final message, use the ring to contact me. I'll decide at that time where you'll be of the most use. Now I must go. Work well, for the tasks I've set you are important."

With that, he faded from sight like the afterimage when you stare too long into the sun. I shuddered and set about gathering my possessions, old and new. As I packed, I realized that beneath the sense of trepidation that had gathered in my gut, I'd also begun to feel a growing excitement. I'd learned to love the wilderness during my youth, and would be spending considerable time in new lands that I'd yet to experience—and that perhaps no living man had seen. More importantly, I had the feeling that should I survive my tasks—and I was confident I would—the places I was going would answer some of the questions that had puzzled me since I read the first of Orgrim's two scrolls. With that in mind, much of my trepidation eased, and I went downstairs to seek my morning meal.

Chapter 9: Into the Southwood

The King's foresters did more than simply guard the woods against poachers and hunt the odd wolf unwise enough to attack a farmer's livestock. Among other duties, we also escorted occasional parties of royally sanctioned huntsmen who'd come to seek their sport in our woods. I endured much mockery at their hands, even when it became clear I knew my business better than they did, and could always find them the game they sought. In exchange, I learned a measure of contempt for these tall, strong men. One or two would face wild boar or a stag on foot, armed with a boar spear, but most stayed a safe distance back and took their trophies with crossbows or—rarely—longbows while I stood before them in case the doomed animal made it through their first volley. It became all too clear that some felt the need to slay something weaker than themselves to feel like men; others simply felt the need to kill something.

An imprudent contempt for these men remains part of me today, though it was sometimes justified. Yet at the time, any sense of superiority I could bring myself to feel, no matter how spurious, helped me endure their taunts.

Perhaps it would have been easier had their mounts not shared the contempt the men showed me. Many of our visitors came astride large, powerful horses worth more than a lifetime of my earnings, and such mounts are a breed apart from your ordinary horse: a good one receives more and better combat training than most footsoldiers, and is more than a match for the average unmounted man. And those horses are wary, allowing none but their masters to approach, and very leery indeed of one such as I who fell below their line of sight and who obviously had no other purpose than to sneak past their guard and slip a knife into an unguarded belly. So whenever a visitor arrived astride such a horse, I walked with care and always kept an eye cocked backwards in case one took it upon himself to trample me.

Don't get me wrong—they were beautiful animals, and I admired their untiring strength and proud spirit, even when one appeared to escape its master's control and pursued me until I found refuge in a tree. Laughing at me from the saddle, my betters would apologize for their horse's indiscretion, but the skill with which they subsequently handled their mounts told me it was no accident I'd become the subject of the hunt, however temporarily. I suppose it's to be expected that from those days onwards, I always carried a deep and abiding mistrust for horses, and somehow they sensed it and returned my mistrust.

Years later, I stood tall enough to look Orgrim's horse in the eye, but some of that apprehension remained. When I called for my horse after breaking my fast, I was unsurprised to discover her awaiting me— though I hadn't come to the inn with a horse and had no idea how the stablehands would know which horse was mine. I was also unsurprised, though not pleased, to find Grey awaiting me atop the saddle that lay amidst a pile of new gear on the immaculate stable floor. As before, he greeted me as if I'd been gone for years rather than what had been little more than an hour. I felt an almost overwhelming urge to be rid of him, then felt bad about it and resisted the temptation. How could I abandon something as defenseless as a cat just because it was proving inconvenient? I could always find it a safe home later if it became an unbearable nuisance. Moreover, I reflected, the cat seemed to provide a foolproof warning of Orgrim's imminence, and I had a feeling that would prove useful.

I surveyed my horse with trepidation, and she returned my gaze with even less confidence, sensing the dwarf within. We were off to a fine start already, and it would grow worse; I'd never gotten a horse ready for riding, and had only ridden a pony a few times in my life—not often enough to be any good at it. The former alone would have posed an insurmountable problem, save that the stablehands were familiar with rich guests and willing to do the work for a few small coins. I watched them work as carefully as possible without being obtrusive about it, realizing I'd soon have to be doing this with no help. They even found a safe place to secure my lute, wrapped in oilskins. The riding part I planned to figure out as I went along, for I was confident I could keep my seat at a walk for as long as necessary, and confident there'd be no immediate need to make haste.

The lad who'd prepared my steed handed me the reins, and I slipped a coin into his palm as he did. He smiled and maintained a diplomatic silence as I crossed to the right side of the horse and tossed the reins up over its head and onto the saddle. Seizing the pommel with both hands, I placed my right foot into the stirrup and gathered my other leg beneath me to push up into the saddle. But as I did, the horse flattened her ears and began sidling clockwise away from me. The stablehand, having seen my obvious hesitation, was ready for her, and stepped in to grasp her bridle without being asked. He held her head down, and stood close against her shoulder to stop her evasions. I smiled my gratitude and pulled up with both hands as I thrust upwards with my leg. My strong new body was proving agile as I grew more accustomed to it, and I'd reached enough of an accommodation with it that I didn't vault right over the horse and onto the other side. Grey joined me atop the saddle almost before I noticed his absence from the floor, and settled atop one of the saddle bags with a look of acute displeasure.

The stirrups were poorly placed, and I had to rely on the servant to lengthen them. The fact that I was so much larger than average was a never-ending source of amazement, and it took some fussing with the gear until I could sit comfortably. Next, he adjusted the reins to an appropriate length, and double-checked the girth strap before stepping away to open the stable doors. With some trepidation, I removed one hand from the pommel and saluted him, but he failed to notice, as his back was to me. My fears proved groundless, for the horse hadn't moved, and showed no signs of doing so. I had vague memories of how to get her moving, so I slapped the side of her neck with the reins. She put her ears back and took a sideways step. Undaunted, I dug in my heels and loosened the reins, and that did the trick. Up went her ears, and she moved forward at a comfortable walk.

Riding was uncomfortable at best, but I managed—or so I assume, for no one laughed where I could hear. Of course, given my size and what might have been a well-swaddled greatsword strapped to the back of my saddle, fear was undoubtedly a more persuasive factor than any skill at managing a horse. By the time I reached the town gates, I was over my fear of falling from the saddle, and beginning to relax. Oddly enough, that made it easier to move along with the horse's gait, and I grinned in pleasure. Maybe I'd make a horseman after all!

That optimism waned as I made my way westward towards Belfalas. The horse showed a distressing tendency to bolt once she saw the open road ahead, and I had to keep a firm hand on the reins and a vigilant eye to keep her in check. Fortunately, horses aren't subtle beasts, and I soon learned to discern the signs that indicated my steed's intentions. But once I'd begun learning how to keep the horse in check, there were countless details I'd never before pondered: Where would I find food and water for my steed? How would I keep her from wandering off while I slept? How often would the two of us need to rest? Did I do the right thing by removing that pebble from her hoof with my dagger when she appeared to have gone lame? Was it really necessary to punch her hard enough to numb my fist to get her to stand still long enough to mount once again?

It was becoming clear there was far more to being a horseman than sitting atop one's mount and watching the miles roll past underhoof.

It also became clear after my first rest stop that sitting a horse involved more muscles than riding a chair. By the end of that first day, my thighs had been chafed into an exquisite tenderness and the stiffness of my muscles as I dismounted warned me of pain yet to come; indeed, the next morning I could scarcely rise from my blankets and set about preparing for another day's ride. And my horse had wandered off some time during the night, and it was agony to track her up into the foothills, where she'd gone in search of water. At least that solved one problem, for she'd managed not to foul the stream beyond hope of replenishing my own supplies. Yet if my face looked anything like I felt, it was no wonder she was unwilling to be caught, and it took me most of an hour to get close enough to seize her bridle. About the only thing that stopped me from killing the creature on the spot was the fact that the exertion loosened my muscles enough to make the concept of riding merely unpleasant; earlier, it had seemed unthinkable.

When I returned to camp with my prize, Grey was just rising from amidst the blankets, and eyed me with obvious amusement. Don't ask me how I knew the cat was laughing at me; I just knew. It took a conscious effort to dump him from the blankets when I gathered them to stow in the saddle bags. By the time I'd struck camp and gotten a fire started, the horse had wandered off again. This time, though, I was better prepared. I took a carrot from my supplies and used that to lure her closer, and this time, I forced my belt knife into the rocky ground, heedless of the damage I was doing to the blade, and tied her to the hilt. That worked well enough I could enjoy a warm breakfast of bacon, cheese, and coarse black bread while the horse ate some of the fodder I found in a saddlebag. That meal revived me, along with the crisp, clean air that was such a pleasant change after months spent breathing the stale, reeking air of Ankur.

Saddling the horse was easy enough, for I have a good memory and I'd watched as the stablehand did the job. Moreover, with my new size and muscle, it was easy to position the saddle and tighten the girth strap. Too easy, as it turns out, for I half strangled the poor horse in my first attempt and had to loosen the girth. Now the problem became how to get back into the saddle. I guess I must have loosened the saddle too much, for the first time I tried to mount, the saddle slipped beneath my weight and rotated nearly all the way beneath the horse, taking me with it and spilling me to the ground with a *thud!* that knocked the breath from me. I was sweating more than the horse by now, and it took an effort of will to calm down enough to start over.

Eventually I discovered a level of tension that both let the horse breathe and supported my weight in the stirrups. But my problems weren't yet over—far from it. No matter how I tried to mount, the horse sidled away from me in a tight semicircle every time I managed to get my right foot into the stirrup. Hopping along on one foot with the other poised above waist level in the stirrup while I pursued the horse was painful enough that after a time I abandoned the whole notion and simply led the horse by the reins. I could have punched her again, but mistreating an animal just to soothe my anger at my own incompetence wasn't my way. It felt odd to be walking when I could be riding, but in fact my legs proved grateful for the rest. In any event, riding was not to be an option unless I found someone willing to hold both the horse and their tongue while I mounted. That combination proved lacking, though many a traveler cocked a skeptical eyebrow at the sight of me leading my horse through the mountain pass, Grey riding atop the saddle with a superior air I found increasingly injurious to my dignity.

Most of that journey to Belfalas is best left undescribed. Suffice to say that by the time we arrived in the rich farmlands surrounding that city, I'd decided that henceforth I'd fare better wandering the land on my own two feet. I'd be happy to sell the horse for what would be a scandalously low price and use the proceeds to book passage on a boat heading downstream towards the Southwood, or perhaps a coach if any ran in that direction. There was a strong temptation just to walk, but had Orgrim intended me to take my time, he'd never have bothered providing a horse in the first place. Given how poorly I'd handled the first task he'd set me, it seemed unwise to tarry about this new one.

As I came down out of the hills, through rich farmland filled with fat and happy farmers, the extent of the city surprised me: Belfalas was huge, and lay nestled in the fork of two rivers larger than any body of water I'd ever seen. I confess that I hadn't traveled enough to claim any expertise in such matters, but Belfalas seemed the largest city in the world, even in comparison with Ankur, which had left me speechless the first time I'd seen it. Belfalas was surrounded by an awe-inspiring expanse of wall, and was filled with broad, winding streets visible even from this distance. As I drew closer, though, it became obvious the city's walls were in sad shape, far more impressive from a distance than up close. Belfalas had suffered grievously during the recent conflict with Amelior, and the walls remained unrepaired even though the war had ended nearly a decade ago. I knew too little of that war to be sure whether leaving Belfalas thus defenseless had been a condition of the peace treaty, caused by a lack of funds, or the result of simple carelessness. Given the magnitude of the task, I'd have bet the war had taught the townsfolk how indefensible their city was and persuaded them to rely on things other than walls for their security.

Whatever the reasons, a large gap nonetheless remained between the walls and the nearest habitations. Long ago, when the city had been much smaller and nearer the frontier, the first farmers had needed a place of refuge from the Goblins, who were said to have periodically invaded these lands from the west. As the city had grown, new walls had been thrown up to contain it and offer shelter in time of need, and though the old walls were still visible here and there, mostly they'd been incorporated into buildings or pulled down to provide materials for newer structures. Judging by the obvious age of the current walls, there'd been no new wall-building for half a dozen generations. At some point, someone had decided it would be more cost-effective to simply restrict the city to its current size and keep all new construction a safe distance from the walls in the unlikely event a war came and that distance became necessary to protect the inhabitants.

The few parts of the walls that had been repaired were those necessary to control traffic and collect tolls. This I observed while I awaited my turn at the gates, which had been repaired well enough to bar the passage of commercial traffic but by no means well enough to hold determined attackers outside. I watched with some discomfort as a caravan of carts bearing night soil blocked the road and fouled the air; a city with that many people generated an impressive stench, and though a different city might have been content to dump the wastes into the river, Belfalas had been founded by farmers; those same wastes would make their way back into the city in a few months in the region's rich harvests.

When my turn came, I paid the entry fee, which—presumably because I had enough money to own a horse—was steep. Had I been here at my own expense and planning to stay, I'd have pursued the matter to learn whether they'd flagged me as wealthy and inflated the fee accordingly, or whether people really spent their entire lives within these walls, unable to afford the cost of leaving and returning. Even without these tolls and with the roads safe for travel after the war, only wealthy merchants or minstrels could afford the luxury of travel. Yet with the current tolls, someone in Belfalas was growing wealthy indeed.

When I emerged from beneath the shadows of the walls, the pungent odors of massed humanity assaulted me. On top of the aroma the carts had left in their wake, there was the scent of far too many unwashed human bodies packed into too small a space; after several days in the wilderness, I'd forgotten just how bad that smell could be, and didn't look forward to reacquiring my tolerance for it. At least it was still early spring, and not yet warm enough to magnify the stench to truly numbing levels. And despite my displeasure, there were also pleasant smells amidst that heavier stink: as I paused to get my bearings, I could smell occasional wafts of fresh-baked bread, the heavy perfumes of incense and spices, and a faint, half-imagined scent of flowers. Grey rode atop the horse, nose wrinkling as he tried to take in the barrage of smells.

Many of the buildings still showed signs of damage from fire or catapulted rocks. Unlike the walls, however, there'd been repairs on the city itself, because such repairs were a more immediate need for people who required shelter more than walls. Some repairs were obvious, in the form of patches of new construction that contrasted with the age-worn original stones, but even the poorest of the buildings had long since been repaired with scraps and odds and ends.

It didn't take long to learn there was no coach traffic from Belfalas. Not surprising, given that this was a recent innovation even in Ankur, whose coaches traveled almost exclusively between Ankur and Volonor in the east, and were an expensive and uncomfortable means of travel. That left travel by river my best option—unless, of course, I was willing to reconsider selling the horse. The fading ache in my thighs made it easy to choose, and I set about finding a stable. Given that I was unwilling to haggle and merely wanted to see the last of the beast, the sale took less time to accomplish than to describe. I'm not sure which of us was more relieved when I patted the horse a final time on the flank and left without a backwards glance, ignoring the ostler's pleasure. I already had more money than I needed, and wasn't displeased if I could do an honest tradesman a favor while eliminating an unwanted burden.

On foot, with Grey riding atop my shoulders, I set off towards the western end of Belfalas, which fronted on the river. It was easy to find my way, for unlike the few cities I'd been in, there were broad east–west avenues leading through Belfalas. By the evidence at hand, these were designed to facilitate the passage of carts bearing produce offloaded from river barges towards the caravans that would bear this material east and west to where it was needed. I passed through an immense marketplace, still mostly empty. I could imagine the throngs who'd be here when the harvest was in and the large, empty areas were filled with the fruits of these lands.

The western walls of Belfalas, which loomed directly above the river, were in far better shape, for much of Amelior's assault had focused on the landward side of the city. Although a fresh breeze blew in across the walls, any benefits it might have brought to the air quality were far outweighed by a broad expanse of warm, no-longer fresh fish drying in the sun, their odor carried inwards over the walls from the fish market. I'd eaten fish before, reluctantly, and hadn't been fond of it even cooked. This was worse. I made my way past the market as swiftly as possible, heading towards a large barnlike structure with the sign hanging from its open door bearing the image of a barge.

Inside the building, it was cool, and there was a strangely pleasant, humid smell of decay. As I approached the small office, I looked around, noting the heaps of rotting ropes and the young man who was busy cutting out such portions as he could salvage. One old boat, irreparably damaged, lay forlorn against a wall where it had been stored for the winter; had it been serviceable, I imagine it would have been on the river even now, earning its keep. In the office, a bored-looking clerk sat playing with a pile of parchment sheets, trying to look busy and failing. He greeted me as I entered.

"Welcome, Sir." His gaze swept me from head to toe, noting the quality of my garb and the huntsman's knife I bore at my belt. "Would I be correct in assuming you need to hire a boat?"

I smiled back. "No, merely passage south." He didn't appear disappointed, so I imagine the lute and the cat had already told him I was no wealthy merchant come to make the man's fortune.

"Very good, sir. And how far south would you be going?"

"As close as I can get to the Southwood."

His eyes narrowed as I said that, and he took time to appraise me more closely. "Not an auspicious destination, but then I'm sure you knew that. You look to be a man who knows his way in the world."

I nodded, and there was a moment of silence as if he'd been expecting more. Then he shrugged. "Very good, sir." He named a price, and as it seemed fair, I agreed with no hesitation and counted out the requisite number of coins. In exchange, he pressed a token into my hand, told me when the boat would leave and from where, then repeated himself to be sure I understood. We parted with smiles, and he returned to toying with his papers.

It would be a day before the boat left, so I took the opportunity to wander the city and spend some of Orgrim's money. It was still early in the day, far too early for the most interesting night spots to be open, so I instead took the time to provision for the journey. All my life I'd carried a sack slung over my shoulder, and I was surprised and pleased to find a large packsack that hung by straps over both shoulders and left both arms free, unless I chose to carry my lute rather than slinging it. This device was so efficient I could fill it with more supplies than would otherwise have been possible; in addition to standard things such as dried meat and unleavened waybread, I had room for luxuries such as mixtures of nuts and dried fruits, clay jars of preserves, and two large metal flasks of strong drink. Moreover, the pack included fasteners that let me carry my sleeping bundle and an oiled cloak on the outside. I even found a cobbler who was willing, for a small fee, to set aside his other work and make me some new boots before I departed.

I ate my lunch at an inn that would have been far beyond my means, bribing my way in past a door-keeper who'd glanced over my attire until I erased his skepticism with a generous handful of coins. The food and wine were uncommonly good, and I toasted my former equine companion, whose sale had funded both my feast and my journey south. Afterwards, I reserved a room for the night and settled down to nap a while and digest my meal. A voice within my head had been whispering suggestions on how I could spend the night, and as I'd soon be leaving all human companionship behind for an unknown period, I began to feel I should heed that voice and seek the companionship of a woman.

When I rose from my nap, I found it near enough to dinner that there was little point in exploring Belfalas further. I went down to the common room for a meal and more wine, and as the waiter served me, I let it be known that I'd also want a woman's companionship that night. He resisted until I slipped him a few more of my still plentiful supply of coins; that persuaded him, and he disappeared for a time before coming back and nodding me in the direction of my room. By then I'd finished my meal, so I headed upstairs to wait for a bedmate, bringing a bottle of wine and a growing need.

I'm not sure how long I waited, but the wine was a good companion, enough so that I almost missed the first tentative knock on the door. I staggered to my feet, then bade them enter. The woman who entered was attractive enough in a worn sort of way, flaxen-haired like most of the farmers who'd settled in this area and big bosomed, and she had an attractive affected shyness. She pulled the door shut behind her, almost catching Grey's departing tail, and came to join me by the bed. The part of me submerged beneath the warm heedlessness of the wine felt appalled at my recklessness, but the voice that had urged me to this form of recreation was stronger and I surrendered to its urging and began to enjoy myself. It was a nice change to be wanted for more than the novelty of spending the night with a dwarf, and that, combined with the soft, warm pleasure of the woman in my arms, distracted me enough that I almost failed to notice the door opening.

The big man who slid into the room and bolted the door at his back was disappointed I'd noticed him, but his gaze took in the empty bottle of wine and a confident grin grew on his coarse features as the woman slipped from my arms and moved to the far side of the room with a knowing smile. I rose to my feet, noting as I did the truncheon in his meaty fist.

"Sorry to be spoiling your evening, Sir, but there's been a slight change in plans. The fee for the evening's entertainment will be the contents of that fat purse you've got over there on the chair."

"And if I choose not to pay?" I tested my balance surreptitiously, and found my legs grown steady beneath me.

"Then I'll be the one who gets the entertainment and you'll still lose your purse. I'd actually enjoy it more if you don't pay willingly." The truncheon smacked into his free palm with a *thwak!* that echoed in the room.

I hesitated, unsure how well I'd be able to fight in my new body. Though I suspected I had strength and speed on my side, what little weapons skill I'd possessed had been acquired against beasts armed with natural weaponry, and skills I'd learned with much shorter arms and legs. In consequence, I had no idea how well those skills would translate to my new dimensions. In fact, the results of my one test thus far of my new body's martial skills, against the kitchen help, didn't inspire confidence about the outcome of this match. The big man took my silence as refusal, and his grin broadened as he raised his weapon and advanced.

Rather than waiting for him to strike, I closed as his arm began its downwards arc, and caught his wrist before the blow had fairly begun. I was pleased by my speed, and even more so by the strength that let me stand that way for a moment, evenly matched. He broke that deadlock by sinking his free fist deep in my belly with a force that brought up all my dinner and the fine wine that had washed it down. He stepped back for a moment, freeing himself from my weakened grip, and when I raised my head from where I'd gone down on one knee, tears in my eyes and not yet finished gasping and heaving up my dinner, he stood ready to resume our discussion. It's not that he was giving me a chance to fight fairly; his look told me he was enjoying this and wanted to prolong his pleasure. I knew I'd never block the next blow, and I steeled myself as best I could for the impact.

Then all at once, the fear that had taken the place of dinner in my belly and begun clouding my mind was swept away by a wave of rage such as I'd only experienced once before. It was as if I retreated behind my own eyes and let that rage seize control of my body.

Everything slowed and grew clearer. I watched without alarm as the truncheon descended, and felt a savage joy as I surged to my feet and caught his wrist in my hand. This time I didn't feel the impact of his fist in my belly, other than as a dull sensation far away at the edge of my consciousness; in its place, I felt a burst of strength like a bucket of ice-water dashed in my face. I had strength enough to whip his descending weapon arm to the side, then rotate it in a vicious arc up and across his front. I felt my snarl of joy as his shoulder dislocated and he screamed his agony and fear, dropping the truncheon and going to his knees before me, his wrist still in my grip. From my vantage point behind my eyes, I relaxed, confident the fight was now over, but to my horror, the part of me that was in control had no such intentions. Maintaining my grip on the man's arm, I forced him to bend at his hips, and as he folded before me, I began kicking him in the belly, continuing even after his screams stopped and he hung limp in my grasp.

Then my world went bright as something crashed upon my head. I released the unconscious man, swinging about to confront my new assailant, the whore who'd planned this robbery. In her hand, she held the man's truncheon. As she met my eyes, she screamed; with an odd detachment, I noted that the man's scream had been higher pitched even as my fist snapped her head back and flung her across the bed, where she lay unmoving. By now, I'd begun to feel sick at what I was doing, but that didn't stop me in the least from proceeding, as if the me who recoiled from what was happening was no longer the me who seized the woman and ripped her threadbare shift from her body. I don't like to think what would have happened had it not been for a pounding on the door that distracted me.

"Open up in there—open or we'll knock the door down!"

The murderous rage that had driven me thus far retreated, sullenly, and I found myself in control of my limbs again. The rage vanished as abruptly as it had arisen, leaving a faint residue of unclean pleasure and an echo of mocking laughter. I shook my head, feeling the blood trickling down the back of my neck and the growing ache in my gut, and there came a series of heavy thuds against the door, as if whoever'd been shouting had begun to follow through on his threat.

"Wait!" I bellowed. "I've been beaten half to death!" As I said it, I realized it wasn't true. Though I was indeed bleeding, the blow to my head and the second and subsequent punches had left me somehow unharmed. I had little time to ponder that, though, for if I didn't open the door soon, that excuse would no longer hold any merit. I drew the bolt, opened the door, and stepped back.

Two men in the uniform of the town watch stepped across the threshold, short swords drawn and angry looks turned towards me, as if I'd interrupted their dinner. Behind them, the innkeeper stood clutching a club. "Just what in the name of decency has been going on here?" The three men took in the scene that confronted them, the naked, unconscious woman sprawled across my bed, her partner in crime lying moaning on the floor in a pool of our mingled vomit, his arm stretched out at an unnatural angle.

"Ask our host. Apparently, the entertainment he arranged tonight included robbery and a beating." I put my hand to the back of my head and removed it, covered in blood. Even then, my wound did not hurt, but I kept my eyes and thoughts on the two guards.

The two men turned on the innkeeper, who'd gone pale and stepped back a pace as if he had no liking for the turn of events. "I... I know nothing of this!" he protested, though his voice lacked conviction.

"So it would appear," the second guard observed.

"Sirs, I must protest this treatment," I went on, seizing the initiative. "I insist that you take these two men away at once and visit upon them whatever punishment Belfalas reserves for such villains!" The innkeeper made as if to flee, but the first guard had anticipated that and caught him by the arm.

"And the girl?" the guard inquired, an eyebrow raised.

I smiled back at him, trying to look as cold as I could. "Leave her to me. We have a business arrangement to conclude."

"Just see that she can walk home after you conclude your business," the guard cautioned. "Under the circumstances, we'll look the other way if you want to play rough, but we won't tolerate murder or anything that prevents her from doing business. This isn't Somorrah, you understand."

"I understand. The guard needs its taxes, after all."

His look hardened, but he sheathed his sword nonetheless and with the aid of his partner, bent to pull the unconscious man to his feet. The innkeeper fled the scene, though not before pressing something into the hand of the other guard, who took a moment to fumble at his purse before lending his companion a hand. It was unlikely the innkeeper would be spending any time in the town lockup that night, and equally unlikely this was the first time he'd escaped that fate.

I closed the door on their departing backs, and bolted it. Part of me wanted to make the woman pay for what she'd done and what she'd tried to do, but that part was no longer in control. I forced it down, and instead, crossed to the room's one table to moisten a cloth in the basin of cold washwater and return to rinse her face. It took a few repetitions before she woke.

When her eyes focused, she gathered her legs beneath her and recoiled across the bed. She made no effort to scream, nor did she reach for any blankets to conceal her nakedness. The coyness she'd displayed earlier was long gone, replaced by weary anticipation and the growing bruise on her cheek, as if she'd been in this or a similar situation enough times before to know what came next. That and the horror of seeing on another face what I'd far too often imagined on my own banished what little lust was left in me. I forced a smile, concealing as best I could the revulsion I felt for what I'd done and had been intending to do.

"Never mind, girl. You've spoiled the mood. Just gather your things and get out of here before I change my mind."

With a certain dignity, she covered herself with one of the blankets we'd knocked from the bed before her partner arrived, and strode to the door, without looking back, though the stiffness of her shoulders told me she was expecting a blow. I sat alone on the bed for a long moment before I thought to rise and close the door behind her. I almost caught Grey's tail in the closing door, and he shot me a reproachful look. The wound from her blow had ceased bleeding, and still didn't hurt, so I took some time to lave it with water from the washbasin, knowing what it would be like to have to deal with blood-clotted hair in the morning and not wanting that additional work. When I was done, I bound the wound as best I could with bandages ripped from the bedsheets. I doubted the innkeeper would object.

As I worked, I recalled something Orgrim had said before he left: "I've given you that which lies within and which will provide you with resources you can draw on in time of need. Should it become necessary, rely on your inner voice for advice." Surrounded by the sour smell of vomit, my own blood still on my hands, the memory of what had just transpired under the urging of that inner voice provided little comfort.

***

The next day, I woke with a mild headache, an unpleasant taste in my mouth, and the room's vile air in my nostrils. I used the chamber pot, then gathered my belongings and set out for the river, bearing the token the riverboat's master had provided as my proof of payment. My gut ached enough to discourage me from breaking my fast at the inn, but once I got moving, my head wound was only evident in the gentle tugging of the bloodied bandages as I moved my head and the dried blood I'd failed to wash away pulling on my hair. Though I shuddered at how I'd lost control the previous night, it appeared my newfound inner strength had at least one advantage: I was quite certain that had I been myself when the woman struck me with her partner's truncheon, I would still have been unconscious, if not dead.

The riverboat that awaited was not much more than a large raft with sides, and the unpeeled logs that formed the flooring were awash by the time I'd boarded along with the rest of the cargo, an anonymous collection of sacks, barrels, and crates, as well as two tired draft horses that undoubtedly found this part of the trip easier than the task of drawing the boat back upstream against the current. I took some faint pleasure in watching Grey's evident distaste for his new environment, but his distaste evaporated when he found a warm, sunlit spot atop some crates where he could curl up. The two burly men who crewed the boat weren't prone to conversation, and ignored me once I'd surrendered my token. The river was no longer swift, the spring rains having ceased, and the boat drifted downstream, propelled by the boatmen's poles on flatter stretches of water. It was a peaceful time, for I had naught to do but examine the scrolls Orgrim had left me and watch the countryside slide past.

The land south of Belfalas was unremarkable—mostly low, rolling farmlands at first, then flat fields of some short grass separating the tended fields. It was pleasant enough if you like fields, but I prefer forests and mountains. Farms covered the land as far as the eye could see, with their fields radiating outward like the spokes of a cartwheel from small fortified manors that had a tangible feeling of age and disrepair. Neat lines of fence made from the fieldstones that heaved their way to the surface every spring imposed a certain regularity upon the land, which was bright green with new crops, not yet begun to tarnish brown from the summer's dry heat, and relaxing to my eyes after so long amidst the city's grey and brown stone.

The sun hadn't yet grown hot enough to make the journey unpleasant, nor was there enough breeze to cool me, so on the whole, it was a comfortable balance. It was far too easy to lie atop a pile of sacks, safely above the water swilling around the bottom of the boat, and smell the clean country air washing away the city's stench. The lap of water against the hull, the gentle swaying of the boat, and the men's grunts as they used the poles to keep our course straight and the boat free of the shore were lulling, and it was easy to fade away and simply exist for a time.

When I'd slept my fill and grown bored, there were plenty of field-workers to watch. Indeed, there were enough laborers it was rare for us to proceed unremarked; like all workers, these men and women were more than happy for an excuse to pause their efforts and wave or watch us out of sight. I saw a few carts headed north or south along the muddy tracks that passed for roads, but we were alone on the river. The people here weren't so fat and happy as the ones I'd seen in the more prosperous lands east of Belfalas, but neither did they appear to be suffering. Evidently, the life of the Belfalasian farmer wasn't nearly so hard as I'd heard.

Towards the end of the day, we came to a large fork in the river, where a smaller but faster-flowing stream joined its waters, and the men began poling our boat towards shore. The town at that confluence was nothing much to look at, a score or two of buildings surrounded by a low palisade of sharpened logs. There was a guard tower on the side facing south, towards the Southwood, but it was unmanned, and indeed, no guards were to be seen anywhere. I collected Grey, who hadn't stirred a muscle longer than necessary to roll onto a different side, and left the boat without a word to my hosts, who were busy enough unloading their cargo they wouldn't have noticed, nor likely replied if they had.

One building just inside the gates had the look of an inn, with a hitching post and water trough, and shuttered windows overhead that suggested the availability of rooms. As I drew nearer, the sun-faded sign by the door, two crossed sheaves of ancient wheat over a battered pewter mug, confirmed my suspicions.

The other buildings looked neither promising nor interesting, and nobody wandered the streets, so I entered the inn without a backwards glance. Early as it was, no farmers nor other townsfolk were present, and I had to pound on the bar for a moment before I caught the innkeeper's attention. He was a fit-looking man with plenty of grey in the mane of hair caught up in a tail that fell between his soldiers.

That worthy looked me up and down before deciding a smile was in order. "Good day, lad, and how might I be helpin' you?"

"A drink first, then a meal and a room."

He nodded, and turned his attention to the kegs behind the bar. "I see you're a minstrel," he shot back over his shoulder. "Would that be meanin' you'll want to play for your room and board instead of payin'?"

I hesitated. Having once nearly been robbed of all my money, I had no desire to announce my wealth and invite a repetition. On the other hand, I'd had little chance to try out my voice of late, and had no idea how well I could sing. While I weighed the two options, he returned with my beer.

"Don't you be worryin' yourself, lad. There's no shame in honest poverty, and we get few enough visitors. People will be happy to pay your score for some songs of the old days and gossip of the new ones." He winked, and headed for the back room. "Pick any room you'd like upstairs. I'll be callin' you when dinner's on, and I'll send the lass with a washbasin."

The amber beer was cool, and very hoppy, but soothed a dryness I hadn't noticed developing. When I'd drained the mug to the thick, yeasty dregs, I headed upstairs and examined the rooms. After my previous night's accommodations, they were a decided disappointment. No beds, but rather heaps of what looked to be straw in large, disheveled burlap bags, and coarse blankets folded at the foot of each bed. I picked the room that smelled cleanest, and flung the shutters wide to let it air.

In the soft light that flooded the room, it was obvious there'd been no recent visitors, and there was enough dust on the one piece of furniture, a small table, that I had some hope the bedbugs had grown bored with waiting and had sought better foraging elsewhere.

As I inspected the room, I heard footsteps in the corridor, and turned to see the maid entering with the washbasin I'd been promised. She was plain but presentable, with the flaxen hair so common among the farmers. A faint aroma of flowers entered the room with her. In response to a sudden whim, I let my gaze dwell on her curves, feeling more lust than awkwardness at how she blushed. My reaction puzzled me enough I almost didn't notice my hand emerging from my purse with a coin and proffering it and—to my horror—winking. The girl's blush turned to anger, and I got the impression that if her hands hadn't been full with the heavy basin, she'd have fled the room to summon help or crossed it to slap my face. Yet her eyes watched the coin like a hawk, and I knew I'd caught her interest. Mustering such of my resources as I could, I scrambled for an excuse.

"Hold, lass, don't be angered. We city folk have different customs from you country folk. I was merely preparing to ask if you could help me wash; a childhood injury prevents me from reaching my back, and it grows mighty itchy some days. That, and I'll need your help to change my bandages." I showed her my head wound.

The anger eased into skepticism as she lowered the basin to the table, without spilling the water. "Then you'd be havin' a strange way of expressin' your wishes, Sir." Taking her eyes off me only briefly, she glanced back to the open door, and some of the tension left her. "I suppose it'd be doin' no harm to help you, provided you mind your manners. I've a loud voice, and the men of the house can be here before you could be silencin' me."

I laughed, moved to the far side of the basin from her, and began removing my shirt. "You have the better of me, then. Don't worry a hair on your head—I won't take anything not freely offered." I laid the coin on the table, pulled my shirt over my head, and let it drop to the floor. Fighting a fleeting urge to reach for her despite her warning, I turned my back to the basin and waited. I heard her sharp intake of breath as she saw the old scars, which hadn't been erased by my transformation. There was a brief pause, then I heard the splash of water and felt her give a tentative scrub at my back, the water dripping down and pooling at the top of my breeches. It felt good, but it also awoke lustful feelings I had to struggle to force down again. By the time I'd succeeded, she was done, and had replaced the washcloth in the water.

"My bandages?"

"Patient yourself, sir. I'll be returnin' in a moment with fresh cloth for your head." She was long enough at her task that my back chilled as the water evaporated. But return she did, with a heavy pair of scissors, and after soaking the bandages, she cut them away, taking no small amount of hair with them.

"Tsk," she chided. "Your hair's a proper mess. Would you be havin' me cut it for you?"

"If you feel you could, then by all means. But mind you: don't go making me look the fool."

She laughed, at ease now, and set about evening out the damage she'd done to my hair when she removed the bandages. Then she took the clean new cloth and wrapped my head once again. "There. Now you'll be on your own for the rest, Sir." The coin was gone from the table, and her face showed more mirth than anger.

"Sadly, lass, I will be. Thanks for your kindness." I felt the beginning of another wink, and closed both eyes to forestall it, but her eyes had gone wide and she was no longer paying attention.

"What a lovely cat you have. Is he friendly?"

"His name's Grey." I opened my eyes again, saw her squatting by the bed stroking the cat, and forced my eyes closed again. The urges that were building within me had grown unpleasantly demanding. I'd felt those longings before my transformation, many times, but they'd never been so insistent; my larger body apparently had larger appetites. I took a deep breath and clenched my hands into fists, opening my eyes and focusing them on my cat. "You'd best leave, lass, for I'll need to wash and have a nap before I play for my dinner." I managed to pick up the washcloth without knocking over the basin and began scrubbing at my chest.

With a last caress of the cat, she rose and curtsied. "Have yourself a pleasant rest, Sir. I'll be lookin' forward to hearin' you play tonight."

The door closed behind her, and I opened my eyes. Grey sat on the edge of the bed, looking smug as I'd ever seen him. "And well you might wear that look, you foul beast. I paid more for less attention."

Grey shot me such a scornful look I was taken aback. Then the look faded and he curled himself in the middle of the mattress while I dropped my trousers and continued washing. I patted away the last of the water with one of the blankets, then set it in the window to dry. Grey sniffed fastidiously at my hand as I sat on the bed beside him, then butted his head against my hand. I stroked him and he purred, a soothing sound that rumbled so deep in his throat it might have been coming from somewhere else. I picked him up, set him at the foot of the straw bag, then lay down beside him to collect my thoughts. I couldn't sleep, for I had much to ponder.

My recent behavior alarmed me. In the past, I'd not been too proud to seek out a whore when my needs grew great, but I'd not believed myself to be so desperate now, and I'd never considered forcing a woman, particularly one who wasn't in the business of pretending to be forced. Then there was that killing rage that had risen in me, and even though it saved me from a beating or worse, the lack of control was something new and unexpected. Something had changed since Orgrim transformed me, and not for the better.

***

When I came down to the common room, drawn by the delicious smell of fresh stew, a smallish crowd awaited me, perhaps three dozen men and women, waiting patiently. The girl who'd brought me the water also brought my meal, a large earthenware bowl of steaming broth plus a chunk of coarse black bread covered with some kind of runny cheese. I ate a large quantity of the food, relishing every mouthful, for it was tasty and I was hungry, and I smiled at my audience in between mouthfuls. No sooner had I finished than the girl was at my elbow with a mug of the inn's bitter ale. Grey had found his way downstairs and settled himself atop the bar, from which perch he allowed the innkeeper to feed him scraps of meat.

I took a long swallow of the bitter drink, then cleared my throat. "Good evening to you all, and my thanks for your hospitality." They nodded at that, some smiling but others too shy to do more than look away. Wiping my hands on my legs, I took my lute into my hands and began tuning it; despite its oilskin wrappings, the dampness of the air this near the river had let some of the gut strings stretch enough to throw it out of tune, and I was grateful for the chance to try out my voice as I tightened the strings, humming beside the chords and slipping into the mood. The fingering differed from what I'd learned, for the strings were closer together now, but my fingers knew where to seek each string and adapted with gratifying speed. I was relieved to note that my voice remained strong, though it emerged deeper from my much larger chest. When I'd done delaying, I played an old tune my foster father had taught me, seeking across the strings and letting my fingers recall the old patterns.

I felt the familiar nervousness that always woke during those first moments before I caught the rhythms and joined them, letting them erase all else while the audience relaxed along with me. I was by no means a true musician or singer, such as came sometimes to Court, but music had strengthened me through my youth, and brought ease and reassurance. It showed when I played, both in the music and in my voice, and that compensated for myriad technical sins. Of course, it helped that these villagers had never heard the Court's better musicians. There was polite applause when I'd done, and a few more smiles.

"What would you have me play?"

"Sing us somethin' of the war," called one man, who was missing most of his right arm below the elbow.

I nodded. "This song's called *The Soldier's Lament*." I picked up a minor key and worked my way through the opening chords twice while I called the words to mind and let my fingers find the patterns.

"When the sunlight fails and the clouds roll in
And the shadows fade to black
Then our hearts grow cold and we're not so bold
As the dark comes creeping back..."

I sang of the minstrels who traveled, in the pay of recruiters to sing songs of valor and heroism and the joys of war, leaving the gullible vulnerable to the recruiters who followed in their wake bearing bright coins and brighter promises, leaving less need for pressgangs. Then I carried the listeners through the disillusionment of the young soldiers, and the deaths and horrific wounds, and the final painful homecoming of the survivors, trailing off on a mournful note. The veteran across the room nodded, tears in his eyes, remembering.

But another voice rang out. "Enough of that, minstrel. Sing of the glory. Help us remember our heroes."

I nodded. "They were, my friend, they were. But not for the reasons we were told." I played with a few chords, then took a long drink of the ale. "Very well. This one's about what happens when we forget the only good reason for war." I flexed my fingers and set up a faster rhythm, moving into the angry words.

"In our hubris we made peace
Oh so sure we'd found surcease
From the pain of war released:
No more need to conquer..."

I sang of what happened when we forgot what we won through those sacrifices, and the cost of forgetting those who preserved what we'd built. I worked in a few sly digs at Amelior, our erstwhile foe with a thirst for empire, and had many heads nodding before I ended the song with a flourish. There were even a few hoots of appreciation. I smiled at the man who'd asked for that song, gratified by his shy smile, and had another sip of my drink. My fingertips were beginning to feel sore, for I'd not practiced as much with my lute as I should have, and the transformation of my body had thinned the calluses on my fingers enough that playing was mildly painful. But there was warmth spreading in me from more than the ale, and I found myself at peace, comfortable as I'd not been in a long time and basking in the acceptance of those around me.

"Enough of all this man's talk of fightin' and killin'," laughed the maid who'd helped me bathe. "Let's have a song for the ladies."

I smiled back at her, hoping for but not getting any encouragement. "And would that be for the unwed ladies?" She colored prettily, and as the others laughed, I sought out chords for a song that might grant me a break from playing when it was done and offer an opportunity to seek some answers as to what lay ahead when I moved southward.

"This one you may have heard, for it's called *The Song of the Elf Maid*." I found a slower rhythm and played with it until I could feel it moving within me, guiding my fingers the way a song did when I had it moving clean and clear in my head and my heart and in whatever linked the two.

" 'Twas just past dawn by Glimmermere, the moon yet in the sky
And not a sound was there to hear, except a maiden's cry.
She sang a song of loud lament, a tale of lover's woe
Her man had left without consent, and none had seen him go..."

It was an old and entirely implausible tale of the romance between an Elven maid and a mortal man, something from the early days when we'd first arrived on these shores and not yet earned the enmity of the original inhabitants. It was pretty and wistful and right at the edge of my skill, for the old musicians had been far more sophisticated than most of us today. Yet I thought I did a credible job of it, and the audience's awkward silence as I set aside my lute told me I'd captured some of that ancient beauty for them.

"Thank you," the girl spoke into the silence. "That was beautiful."

"You're welcome." I sipped the ale again, keeping my eyes as guileless as I knew how. "It's a silly sort of song, though, for as we all know, the Elves were never more than a fable for children." Most heads in the room nodded, but there was one older woman at the back of the room whose distant gaze and haunted eyes spoke of some memory. I resolved to question her later. As I planned what I would ask her with one part of my mind, I chatted with the audience, telling them choice bits of gossip from Ankur between sips of my drink. Ankur was a place so far away that none had ever been. The tale of the marriage of the commoner general, John, to the princess Amanda after the old King died on the eve of war with Amelior was so popular I had to tell it twice, the second time in tedious detail. I had little news of Belfalas, which, though a short journey upstream by boat, was farther than most had traveled.

I played a few more songs as the night closed in around the inn, letting each one carry me somewhere different I might strive to bring my audience. I took long breaks between each group of songs to rest my fingertips, then in response to the maid's request for a song from the Exodus that brought us to these lands, I began fingering a tune that had been lurking at the back of my mind for weeks now. Playing it while in this contemplative mood might help me discover why it had haunted me, when I hadn't thought of it at all for years. Once again, I set about finding the right chords, and though it had been long, I found what I sought and fell into it.

"Let me talk a bit of malice, let me speak a while of wrong

Tell a tale of so much ill—let me spin for you a song.

There was once a man of learning, one whose knowledge spanned all time

And whose knowledge brought him power that erased our peace of mind..."

The song was awkward by design, and unsettling, striving to convey at once the seductive power of magic and learning and all the good things they'd brought our ancestors, while reminding us of the consequences of that learning and why it was now forbidden. The deeper meanings that lay behind these contradictions eluded me, the more so now that I'd made them tangible once more, but the surface meaning was clear: it had echoes of Orgrim and his mysterious past in every note.

Sharp claws on my leg interrupted my thoughts as Grey climbed until he could rest his hind legs on my thigh, then sprang up onto my shoulders, purring. Some of my audience smiled, others yawned, but all drained their drinks and began the familiar motions that told of preparations for leaving. It was still early, but farmers work while they have light and rest while they have time. Resting my lute against the bar, I rose and crossed the room to the old woman.

She looked up as I approached. "That was a fine evenin', lad. You have a lovely singin' voice. It's a gift you've given us, for sure."

"Thank you." I started to bow, felt claws sink into my shoulders as Grey struggled to retain his perch, and thought the better of it. "I know it's late, but I wonder if we might talk a moment."

Her eyes narrowed, but she nodded and gestured for me to be seated. "Speak your mind freely, and I'll answer best I can."

I paused, uncertain how to begin, then settled for the direct approach. "I couldn't help but notice your reaction when I sang of the Elf maid. It seemed almost as if you knew of such folk."

She snorted. "The Elves? Naught but fairy tales, lad, naught but that, though you're not nearly the first who's come here seekin' such things."

"And?"

"And you'll not be the last neither, nor will you be havin' more luck than any of the others."

"What happened to the others?"

"Will you be wantin' me to tell you that few came back, and the few who did were changed?" She laughed with both her mouth and her eyes.

"Were they?"

She met my eyes then, and a solemn look replaced the mirth. "I apologize for teasin' you, which is a poor way to repay the gift you gave us this night. No, lad, they all came back, and as for the ones who didn't, I'd wager they simply chose another path home rather than bidin' another night in our poor village. The only changes I could honestly say I saw were from fatigue, exposure to wind and rain, and a certain gauntness that comes when a city man tries to live in the woods without enough rations or wit. Nothin' strange about that."

"So you didn't see an Elf either? Then I'm sorry for keeping you from bed." I began to rise.

"Bide a moment, lad. I didn't say *that*, now did I?" A touch of strangeness entered her eyes. I sat again, excitement growing. Knowing the forest folk existed was a different thing from *knowing* that they existed.

She took a deep breath, and continued. "When I was a young girl, I did what many did in those days. There was a fairy ring by the edge of the forest, toadstools and the like that formed a circle in which the grass grew greener than anywhere else, round the year, never covered by the snows of winter nor the leaves of autumn. I went there to spend the night, for we all believed that doin' so would reveal our own true love, and perhaps even an Elven prince. A silly thing, but we were young and it was excitin' to disobey our parents and seek magic.

"I found the ring easily enough, for there was a well-worn path to it leadin' from some ruins that lie by the river near the forest; you can follow the river tomorrow should you wish to find it. I spent the night there, bedded down amidst the toadstools; to be honest, the ruins scared me. The grass was warm despite the chill beyond the ring, and it was temptin' to close my eyes, but I was too excited to sleep. Some time 'round moonrise, I felt sure I was bein' watched, but the harder I looked, the less I saw. Yet there was motion at the corner of my eyes, and after a time, I realized it was the turnin' of my head that made it go away. The next time I saw the motion, I stayed where I was, and looked at it sideways like."

"And what did you see?"

"One of the Elves, naturally. He was beautiful far beyond the way of our folk, and strange, as if he were equal parts moonlight and flesh, and he moved as if he never touched the ground. He was smaller than we

84

are—you bein' a strappin' young lad, you would dwarf him—and finer of feature, and had great glowing blue eyes that saw everythin'. And that's all I know of him, for he knew I'd seen him and he smiled and was gone in an instant, as if he'd never been."

"Were you dreaming?"

She smiled. "Some would say I was, for there was much of the dream in him. But I know it wasn't so." She put her hand to her throat, and I noticed the thin leather cord that went around it and vanished into her bosom.

"You have proof?"

"Aye, I have."

"Would you show me?"

She hesitated, distrustful, then reached a decision. "Aye, that I will, providin' you be willin' to look without touchin'."

I nodded assent, and she drew the necklace from within her clothes. There was a small leather bag there, sweat-stained and worn until it was well-nigh translucent, and she worked at the straps until it opened. As it did, a faint silvery light emerged, like the moon's glow seen through clouds. She left it open long enough to see, then closed the bag and concealed it once again. "It only does that at night, long after sunset, as it did that first night when he left it."

I smiled, excited again by what lay ahead. "My thanks for your kindness and for sharing that special gift."

She smiled in return, rose, and left the inn.

I gathered my lute and with a nod to the innkeeper, returned to my room. I was tempted to pursue the maid who'd helped me bathe, but resisted—not without effort. I had things to think about, for tomorrow I'd be entering the woods and would have my own chance to seek the Elves. Knowing that I'd have a much better chance of meeting with the legends than any who'd gone before was more stimulating—if less pleasantly so—than bedding an inexperienced country girl, particularly with her kin likely to hound me out of town the next morning. I put aside my disappointment at that decision, and lay down upon the lumpy, uncomfortable mattress, burrowing beneath the coarse blankets.

I slept without dreaming, as was my wont, though it disappointed me that I hadn't dreamed of what the woman told me. They say that dreams reveal insights hidden to the waking mind, and perhaps their absence explains why my insights always seemed to take more physical forms by day.

***

The next morning dawned bright and clear, and I lingered over my breakfast. When I was done, I bought fresh provisions for several days and set out southward at a comfortable, sustainable pace, following the river towards where it entered the woods. With my long legs and the land's gentle contours, the walking was easy at first, though the wild grasses that sprang from the earth beyond the farthest of the outlying farm fields were taller than my waist and caught at my feet as I walked. About the time we reached those grasslands, Grey began tugging at my breeches with his claws, wanting to be carried, so I slowed and bent to seize him. As I did, he clambered up me to reach his perch on my shoulders before I could lift him there. His claws drew blood several times along the way, and his weight lay heavy across the back of my neck. I could feel the sweat pooling there and growing itchy, and I was half tempted to remove him from his perch, but when I tried, he mewed so piteously I lacked the heart to continue.

Around noon, when my hunger and fatigue began to get the best of me and the edge of the forest had risen above the grass to form a green wall that spanned the horizon, I paused by the riverbank to eat. I sat on a flat rock by the stream, laid my boots beside me, and set my feet to dangling in the cool water once I saw it was moving fast enough there'd be no leeches. Across the stream, a sleek-coated fisher paused to assess me and my cat, then seeing we posed no threat, continued its hump-backed progress, turning over rocks and darting its nose beneath the water to grasp at something. Grey took the opportunity to spring from my shoulders and seek his own meal. As he vanished into the grass, I filled my cup with water and poured it over my head, cooling me and washing the sweat and cat fur from my neck.

Grey returned with a tailless mouselike thing that he proceeded to devour daintily. I ate, watching the world going about its business around me. The grass swayed in a gentle breeze that carried countless fresh scents and the shrill buzz of grassland insects, loud enough to ring in my ears, while the river murmured to itself. There were birdsongs, some of which I recognized, and a hawk soared high overhead, wing-tips spread like fingers against the sky. Grey finished his meal first, and began cleaning himself without taking his eyes off me. When I'd done eating, I brushed the crumbs from my lap, then gathered the cat up and placed him back on my shoulders before he could inflict any more damage climbing there himself. Once he'd settled into place, I continued my walk.

It wasn't long before we came close enough to the woods to make out individual trees and the ruins the old woman had mentioned. In broad daylight, and from a distance, these were unintimidating, but I kept an open mind and watchful eyes, just in case. My legs and endurance had both been hardened by my passage through the mountains, and I was pleased at how tireless I'd grown; the woods came closer with each stride, and my anticipation of what lay ahead grew until it was well-nigh irresistible.

It was mid-afternoon when I arrived where the woods met the grass-land and the river rushed past the ruins, and it was then I felt my first hint of strangeness. The ruins themselves held little interest, as they were nothing more than a jumble of weathered, lichen-encrusted rocks perhaps a hundred paces across and rising from little more than head-height above the grass to some four times my height in places; they might once have been anything from a small castle to an immense cairn, for whatever structure they'd once possessed was only a faded memory. Though there were hints of an open area at their center, I saw nothing that encouraged exploration. I did climb my own height among the tum-bled stones to survey the lie of the land, but I felt nothing extraordinary as my hands sought and found purchase on the rocks.

The strangeness came when I scanned the sweep of forest that stretched to both horizons. The trees extended eastward into the dis-tance until they butted up against lowering mountains, which I knew, from studying maps, swept southward to the sea. But to the west, the trees vanished against the featureless horizon. It was a humbling vista, for I'd never seen such a broad expanse of open, empty land, but that wasn't what bothered me: it was the boundary between the woods and the grassland, straight as a sword blade, with not so much as a shrub reaching out to extend the forest's dominion into the plains. At first glance, it might once have been farmland cleared by human hands, but apart from the ruins, there was no sign my kind had ever imposed our will: no stumps—though they might have rotted after the passage of enough time—but also none of the heaped fieldstones that defined farms throughout this region.

After a time, I turned my gaze upon the forest itself, and the sense of strangeness deepened. The woods were thick with oak, pine, and a sprinkling of other trees I was familiar with, but despite that diversity, there was a curious absence that took me a few moments to discern. The problem was there were no trees smaller than a double hand-span in diameter, and most were so large I couldn't have reached around them to touch fingertips on their far side. There was little understory vegeta-tion, though enough light filtered through the canopy to the forest floor to illuminate the mosses and ferns that grew there in profusion. The woods were silent and motionless, with not so much as a bird call or squirrel scolding me from amidst the leaves. Even the insects had gone quiet—not silent, but rather hushed—and though I was grateful for the respite from their shrill chorus, I'd failed to notice when their voices became muted.

A peculiar feeling came over me. I've often been watched before, whether by boars and other forest animals intent on doing me no good or by the men and women of the Court with even darker motivations, but this was nothing like that sensation. There was something in that feeling of nights spent alone in the forest when I was younger, practicing the wilderness skills my foster father had taught me; I remember the mistaken feeling of being watched by the trees themselves, not yet confident in my skill and less comfortable with solitude and stillness than I'd eventually become. What I felt wasn't exactly like that either. Neither was it like the brooding animosity you hear about in fairy tales, right before the hero vanishes for good or meets the monster he's set out to slay. It was... I guess the closest I can come is that I sensed an otherness with something more than the five familiar senses.

Shrugging, I shook off the feeling. Nothing the old woman had said gave me cause to fear for my safety, and the tales foresters told of the Southwood suggested a cautious man had nothing to fear. Besides, during my survey of the ruins I'd spotted the fairy circle the woman described—it would have been difficult to miss—and I wanted to gather firewood and investigate the circle before night fell. When Grey saw my intent, he leapt from my shoulders and settled himself on a fallen stone that had spent the day warming in the sun. I laid my backpack on the ground beside him, and entered the woods.

The first task took no time at all, for there was plenty of wood scattered beneath the trees, much of it dry despite the shade. The strangeness was more intense beneath that shade, but not hostile. Having piled my wood near a small angled opening in the rubble that would help reflect the heat when I built my fire, I turned my attention to the fairy ring, which lay beneath the boughs of an enormous oak. It was an impressive thing, nothing like the humble rings in my familiar forests to the north. Here, the circle was broad enough for two of me to lie head to head without touching either side. The toadstools that marked its boundary were enormous, some the size and solidity of a wheel of cheese, and even the smallest was big as a man's head. Within the circle lay short grass of a vibrant green that made the grass outside the ring, though still in the flush of its late-spring vigor, pallid by comparison. The final noteworthy aspect of the circle was that it shared the sense of otherness projected by the forest.

I stepped into the circle, then out again, but nothing happened apart from a momentary intensifying of the sensation. Unlike the old woman, though, I had no intention of spending time within the circle. I'd heard—

and sung—far too many tales of those who'd spent the night in a circle and awoken to find weeks or even months vanished like the morning dew. No, I'd observe from a safe distance, hoping but not really expecting to meet my first Elf while I stayed in the grassland's comparative safety. After a last look around, I returned to my piled wood to nap and prepare for dinner and a night's vigil.

Some restless part of my mind woke me around sunset, though not with any sense of alarm. Rather it was a sense that something had changed beyond the fading of the light and the decreasing warmth. While my sleep-dulled mind began to function again, I used my firepot to kindle a cook fire; the coals in the pot were almost extinguished, but I'd done this enough times to succeed in coaxing them to more vigorous life with gentle breaths. Soon the fire was strong enough to cook the fresh meat and toast the bread I'd brought. I ate slowly, relishing the good food and the clean, still air, and watching with considerable pleasure as the sun set in a red sky that limned the wall of the forest running off to the west. Grey stalked about the fire, chasing shadows and trying to catch my attention, but he distracted me only briefly, for as the food worked its magic on my hunger, something else worked another magic on my senses, sharpening them and leaving me alert.

It wasn't a worried alertness—more the sort of anticipatory feeling that presages a thunderstorm, though the clear depths of the sky told me no storm was in the offing. Although Grey still hunted shadows, these were innocent and harmless, not the shadows I remembered from the nightmare of my transformation. I'd felt no sense of being watched earlier in the day, and there was still no sense of hostile intent around me. Yet the birds remained silent, and the only sounds were the crackle of the fire, the soughing of the wind flirting with the edge of the forest, and the susurrus of water a stone's throw from where I sat. It was that sense of otherness, the same one I'd recognized when I first arrived here but now grown stronger with the fading of the sun, grown to the point where I fancied I could reach out and touch it if I tried.

That sensation extended to the heap of stones that faced me across the fire, for now that the sun was gone, their appearance changed subtly. I had to step beyond the circle of light from my fire to understand what had happened, and when I did, the change was obvious even to human eyes. Earlier, there had been naught but heaps of sun-warmed stone, solid enough to stand on and not obviously different from any other rock; now, there was a strange feeling of absence, as if I could reach out and pass my hands through the stones. The sensation was sufficiently odd that I tried this, and though the stones remained solid beneath my probing fingers, there was a curious sensation in my fingertips as if the stones were only feigning solidity—almost the way the vibrating strings of my lute were there, yet not there, when I played. I rested my hands against the stone, still warm from the sun, trying to understand what I felt, and all at once, the moon rose. The change was sudden and complete: the stone softened beneath my touch as if it were nothing more than dense cobweb.

I pulled my hand back, having no desire to become as insubstantial as the stones, and no sooner had I done so, than the feeling of cobwebs vanished. Intrigued, I moved my hand closer to the stone once again, and as my fingers came in contact with it, that clinging feeling returned. With a shudder, I withdrew my hand.

The moon had wrought another change. The forest at my back, gone monochrome now beyond the warm light cast by my fire, had come alive. The quiet calls of nocturnal birds drifted out of the woods, and bats began hunting overhead, their shrill squeaks clear against the wind's gentle background noise. Things moved in the shadows beneath the trees, but normal forest things—a raccoon on its way to the river, eying Grey with a hungry look before spotting me and thinking the better of it, and a small, short-eared rabbit with ginger fur and the perpetually terrified look of its kind. I half reached for the large stone I'd carried against just such an occasion—fresh meat would be a pleasant change from jerky tomorrow—but something distracted me. The fairy circle drew my eye, for the grass within caught and held the moonlight, as if dipped in silver, and the toadstools had begun glowing with a golden light.

Placing my back to the fire, I sat and prepared to watch the circle and the forest beyond it; I had no idea what to expect, but the feeling of magic was so strong I was certain something would soon happen. My companion was oblivious; Grey, bored, slipped off into the grass to hunt up his own dinner, perhaps even the rabbit. By the time I remembered the raccoon, the cat was long gone. I called his name, but he didn't return. I hoped he'd be all right.

I watched until the waning moon was nearly straight overhead, but saw nothing I could claim as evidence I was no longer alone. I'd sat with the patience I'd learned as a hunter, and I'd watched from the corner of my eyes as the old woman advised, yet still I saw nothing. I was beginning to grow resigned to having spent a fruitless night when a commotion erupted beneath the trees. A small patch of ferns began thrashing to and fro, as if a silent hunter had caught its dinner, and I narrowed my gaze, curious to see what had drawn so close yet unseen. To my surprise, the thrashing stilled, to be replaced by a thin wailing, as if a child had been caught out after dark and feared both what the dark held and what its parents threatened when they returned. I shuddered at the memories.

All at once, Grey emerged from the ferns, carrying something limp in his mouth, and no longer able to restrain my curiosity, I hastened to investigate. Head held high, he glided across the short distance between us and proudly deposited his burden at my feet: a beautiful woman, but one so tiny she would have fit in my hand with room to spare for her twin. A fairy! The wailing stopped as she struck the ground.

Knowing something of the ways of cats, I knelt to determine whether she'd been damaged; I'd no idea what aid I could have given, but it would have been wrong not to at least try. But before I could touch her, the fairy gave a start and opened her eyes. They were a pale and luminous blue, with no whites and no pupils, and held infinite depths. I withdrew my hand.

"Save me, Man, and all my considerable resources shall be thine!"

I blinked, but was speechless with surprise; the fairy's voice had been faint and tremulous with fear, and bore an archaic accent, but the words were in my own tongue. I was at a loss for words, overcome with the wonder of what I was seeing.

The fairy mistook my intent. "If you lack greed, then have you no pity in its place?" Now, there was angry pride in that voice, beginning to cut through the terror. I shook off the spell and hastened to reply.

"My apologies. I've normal amounts of both. But you startled me so, I could find no words to respond."

"Abandon then this wordplay, and restrain your beast before it makes a meal of me. If neither greed nor pity can move you to intervene, then perhaps the threat of my death curse will move you!"

Although I'd heard more than my share of stories of fairy gold and fairy magic, I had until tonight been certain they were naught but the tales simple folk told to explain the many things beyond their ken. I no longer knew what to believe, and whether any of what the fairy promised or threatened could be real. What was foremost in my mind was that having often been in the situation of a small creature at the mercy of far larger tormentors, my heart went out to her even as my hand went out to Grey. Grey arched his back in pleasure at my caress and began purring, but his eyes remained fixed upon the fairy.

"Have no fear, small one. You're in no danger."

"And you who had me brought here in the mouth of that great hunting cat would have me believe that?"

I laughed, overcome with the novelty and strangeness of the situation, feeling increasingly pleased that such things as fairies existed. "Your point is telling, but as you have little alternative than to trust me, it's moot. I want none of your treasure, and I fear none of your magic. What I do want of you is easy to give."

"You fear not my magic?" The voice, less fearful now that I'd restrained Grey, held a certain disbelief. The fairy's eyes widened as she looked at me, then a look of horror transformed her face. "Woe! You have reason indeed to have no fear of me nor yet desire aught that I could provide. I would have better remained in the cat's mouth." There was a tremor in her voice.

"What do you mean? You have my word I mean you no harm; indeed, I've saved you from my cat and offered you no threat of harm nor any insult. Neither am I playing with you, ready to betray your trust upon the first opportunity." For the second time in less than a week, I felt the first stirring of a deep anger within me, and it surprised me, for I'd never been quick to rage, and that emotion clashed with the wonder I'd been feeling.

"So you say, and were I one to listen to your *words*, that would reassure me. But it would seem I have scant choice other than to trust. Very well, Man; ask what you will, and for the boon of my life I shall essay to provide what you require."

Though I was tempted to ask what she'd seen that scared her so, the anger rising in me would brook no further delays. "I require only that you bring a message to the Elves."

"A *message*? *That* is all you require?"

"Nothing more. I ask for your word that you'll find the Elves and tell them that I come bearing a message from one Orgrim, a powerful sorcerer. When you've told them that, you'll have discharged your service."

"Only *that*?" There was skepticism in her voice.

"Only that. But I require your word—and my companion and I shall take it amiss should you violate that oath. My companion knows your scent now and might be far less gentle next time he finds you."

She shuddered from head to toe, and a part of me enjoyed that unaccustomed power over another. "It shall be as you say. You will await them here, should they choose to come?"

I felt certain they would so choose. "I'll await them here. Now begone, and bear my message."

The fairy rose, tiny translucent wings unfurling from her back. With a last terrified glance at Grey, she fled into the cool night air, vanishing into the woods like a bat that had flown into a chimney in pursuit of moths. All of a sudden, my anger departed, and I was exhausted despite my long nap; evidently I'd not grown as strong as I'd believed. I banked the fire with dry stones, and lay down to sleep beside it. Grey came to lie close against me, between me and the warmth of the fire, but that was the last I remember.

***

In the morning, I woke to find the cat gone again. The previous day's silence was back, the inanimate noises of the river and the breeze reassuring me I'd not gone deaf. I was stiff from my vigil the previous night, as my long time spent in the city had softened me more than a few days' hike could cure. Moreover, I could smell myself over the clean smell of the grasslands and my skin itched from insect bites and perhaps from small guests I'd picked up at the inn. I'd need to bathe soon. Fortunately, the sun had already begun to burn the dew off the grass, though it was yet early, and it had all the signs of a warm day. I broke my fast on cold cheese and bread, not yet gone stale, and set about stretching to ease the night's stiffness.

When I'd done with those exertions, I approached the stream with trepidation. The water had been cool but not cold near Belfalas, but here, south of the fork where the eastern stream from the mountains had merged with the river, it was icy cold—delightful to drink, but quite another thing to wash in. I knelt to splash some on my face, and it was as brisk as I'd feared. No, I'd wait until later in the day, when the sun would be hot enough to warm me afterwards.

I had little to do but wait, for there was no sign of the wildlife that had emerged last night, my gear was too new to need repairs, and my fingertips were still sore from their work at the inn. It was too soon after my waking to have another nap, and nothing I'd heard of the Elves led me to expect a visit before sunset, so all that was left was to have a closer look at the heaped stone. To my relief, the stone was solid once more in the bright daylight, with nothing to remind me of its disturbing behavior the previous night. It was a few breaths' effort to climb to the top of the heap, and it took that long only because I trusted no stone until I was certain it wouldn't roll beneath me and deposit me ungently upon the ground.

I gained the topmost part of the heaped ruins, glorying in the reach of my new arms and the powerful thrust of my legs. Once there, I sat upon a level floor some twenty feet above the ground and about the same size across, and save for the gaps between the sagging stones, that floor was featureless as the stones themselves. There was nothing here that told me anything about what this heap of stones had once been, save for one clue: the too-regular shape of the stones told me they hadn't formed naturally, nor had any natural mechanism deposited them here in such a quantity this near to the river and this far from the mountains. Someone had carried them here. It was a mystery, for certain, and one I would love to have solved.

There was nothing to be done atop the piled stones, and the view was no better than what I could see from the ground, so I descended the way I'd come and set about busywork. I had enough firewood for another night's fire, but I collected several armfuls anyway. There were mushrooms I recognized as edible, and I gathered them too, along with fiddleheads I spotted when I knelt by the ferns to set a rawhide snare for the rabbit who'd happened along last night. Then I returned to the woods to look around and try to better understand what felt so strange about them.

The woods retained that sense of otherness, more obvious now I'd become more familiar with it and could feel it like a tickle in my mind. It was easy to ignore, though, once I began exercising my woodcraft and watching for signs of life. The light was dim beneath the forest canopy, but there were nonetheless obvious signs that I'd not dreamt the awakening of the woods last night. There were faint tracks here and there, the feather of a chickadee next to the seeds it had tucked into crevices in the bark and forgotten last fall, the remains of a wide variety of defecations, and once, the cracked and dried bones of some small animal who'd fed a predator; there were even the marks of a buck who'd rubbed the velvet from his antlers on the seamed bark of an old pine. But despite these signs, nothing living moved through these woods save me.

The sun had risen high enough in the sky I could no longer delay the inevitable, so I returned to the stream, gathering my bedclothes along the way. With a quick, reflexive look around to ensure I was alone, I began removing my clothes. My clothing and blankets needed a good washing, so I soaked them well and left them under water, in an eddy where the current slowed. I weighted them down with several rocks, moving as fast as I could, but by the time I was done, my hands were numb from the cold. I warmed them by holding them in my armpits, clutched tight to my side, until feeling returned. That done, and before I could think the better of it, I stepped into the stream and flung myself flat into the water. Had I been any weaker of will, I'd never have done it, and I'd never have stayed long enough to scrub from top to bottom. It was cold enough that I soon had not one, but two, lumps in my throat, and it took a good hard swallow to return them to their proper position in my loins. But I kept at it until I was done, and emerged to stand dripping on the mud of the riverbank. Grey lay atop the bank, smug and dry amidst the tall grass, watching me with evident amusement.

"Be glad you can bathe yourself, cat, or you'd be next."

His gaze dripped contempt, and he rose and padded away in the general direction of our camp. I turned back to the river, shaking from the chill, and recovered my soaking gear, careful lest my numbed hands slip and send it on a long ride downstream. With my damp gear in tow, I returned to the sun-warmed ruins by my camp, where I wrung out the clothes and blankets as best I could and hung them to dry. That done, I climbed back to the top of the rocks with my lunch. The breeze was chill at first, but the sun soon warmed my skin, after which the breeze became a comfortable respite from the warmth. When I'd done with my lunch, I stretched full-length across the stones and closed my eyes. It wasn't comfortable, as such, but a full belly and the absence of my former itch—the icy water had done its work nicely—combined to lull me into a light sleep.

I woke towards sunset, the sun's warmth having faded but the light still good enough to climb down safely and retrieve my gear. I was stiff from my uncomfortable bed and from the sunburn that had grown over the course of the day, but those complaints notwithstanding, I felt wonderful; my swarthy complexion had spared me any serious hurt, and the warmth had penetrated right into my bones. The clothes were dry and warm from the sun, though stiff and scratchy across my shoulders. Grey awaited me at the camp, and after a cautious sniff, came to lie in my lap to be petted and fussed over. When he'd had enough of that, he left me in search of his dinner and I set about getting the fire going again. There were still coals smoldering where I'd banked them beneath the ashes, so that took little effort.

I ate my evening meal and savored another glorious red sunset. And as the light faded, the sense of otherness I'd grown accustomed to during the day strengthened, becoming a tangible presence again. This time, I resisted the temptation to touch the rocks, for my memory of the feeling was not a pleasant one. Once again, the forest came alive as the moon rose from behind the eastern mountains, and I watched and listened with pleasure as the animals whose traces I'd seen earlier in the day began moving about their usual business. It was a simple show after the frenzied entertainments of the city, but it repaid one's patience.

After a time, I grew certain I was being watched, yet I could see and hear nothing to confirm that it was so. Despite the moon, it was dark, and my night vision was no better than that of any other man, so the fact I couldn't see my watcher meant nothing; there was not even movement at the corner of my eyes, as the old woman had led me to expect. I thought of several strategies, then settled on the first one I'd come up with. Keeping my hands well away from the weapons I'd left in plain view atop my blankets, I cleared my throat and raised my voice. "I know you're watching me," I spoke to the forest. "I mean you no harm, and have a message." Then I waited.

Almost immediately, my watcher rose from behind the ferns I'd inspected earlier that day. The Elf stood a foot shorter than me, just over five feet tall, and his two most obvious features were his hair and his eyes. His golden hair glowed with an inner luminance tinged with the moon's silver, until it seemed almost more aura than hair. His eyes were the green of day-old leaves, and like those of the fairy I'd rescued from Grey last night, they were a single, solid color, with no trace of pupil nor white of eye. The combination was unutterably strange, and yet beautiful. I've called the Elf "he", for such was my first impression, but his was an equivocal beauty, and it was mostly the absence of obvious female characteristics that suggested his sex. That same otherness I felt surrounding me was magnified a hundredfold in him, and he moved as a shaft of moonlight, leaving no trace as he parted the grass with his small feet. The grass closed behind him as if he'd never been there—indeed, as if he came out of dream rather than existing in the same reality that was my home.

The other things that caught my eyes were the long, thin sword that swung at his waist and the strung longbow clutched in his right hand, the silver-tipped arrow resting beneath his right thumb while his two left forefingers gripped the bowstring and fletching loosely. I watched him, but made no effort to reach for my own weapon nor to gather my feet beneath me. I'd worked with master archers before, and knew from the casual ease with which he held the bow that I'd not live to complete either motion should I alarm him. His own eyes roved about, as if seeking something, though without pupils to watch, it was difficult to be sure where he was looking.

"My name is Modred. Be welcome to my camp," I said, making a conscious effort not to scan the woods at his back to determine whether he was alone.

When he spoke, he used my own tongue, and like the fairy, the words rolled smoothly off his tongue, freighted with an antique accent. "This is not about welcomes, for you are not welcome here, but circumstances nonetheless force me to accept your hospitality." He folded himself into a crouch, on the far side of the campfire, squatting and letting his bow rest across the front of his legs, the arrow pointing more or less in my direction and his fingers relaxed upon the string.

"You have my apologies. As it happens, I'm not my own agent in this matter."

His eyes sought mine, then, and the relaxing of the small muscles around them made them seem unfocused, as if he were seeing *through* me more than looking at me. After a moment, his eyes widened in shock, and though he mastered himself, his grip tightened on the bow. "So I see. You should know that this makes you less—not more—welcome here, for it's painful for us to deal with such as you."

"If I'm not welcome, then why are you here?" I watched him carefully as he replied.

"To determine whether you pose us any threat."

"And if I do?"

"That will become clear once I understand the nature of the threat." He smiled coldly. "I've come to receive your message and to bear it back to my elders."

I shook my head: no. "I'm afraid my message isn't simply verbal. I have that which I must deliver."

His eyes widened and he surged to his feet, bringing his bow to bear. It took all my courage to remain seated, immobile, though I couldn't quite prevent a flinch. After a moment, he relaxed and let his aim drift aside. "My apologies. My misgivings led me to mistake your meaning."

There was no warmth in his voice, but at least he'd not slain me where I sat. I released the breath I'd been holding and took in another deep breath, equally slowly, to calm myself as I'd learned to do before other, far less important performances. "It's my turn to ask your forgiveness. I know not what it was that worried you so; please believe me. We speak different languages, though you use the same words I do, and we can expect other such misunderstandings... I truly mean your people no harm, and should my words give you cause for doubt, please reinterpret them in that light."

"I shall endeavor to do so," he said. "You claim you bear that which must be brought before my elders. I must see it before I can permit that."

"That's a fair request." I tried to meet his eyes, and though I succeeded, I wasn't sure what I saw there; it was disconcerting to gaze into those green depths and have none of the normal clues to tell me what he was thinking. Nonetheless, his body language told me he remained under as much tension as his bow, and that caution was recommended. "I'm going to reach into my backpack now, and remove a scroll. Please don't mistake my intentions."

Without rising, I eased my arm towards my backpack, hoping he didn't catch the faint tremor I couldn't conceal, and opened the top flap. Then, using my fingertips, I teased the two scrolls free of the smooth leather until I could see the colors of the seals. When I was sure he'd seen they were scrolls, I removed the one with the green seal and swung it in front until I was holding it towards him, but not pointing directly at him; I had a strong premonition that doing so might have been more than his forbearance would permit.

"I have two such messages: one for your leaders, the other for someone else who need not concern you."

His head turned towards the scroll and his eyes unfocused once again, then he frowned and looked again at me. "I sense no ill intent, yet there's nonetheless a powerful magic in that scroll. There's something here I understand not at all, and that the elders shall have to deal with. Very well. Yet there is one more thing I must ask before I can bring you to them."

"Ask, and if it's within my power, I shall comply."

"You're nothing if not courteous, Man." There was the slightest hint of irony in his voice, and I began to relax. "Very well. You must leave your weapons here, both as an act of good faith and as a courtesy, for your iron is uncomfortable at best to my folk."

I fought down the unease that rose within me, vanquishing it with the realization that I was no great warrior anyway, and that even were I such, I'd be outnumbered beyond even a hero's ability once I returned to the Elves' home. Should they want me dead, my knife would do little good against bowmen firing unseen from cover. "I accept your conditions," I replied, "with two conditions of my own. First, I must put aside my weapons so they will remain safe against my return. Bide a moment."

I gathered my weapons, careful not to make any moves that might be misconstrued as hostile, and wrapped them in a spare oilskin I'd carried as a shelter against the rain. When I'd done, I overcame my revulsion as I forced the bundle past the cobwebby cling of the ancient ruins and left it deep beneath their surface, where it would be concealed from a casual search. Moreover, I had the suspicion that nothing short of magic would permit its removal from the stones by day, while no wanderer by night would think to seek them there. The Elf unstrung his bow and began extinguishing my fire, careful to ensure it wouldn't spread. He turned at my approach.

"You mentioned two conditions."

"Yes. The second is that you must arm me so I can defend myself should we encounter something wild with even less liking for humans than your kind feels."

He laughed, a brittle sound that only hinted at true mirth. "You'll be safe enough, but if it will ease your fears, I shall provide a means of protection." He reached a hand behind him and unclasped a leather belt sling that held a hand axe. He tossed it gracefully, and I caught it by the haft, grateful I hadn't been humiliated by missing entirely or grabbing the head. The axe head was light and made of an unfamiliar metal, but felt sturdy for all that. I hooked it to my belt.

I reached to collect my backpack. "My thanks for your trust."

"See that you justify it." He turned his back and moved off towards the forest, flowing across the grassy ground like a moon shadow. I followed as best I could, conscious of how graceless my movements were by comparison. He paused at the edge of the woods.

"Take my hand for the crossing."

I looked about me as best my human vision permitted, but saw nothing to cross. I shrugged, and took his hand. It was cool and dry, and when I squeezed harder than necessary to let me gauge his strength, he returned my grip without wincing. I relented, remembering what I'd done to the man in the inn and not wanting to hurt him despite my impulse to test his strength; he was more graceful than any dancer I'd seen, but by no means weak.

Something changed in that moment of contact. The Elf stepped between the trees, drawing me with him, and in an instant, the sense of otherness vanished. He relinquished his grip immediately, as if my touch were unpleasant, but the world had already changed, and it wasn't until I paused that I noticed the nature of the change. As we came abreast of the cluster of ferns in which I'd set the rabbit snare, I paused and knelt beside it.

"Why have you halted?" His tone was impatient.

"I set a snare earlier, and must remove it so no animal will come to harm in my absence." That was true enough, but it also provided an excuse to cast a look first backwards at the camp and then another downwards at the ground, where the Elf had hidden. The yellowish flash of moonlight in a cat's eyes met my first look, and I knew that Grey had seen me and would follow. I was more interested, though, in the ground around the snare. Though the Elf had lain here to watch my camp, and must have crawled or wormed his way on his belly to reach this position, even my wood-wise eyes could see no sign he'd been here.

"You surprise me, Man. Few of your kind would bother, and I had particular cause to doubt you." He looked troubled, as if I puzzled him.

I smiled, friendly as I could. "I remember what it was like to be small and powerless before my tormentors, and would not wish that even on an animal." He missed the deeper meaning in my words, and I duly noted that; whatever it was he'd seen when he'd first appraised me and grown alarmed, he couldn't read my thoughts.

The change in my circumstances now became clear, for try though I might, I could see but not touch the snare. It was as if I were brushing my hand through cobwebs, though the ferns were solid enough beneath my touch. I heard a snort of laughter and turned to meet his amused gaze.

"You're in Eald, now, Man. That which you left behind you is beyond your grasp."

"And the snare?"

With a motion too rapid to follow, his silver sword cleared its scabbard and flashed in the moonlight. The rawhide snare parted beneath that stroke. "Some things there are that exist in both worlds at once."

Not trying to hide his amusement, he resheathed the sword, turned away from me, and glided deeper into the woods.

Chapter 10: Messages and departures

Walking through the woods by night has always been a surreal experience, for nothing looks as it should, and the near absence of light robs my eyes of the certainty I feel by daylight. You never appreciate how important vision is to human arrogance until you have to do without your sight for a time and rely on other, lesser senses. No matter how self-assured I grew over the years, there was always a sense that something lay just beyond what I could see, cloaked in shadows. If I could hear that something or catch its scent, it was easy to name it and relax, or at least to take the necessary precautions should that name signify a predator.

But when you can neither see nor hear nor scent what accompanies you through the dark—*then* you must be vigilant. The older foresters often told tales of things that moved about the forest by night, and that kept to the deepest shadows, and warned us to never travel alone by dark—though we often did so from necessity despite those warnings. "After all," we reassured ourselves, "no living man could claim to have seen any of those anonymous things that crept about in the dark." With quiet voices that were far more disturbing than had they mocked us, the older foresters gave the same answer. "Yes, no *living* man." So although we publicly mocked their warnings, privately we took care to avoid being caught alone in the woods by night unless it was truly necessary.

Our walk through the Southwood that night had a different feeling, one akin to what I imagined one would feel in a dream—if one were the sort to remember one's dreams. I'd heard enough tales from those who did to recognize the strange distortions of time and distance as we walked. The forest was at once familiar, like any other forest I'd spent my days and nights traversing, yet at the same time unreal. The deeper we penetrated, the stranger things became. It wasn't that the shapes changed beyond recognition or anything so drastic; rather, everything took on a great clarity, the sort of crystalline focus one feels in the grip of a fever, and *that* despite the darkness and the thick shadows that gathered here and there. Indeed, the moonlight bathed me with a physicality beyond any poet's metaphor, the stars shone brighter than I'd ever seen them shine before, bright enough to cast shadows, and there were many lights in that sky that were unfamiliar despite years spent gazing up at the constellations and memorizing as many as I could. Sounds rang in the still air with almost painful sharpness, and the smells of leaf mould and night-blooming flowers intensified.

Small though my guide was, he moved fast, and I was hard pressed to keep up despite my longer legs. The world continued changing as we walked, enough so that I was lost within moments of our departure; the moon had changed position when we crossed over into Eald, and though the stars overhead remained familiar enough I could have set a course by them, the Elf set too rapid a pace to do so without running into a tree or other obstacle while my gaze was turned upwards. I consoled myself with the notion that I would either be escorted from the woods once I'd delivered my message, or would have no need to worry about ever finding my way home again.

Soon, the trees closed together overhead, though the light of the moon penetrated even so and lit our path as well as the sun would have done. As we walked, the forest became dominated by oaks, many broader than I was tall. I'd originally thought that given the light's silvery hue, all illumination must have come from the moon, but now that the forest canopy obscured the moon, the light appeared different indeed—directionless, almost. More animals than I'd expected moved about us: deer paid us no heed, browsing on acorns that should not have been on the ground this early in the year, rabbits hopped about as if they'd not a care in the world, and a huge boar rooted beneath a tree, seeking mushrooms. I gripped my axe, conscious of how poor a weapon it would prove against a boar, but after an unworried glance in our direction, it too ignored us. My guide ignored them all, striding along as if he had not a moment's doubt where he was headed. Shaking my head, I followed, savoring the strangeness of the situation and abandoning any hope of understanding it.

We walked for long enough that my legs tired before we saw the first sign of our destination. That sign was the familiar and comforting warm glow of a fire's light lapping at leaf-shrouded pillars that soared upwards until they vanished to form a roof high as the night sky above. As we drew nearer, I slowed my pace, not caring whether my guide outdistanced me, for I wanted to see what I was getting into. It wasn't so much that my caution would make any difference, for I'd already committed to this adventure; rather, it went against my nature to walk blindly into a situation without understanding it.

Despite my vigilance, two sentries emerged from the woods around me like moonbeams from behind a cloud: one moment, nobody was there, and the next, two Elves armed with bows had slipped into view, flanking me, but far enough behind for each to be outside the other's arc of fire. Were it not for slight differences in their clothing, it would have been easy to mistake them for two reflections of my guide. I acknowledged their sudden presence with a slow nod, but gave them no sign that their presence concerned me. Instead, I held my head high as I approached the fire.

As before, I took a long, slow, calming breath before stepping around a tree root as high as my knee and into the circle of firelight. My two escorts slipped back into the woods like an otter entering a river. In addition to my guide, three Elves awaited me, each enough alike to have been brothers or sisters. I'm sure I could have distinguished between them in better light, or with more time spent growing familiar with their features, but in the strange light of Eald and with the dancing light from the fire that lay between us, the three seemed identical. Their inhuman gazes compounded the strangeness of that sight, and despite myself, I shivered.

Two of the three who awaited me were standing, each clasping a long, slender, silvery sword and garbed in shimmering chainmail of the same unfamiliar metal. The third, who'd been sitting, rose, and with the firelight now limning her face, it was clear she was a woman. There were signs of age on her face and in the grey tinge that lent her golden hair the color of firelit pewter rather than the white gold of her guard.

"I bid thee welcome to our encampment, Modred, for though your race is not welcome here, yet would I not show discourtesy to one who bears a message from one as important as Orgrim."

There was wariness in her voice despite the formal politeness, but allowing for that and the strangeness of those eyes, I found I was enjoying the ample evidence that she was female. I let my eyes range over her body, relishing the sight of her; yes, I would take such a one as a bed partner without a second thought should the opportunity present itself. Alarmed, I bowed deep to conceal my discomfiture, and when I rose, I'd wiped away any trace of those thoughts.

"Forgive my intrusion, Lady. I come bearing a message from my master. Had it not been for his command, I would not have entered your woods of my own volition."

She bowed her head graciously, though her gaze never left me, and she signed for me to be seated. I did so, savoring the sharp aroma of the burning wood and awaiting her next words as I glanced about the encampment. The two who'd been standing remained on guard, eyes roving over the forest around us, which struck me as odd given how plainly I was within their power and how impossible it was for any other human to have followed me. I felt sure there were more of the Elves in the darkness about us, but it was a hunter's instinct, not any sight, that told me this.

"Let me see what you have brought us."

As before, I reached into my backpack and eased out the scroll, careful not to let it point at anyone. I held it before me, certain that it would be unwise to approach the old woman, and waited. My former guide stepped into my peripheral vision, and took the scroll from my outstretched hand.

Still making no sound, he moved around the fire to stand before the woman, holding the scroll illuminated in the firelight. For a moment, all three pairs of eyes across the campfire attained that unfocused look I'd first seen in my escort's eyes as they stared at the scroll, then the two guards resumed their appraisal of the surrounding woods. The old Elf's gaze remained on the scroll for several moments longer, the snapping of the fire the only sound, then she sighed and her vision grew focused again.

"There is peril here, but nothing beyond my skill. Open it."

The Elf who'd accompanied me thus far bowed, and with a flourish, ran his finger down the scroll until a fingernail snapped the seal's green wax. Then in an instant, even before the first tiny crumbs of wax had begun their descent to the forest floor, the scroll unrolled itself violently and flung him backwards into the night. An oily black cloud burst forth from inside the scroll, even as I heard the Elf's body strike the ground some distance from the fire, but I dared not look away to see what had happened to him, for my gaze was snared by what was happening before me.

The scroll had fallen into the fire, where it smoldered, emitting a foul black smoke that rose to twine with the black cloud that grew thicker and less pleasant with every passing heartbeat. I heard gasping intakes of breath from the Elves—all save the old woman, face grim with concentration, who'd begun circling her arms, bent at the elbows, counter to each other in the air before her, passing outwards below her waist then up across the center of her torso. Several more Elves emerged from the shadows, bows strung or swords drawn, and interposed themselves between the woman and the apparition. Chill fear took hold in the pit of my stomach, and had it not been for the fact that my legs would disobey me—and the sure knowledge that I would have been slain instantly had

I tried to run—I would have run into the night like a child fleeing a beating.

The darkness had by now solidified into a humanoid shape, but with muscles that would have been impossible on a human both for their size and for their alien configuration. The cool moonlight and warmer firelight seemed not to touch that figure, save for the pair of fiery red eyes that surveyed the encampment and caught the fire's flames in their depths. Its laughter was the slow rumble of a rockslide, and I could see the fear of several Elves as the creature raised a heavy arm, palm forward and wicked black talons gleaming, in an incongruous gesture of appeasement.

The old Elf hadn't paused for an instant, and in the wake of her still-circling arms, arcs of light began to trace a path in the air before her; indeed, it was as if she were drawing moonbeams out of the night and wrapping them around her arms. As the creature raised its hand, the circling of her arms slowed, then stopped. A disk of light hovered before her, seeming no more solid than fine lace. It seemed a feeble barrier between her and the creature above the fire.

But the creature did not attack. Instead, it spoke in that same gravelly voice. "Hear you: I bear a message from my master, and am commanded to tell you that Orgrim has returned to your lands. Know you that you are in no peril so long as you choose not to interfere with his workings among the humans. But should you interfere, I am to warn you that I am but one of many who will be unleashed upon you for your temerity."

Several of the Elves had taken a step back as the monster spoke, weapons raised, but the old Elf stood her ground. "We take your meaning, demon. Return to your master with *our* message: We care not at all what passes among the humans, and would have had no intention of interfering in human affairs even before hearing his message. But bear also this message with you: the Elves have no fear of such as you, and the manner of delivering your master's message shall give us cause to reconsider our intentions."

With that, she clapped her hands together, and the silvery shimmer in the air before her flew at the "demon", expanding to wrap itself about that mighty frame like a fisherman's net. The demon laughed, mocking her, and shrugged its mighty shoulders, but found itself unable to move; then, the net of light began tightening, crushing the demon in upon itself and distorting its shape. But even as that foul blackness dwindled, the burning eyes turned in my direction.

That gravelly laughter once again tainted the night, even as the blackness collapsed in upon itself. "Farewell, Brother. I hope you shall find it more comfortable in your new home than I find my current prison!"

Though I'd thought my voice paralyzed with horror, I felt the movement of my throat and recognized my own inadvertent laughter. "It's tolerable, Brother, made bearable by what I've been promised when all is done." As one blackness waned and faded, leaving that mocking laughter in its wake, another blackness grew in me, and I collapsed to the soft ground.

The last thing I remember was the chill as that second voice spoke inside my head, a greasy caress upon my mind: "Yes, Morley, I've been promised much when all is done."

***

I awoke to the touch of gentle fingers upon my temples, and an insistent pressure upon my mind. Unable to resist that pressure, I opened my eyes, and gazed up at the old Elf. I still couldn't read what lay in those inhuman eyes, but there was what appeared to be wariness in the lines around them and their companions graven upon her face.

"I wake you, Man, against my better judgment. There are those among us who would have slain you as you slept."

A sense of my body returned, revealing that I'd been staked to the ground, spreadeagled, but not tied so tight that I was in any pain. "I'm grateful for your mercy."

She frowned. "Don't be. It was fear of what your death might release that stayed our hands as much as any mercy—for though I have no doubt I could banish what lies within you, such spells open a gateway to somewhere perilous beyond your imagining, and there's no knowing what might come through that opening. No, we're safer with you as you are."

I licked dry lips. "And what am I?" I spoke that question as casually as I could manage, but at that moment, the answer was more important than anything else in my world.

"Know you not? How could that be, Man?"

Those strange eyes bored into mine, and I flinched away, not knowing how to meet her gaze. "I know you have no reason to believe me, but I'll tell you my tale nonetheless in the hope it will explain how I came to be what I am." I told her of my nightmare and my transformation, and watched her eyes widen with surprise. Then the wariness in her eased. "So you see," I concluded, "until tonight I was convinced I'd merely dreamed what happened—for it was so far beyond my experience it could be naught else but a dream."

Her voice was gentler now. "It was no dream, Man, as you now know." She paused, and spoke back over her shoulder to the other Elf. "He's an unwilling servant in this, incomprehensible though it may seem. Killing him would have been not just unwise, but unjust."

An unfamiliar voice replied. "So you say, Elder, and we must perforce believe you. And what shall we do with him now?"

"I see no alternative but to release him. We aren't yet ready to face our ancient betrayer, and harming his messenger would precipitate a confrontation before we have had time to understand our situation." She got to her feet. "I've told them to release you. Though no friend, you're largely innocent in this matter."

Belatedly, I realized that the conversation I'd overheard had not been intended for my ears, and that I would have heard none of it had they known I understood their tongue. As I pondered that, ungentle hands pulled the stakes from the ground and released my limbs from the ropes that bound me. I sat up, not wanting to tempt the Elves into reconsidering their decision. A wise choice, for I now saw the several bows trained on me, their owners pitiless and wary. At my feet, the fire had been extinguished, and it was clear the Elves were preparing to leave.

"Wait!" I cried. All eyes turned in my direction.

The old Elf spoke. "For what reason? You've delivered your message, and we must bear it to the council of Elders that they may debate our course of action. We bear you no more ill will than we bear the rest of your kind, but neither do we owe you our time."

My words came out in a rush. "I had not presumed any such debt. Yet as one who would not be your enemy, I would benefit from your advice. Any knowledge you can give me of my present situation would be invaluable in escaping Orgrim's control. Though I may never be your ally, it would nonetheless be better for you if I were not your enemy—not that I'm a fearsome foe, but your true enemy would be weakened by my escape." As I said this, I understood that it was true and that I'd been overlooking or perhaps willfully denying that I'd not been my own man these past weeks. I misliked what that said of me, but had no time now to ponder that further.

The Elves spoke among themselves, this time too quietly to hear. Then the largest part of their group faded into the woods, as if they'd never been present, leaving the old woman and (so far as I could tell) my former guide, whose bandaged head testified to the consequences of having opened the scroll. It was the woman who spoke.

"There's enough truth in what you say that I shall endeavor to answer your questions. Ask, Man."

I took a deep breath to ease the tightening in my chest. "I asked you what I am..."

"You are who and what you were before your dream. But there's a demon within you that bides its time, and emerges when doing so serves its purpose."

"That's the second time you've used the word *demon*. The word is unknown to me."

"And so should it be. Your race vowed to abandon magic when first you came to our lands, and as a consequence of that vow, you should know nothing of those foul creatures. And it would have been far better had that promise been kept; had we known it to be this badly broken, we would have refused you entry into Eald." She shot a hard look at the other Elf, who turned his head away, shamed.

I thought of what I'd read in Ankur. "I've read something of what you say. But I sense another reason."

She nodded gravely. "The second reason is one unknown to you, and one that cannot be known by any of your race."

I thought of the unreadable words in the scroll, and comprehension began to dawn. "*Cannot*? Do you mean we're incapable of that knowledge as a result of some great spell?"

"You're astute. Yes, there was a great spell, and anything that I could tell you would be as our own sylvan tongue to your spellbound mind." She paused, and frowned. "Also, there are depths here beyond what you imagine. That spell has implications even for the Elves, and we ignore them at our peril."

"I won't ask you further, then." In fact, I would have liked nothing more than to press her to reveal enough I could understand. Instead, I forbore. "Can you tell me more of these things you called demons?"

My former guide's eyes narrowed, and his knuckles whitened on his bow. "You have seen all you need to see to answer that question." I tried to meet his eyes and failed, for he avoided my gaze as if he now feared me. I noted the smear of dried blood that had run down his neck and stained the collar of his shirt, and the whiteness of his pursed lips, and my own recently healed head wound twinged. I reflected that he had good cause to fear me.

"For an Elf, that would be true enough. For me, it's not. You agreed to answer my questions, and if I'm to help you—or at least to weaken our mutual enemy—it behooves you to speak more freely."

The bowman was about to reply, but his companion cut him off. "He speaks truth." She paused a moment in thought. "This is difficult, for I must speak in terms that you can understand, and the more important terms are forbidden you. Very well, consider this: The demon you witnessed is a being not unlike yourself, but without a corporeal body and with the ability to wield certain powerful magics under the right conditions. Your Orgrim is one who can summon and control such creatures." Her lips wrinkled as if she'd tasted something unpleasant. "From what you've said, I believe that he summoned one such and bound it deep within your body; in exchange for the freedom to act upon our world, the demon was to use its power to shape you into the giant you are today. Though your demon allows you a measure of freedom, it also exerts a measure of control over your will."

"It mentioned a promised reward." I felt a chill spreading through my breast.

"All such dark magics bear a terrible price, Man. If Orgrim is true to his old habits, it will be you who bears that price, for he's too wise to let such burdens fall upon himself."

I still didn't understand what she was saying, and at that moment, did not want to know more. Ignoring the faint echo of laughter at the back of my mind and the painful knotting of my stomach, I pressed on with questions whose answers I did want to learn. "You speak as if you know Orgrim." Could she be that old?

"Yes, though I do not say it with pride. Your Orgrim was he who first made contact with us after your people destroyed their own lands, and he who bargained with us for their right to come here seeking sanctuary. We accommodated his request, for we were a hospitable people in those days, but he concealed his true nature and then betrayed us. Your people convinced us they'd abandoned all magic, our first condition for letting you come to our lands, but in time we discovered you had brought the worst of your old magics. Then you began destroying our forests to make room for your farms and cities. When we resisted, there was war, and we fared poorly at first; our magics are not those of war, and we needed to learn new tactics to fight foes armed with a terrible magic unknown to us and the metal that separates our race from Eald when it does not slay us outright. Eventually there was peace between our peoples, or at least an end to war, but we haven't forgotten. Nor have we forgiven."

I bowed my head. "If what you say is true, I'm ashamed for my race. Yet I would say to you that not all were involved. As you said, magic was unknown to my people, and the sagas tell that most were seeking safety from some terrible cataclysm. I make no excuses for our leaders, but surely the people were guiltless?"

"As guiltless as you are for bringing two demons among us and destroying our peace." She saw the look growing upon my face and spoke before I could defend myself. "I don't claim that you serve our ancient foe willingly, for you acted honorably to discharge what you saw as your debt. Yet the burden that lies heavy upon you was assumed of your own free will, and you must endure the consequences. Your crime lies in extending those consequences to us."

"Forgive me." I felt very small indeed, and there was a terrible weight upon my heart along with the simmering fear my new understanding had awoken. "I suspect my people will suffer as much as yours if what you've told me is true."

"If that be the case, then Teah preserve us all." There was sorrow mingled with apprehension in her voice.

"Teah?"

"She who gave us Eald, and many other fine things beside." The Elf's eyes sought the moon, obscured by the trees but whose light was all around us in the twilight of Eald. "But that is something of which I may not speak to you."

There was something here I felt sure I should understand, but it eluded me, and the harder I tried, the more distant that understanding grew. I shook my head, trying to clear an intangible pressure on my thoughts. "I don't want to abuse your patience, but I have one more question." I paused, fear vying with hope. "How can I save myself?"

"There's nothing you can do."

The fear was winning. "You claimed you could banish the demon within me."

"But not that I *would*. You have no such call upon me, and even had you, I would not risk the consequences."

The fear acquired a tinge of despair. "Then you're afraid to confront Orgrim?"

Her eyes flashed, but it was the bowman who responded. "Your temerity's inexcusable. If she refuses, it's neither from fear nor yet from enmity."

"Indeed, neither would influence my choice. But there are depths I don't yet understand, and cannot explain, and until I've plumbed them, I shall act no further. You're on your own in this matter."

The old Elf turned to go, the bowman covering her departure. I fought down the wave of despair rising within me and realized I had another question. "Wait. There's another question I must ask." Before she could deny me, I swept on. "How can I return from Eald to my own world? Surely you would not strand me here and risk the consequences?"

"Consequences? You fear perhaps that your master would come to retrieve you?" I remained silent. "Fear not. Your race cannot remain in Eald other than in our presence. Once we leave, you'll soon return to where you—" All of an instant, her head turned, paralleled by that of the bowman. I followed her gaze, and into the open space before me walked my cat.

Grey didn't have the look of a cat that had spent the night walking through deep forest; he didn't limp, and neither burrs nor mud marred his sleek coat. And despite the fact I'd led him a long chase, he crossed towards me and tried to rub himself against my leg, purring his anticipation. I think I was more surprised than he was when he passed right through me, as if I were no more substantial than a morning mist. Unperturbed, he folded his hind legs beneath him and sat before me, watching me expectantly with his head cocked to one side.

The two Elves stared at the cat, wide-eyed with wonder. The bowman's aim had shifted from me to the cat, then back again, but the sorceress approached and squatted before the cat to examine him. Her eyes took on that unfocused look the bowman's eyes had held when he first examined the scroll, the net of wrinkles relaxing for a time, and when she rose, a look of astonishment had erased her tension.

"This is no ordinary animal you choose as your companion."

This too was something I'd been denying, but I made no mention of that in hope I'd learn more from her reaction. "As it happens, *he* chose me. He's clever for a cat I'll grant you, but he's just a cat."

"He's far more than that." She fixed me with her gaze and spat an unfamiliar word into the air. A heaviness came over my mind, then faded. "I speak this for your ears alone, Man. This cat bears within him that which is either your salvation or your doom. Keep that always in your thoughts and think twice before ever you abandon him again to fend for himself."

As the last of the heaviness faded from my mind, I felt anger growing in its place. The Elf's words had burdened me with fear, a crushing lack of comprehension, and little new understanding in compensation. I'd begun to resent that. "Could you be more specific?"

"I judge it unwise to do so. You'll discover the truth in time, on your own, but were I to tell you what I know, I'd be doing you a grave disservice. Orgrim would learn of this as soon as he met you, and that discovery would bode well for none of us." She paused a moment and looked to the sky. When her gaze returned, it bore what I took to be humility. "I have no love for you or your race, Man, but I nonetheless wish Teah's blessing upon you. I have a feeling you shall need it."

With that she turned, and vanished into the forest with her escort. Overwhelmed by the whipsawing my emotions had been through that night, I stood, numb, and watched her leave.

Chapter 11: Message to the Goblins

Shortly after I'd fled the place where I lived with my birth parents, I faced an impossible dilemma: I couldn't stay in the town where I'd sought refuge, for it had become clear I would soon die of hunger if a knife thrust didn't take me first while I slept in some noisome alley. Neither could I return home, for it was inevitable that some day I'd fail to rise from a beating—and despite my predicament, I wouldn't have sworn I could muster the courage to return to the terrible place that was all I had of security in this world. (And later, as I've previously reported, even that place was denied to me.) I can remember the numbness in my head as my thoughts went around in circles, unsuccessfully seeking a way out of the dilemma, too far gone with fear and pain and hunger to force my mind to solve the problem. All I wanted to do was close my eyes, sleep, and wake to find my problems solved. Or to never again wake.

Of course it's never that easy. I'd long since learned that nobody would help me solve my problems, and that those problems would be the death of me if I couldn't find a solution or a way to endure them. Although death was always an attractive alternative, offering a final way out, it was an alternative I'd staved off for too many years to just give in. In the end, I returned to what I knew, steeling myself against the beating I knew awaited me, yet at ease knowing I was returning to the one place in the world I could call home. But as it turned out, all that preparation was for naught—that final time, they wouldn't even unbar the door. Though I nearly collapsed from the shock of that rejection, I somehow found strength to take the steps that led me away and to an unexpected home in the forest. Where I'd returned, many years later.

With the Elves gone, the strangeness of that forest combined with my fears to overwhelm me, and I slept on that very spot, lacking the energy to make a start on returning to my old camp. As always, I dreamed no dreams I can recall, save for the overwhelming feeling that my memories of the previous night had been nothing more than a dream. But by morning's light, it was plain I'd not dreamt the events of the past night. The marks of the stakes that had held me down still showed on the ground, as did the extinguished campfire and the warm grey cat sleeping on my chest when I awoke.

The sunlight that filtered through the trees disoriented me, for the sun had risen far to the north of where I expected to see it. After I'd broken my fast on the stale remnants of the bread I'd brought from Belfalas, made palatable by liberal application of jam, and gnawed on some tough jerky until it softened enough to swallow, I coaxed Grey back onto my shoulders and cast about for a time, seeking our back trail. But search though I tried, there was no sign other than the remains of the Elf camp that anyone had ever been here, or that I'd ever entered the camp. Since I'd made no particular efforts to conceal my tracks the previous night, this was passing strange. There was not even a sign of the spot where the Elvish bowman had landed, bleeding, after having been hurled backwards by the demon. Worst of all, I had no idea where in the woods I was, save what the position of the sun told me: if my estimates were right, I was much farther south than I could have walked in a single night. It became clear I'd have to sacrifice everything I'd left behind at the ruins, and continue on to my next task, a visit to the Goblins.

I unfolded the cloak Orgrim had given me, and examined it. Including the odor of old sweat, it was indistinguishable from any other cloak, but I'd learned enough of Orgrim to know it must be far more than that. I pondered a moment to be sure I remembered Orgrim's instructions, and when I was done, sat in a clear spot on the forest floor and gathered Grey into my lap. He knew what was coming, for he closed his eyes at once and curled his tail across them for good measure. No ordinary cat, whatever I'd told the Elves last night. Taking a deep breath, I cast the cloak around my shoulders and gathered it together in the front. There was a chill within the cloak, though its thick weave had promised warmth. Before pulling the hood over me, I took the silver axe the Elf had left me in hand. Where I was going, that measure of security would be welcome.

All preparations completed, I pulled the hood over my head with my free hand and closed my eyes. For an instant, nothing happened, then that slight chill intensified to a deep and numbing cold. That sensation faded almost as soon as it began, followed by the cloak itself, for wherever I'd traveled to, the cloak had not accompanied me. I opened my eyes in the sudden warmth, and looked around, not without trepidation. Save for my furry companion, I was alone, seated amidst tall stalks of grass that rose well above my eyes. Assuming I was still facing in the same direction as when I'd sat down, the sun now rode in the sky far to the south. I shook my head to clear it, disoriented for the third time in less than a day.

I spilled Grey from my lap and rose for a better look around. To the south, a solid wall of forest concealed the horizon, and to the north, there was nothing but flat plains and the dim smudge of what might be mountains on the horizon. Something was wrong with the vistas, and it took a moment before I discerned what it was: the grasses were taller than I'd remembered them being before I went to visit the Elves, and had begun yellowing as they did in late summer. The leaves on the far-off trees were naught but a blur on the horizon, but there was no mistaking the fact they bore none of the pale, youthful green of spring leaves. There'd been many strange things about my stay in Eald, but could I really have been there long enough to miss the spring and much of the earlier part of the summer?

I shrugged, and tried to dwell on more practical matters, for if I'd lost that much time, there was nothing I could do to regain it. There was no hint where I must travel next, and I was toying with the idea of using Orgrim's ring to seek suggestions when something caught my eye. Some distance to the west, a considerable flock of ravens rose amidst the grasses and took to the air. They circled for a time, then descended. Though ravens were by no means solitary birds, the only time I'd heard of them gathering in such numbers was on a recent battlefield. On the one hand, the last thing I wanted to do was come anywhere near a battle, yet on the other, there might be wounded who could be persuaded to provide directions in exchange for such aid as I could offer. That eased my decision.

I put Grey back onto my shoulders, rearranged my gear so my arms would be as free as possible, then strode off to the west, keeping my axe in hand and my eyes roving for any sign I was no longer alone. The grass here was variable, often lower than my thighs then rising to chest level or higher; where possible, I skirted the taller patches, not wanting to blunder into an ambush. It was closing on mid-day when I came across the first signs of what had drawn the ravens. As I rounded one tall stand of grass, I stepped into a long stretch in which the grass had been beaten down by the passage of many feet, with the hoofmarks of horses over-lying and nearly obliterating those original tracks. I knelt to examine the tracks, but far too many creatures had passed this way to make any sense of what I saw.

I followed the path as it veered north of west, in the direction of the ravens, and soon came across the first clear proof that battle had passed before me. Streaks of old blood daubed the grass, here and there com-bined with patches of coarse cloth and an occasional tuft of rank, oily hair. Now and again, one or a few of those who'd been pursued had bro-ken from the path taken by the main rout and fled along their own paths. The horses hadn't pursued them, but had kept on, traveling fast along the clear, trampled trail.

After a time, I came to a more chaotic area, where the fleeing crea-tures had made their stand. Here, there was more blood, and my first sight of a Goblin. Perhaps a score of torn bodies lay hacked and tram-pled into the earth until they were almost beyond recognition. About all I could tell of them was that they were small, perhaps no larger than I'd been before my transformation, and had mostly hairless heads. The one face that remained intact was vaguely human, but with pointy ears and a snaggle of teeth that were those of a carnivore. I shuddered, and con-tinued on my way, certain I didn't want to carry on but that there was no other way to go if I were to fulfill this part of my mission.

There was more blood now, and in a short while, I came to a much larger trampled area where the final battle had been fought. I stopped on the edge of that area, under cover of a taller clump of grass, and was appalled by the scene before me. Though a few dead horses lay there, round bellies beginning to bloat beneath the sun, the bulk of the slaughter had fallen upon the Goblins. There were at least two hundred corpses, many hacked apart, with several times as many ravens feasting among them, not the least bit perturbed by my presence. From the signs I'd seen while approaching, the battle had occurred less than a day in the past. I looked away, for though I'd butchered innumerable forest animals in the past, I couldn't encompass the magnitude of the carnage. What had once been sentient beings like me, however unpleasant and hostile to my race, were now nothing but carrion.

I had no desire to pause here for my noon meal, for I found my appetite gone; neither did I want to inspect the bodies with so many ravens present. Though I'd never heard of a raven attacking a healthy man, particularly in the presence of this much food, such great numbers intimidated me. For a moment, I wasn't a six-foot-tall man, but rather a small, scared dwarf not much larger than these great black birds. I shuddered, and began circling at a comfortable distance around the battlefield, careful not to attract the attention of the birds. I still wasn't certain where I should go, but it was a good bet that the Goblins had been fleeing towards what they thought would be safety. That same refuge could prove a good choice.

I managed to avoid disturbing the ravens and passed into the tall grasses beyond the battlefield; had they not been torpid from their feast, I doubt I would have succeeded in escaping their notice, shaken as I was by what I'd seen. On the far side of the trampled grass, I came across traces of an old path, made by something small, moving on all fours. The frequent traces of blood led me to suspect I'd stumbled across the trail made by a fleeing Goblin. This was fortunate, as it meant I might find one of the creatures still alive and able to provide an opportunity to learn of my destination before proceeding. I moved a little faster now, though no less warily, eager to learn more of these lands before I blundered into some situation that could prove fatal.

It wasn't long before the trail grew clearer, and the signs of blood became fresher. It appeared my prey had crawled only a short distance before passing out from blood loss; then, after a time, it had regained consciousness and begun moving again, losing more blood in the process. When I came across a still-wet patch of blood, I slowed my pace, not wanting to meet an armed foe unexpectedly. As it turned out, I had nothing to fear.

Ahead in the grass, prone, was the Goblin, still striving to place more distance between itself and the scene of the battle; it was exhausted, for it had made little progress since this most recent fall and seemed unaware that those who had slain its companions were long gone. The Goblin was barely conscious, and failed to notice my approach; having abandoned its gear on the battlefield, all that it still possessed was the patched and torn cloak that hid most of its pallid, unhealthy flesh from the sun. Its only weapons were long, sharp nails that scrabbled at the earth, striving to draw the small body forward. The head was hairless, with an unhealthy pallor despite a day or more spent beneath the sun that was beating down upon our heads. The one pointy ear that remained was surprisingly delicate; a stump remained where the other ear had been, splashed with blood and merging into a long wound that ran down its neck and into its back. Flies buzzed about the wound.

Grey leapt from my shoulders and vanished into the grass. Steeling myself against the sight of this unpleasant creature, I approached, and rolled it on its back with the tip of my boot. The Goblin's deformed face had a prominent jutting lower half and an odd mottling to the waxy greyish pallor. It gave a shuddering gasp as its belly became vulnerable, and its eyes widened in horror. The eyes were the same strange, flat greyish color as the skin, and like those of the Elves, had no pupils; unlike the Elves, its were bloodshot and rolled about, like curdled grease flowing from a gravy boat. I took a step back, repulsed, even as the Goblin's mouth opened to emit a faint shriek of terror, revealing an impressive array of sharp, meat-cutting teeth. The Goblin gathered its breath to shriek again, and not wanting it to attract any more attention, I kicked it in the nearest leg, which appeared unwounded.

"Silence, or I'll give you good reason to scream." Its terror made me regret my words as soon as I'd said them, but at least it obeyed and stayed silent, apart from the heaving gasps of shallow, too-rapid breathing. Belatedly, I wondered whether the Goblin spoke my tongue or whether Orgrim's magic changed my words into my captive's tongue. I continued. "That's better. I'm not one of those who attacked you, and if you'll trust me, I'll do what I can to help."

The Goblin heaved itself—himself, as a gap in his cloak revealed—to a sitting position, and blood began streaming down that unpleasant face from a gash on his forehead that, distracted by his hideous appearance, I hadn't noticed. "Aid from a Man? I believe you not. Kill me and be done with it, foul creature, and my curse be upon you and your misbegotten kind for your cruelty."

His fatalism amused me. "If that's truly your wish, I can leave you to die." I turned as if to go.

"No—wait. Mean you what you said?" A calculating look grew beneath its mask of old grime and fresh gore.

"I wouldn't have said it otherwise."

"Then I accept your aid—but, you must set aside your axe before you approach."

A cunning look grew on that face, and I found it hard to conceal a grin as I tossed aside the axe. When I drew close enough to examine his wounds, I wasn't the least bit startled when he lunged at me with surprising speed, snapping his teeth at my hand. I'd been ready for just such an attack, however, and whipped that hand aside, my other hand catching him by the back of the neck and driving him into the soft earth. I resisted a momentary urge to grind his face into the muck, and held him down, my flesh crawling at the contact with his oily skin. This close, his rank odor was too strong to ignore, equal parts fear sweat and curdled milk.

"Is this how you treat one who'd help you? Perhaps I should leave you for the ravens!"

The Goblin shuddered, then went still. I released my grip, and moved back a pace. "Let's try again. I said I'm here to help you. If you'll let me, I'll bind your wounds, feed you, and give you water. In return, I expect you to leave me in peace while I do so. If you don't, I'll bring you back to the ravens and see whether they prefer their meat still squirming. Do we understand each other?"

"I would sell my firstborn to the Elves before I'd return to the ravens." He rubbed at the stump of his ear, oblivious to the new flow of blood that motion evoked. "Very well, Man. You have a deal."

I approached the Goblin, ready for treachery, but he only flinched as I touched him again. His wounds were shallow; the missing ear was the worst of it, and there was no sign of the rot that would spell a human's end. Perhaps the steady flow of blood had kept the wound from going bad, or maybe the fly maggots that had already begun foraging there saved him. I tore a strip of cloth from the small supply I'd carried for my own bandages, soaked it in water, and laved the wound so I could inspect it more closely. The Goblin bore my investigations stoically, not so much as whimpering even when I used a small wooden scraper to remove the maggots and a few unhatched eggs the flies had laid in his wounds. When I was done, I took a larger piece of cloth and bound it across his wound, careful to cover both the scalp wound and ear.

"There. That will do until we reach somewhere with more supplies."

The Goblin recoiled, hissing in fear and baring his teeth. "Take me to your kind for torture and humiliation? Never! Better I should face the ravens and the clean death they offer!"

I was nonplussed. "Take you to my kind? That wasn't my intention, else why would I lend you aid?"

The Goblin frowned, thinking hard. "If not to your own kind, then..."

"To *your* people, yes. I bear them a message from my master, and if you lead me there, in return I shall see you there safe and find you better care."

The cunning look returned to that unpleasant face. "Take you to my people? Yes, Man, that I'll do." The predatory look in those disturbing eyes left no doubt as to his intent, but I had little choice if I wished to complete this second task Orgrim had set me.

"Good. Then lead on."

The Goblin made a hesitant motion to rise, then fell back. "I can't walk. My wounds have weakened me."

I retrieved my axe from where I'd tossed it and attached it to my belt, ignoring a sudden apprehension. "And I cannot carry you, so walk you shall."

"And what will you do if I don't? Without me, you've no hope of finding my people."

I laughed outright, watching anger contort his face. "You place an undue worth upon your life. The trail your people left during their flight leads straight as an arrow. It might cost me another day, but I'm confident I'd soon find your home."

What the Goblin might have replied I'll never know, for Grey emerged from the grass, and strode before me to confront the Goblin. There was something in his stride that spoke of a hunter stalking a mouse, and having been warned about the cat by the Elf, I watched, eager to detect any sign of enchantment. Thus, I was unsurprised to see a new pallor creep across the Goblin as he swallowed his words and shrank into himself, as if he were indeed nothing more than a mouse being stalked. Something intense quivered in the air between the cat and the Goblin, half-felt now that I was alert for it.

"You promised me food, but oathbreaker that you be, I shall walk," the Goblin moaned, and that suddenly, the tension fell apart and Grey was nothing more than a cat again. I picked him up and placed him back upon my shoulders, rewarded by the deep rumble of his purrs, and by the time he'd settled around my neck, the Goblin had levered himself to his feet and stood there, tottering.

I handed him a chunk of jerky, which he snatched from my hand. "You must taste it first."

I laughed, bit off a chunk, and began chewing. "As I said: lead on."

The Goblin cast his gaze across the horizon, then stumbling from weakness, set out westward, casting an occasional frightened look back at the cat as he gnawed at the jerky. We walked for hours, and I grew increasingly impressed by the Goblin's stamina. Even unwounded, I found the day's heat unpleasant, enough so I took Grey down and made him walk, for the back of my neck grew sweaty from the heat generated by that small body. The cat disappeared again into the grass, moving with the disconcerting grace of his kind. Though the Elf had warned me not to lose him, I wasn't worried; Grey had always seemed more interested in my company than I'd been in his, and I was confident I could rely upon him not to lose me.

As it turned out, we hadn't far to go. Long before the sun began its descent, we reached a large sunken area in the grassland. Its bottom lay several score feet beneath the surrounding land and the bowl itself was a long stone's throw across. Until we were almost upon it, the depression was concealed by the waves of grass that flowed as far as the eye could see towards the horizon. At its bottom, a cave mouth gaped wide enough for three men to enter abreast. I scrutinized it, and saw hints of movement just out of sight in the dark. My guide entered the depression along a well-trodden trail, and I followed close behind, not wanting to give him the chance to flee beyond arm's reach. Suddenly, that hidden movement became overt, and a dozen or more Goblins boiled from the cave mouth. Of these, a few rushed towards us brandishing short spears; the others, fear plain, raced upwards until they could look over the rim of the depression, desperate to see whether I was alone or the vanguard of a larger force. I mastered my urge to flee, bent to place my free hand upon the Goblin's shoulder and hold him near, then stopped walking. Feet planted, I prepared to fight for my life if it became necessary, and hoped it wouldn't be.

"Halt!" I bellowed, and with the power of my large lungs behind that shout, it was an impressive noise in the enclosed space. The volume and the fact that I'd seemingly spoken the command in their language broke their charge, and the spearbearers slowed and approached cautiously, forming a wide circle. Confident hoots came from the scouts who'd reached the top of the depression, and now it was obvious I neither presented an immediate threat nor foretold an imminent invasion, many hidden Goblins surged from their hole like ants from a trampled anthill. My resolve wavered in the face of the numbers the cave had sheltered. With this many so close, my companion's rank, unwashed smell was multiplied enormously.

One Goblin, a head taller than the others and wearing primitive chainmail, approached close enough to talk without shouting, but not so close I could reach him with a quick sortie through the crowd that separated us. "Fool! What's the meaning of this, bringing our foe into our midst?"

My guide cowered, beaten down by the contempt and anger in that voice and weakened by his long walk. "He claims to bring a message for our leader."

"A message? We'll carve his liver from his dying flesh and bring it to our leader to feast upon—that shall be his message. For your part in this, you shall have the privilege of watching his fate until we find time to disembowel you and scatter your guts for the ravens." My guide fell to his knees, moaning, and the Goblin raised an arm to give a command, but I forestalled him.

"I'm sorry to disappoint you, but there will be no disemboweling and no feasting until I've delivered my message." A strong sense of arrogant confidence was rising in me, banishing the momentary fear I'd felt.

Their leader scowled. "You speak our language well for a Man. I wonder how well you'll speak it with your tongue ripped from your mouth?"

The confidence crested, and I surrendered to it. I laughed, and locked my gaze on the leader's eyes. "We're not going to find out, are we?" He couldn't escape my gaze, and something within me looked deep into those strange and unpleasant eyes as easily as if they'd been human eyes. I saw right down to the fear that danced at the bottom of his soul, and smiled a predatory smile whose power was strong enough to feel, thrumming in the air between us like a gallows rope bearing its unhappy burden.

The Goblin fell back, sweat streaming down his brow. When I released him from my gaze, he wouldn't meet my eyes, and his voice rang hollow with false bravado. "A message, you say. Well then, we'll bring it to our Shaman and let him deal with you. And when he's done, we'll see who feasts and who provides the meat."

With that he spun on his heel and headed for the cave mouth, shoulders hunched as if anticipating a blow. The Goblins before me melted away like the dew on a bottle of wine brought fresh from the cellar, and cleared a path. Whatever had shone in my eyes and rung in my voice, they'd seen it too, or felt it, and each made sure to keep well clear. The confidence that filled me subsided, enough that I began to feel traces of apprehension at the ease of my victory, but the arrogance never entirely left me. So I strode without faltering behind the leader, abandoning my guide to his companions' tender mercies. I've no idea what happened to him, and though I owed him nothing, his fate weighed upon my conscience.

The cave mouth opened onto a tunnel that led first through soil shored up with long slabs of stone, then deeper, through a thick layer of dark rock that had surrendered to the assault of legions of pickaxes and stonecutting implements. Though I'd expected a difficult time navigating a tunnel built for such small creatures, the roof was tall enough I only had to stoop occasionally. There were no torches to light our way, and the only illumination was an almost imperceptible silvery glow from the Elvish weapon. Despite that, it was so dark that I marveled I could see; I fought down the memories of awakening, blind, in the palace crypt and turned my attention to the mystery of my sight. I'd never seen well in the dark, not even as recently as my visit with the Elves, so this could be Orgrim's magic or—and I changed the focus of my thoughts as soon as the idea occurred—that which now dwelled within me. Instead, I concentrated on the world around me.

There was a surprising amount of air movement in the tunnel, more than could be accounted for by the numbers of moving Goblins alone, yet despite this, the air was thick with their rank scent. The tunnel's size and the work that must have been required to carve it from the rock suggested this tunnel led to a large community, and one that had been here for considerable time. After a short walk, the tunnel opened into a wider passage that showed fewer signs of Goblin hands; evidently some natural fault in the rock had hosted them until they could tunnel to the surface.

Here and there, other tunnels led off from the main one, some spearing upwards and others diving deeper, but each guarded by a small squad of soldiers with sour expressions on their faces, armed with a bewildering array of hacking, stabbing, and bludgeoning implements. Their weapons lacked in sophistication, but looked no less effective should enough of them wield those weapons at once. There was dismay at my presence, for though the guards roared their approval at my capture, that approval became apprehension when they saw my unbound hands and the silvery Elvish axe.

Eventually, the tunnel opened into an immense cavern whose roof soared high enough overhead I couldn't see its roof, even with my new-found ability to see in the dark. The cavern floor was pockmarked with pits, some filled with water, others bearing small fires of what looked to be coal or peat, still others little more than holes that vanished to unknown depths. At the distant edges of the cavern, I saw herds of small, pale creatures that might have been sheep had it not been for certain irregularities of outline and the fact that no sheep could have lived long under these conditions. Elsewhere, there were wide expanses of crops I couldn't identify from this distance, though the nature of any crops that could grow this far underground was a mystery. Enveloping it all was that same rank stench, but also a pleasant warmth and humidity.

Goblins surrounded me in numbers beyond any man's ability to count—large ones, small ones, young ones, old ones, healthy and vigorous ones next to Goblins so scarred and mutilated they might have been the walking dead save for the sullen glow in those disturbing eyes. A continuous murmur of noise beat on the air like wind on a forest: voices raised in anger, quieter conversations, coarse laughter, and the cumulative effect of hundreds and hundreds of bodies breathing in a space that was, despite its size, enclosed and deep beneath the earth. Here and there, a stronger Goblin beat a weaker one over some dispute or perhaps an imagined slight, and the sounds of that beating rose to merge with the rest of the susurrus.

But as we penetrated deeper into the cavern, those Goblins near enough to see me fell into shocked silence that spread away from us like spilled lamp oil. In our wake, that silence became an angry muttering that swelled until it filled the space behind us like the sound of my rushing blood in my ears. I repressed a shudder, maintaining a confident stride on the strength of the arrogance that still filled me despite certain knowledge that the confidence wasn't mine nor yet under my control. Though I could have forced down that otherness and assumed control, I couldn't make myself do so. Whatever it was that lay within me, it gave me strength to face this multitude calmly, and I was prepared to accept this loss of control as the price of that calm.

As we reached the cavern's center, the crowds thinned, until at last my guide and I stood alone in the center of that sea of Goblins. We halted before a large, flat stone that rose several feet above the cavern floor, and I stopped behind my host. We didn't have long to wait.

On the far side of the cleared area, an enclosed sedan chair moved toward us through the crowd. As it drew nearer, I saw that it was borne by eight brawny Goblins, giants of their kind who stood almost four feet tall and who were armed with large, finely crafted swords and matching armor that must have been manufactured by my own race, though I didn't want to speculate how it had reached this place. The chair approached the large rock and swung broadside to it, the eyes of its bearers meeting mine with no fear. Then a door swung open and a small Goblin stepped out onto the top of the rock.

Immediately, a heavy silence fell upon the cavern; even the breathing hushed. The Goblin was neither particularly old nor particularly frail; indeed, there was nothing remarkable about him as he surveyed the crowd from his elevated vantage point. It was when he turned toward me that I glimpsed what made him special. His eyes held an inner glow that, though it shed no actual light, reached out with a near-physical presence; there was not the slightest trace of fear or hatred in those eyes, only a massive self-confidence as solid and imposing as the rock around us. As that inspection penetrated the depths of my being, I imagined I knew what my guide had felt when I turned my own gaze upon him.

When the Goblin spoke, his voice was steady and quiet, yet so strong it was like the pressure of a storm wind. The thing within me that had fed the arrogant self-confidence that carried me here grew uncertain, and withdrew, leaving me more in control. This dubious victory failed to reassure me.

"We have an enigma," the Goblin pronounced. "I see before me a Man, a demon, and a dwarf all in one, and the coming of you three was foretold. I'm the Shaman of these people, and knew to expect a messenger. But although your presence here is message enough, I doubt that's the sole message."

I called upon years of experience as a minstrel to calm myself and steady my voice, and when I was confident I could reply without it cracking, I did. "Your foretelling hasn't betrayed you. I'm here by the command of the mage Orgrim, who bids me bear you a scroll that bears his words." The leader's guards had laid down the sedan chair, and were scrutinizing me with clear hostility. As casually as my nerves permitted, I removed my backpack and withdrew the scroll with the black seal upon it.

The Goblin atop the rock glanced at the scroll, and his gaze darkened. "You dare bring such a thing among us, Man? Such arrogance astounds me!"

I felt the presence in my head withdraw and disappear, and fear rose to fill the void its absence created. As full control returned in the wake of that withdrawal, I felt the dampness growing in my armpits and upon my forehead, and worried that should this scroll behave as the last one had, I'd soon be in serious trouble indeed. Working on instinct, I went to one knee and bowed my head, proffering the scroll.

"Surely you can see I'm not here of my free will? While that may not excuse my actions, I beg your understanding. To the extent that such is possible, I'm guiltless in this matter."

The Shaman muttered something I didn't hear, and I felt the scroll plucked from my fingers. I looked up to see who'd done it, and watched the scroll float across the space between us, with no one present to bear it across that distance. The scroll settled into the Goblin's small hand, and I watched in fearful anticipation as he snapped the seal with his free hand.

Once again, that thick, oily black shadow boiled up from the open scroll, but unlike the Elf, the Goblin only widened his stance as if to brace himself against a wind. The demon swelled to its full size, and stretched mighty arms wide, as if trying to encompass the Shaman. Again, that voice, like heavy stones rubbing together, shattered the silence.

"Hear you: I bring you greetings from my master, and a warning: Orgrim walks once more among Men, and will brook no interference from your race. I bring you this token of what shall happen to any who chooses to interfere."

Before anyone could react, the demon's arm stretched an impossible distance to seize the nearest of the guards who'd borne the sedan chair. The Goblin, until then steadfast, shrieked his terror to the assembled multitudes as that arm carried him within reach of the other mighty arm. Talons sank deep into the Goblin's chest, silencing that scream in an instant. Blood and scraps of flesh and ruined armor rained upon the rocky floor as the demon tore the guard apart and feasted, and though my bowels heaved and nearly emptied themselves at the sight, I couldn't avert my eyes; worse, that unpleasant new part of me that had hidden until then rose again, relishing the sight. Through this all, the Shaman watched, unperturbed, until the demon finished its meal. The Goblin's lips were moving, but my gaze was focused elsewhere, at another of the creatures who had called me "Brother".

The Goblin leader pointed his arms to the ground before him, anger growing. "You've delivered your message, and now I have my own message for you to bear. Tell your master we've not forgotten the one who scorned us so long ago, and that we're not to be so lightly dismissed now."

The demon slurped at the marrow in the dead guard's shattered thighbone. "Bear your own messages, Goblin. You have no power over me."

The Shaman smiled, and the power in that smile caused the demon to halt its meal, bone still projecting from its lips. "Perhaps not, but I serve one who does. I invoke Gorm's power, and banish you!" With that, he raised his lowered arms high in a sudden, violent thrust. One moment, the demon stood frozen, the bone half falling from its mouth, and the next, there was a silent concussion that knocked me to the ground. When I picked myself up, the demon was gone.

The Shaman turned his attention to me, anger increasingly evident. "Orgrim has returned after all these years, and his arrogance has grown. He dares much to threaten us, and by Gorm, you shall pay for his temerity." He looked down on his people and raised his voice. "Kill him and let all divide his flesh!"

The Shaman started to turn away, amidst a swelling murmur of anger, and the many Goblins who'd drawn closer while my attention was elsewhere began brandishing their assortment of knives and other weapons. With the Shaman's back turned, the part of me that had risen when that first Goblin mob had threatened me rose up and stifled the fear that should have overwhelmed me, imposing an odd calm. As that part gathered force, I stood, a change coming over my face as the presence rose in me and swelled as if striving to burst from my flesh. I didn't even bother to take the Elvish axe in hand, for I was mighty beyond the need for such feeble tools.

Among my own kind, I was larger than average; here, I was enormous, and that, accentuated by the transformation in my posture, kept even the largest Goblins away; none wanted to be first to approach. Still, they'd been given their orders by someone it was dangerous to disobey, and the rear ranks began pushing the front ranks forward. The energy surged in me, and I felt my arms reaching out to rend any Goblin that came close; indeed, I was losing patience waiting and past ready to carry the attack to them, when the Shaman's voice rang out over the assembled voices.

"Cease! Leave the Man in peace."

A profound silence met that command, and all eyes turned towards that voice. I blinked. There, atop the rock platform, the Shaman stood facing Grey, who was licking his fur as if nothing untoward had happened. A look of awe had replaced the Goblin's anger, and as I watched, he put his hands to his temples and closed his eyes as if concentrating on something. When his eyes opened, he shook his head as if to clear it.

"Gorm speaks: the Man is not to be harmed, for he features in Gorm's plans for us all."

There was a collective sigh of mixed relief at not having to face me and disappointment at not reaping the rewards. I felt that disappointment, for it would have been glorious to have slain them by the score, and the power of that thwarted lust staggered me. As I fought down that inhuman feeling, hearing the laughter in my mind as the insolent presence in my head withdrew beyond conscious awareness, the Goblins who'd begun crowding towards me retreated hastily, the pressure at their backs released. I seized the reins of my mind, angered at having lost control again and increasingly disturbed by that loss.

I scanned the Goblins around me. Some showed thwarted anger but most appeared relieved at having avoided a dangerous confrontation. A very few showed speculation, as if they were wondering how they might take advantage of the changed situation. As there was no Goblin close enough to pose a direct threat, I turned my attention to the Shaman, who was watching me with a fascinated look.

"I wouldn't have you think me ungrateful," I said, "but your change of heart puzzles me."

The Shaman spat at his feet, and a look of sly malice crossed his face. "Then be puzzled, Man. For though Gorm commands me to spare your life, he gives no instructions to aid you nor this creature that accompanies you." He half stretched an arm towards Grey, then withdrew it as if thinking the better of the idea.

The guarantee of my life emboldened me. "Again I ask: what were you told, and who told you?"

The Shaman frowned. "Hold your tongue, Man. Though I must spare your life, that doesn't mean you must leave here with all the parts you arrived with. Your role in Gorm's plans doesn't require you to be able to father children, nor to walk with all your toes, nor to have your ribs unbroken." Grey hissed at the Shaman, then jumped down and strode to my side. "But I misspeak. It wouldn't do to risk your life unnecessarily, pleasant though that risk would be. Leave, before I change my mind on that matter too." With that, he spun on his heel and returned to his sedan chair. Before entering, he bent to whisper to one of the bearers, who hastened away into the crowd.

I knelt to pat Grey, and the cat purred loudly enough to be heard halfway across the cavern. I'd not expected my salvation to come in the form of a cat, yet there was no longer any possible doubt the cat was more than it seemed. I had strong suspicions why this "Gorm" had instructed the Shaman to free me. "You're no ordinary cat, Grey, that's certain. Someday soon I must discover what you are." The cat rolled onto his back to have his belly scratched. As I rubbed my small companion, a hand gripped my elbow. I turned to the Goblin who'd led the troops that brought me here.

"Come now. For bringing you here among us, I've been cast out of the caverns and ordered to take you with." Though his face bore a sour look, he didn't appear perturbed by his fate and his voice was less bitter than contemptuous.

"And that doesn't bother you?"

He spat on the ground. "Your people will be here any day now to exterminate us in this Home, and as a leader among warriors, I'd be one of the first to die. Better to live another day, in another Home, and there regain what I've lost here. I was powerful once, and I will be again wherever I may be. But enough—we must flee, for whatever guarantees you've received won't protect me."

He still gripped my arm, and though I could have resisted the pull, there was no point. I'd never find my way out of these caverns without his aid. I lifted Grey back onto my shoulders and rose to my feet, shaking off the Goblin's arm. He scowled, then turned his back and set off at a good pace deeper into the cavern.

"Wait!" I called, my long legs letting me follow at a more comfortable pace. "Did we not enter from the other end of the cavern."

"You think so? Well, then it was so. But did you not listen to what I said? *Your* people lie in that direction, and though I expect you'll want to rejoin them, that's hardly my plan; I doubt they'd show me the courtesy that we showed you."

I pondered that for a moment. I had no idea how I was going to return home, particularly given that the people of Amelior would not welcome one of their race returning in the company of a Goblin. "You have a point. Very well, I'll follow."

The Goblin moved fast, for all his bravado, with many a glance over his shoulders at the crowd of his folk who stood and watched, muttering; word of my guide's banishment had spread with surprising speed, and there were many looks of eager cruelty. Several threw things—mostly curses, but also offal and scraps of the unidentifiable garbage that littered the floor—but none dared approach. We were struck countless times, but never by projectiles that did more than sting, and apart from that, we were left unmolested. After a hasty crossing of the cavern floor, my guide darted into a dark tunnel and began climbing. The upward passage was steep, but not so steep I had to save my breath for walking.

"How can you find your way through this maze?"

The Goblin was panting from the pace he'd set, and had to stop to gather enough breath to reply. "What matter? We'll never return. As well ask why you see as well in the dark as I do, though your kind should be blind and unable to walk. Save your breath for important things, like leaving this place before they gather courage to tear me into bits."

I repressed a smile, for though I was breathing deeply, I was keeping up with little effort. Nonetheless, I complied with his request, for I had much to think about, and keeping him in sight took little of my attention. My immediate concern was what to do when I reached the surface, for as he'd noted, it would be foolhardy to accompany him to another place of his people, and no wiser to return to my own people with him at my side.

For that matter, did I really want to return? Orgrim had given no instructions beyond delivering his message to the Goblins, though he'd said I could contact him with the ivory ring once I delivered that message. On the one hand, I was worried there'd be difficult questions to answer if I delayed too long before using the ring; on the other, had there been any obvious way Orgrim would know that I'd completed my task, he would not have left me the ring. On balance, it seemed likely I had at least a day, and perhaps several days, before I'd need to contact him, and that time would prove useful. After the events of the past few days, I knew one thing for certain: whatever Orgrim had done to me, it had not been for my benefit, and my eventual ending should I return was unlikely to be pleasant. I had no knowledge of the ways of demons or wizards, but what I'd seen and heard didn't reassure me.

Leaving his service was an obvious solution, but I doubted that tendering my resignation would achieve that goal. Perhaps it would be worth appealing to the demon within me, for it was likely that he too served Orgrim unwillingly, and perhaps together we could find some way to escape. I considered waiting until the Goblin and I parted company, but I couldn't be sure that would be within a day nor that I had more than a day before Orgrim reclaimed me. So—now. I had no idea how to speak to the creature who shared my body, so instead I spoke the words in my head, but moving my lips to reinforce them.

"Demon, I would talk with you." There was no response. "Demon, I know you're there within me, and that you can hear my words. Answer me, for I would speak of matters of interest to us both."

The Goblin had paused to catch his breath, sweat beading on his greasy brow and trickling unnoticed down his face. "Do you talk to yourself, or cast some spell that eases your passage? Would that you would share it to ease mine, though I suppose that's too much to ask of a Man. Therefore, I urge you to save your breath, for we have a ways to go before we escape, and further still before we're in lands where the Shaman's power doesn't reach, and your cruelty in ignoring my needs will not go unremembered."

I ignored him, for deep in my mind, there'd come an echo of mocking laughter. "Demon, we must talk. Mock me though you will, you can't deny that we're both Orgrim's unwilling servants. Alone, we shall remain that way; together, we may devise a way to escape those bonds."

The laughter waxed, then became a voice. "Man, you are foolish as all of your kind. Though I'm bound, I've been promised my reward once my service ends and I feel no need to escape my bonds just yet; you, though unbound, have already been granted your reward, and have naught better to look forward to than an unpleasant end."

I grew angry. "And what reward do you seek—my body? Lest you forget, it remains within my power to end my own life and thus rob you of your reward."

I placed my hand on the shaft of the Elvish axe, ignoring the Goblin's gasp of dismay.

"Have I offended you, then? Forgive me. It's only my life I sought to save, worthless to you though it may be. Ease your own way as much as you must, and let me live to bear my own suffering with admirable stoicism." His plaintive voice echoed in the narrow tunnel, and his skin paled. But my attention was for the voice in my head.

"It's the curse your race took on freely that you believe only your life has worth, Man. I assure you this is *not* all you have to lose, and in time, you'll learn what I mean by that." There was an oily, unclean lust in that voice that clung inside my head. "But it wouldn't do to tell you that, for it's not yet time for you to learn what you sold to Orgrim."

My own anger, natural and clean, rose in me and burned away the foulness the demon had left upon my thoughts. "You speak in riddles, and, I think, choose your words to unman me. It won't work. Whatever Orgrim's promised you, there are things no creature may take from me." I drew my axe; at the edges of my vision, I saw the Goblin recoiling hard against the wall, a thin wailing rising from his mouth, until I brought the keen blade to my own throat.

The laughter echoed again in my head. "Cling to that hope, Man, for it serves me well." Then the voice stopped, leaving not so much as an echo.

"You're mad, even for one of your race!" hissed the Goblin, eyes wide, the rank smell of his sweat fouling my nose.

I reslung the axe. "Think what you will. In the meantime, you've tarried long enough. Get us out of here before your former masters change their minds about you and deprive me of my guide."

Without a word, the Goblin turned and resumed his rapid pace upwards.

***

After a time, the increased movement of air told me we were nearing the surface, and it wasn't long before I saw the dim glow of daylight. When we reached the tunnel's mouth, which emerged from beneath a low earthen bank in another of the hidden depressions in the flat grassland, the rain was beating the grass flat. We stood there beneath the overhang, watching the walls of falling water and the distant lightning flash, and I breathed deeply to clear the taint of the cavern from my lungs. I still hadn't decided what to do with my remaining interval of freedom, and while I was here, it would be wise to gain what knowledge I could from the Goblin.

"How is it the rain doesn't flood your caverns?"

"What am I, a builder, that I should know these things? My people have lived underground since time began; surely it's enough to know that someone learned to keep the rain out, and shared that knowledge with those who build?"

I reflected a moment. "Forgive me. You're justifiably angry, and scared for your life. If I swear that I'll do you no harm, will you at least listen to what I have to say?" I eased to a sitting position, back against the stone wall, so I could meet his gaze without having to bend my head downwards or forcing him to look up. Grey slipped down from my shoulders and onto my thighs. Reflexively, I began stroking him, and he closed his eyes and melted into my lap.

The Goblin glared, but there was less heat in his voice. "Do no harm? Do you mean no harm greater than exiling me from my Home, Man? No harm greater than crushing my heart with terror at your mad behavior? No harm greater than squeezing me to extract such information on my folk as you couldn't collect on your own, information you will bring back to your people so they may more efficiently exterminate us? I'm relieved, Man, for now my fears are eased."

I winced. "My name is Mo... dred, Goblin. Stop calling me 'Man', for it leads you to assign me the wrongs of my race rather than hearing my words and judging me by my own deeds."

"Moh-dred? Since I am in no position to bargain, I shall henceforth call you by that awkward name, and assign you only the wrongs you've already earned."

Despite those harsh words, his anger had eased, so I went on. "Fair enough. And your name?"

"My name is of no importance. Call me what you will; call me even *Goblin*, for then you can ignore my own wrongs and assign to me those of my race." He glared defiance, but I kept my expression calm and open, trying to persuade him that I neither judged him nor showed any of the frustration I'd begun to feel.

He shook his unpleasant head, puzzled. "You have patience beyond the way of your kind, Moh-dred, and you haven't yet slain me, even though I can no longer be of any use to you. Why do you forbear, you who bear the axe of our enemies and the will to use it against me?"

"Because I too know what it is to be small and terrified and impotent, unable to strike back against my tormentors, and I would not inflict that humiliation upon another."

The Goblin started another of his sharp retorts, then saw something in my eyes I'd been unable to hide. "Were it not for the truth in your face, I'd think you mock me and call me those things. But you, small and helpless? This cannot be. How can I be talking to a Man with no intention of killing me?"

Mistrust showed once more upon his face and in his voice, so I smiled my gentlest smile. "I told you once not to judge me by the wrongs of my race. It would have been as well said had I told you not to judge all of my race by those few you've seen hunting your people; indeed, until a few days ago, I and most of my people didn't believe your race existed. We're a diverse people, and the larger part of us live far from your lands."

"Not so diverse you overcame the need to threaten me with your axe, nor so diverse that you remember they were all our lands before your people stole them from us."

I laughed a single harsh laugh. "I think the Elves and the Dwarves would dispute that conclusion, friend Goblin. But as for threatening you—no, Goblin, 'twas myself I threatened. You accused me of madness, and your barb fell not far from the mark. There is that within me that is indeed mad, and I'd rid myself of it at any cost, even at the price of my life."

"At the price of your *soul*, you mean, for Gorm forbids us self-murder, and the same laws govern your kind, whether you know it or not."

I stared at him, for this was the first time a Goblin or Elf had used a word I was unfamiliar with. "You used a word I don't understand, and I understand even less how the laws of your ruler might bind my people."

He glared. "How can you misunderstand? Do you not speak our tongue better even than I do?"

I reflected on the paradox of my ability to comprehend a language I'd never before heard, yet not these few words. "Nonetheless, you have used a word I don't understand. What did you mean by 'at the price of my soul'?" I tripped over that last word, but managed a credible attempt.

The Goblin was silent a moment. "Can it truly be that you don't understand? Then what they say of your race is true: you are soulless and godless and less than the dirt we tread beneath our feet." His face hardened into a look of open contempt.

"*Soulless? Godless?*" I spoke the words as they'd sounded, not knowing what I said. "If not knowing proves your point, then I suppose we are. But that's no proof. Tell me your meaning so I can better judge."

The Goblin appraised me a moment, his expression wavering between contempt and disbelief; disbelief got the better of him. "You mock me still? Very well, I shall play your game, for there's naught else to do until the rain stops." He cast his eyes upward, as if thinking, then met my gaze with those disturbing eyes. "Gorm, who created my race, instilled in each of us a part of Himself, the spark that gives us life and consciousness, and which returns to him when our brief span of existence ends."

"He's the father of your tribe? Are you all descended from one sire, then?"

The Goblin blinked. "Father? Are you a fool, Moh-dred, that you blaspheme so? I wonder that the lightning does not strike you down where you sit and immolate you even to your soul!" He cringed, his eyes going to the skies. Lightning flashed, but far away, and the drum of the rain upon the earth was loud enough to drown out most of the distant thunder that followed.

"*Blaspheme? Soul?* You speak beyond my ability to understand." Try though I might, and despite the language skills Orgrim had bestowed upon me, skills that let me speak with the Elves and the Goblins as fluently as with my own kind, I couldn't wrap my mind around those words and the concepts they represented, and I felt the same frustrated pressure growing in my head that I'd felt when I tried to read parts of that ancient scroll in the library. But that had been my own tongue. Whatever it was that blocked comprehension of those words, it failed to completely block the Goblin's strange words.

My companion looked on me with what might have been pity. "Then either you truly are mad, or you mock me beyond any Goblin's ability to forbear. You coming here, risking your poor life by insulting our Shaman... you are mad, and can't be held responsible for your actions." The Goblin's face showed pity.

"Think what you will, but let us talk of other things. My head aches abominably when I try to understand you. Tell me instead of your claims that my people have wronged your people by coming here."

"Such foolish questions you ask! No wonder your people cast you forth to wander far from their stolen lands." The Goblin shook his head sadly, but frustration distorted his already misshapen face. "Very well, let me try. How can you think these were your lands, when Gorm Himself gave them to my people? How can you excuse waves of your fearsome warriors trampling our lands on their terrible steeds to spear us, leave our corpses for the ravens, and pour fire into our Homes? How can you consort with our ancient foes"—he gestured at my axe—"and expect us to abide peacefully here, on the impoverished fringes of our stolen lands?" The anger in his voice and on his face grew increasingly evident until, at that last comment, he rose to his feet and stood over me, his jaw muscles working with the intensity of his emotion.

"You pose questions I can't answer."

"Of course not, for there's no defense possible against these accusations."

"I beg to differ, and if you'll let me, I'll play the apologist for my people. To your first question, I must say that when we arrived here, there were none of your people to be found in the east. There were the Elves and the Dwarves, and both races welcomed us."

"And yet those lands were no less ours, and stolen from us by those two ancient foes before the thought occurred to your folk. They gave away what was not theirs to give."

I ignored him and went on. "As for your other question, I can't answer for the people of Amelior, save that they claim your people kill them, and that they only defend themselves. My own people live so far away that none of us has ever seen one of your race, let alone slain a Goblin."

The Goblin's voice became bitter. "And so they would say, godless creatures that you all be. But the truth is different. Though we drive them from our lands where we may, it is done by Gorm's command; we but reclaim the lands that were ours, and should they refuse to leave, what else can we do but slay them? And in turn, what do they do? They hunt us to extinction!"

I shook my head to clear it. There was logic here, uncomfortable though it was. "Be that as it may, I can only repeat what I was taught. I'm no Ameliorite, and I can't speak for them. The answer to your final question is easier than that to the first two: we consort neither with the Elves nor with the Dwarves."

"The evidence of my eyes betrays you. *You lie!*" He rose to his feet and stabbed an accusing finger at me.

I fought down a sudden anger, trying to escape my control and spend itself on the Goblin. "And now it's you who tempt my forbearance. The Dwarves and Elves have shunned my race for generations. I bear this axe for one reason alone: my master sent me to bear his message to the Elves before sending me to your people, and they gave me the axe in compensation for surrendering my iron weapons before I met their elders." I thought of the old Elvish woman, but let the matter drop, not wanting to explain it. "That would be the first time one of my race has seen an Elf since soon after our arrival in your lands. Indeed, they would have slain me had it not been for the cat I bear."

"You claim the cat persuaded the Shaman to spare your life? Of all your—of all your *impossible* stories, that's the least plausible." The Goblin's look turned sullen. "Very well, enjoy your joke. You wonder why it is that we Goblins hate and fear your people? Your godless blasphemy, your theft of our land, and now, your contempt for my intelligence are ample reason. Leave me in peace, Man; our conversation is done."

I shrugged and left him in peace, disturbed by our discussion. I turned my attention to the rain that beat down near where we waited. He'd given me much to ponder, and the rain's hypnotic beat lulled me half to sleep as I tried to puzzle out what he'd said. It was obvious the Goblins were ruled by some great wizard, Gorm, who may even have been as powerful as Orgrim, and that he was served by a variety of lesser wizards called "Shamans". The whole race had been intimidated or perhaps even enchanted into believing we were their mortal enemies, and that the fault was ours in the ongoing war for possession of Amelior's lands.

All this was logical, and yet I felt doubt; there were parts of the Goblin's argument I couldn't understand, and parts that were deeper than their surface logic suggested. This would require considerably more thought.

I must have dozed, for after an indeterminate time, the rain stopped and the sun emerged from behind the clouds. I looked around with a start, and found the Goblin gone. That solved one problem, for I couldn't have accompanied him much longer, nor did I trust him enough to leave him free again while I slept; from his obvious hatred for my kind, he'd soon forget his Shaman's order to let me live, and try to slay me in my sleep. I rose, knees creaking, and gathered up Grey. I knew from the rumbling in my stomach it was early afternoon; that and the angle of the sun gave me my bearings. I set out into the wet grass, the sun at my back as I headed eastward towards the lands of my kind. I wanted to put some distance between us and the Goblins before I'd risk contacting Orgrim.

My boots and leggings were soon soaked through, and I walked with difficulty through the matted grass, leaving a trail a child could follow. All around us, steam rose from the grass as the sun's heat began drying the land. I walked for perhaps an hour before hunger got the better of me and I paused to consume my scant remaining provisions. I'd need to find supplies soon, else I'd have to test my hunting skills in these unfamiliar grasslands. Grey had already vanished, gone to seek his own meal.

When I'd done eating, I brushed crumbs from my lap and began contemplating the ring Orgrim had left me. His cryptic instructions weren't reassuring: how does one "sink" into a ring just large enough to fit on one's small finger? I closed my eyes and concentrated on the cool, smooth feel of the ring where it lay against my skin. It was easy to imagine my mind following the path of my finger through the center of that ring, but that wasn't what Orgrim intended, for I felt nothing. Next, I held the ring to my forehead and tried the same trick, with no more luck. Finally, I opened my eyes again and glared at the ring. At first, it was difficult to focus on it, for its surface was featureless, and it drew uncomfortably at my eyes if I stared too long.

It was that discomfort that gave me my clue. I once again focused my gaze upon the ring's smooth surface. When the pull began, this time I tried to yield rather than fighting, and after an uneasy struggle, succeeded. One moment I was staring at the ring, and the next I was surrounded by whiteness that was the opposite of the blackness you see when you close your eyes; the feeling of unseen distances was identical. But there was a plucking at my mind that frightened me, and in panic, I drew back, calling my master's name into that void as I did so. In an instant, I was back, fingertips white with the pressure they were exerting against the ring. Orgrim hadn't answered my call, and I couldn't muster the strength of will to try again. Perhaps tomorrow.

I looked up to find Grey still gone, and as my attention focused back upon the grassland around me, I heard a familiar noise: the drumbeat of hooves upon springy ground. I rose to my feet and looked to the southeast from whence that sound came. There, approaching at a tremendous rate, were six horsemen, long lances tucked beneath their arms as they drew nearer. I had no doubt they were expecting a Goblin, but as they had no reason to harm me, I stood my ground and made no effort to reach for a weapon. That logic was far less persuasive than the certainty any defense would prove fruitless, for not only was I ill-equipped to withstand such a charge, my skills were inadequate to the challenge even had I the appropriate equipment.

Instead, I watched and enjoyed their skill, wishing I had even a tithe their ability with a horse. As I waited, I drew my lute from its protective sack and set about tuning it, hoping to appear more innocent than might otherwise be the case.

As they drew nearer, the leader gave some signal and the charge slowed, lances lifting to vertical when it became plain I posed no threat. Sun glinted off the leader's oiled chain hauberk as he slowed to a trot and his men flowed past him to encircle me. Most wore boiled leather armor with scraps of metal sewn to it, evidence of the recent rains still plain on the clothing that showed beneath the armor and on their mounts. Each man wore a round steel cap strapped to his head with a leather band beneath the chin, and several bore scars. When I'd been encircled to his satisfaction, the leader sidled his horse closer so he could better inspect me.

"Tell me what unit you belong to, and how you find yourself so far from our main force." He had a faint accent that struck me as familiar, but nothing so strong as to make him alien, at least not compared with the beings I'd lived among the past few days.

"In fact, Sir, I'm not part of your force at all—I'm here on Ankur's business." I had no desire whatsoever to tell him why I was really here, but having had no time to prepare a suitable explanation for my presence, I felt it wisest to stick close to the truth.

"So your accent indicates, but you're a long way from home, Ankurite, and in another King's lands."

"Would that be the King of the Goblins?" I responded, buying time while I assembled a story that would make sense.

There was a snort of laughter from close behind my back, and my skin prickled as I realized there might be a lance inches from my chest. I resisted the temptation to turn, and watched the knight's face harden.

"Your wit does you credit, but I note that you haven't answered my question."

I bowed. "Forgive me. I was unaware you'd asked me a question." My story was beginning to come together, and it was simple enough to remain consistent if questioned.

Rising in his stirrups, he half-bowed, mocking me. "Allow me to rephrase my question, then. What brings an Ankurite uninvited into Ameliorite lands, so close to our foes that one might think you had but recently broken your fast with them or used that instrument of yours to entertain them?"

I laughed and restored my lute to its bag, careful not to back into the lance that undoubtedly hovered at my back. "Now it's *your* wit that does you credit. Surely I wouldn't be here without the approval of your leaders, for is it not true that our kingdoms now work together under the truce negotiated these seven years past?"

"In *principle*, Easterner, we work together, though my people handle the work while yours worry about the together." He brushed at an old scar, and met my gaze, unperturbed and clearly expecting a reply this time.

"You seek more? Very well. I serve Bram of Ankur, who serves King John in the capacity of advisor on western affairs." There was a gasp behind me, answered by a sharp look from the leader of the knights, and I recalled why the man's accent was so familiar. Bram had been an Ameliorite before he came east.

"You serve that traitor? He's no friend of ours, and by extension, neither are you."

A bead of sweat trickled down my forehead as I fought the temptation to look behind me. "I believe you wrong him. Though he no longer serves Amelior, he instead serves both our peoples, and I take it amiss that you'd slander him so." I gambled and placed a hand on the head of my axe, meeting his gaze.

He backed down, shaking his head. "This is beyond me. We'll bring you back to our leader and see what he makes of you." He nodded to the man at my back, the one who'd been holding that lance during our conversation, and this time, I turned to face him. There was no lance. The rider had the largest of the six horses, and he offered me a smile. I returned it, and moved to walk beside him as the troop returned to their previous formation and set out toward the southeast, back from whence they'd come, moving at a fast walk.

I held up my hand within easy reach. "Modred."

"Kelvin." He offered me his hand, and I shook it hard. He was big and strong, but not in my league, and I think I surprised him. "And what really brings you so far from home, Modred?"

I reviewed my story, and added a new twist to do my friend and protector in Ankur a small favor. "It's as I said. Your former country-man serves both our lands. As you know, Ankur and the East have been less than forthcoming in offering their aid against the Goblins. Bram knows full well what you face here, and would persuade our King that your cause is just and that our assistance is crucial. Since he cannot come himself—nor would doing so offer any additional assurance of his word—he's sent me in his place."

"And he believes that your word would add anything to the words of those who have come before you bearing bright promises, then returned eastward, leaving only promises behind?"

I watched the tightening of his eyes, and realized this was a sensitive subject. "Just so. Have you spent any time at Court, Kelvin?"

"Some. When I was younger."

"Then you know something of the maneuvering that goes on. Here, your people are fortunate in one way mine are not: you have one enemy now. We have many, both within the Court and without, and it behooves us to move with care. Bram and our King know that to be of use to Amelior, we must first retain our grip on power. A hasty move might jeopardize that."

He nodded. "There's truth to what you say, yet seven years is a long time. Couldn't you at least send us troops?"

"Food, arms, and other resources are all we have managed. Were we truly your foes, we wouldn't have sent even so little. That's not to say Amelior has no enemies in the east, but rather that Bram and our King are not among them."

As we talked, Kelvin had been casting his gaze around with the wary caution of someone experienced in these lands; indeed, none of the six horsemen had relaxed their guard for an instant, for all knew how close we must be to the Goblins, and their scars testified that such vigilance was the price of survival. I'd been doing much the same, but seeking my strange four-legged companion rather than any threat from the Goblins. I saw no sign of Grey, but was nonetheless confident he wouldn't abandon me for long.

We continued, but the conversation ended, for the leader set a pace brisk enough to force me to reserve my breath for walking. Fortunately, the Goblin had been right that Amelior was planning another raid; we walked less than an hour before the drumbeat of hooves announced the arrival of more horsemen. They greeted us with whoops of welcome and continued off on their own patrol. The Ameliorite camp was nothing more than a cleared area of trampled grass and a small cook tent. Hobbled horses stood everywhere, and the men sat in their oilskins, damp and uncomfortable. There were few wounds, and none seemed serious.

The Ameliorite strike force was large, perhaps two hundred mounted men, each of whom carried all his own gear. I would have expected at least a small supply train, but there was nothing of the kind. Were we that close to Amelior? That seemed improbable. On these plains, cavalry would value mobility over comfort, and wouldn't want to stay long in one place lest they be surrounded and overwhelmed. A larger camp or other source of supply must lie within a day's ride to the east. I was no military man, but there was no way they'd leave their supplies unguarded; if their advance force was this large, it implied comparable numbers at that base camp, and even more if there was another strike force in the area. More than four hundred men was an impressive force to put in the field, and it wasn't hard to understand why the Goblins worried.

There was considerable loud commentary as we entered the camp. One man wondered loudly where my companions had found a town nearby, and whether they also had a brothel. I smiled at him and bowed as best as I could with legs and back stiffened by the brisk walk. I had little wind left, despite all the miles I'd put behind me in the past week or two, and I wanted to arrive capable of talking to the commander.

The leader of the force was a small man, just over five feet tall, but he had a look about him that left no doubt he was in charge. He swept my escort with his gaze, made a judgment from what he saw, and rose to greet me. His smile was warm enough to charm the dew off the grass, but his eyes remained vigilant. I met his gaze, but couldn't hold it, and I looked down instead at the strangeness of his handshake. He was missing the ends of the last two fingers on his right hand, and the wound was fresh enough that blood still stained the bandages.

"Welcome to our humble camp. I'm Colin. And you are?"

"Modred of Ankur, and here on official business."

"Do tell." The smile stayed, and his voice was pleasant, but his gaze didn't soften.

"I'm working for Bram, King John's advisor, in an unofficial capacity. I've been sent here to scout out the lie of the land and report back to His Highness."

Colin's smile vanished when the name registered. "The traitor dares much in sending his man to spy on us."

I shook my head in denial. "You wrong him. Whatever his past, Bram's an honorable man. The intelligence I gather will serve as fodder for those who would help you. Not every easterner is your enemy."

Colin glanced down at his wounded hand and frowned. "Nor are they our friends. So, Modred, if friend you be, tell me what you've seen and what you'll report." This time he pinned me with his gaze, and I couldn't look away.

"I've seen enough Goblins to understand the threat they represent, and enough to wonder how Amelior has stood alone so long." That was a slight exaggeration; my Goblin companion had hinted that there were several "Homes" nearby, and if the others were anything like the one I'd visited, then each was larger than even Ankur. The Ameliorites were outnumbered—for that matter, we all were, even back in Ankur.

"Would that the rest of your countrymen felt the same." Colin spat on the ground. "And you say Bram is on our side in this matter? I confess to being glad to hear it; he was a good man in my experience, and it shocked me to hear of his betrayal. When next you see him, tell him that Colin sends his regards, and wants him to know there are still those who want to believe him innocent of the charges." For a moment, there was a warmth in those eyes. Then that softness faded.

"Very well. You shall stay with us until we return eastward. Can you ride?"

I laughed. "Poorly, I'm afraid. It's not a skill for men of my class. I'm safer on two legs than four."

Colin's smile warmed. "Then I hope you can play that lute better than you can ride. It's been many a day since we had a chance to relax and hear a good ballad."

"I'll do my best."

"In the meantime, we'll find you a docile mount. We'll be traveling far today, and you'll never keep up on foot." He shouted a command at one of his men, who leapt to his feet and moved off towards the horses.

Colin excused himself and began moving about the camp, seeing to his wounded and passing on orders. The camp had been quiet, but now there was much movement as men began saddling their mounts and checking their weapons. I watched, bemused, as the disorder became order, and almost missed the approach of a rider.

"Modred?"

I turned, and it was the man Colin had sent off in such a hurry. I say "man", but despite his height, he was a youth of no more than fourteen years; even so, his face was older than his years, and he handled the two horses that accompanied him with unconscious ease.

"I've brought your horse. Colin bade me ask whether you've fought on horseback before."

"Only *with* my horse, I'm afraid. Any fighting I do had best be on foot."

The youth nodded. "He suspected as much. I'm to keep you safe from harm in the event of an attack. We need such allies as we can get back east, and you're too valuable to risk in a fight."

"You're planning a raid?"

"Just returned from one, and we left more of those monsters than I could count rotting beneath the sun. As you might imagine, they don't take kindly to that, and they'll want to hunt us back to our own lands. We'll try to place as much distance between us as we can, but the grasslands are crawling with Goblin war groups and I doubt we'll get far without meeting one."

He showed an eagerness I found disconcerting. "That's a strange hope. Were it me, I'd be just as happy to make it home without seeing so much as a mouse."

He laughed. "Had we not found you out here, alone in the heart of the enemy's lands, I'd think you spoke the truth."

"But I do speak the truth."

His expression grew uncertain. "Is it so? But of course. You easterners live far from our wars, and don't understand."

"Understand what?"

"That each dead Goblin is one less chance for a burned-out farm, and one more chance those creatures will leave us in peace."

"And you believe that?"

"How could it be else?"

I was spared having to answer by a low whistle that wouldn't have carried much further than the edges of the camp. Everyone save me had mounted before the whistle faded away on the breeze; I managed a credible mount, but it took me long enough there were many smiles at my expense by the time I could devote any attention to my companions. Wary looks replaced the smiles as Colin led us eastward at a brisk pace and we moved into denser grass. The wind blew at our backs, clearing what was left of the storm clouds, but I had little attention to devote to the scenery; instead, I concentrated on staying in the saddle.

Nobody spoke, and every pair of eyes scanned the grasslands around us. I felt the tension despite my focus on not falling, and for the first time, it struck me that any Goblins we met wouldn't know I'd been given safe passage by their Shaman. I remembered Colin's recent wound, and my carefree mood vanished. I began to watch more vigilantly, despite knowing my companions would likely spot any enemies first.

We'd ridden for perhaps half an hour, the sun lowering, when something changed. The wind had freshened at our backs, enough to whip cloaks about us and dry the sweat from the horses' backs, and the troop had slowed without my noticing, enough to make me nervous when the change registered. I kept a tighter rein on my horse, for he'd grown restive, ears cocked forward as if listening and pace grown erratic, as if he couldn't decide between slowing to a cautious walk and charging ahead.

My bodyguard rode up beside me, close enough to lean across the gap and whisper in my ear. "Prepare yourself. The horses have scented something ahead."

"Scented? How can that be? The wind's at our back."

He laughed. "Forgive me. I spoke metaphorically. They have an uncanny way of knowing when Goblins are about. I said *scented*, but nobody understands how it is they know what they know."

Colin rode back to join us. "Modred, I want you to hang back here with James. He'll keep you safe once the fighting starts. Your presence here means you've nothing to prove about your courage, and you're more valuable to us back at Ankur than here, in battle. Watch, learn, and survive to bear your news to our eastern kin." There was the snap of command in his voice, and even had I been a braver or more warlike man, I'd have thought twice before disobeying him. Without pausing to confirm whether I'd heard him, he wheeled about and began moving through his men, communicating with hand signals. Almost imperceptibly, the horses began to collect into small groups, as if each man were being careless about where he rode. But I noted swords being loosened in their scabbards, and the long lances being clutched tighter.

All at once, there came a shrill cry from hundreds of small throats, and a mass of Goblins surged from where they'd been concealed in the grass ahead, as well as flanking us in a broad crescent. There were so many of them, all moving fast, I couldn't begin to count their numbers, and they hurled themselves at the lead riders like rats upon a mongrel. I took a deep, involuntary breath, but even as the Goblins charged, the Ameliorites responded, accelerating at an astonishing rate. Colin had read the attack well, and his men hit the Goblins almost before the small creatures could attain a full run. A shrill wailing rose on the air as the lances struck home and the horses broke through the first ranks, the lances sweeping backwards to clear themselves of impaled Goblins. Then, without slowing, each rider raised their lance again and drove hard into the next rank.

The wailing merged with the cries of the dying, but the charge had begun to falter; there was no room to continue amidst the packed ranks of Goblins. Each rider cast his lance at the nearest Goblin in a practiced motion, and drew the long sword or axe he carried. The riders moved together, swirling about in a complex pattern that must have taken years of training to perfect and that left no man's back unprotected for long. No sooner did a Goblin come within sword range than it fell, pouring blood from a deep slash or trampled underfoot by a horse. No Goblin came close enough to strike at an unprotected back—not even those with spears or other weapons long enough to reach that high—and though I saw flung weapons strike several riders, no Ameliorite fell.

It was slaughter more than combat, but despite that, the Goblins never faltered right until the end. In the short time the encounter lasted, not a Goblin fled that I could see, and when the last sword stopped rising and falling, only the wounded still moved. When the wind shifted, the scent of blood and other things even less pleasant was overwhelming. I turned away, appalled, to see James smiling from ear to ear.

"Aren't you proud to witness their valor?"

I said nothing, but nodded to forestall his suspicions. Colin rode up, fresh blood coating his sword arm. The bandage on his right hand was also stained red, though whether with his blood or that of his foe I couldn't tell.

"This too I'd bid you bring to Ankur: We were fortunate. No deaths, and only minor wounds. We aren't always so lucky." He wiped sweat from his eyes with his right arm, smearing a faint bloody streak across his forehead, and wheeled to return to his men. They dismounted and went about efficiently retrieving such of their lances as had survived intact. Not a man spared a glance for the fallen Goblins, some of which still twitched or strove to crawl away into the tall grass.

Colin regrouped us, then ensured that none of the wounds were more serious than they looked. When he was done, he smiled, congratulated his men on the fight, and signaled us to move off again. As we left, the first ravens began falling from the sky and I shuddered, remembering the last time I'd seen them. We continued riding east, still on guard, but our ride was uneventful. The ride continued until just before nightfall, when we reached the supply camp whose presence I'd inferred.

There was no evidence of any other force save for the wagons and those who manned them. The number and size of those wagons, however, were evidence that at least one more group the size of Colin's was supplied here, and that brought home the magnitude of this expedition into the lands of the Goblins. I caught up with James, who'd dismounted and was waiting. With a certain air of superiority, he held my horse while I dismounted, wincing.

"I'll be glad to never see a horse again."

He smiled. "You're no Ameliorite, that's certain."

"Though I don't see many horses now," I observed, turning to my horse to untie my lute and inspect it for damage.

"No," James enthused, "the others will be raiding north and south of us, perhaps even far enough to link up with our other forces."

I kept my back turned until I'd mastered my surprise and banished it from my face. "You've fielded your full army, then."

James seemed unaware of the implicit question. "Perhaps smaller than usual this time; the Goblins have been getting harder to find of late."

Perhaps as many as a thousand men in the field, and this was *smaller* than usual? The numbers were more than I could comprehend. Colin's arrival saved me from a reply.

"Welcome to our home away from home, Modred. Find yourself a comfortable spot by the fire; it's been long indeed since we had aught but our own voices to entertain us, and tonight you shall play for your supper."

I did as I was bidden, and watched with interest as the riders unsaddled their steeds and hobbled them for the night. Those who'd remained behind to maintain the camp were all older men, save for a few cripples, and they moved efficiently about their tasks. I was soon savoring the smells of fresh meat roasting on the fire and fresh skillet bread cooking on the coals. Only then did I realize the meaning of their proximity to our recent battle: they'd come this close to the battle knowing full well that if the Goblins turned east instead of laying in wait for the horsemen, the warriors would return to a scene of slaughter. I shivered.

As their guest and their entertainment, I ate first, and did so with relish. The food was plain but good, and filled a void that the afternoon's slaughter had made me forget. I was thirsty too, and drained a large leathern flask of hard cider to wash down my meal. When I'd done, most of the Ameliorites were still being fed, so I tuned my lute and set about earning my keep. I played them a great many martial tunes, including *The Recruiting Sergeant* and *Blood on the Beach*. Then, the cider and my fatigue having begun to work its spell, I played something darker to exorcise the afternoon's memories. "This one's called *Moonchild*," I remarked, feeling my way into the chords until they were as dark as the song called for.

"With the rising of the moon comes a sense of wild elation
That enfolds me like a blanket in a clinging, sweet sensation.
And it builds 'till after sunset, all the changes come upon me
In a burst of pain and pleasure that I have no urge to flee..."

It was a strange song, not often sung these days, of a man who became a monster by moonlight and hunted by night for blood, with little concern over its source—something that had a new resonance for me. There were thoughtful looks, but most just grinned, remembering tales told by the fire to make children sleep more lightly. I set aside my lute after that song, and making my excuses and blaming the long day's ride and my incompetence therein, I retreated beyond the firelight to seek sleep. Sleep that wasn't easy to find, for the massacred Goblins haunted me, and the raucous singing from around the fire rang in my ears. I was lying on my back, staring up at the sky and feeling its void echo within me, when there came a gentle touch. I sat up, startled, and it was Grey who sat beside my blankets, patience personified and a disapproving look upon his small, pointy-chinned face. I reached out to pet him, and just as I touched him, he lunged at me and bit me for the second time since I'd known him, sinking his teeth into the sensitive fold of skin between my thumb and forefinger.

I yelped and yanked my hand back, licking at the blood that welled up from the puncture marks. Grey licked his lips fastidiously, then sprang away into the night before I could so much as curse. Shaking my head and dabbing at the blood with a cloth, I lay down, my mood foul; even my steadfast companion had deserted me now. I tried again to sleep, but my thoughts were awhirl—so much so I almost missed a light touch on my shoulder. I sat up, ready to swat the cat should he be preparing another assault, then relaxed my fist when I saw who it was.

Orgrim squatted beside me, stern but patient.

"You've done well, Modred, but now it's time to set you another task. Here's not the place to speak of it, though. We must depart."

"It's a long walk to Ankur, and I've no intention of riding." I said that partially in jest, for my thighs hurt enough to warn how bad they'd feel on the morrow after a night spent sleeping on cold grass.

"There's no need for either." He rose and spread wide his capacious cloak. "Step within my cloak and we shall be there before you can draw another breath."

I took a closer look, and saw nothing but blackness—not the dim outline of his legs, nor the least flicker of light. Orgrim sensed my hesitation, and frowned. Not wanting him to learn what had been passing through my mind these past days, I looked back at the camp, half hoping to see the cat, but Grey was long gone. I took hold of my lute and my small stock of gear, and stepped forward, ducking beneath his arms to fit beneath the cloak. The space within was colder than a winter morning with the hearth fire gone out, and darker than the darkness I'd known in Ankur's crypt, but it lasted only an instant. The cloak swept over me, brushing the back of my neck like spiderwebs, then opened before the hairs on the back of my neck had time to rise.

I took a deep breath and emerged from the cloak's shadows to stand in a broad moonlit street, surrounded on two sides by stone walls that rose to frame the same sky I'd been gazing at earlier. But now, overhead, the stars lay far to the west of where they'd been but a moment earlier, and in many directions, dark shadows against the sky blotted out those stars.

The night air that bore the unmistakable stench of a large city mingled with an unfamiliar tang of salt on the air. "Welcome to Volonor."

Chapter 12: Volonor

The first time I visited a large city, I was fleeing my home, and far too upset to pay attention to my surroundings. Survival first, then shelter and food, had been my priorities; the adults who towered over and menaced me had been my most important concerns. The architecture didn't even register for days. Now, I was once again in a strange city, friendless, facing someone older and more powerful who could kill me as soon as help me. I shrugged off those memories, and with an effort, reminded myself I was no longer a scared, helpless child; indeed, as I straightened, I became taller and far stronger than the man who stood beside me. Not that those physical gifts would do me much good should I be forced to exercise them against someone armed with magic.

I shivered, trying to conceal the movement by shrugging to settle my clothing about me. When I'd mastered myself at least that much. I faced Orgrim.

"Did you say *Volonor*?"

"You heard me. Surely by now you've grown accustomed to unusual means of travel?"

"It's not the mode of travel," I lied, "but the destination. What business have you here? Am I to rob another library for you, or bear another demon into the presence of someone who will want to kill me for it?"

Orgrim met my gaze, unperturbed. "The latter, of course. Bear your message to the King."

"And this time, how shall I survive to perform your next task? This time I'll have neither the forbearance of the Elves nor the fear of the Goblins to preserve me."

Orgrim laughed. "No, you shall have your native wit—that and the fact that I'm not yet done with you."

"I find little consolation in that notion."

He laughed again, this time not bothering to mask the cruelty. "Why, Modred, one would think you no longer trust me." He turned away and took a step into the night.

"Wait! Have you no scroll to give me?"

His eyes gleamed with what seemed reflected starlight. "No. This time, you bear the message within."

And with that, he turned and faded into the night. I crossed to where he'd stood, and knelt to examine the ground. There was mud there from a recent rain, and I was a skilled tracker, but I saw no trace of his footprints. I shivered and rose to my feet.

I'd need a safe, warm place to spend the night, and enough strong drink to give me a night's sleep. Having no reason to choose one direction over another, I set off in the direction I was facing, confident that in a city as large as Volonor, I'd soon find clues that would point me in the right direction.

***

I awoke next morning to the dull pounding of a large hammer in my head and a foul, fuzzy taste on my tongue, as if something furry had died there during the night. I also awoke to the feel of warm flesh beside me, and turned my head at once, alarmed, to see who shared my bed. Blinding pain struck between my eyes, obliterating the hammer's strokes but bringing me to full, if muddled, alertness. When my vision cleared, it was to the sight of long blond hair spilling across the pillow beside me. I frowned, irritated that whatever had chanced the night before was now lost to my memory. Gingerly, so as not to disturb my bedmate—or awaken the pain in my head—I slid from beneath the covers.

The room was unfamiliar, but of good quality. My clothing lay in a tidy pile atop the table beside the window, and I moved towards it as best I could manage, which is to say not very. I lowered myself onto a chair, the pounding in my head growing stronger, but by gritting my teeth and concentrating on the task at hand, I managed to reach the floor where the rest of my gear lay. With clumsy fingers, I teased open the flap of my medical kit and reached for the vial of willow bark powder I carried as a sovereign remedy against headaches. There was no water in the ewer, so I took my medicine dry. The bitter, gritty powder stung my tongue and burned my throat, but was better than the foul taste I'd woken to. I closed my eyes and breathed deep for a few moments, giving the powder time to work its magic, and when I opened my eyes again, the pain was more tolerable.

I dressed, astonished and pleased to find my clothing cleaned and mended overnight, but not so pleased I dared any sudden head movements. Dressed and feeling more human, I eased from the room, taking care not to jar my head with each step. The edge of the door caught one of the strings on my lute as I left the room, but the answering hum wasn't loud enough to wake my bedmate. I was in a hall, lit by flickering oil lamps, with a flight of stairs at one end. I made for the stairs.

In the common room below, the landlord met me with a broad smile, then replaced it with a solicitous look as he caught the look in my eyes.

He crossed the room, took me by the arm, and helped me to a table. Ordinarily, I'd have resented his familiarity, but today, I was grateful for any help I could get.

"You'll be wanting more of the medicine that ails you, no doubt?"

My stomach, which up until now had behaved itself, began to churn. "Perish the thought. The drink would be wasted on your floor." The coating in my throat and the effects of holding my jaws clenched in an effort to keep last night's meal down where it belonged made this less clear than I'd intended.

The landlord nodded. "I've just the thing for you." Without awaiting my reply, he strode off behind the bar and passed into the kitchen.

While he was gone, I looked around, trying to figure out where I'd ended up. The room was paneled in light wood, bright and fresh. Two broad, shuttered windows flanked the thick oaken door, which was open too little to look through. But neither the windows nor the door were clad in metal. This, then, was a neighborhood wealthy enough that the watch could be relied upon to do their jobs and keep establishments safe from common thieves. More evidence of the quality of the inn lay in the decor; in place of the heads of dead animals, rusted weapons, and other bric-a-brac, there were polished brass implements of diverse and mysterious sorts accompanied by a collection of oil paintings—not one of which featured nude women. If I'd had any doubts remaining about the quality of the inn, the landlord banished them when he returned.

I turned my head to see what he'd brought me, and was rewarded by only a slight increase in the throbbing in my head; the willow bark was working. "What's this?"

An exquisite ceramic mug lay before me on the table, so thin I fancied I could see my fingers through it as I wrapped them around its rim. Steam curled from the thick black surface of the oily liquid within. "Try it. It's brand new, something the traders brought from the south. They call it *coffee*."

I grasped the cup delicately, afraid I'd crush it. I held it beneath my nose and sniffed. The odor was bitter, like so many medicinal herbs, with a skunky hint of musk, but there was also a rich, pleasant aroma that dilated my nostrils. I touched the cup to my lips and took a sip. It was every bit as bitter as its smell had hinted, and it burned the wool from my tongue, replacing it with a scalded patch, but there was something special to this coffee.

The landlord placed a matching ceramic creamer on the table before me, and a small pot of amber liquid. "If you find it too bitter, add cream or honey." He watched as I complied, and smiled with deep satisfaction as I drained the cup, including the dregs. The liquid lay heavy on my stomach, but also soothed its unease. Better still, my head began to clear.

"Would that all medicines were so palatable!"

The innkeeper's smile broadened. "I'll bring you more. When you're feeling human again, let me know what you'll be wanting to break your fast."

He soon returned with a steaming pot that held several mugs of coffee. I drank it all to the dregs, and was tempted to call for more, save for two things. First and most urgent, I had developed a sudden urgency to visit the privy, accompanied by a distinct trembling of the hands; this new drink had dramatic and not entirely pleasant side-effects, whatever its efficacy at curing hangovers. Second, something this new to our land would be expensive, and I wanted an opportunity to verify the state of my purse.

By the time I returned to my table, I was relieved on both counts. The landlord awaited me, looking smug. "Feeling better, sir?"

I smiled my gratitude. "I'm a new man, and ready to eat like one. Bring me your best, and enough for someone my size."

He didn't disappoint me. Breakfast was a loaf of bread whiter than any I'd been privileged to taste, bread that melted in my mouth almost before I had time to savor its delicate texture. Thick butter, with just the slightest dew of cream still upon it, fresh from the churn. Several eggs, pan-fried so their golden eyes gazed up at me until I soaked them up with that delicious bread. A slab of ham so thick it would have made good saddle material. Potatoes, fried in the grease from the ham, and smothered in ham gravy. A pitcher of chilled cider to wash it all down. For a time, I forgot about my troubles and concentrated on enjoying the meal.

When I was done, I asked the landlord the score, and managed to conceal my shock at the sum I'd managed to accumulate in a single night's stay. I paid him with the heavy coin of Volonor, grateful I had no need to earn my keep in this city. I'd no idea how the coin of Ankur had been replaced in my purse overnight, but replaced it had been, and although the cost of my stay was heavy, there was more than enough coin to leave the landlord a good amount beyond what I owed as a token of thanks for my miraculous cure. Sighing, I gathered my gear and headed for the door to begin my day. I didn't quite make it, for as I stood, my bowels told me that despite their earlier patience, they'd brook no delay in my tending to their needs. I returned once more to the privy, wondering again about the medicinal properties of this new drink he'd called coffee. When I'd done what was necessary and returned, I managed to persuade the landlord to part with a small pouch of the brown beans he'd used to make the coffee. I had plans for those beans.

It was still early in the day, and only servants trod the street, returning from market with the day's fare for their masters. The stone houses across from my inn rose two stories above the street, and had unbarred glass windows at ground level; though each had the weathered appearance of considerable age, the quarried blocks that made up their fronts remained neatly fitted, with little or no mortar missing. The distance between doors suggested each house was large enough for several families to live in. Small but tidy flower gardens butted up against the walls, and a few shade trees grew from earth-filled wells set amidst the cobbles. There was little detritus anywhere along the street, and my eyebrows rose along with my estimation of the neighborhood.

I sidled along, nodding a polite good morning to the dwindling stream of servants returning home from the market or other errands. The wealthy neighborhood turned out to be rather smaller than I'd thought—no more than a few moments' work to move beyond it and into more typical scenery, older buildings less well maintained, more litter upon the streets, and no vegetation save that which peeked through gaps in the cobbles. The watch passed me as I left the wealthier area, and having assessed the state of my clothing and the confidence of my demeanor, made no effort to stop me. That in itself was a relief, for under other circumstances, a minstrel wandering alone might have been stopped for questioning.

I kept on for a while, stretching out the pain from muscles abused by one day more spent on horseback than I'd ever again intended to suffer and trying to get a feel for the new city. It was early enough the streets had little traffic apart from the servants, but after a time, I came across a shopkeeper just opening his doors to throw out the first sweepings of the day. He was a merry sort, and was pleased to direct me to the palace.

That wasn't hard; all I had to do was follow the sound of rushing water, crashing against stone. The palace lay on the edge of town, overlooking a broad expanse of water. This was the first time I'd ever been within sight of the sea, and it proved a mixed pleasure. Long before I escaped Volonor's confining alleyways, I caught hints of that unfamiliar salt tang I'd smelled yesterday and heard the shrill cries of what turned out to be seabirds. The scent strengthened as a brisk wind caught at my hair and fluttered it behind me like a banner, but along with it came the unmistakable and pungent stench of sewage and other, less familiar, decaying materials. A strong breeze washed these smells from the shore into the city, and though I'd lived in a city for most of my life, I'd spent too long in the woods to ever do more than endure a city's stench.

When I emerged from between the buildings, the sound redoubled and I found myself on a narrow, stone-walled promenade that let me gaze out upon the ocean. The horizon drew my eyes right past the massive palace that dominated the beach. It was all I could do to repress a shudder. Always in the past, there'd been something to bound my world, whether mountains, the green of grasslands, or distant forest; here, there was... nothing. It was as if there were no end to the world save that imposed by the limits of my sight. Endless green waves whose like and size I'd never imagined swept towards me in tight ranks from the horizon, surging as if the world itself had gone crazy and there was neither sense nor solidity anywhere. Only in the far distance, where the sky descended to grapple with that unsteady mass of green, was there anything resembling a stable boundary between what lay below and what lay above. I couldn't imagine the desperation that had forced my ancestors to take to their ships and flee into such a vast emptiness, for the restless waters met the sky as if the two were vying for supremacy, neither deigning to notice the land that until then had been my whole world. Worse, if the stories of the journey had been at all true, there would have come a point when that ceaseless motion had surrounded them on all sides. It struck me like a near-physical blow that perhaps our ancestors had fled that emptiness itself, and that perhaps even now that emptiness slid ever closer to our shores.

I clutched the stone wall with a painful grip, grateful for any anchor that could safeguard me against that vast, terrible expanse of water and sky. Unable to repress a shudder, I tore my eyes from that disquieting sight and forced them landward, back to the more familiar and comforting works of Man. Or so I'd hoped, for there was unpleasantness near at hand too. On the pebbled strand that stretched before me, several bodies had washed up against the rim of the ocean, and were lying amidst the sewage and other unidentifiable rotting things. From this distance, there was no sign of how they'd died, though their exposure to the ocean had left them bleached and bloodless. The shrieking seabirds I'd heard were now revealed: strange, pallid birds the size of ravens fought over the bodies and other offal, doing combat with small, scuttling things that emerged from the wave-washed edge of the strand to seize small morsels and retreat into the water. Every dry surface was coated with a thin white film, which I imagined to be salt, and perhaps it was that same film that coated the birds and the bodies.

That vision was no more pleasant than the last, but there was something else to distract my gaze, if not my thoughts. The palace I'd glanced at would draw any man's eyes were it not for the greater wonder of the sea, and in its own way, it was no less compelling. Ancient and monolithic, the building at the heart of Volonor squatted on the beach like a small mountain. Of course, the scale was all wrong for a mountain, as I could see the faces of the guards atop those clifflike walls, yet that massive pile of stone had the same sense of weight one felt at the foot of a mountain. Calling it a *palace* was wrong, for it was more a castle, a fortress, a bastion against that terrible ocean and all that it represented. A broad stretch of open land separated the stronghold from the nearest buildings, and what appeared to be a moat ran below the walls; that same deep trench, partly filled by the sea, ran along the walls and out across the strand until it met the waves, forming a curious link between the present and the past. Every so often, a monster of a wave swept in past the strand and broke upon the seawall beneath the fortress with a force I could feel in my feet, sending white spray surging along the wall and into the moat and crashing high into the air above the seawall. It astonished me that even the quiet strength of rock could resist the unrestrained power of the waves.

The fortress was a relic from that distant age of warfare, when impervious walls were necessary to keep out Goblins or other foes, and I'd neither seen nor imagined its like. Indeed, given its size, I couldn't imagine how those refugees from another land found time and resources to construct such a thing, unless it had been with magic. (That contradicted what I'd read, but as I'd learned, the old tales were neither complete nor entirely honest.) The fortress overhung the harbor like a cliff, and the ugly snouts of catapults and other powerful engines of war projected beyond the crenellations. I knew little of siegecraft, but their height and size suggested that no ship entered or left that harbor without the harbormaster's permission.

There were no ships in evidence, and thinking of the sea set me to wondering just what it was those weapons guarded against. Though I'd traveled little before meeting Orgrim, I'd gathered any lore I could from those who traveled farther, and not a one had spoken of another seafaring kingdom along the shore or out to sea—but then I recalled the traders who'd brought coffee to these shores. I remembered what I'd read of our past in the library, and apprehension grew within me. Could those weapons be guarding against whatever lay beyond that chilling emptiness?

I felt small and vulnerable here, for large though I'd felt on a human scale, this was different, and my self-confidence deserted me. This was something I'd never have expected, for I'd stared up at the limitless night sky all my life, and more recently, I'd watched the grasslands recede to a distant horizon, and in neither case had I felt such discomfort. Yet now, I confronted the certainty there were strange and terrible things beyond even what I'd experienced, things that were all the more terrifying thereby. From the Elves and the Goblins I'd come to understand that Orgrim was a relic from the distant past, and for the first time, I wondered whether he might have been part of that disaster that lay at the origin of our travel to these lands. Could he have been the cause?

Being Orgrim's message bearer took on a far more sinister feel, and bringing his next message to the King was something I could no longer be party to without understanding more of the events that surrounded me. With the Elves and the Goblins, I'd been unaware of the message I brought and, later, not concerned, for neither race was my kin and neither awoke any sense of duty. But here, I'd be bringing that same terrible message to my own kind, with consequences hinted at by every beat of the waves on the shore. Now, confronted by the sea that bridged our past and our present, I began to suspect what his message truly meant. Though a life full of abuse and torment had given me scant reason to love my race, I'd encountered two other races with whom I'd felt even less kinship, and for the first time I felt part of something greater. I wasn't yet ready to forgive my people for how they'd treated me, yet neither was I eager to bring their old doom upon them—upon *us*. Staring at those massive, ancient walls, I resolved to flee Volonor and seek shelter until I had time to ponder how to break the ties that bound me to Orgrim.

I gathered my resolve to leave and tried to walk back the way I'd come, but my limbs betrayed me and left me rooted in place. For a moment, I wondered whether I might be dreaming, but the voice in my head dashed that thought.

"Flee Volonor? No, Morley, you have a task before you." It was the voice of my demon, and even as he spoke, I felt my limbs begin moving without my volition, propelling me towards the palace.

"Wait, Demon! We've talked once, and must talk again."

"For what purpose? You offered me an alliance against he who would give me something of inestimable value. Waste not your breath, for I spurn your offer as I did before."

I thought fast, alarmed at my complete lack of control over my body and having difficulty focusing my thoughts. "I won't make you that offer again. This time, I appeal to your sense of self-preservation. Why would you believe our master would grant what you desire, when you know how he plans to betray me?"

There was an uneasy pause, then the voice resumed, confidence in every syllable. "You're clever, Man, but not clever enough. Though Orgrim's powerful, even he cannot break such an oath as he swore. I shall have my reward at the end, never doubt it."

"But will you be alive to enjoy it?"

"What mean you, Man? Think you he could destroy me after I take my reward? I cannot be destroyed here in your world, only returned to my own. The pain of that return would be transitory, and nothing next to the pleasure of what I shall bear with me."

"You sound confident, Demon, and perhaps with reason, but I urge you to consider one thought: if Orgrim is he who destroyed the world from whence my people originated, he has power beyond your imagining. Are you certain that by serving him you aren't helping to bring that same doom upon your own kind?"

The demon laughed, a chilling sound. "And what care have I for them? I shall have my reward—let the others fend for themselves."

As we talked, we made rapid progress towards the palace, and were drawing close enough to see the faces of the guards who watched our approach from the far side of the drawbridge that spanned the moat. The guards were clad in shining steel hauberks that must have been heavy and already uncomfortable in the early-morning sun. The demon's logic struck me as unassailable, for if he had no fear for his own kind, what hope had I of reaching him with my fears? Sensing that I'd abandoned our conversation, the demon withdrew into a brooding silence, but maintained his firm grip upon the reins of my body. I resigned myself to whatever was about to befall me, and let him drive me on towards the palace.

It wasn't long before we set foot upon the drawbridge, a wooden structure so thick and massive it muffled the sound of our feet, giving back no echoes. The guards watched us with casual alertness until the last moment, when one stepped forward to bar our progress with his halberd.

"Halt! State your name and business."

To my horror, I reached out and pushed the halberd out of my way. "Stand aside. I bear a message for your master from my master, and will not be delayed." With that, my limbs were my own again, and I staggered before I could adjust to the sudden change and reassert control over my body. The demon's mocking laughter echoed in my head.

A second guard stepped behind me and I felt an ungentle prod from something large and presumably sharp at my back. "You speak boldly for a single man. I think you need to learn courtesy before we take you to our King." With no warning, he swept my feet out from beneath me, leaving me scant time to twist aside from falling on my lute. I stared, winded, up at the point of his pike hovering just before my eyes.

Not knowing what to say after my unfortunate first impressions, I kept my mouth shut while his companions searched me, taking care to disarm me. They were thorough, and left nothing but the clothes on my back. When they were done, one of them rolled me onto my side and tied my hands behind me with coarse rope that abraded my wrists, then used that rope to jerk me to my feet, my shoulders protesting the sharp pain. In despair at what had befallen me this morning, I kept a resolute silence as two laughing guards exchanged their halberds for truncheons and used those weapons to propel me before them and into the palace.

We passed through a dark opening that led inward through what turned out to be the outermost walls that encircled the palace. Up close, the palace itself, which had been hidden behind those mighty walls, loomed over me with even greater scale and weight than it had possessed from a distance, even though it lay two-score yards behind the walls, across a courtyard of cobbles. I had little time to inspect the scenery, for the guards moved briskly and soon had me inside. I had no idea what I would say when I met the King, as Orgrim had given me no message, and though I had an idea of what he'd want me to say, the thought of trying to put it in my own words and bear the consequences horrified me.

In short order, I entered a room with an elderly man at a heavy wooden desk heaped with scrolls and an impressive collection of writing implements. He ignored me and the *thwack!* of a truncheon across my shoulders as the guards forced me to my knees on the stone floor. Instead, he continued his work on one of the papers that lay before him, and when he was done, raised his head.

"What have you brought me?"

The guard at my right cleared his throat and tugged me to my feet, turning me half sideways to the man. "Sir, we've brought a fool who claims to bear a message to the King, and one so important he had no intention of explaining himself further."

The scribe met my eyes with a too-casual gaze. This was no man to play games with. "You don't say? Tell me, sir, what's so important you felt confident we'd let a stranger walk unescorted into the presence of our King."

My mouth was dry, but I found my voice and replied as best I could. "Sir, I bring a message from a powerful sorcerer that the King must hear at once. More than that, I cannot now say."

The scribe's eyes widened, and his gaze went to the ropes that bound my arms. He turned to the guards. "Leave him. Bound as he is, he poses no threat. But wait outside lest I should need you." The two guards left promptly, and shut the door behind them.

"Very well, we're alone. Tell me what message you bear for the King. Speak as if you were speaking to the King himself. If you convince me of the importance of your message, I'll see to it the King hears your words."

I licked my lips, and the words I'd feared would elude me rose from the depths of my mind, spoken by a familiar, mocking voice. I intercepted them on their way to my lips, and took as much of the edge off them as I could without losing the message itself. "Know, Sir, that I come before you unwilling, compelled by the spell of a powerful sorcerer. I bear your King the greetings of my master, one Orgrim, who bids me inform you that he has returned and brought with him the reign of magic." The man's eyes widened when he heard my master's name, but he controlled himself as I continued. Only the tapping of his fingers on the table revealed his thoughts.

"I'm to tell you that you shall have a new master soon."

"And that was all?" He tried, but failed, to conceal the tension in his voice.

"Sir, to the best of my knowledge, that's all. Please forgive me for being the bearer of such a message. I beg you to believe that I do this against my will."

He raked me with his gaze, anger and something else—fear perhaps?—vying for dominance on his face. "Though you speak an ancient name that has deep resonance, I'd have proof of what you say."

"Then proof you shall have!" It was the demon's voice that rose in my throat, bursting past my feeble attempts to control it. Once again my limbs were not my own. With a mighty wrench of our arms, we parted the rope that bound them as if it had been a seamstress' thread. My wrists, which should have been slashed to the bone by that effort, bore not so much as a scratch, and without pausing to marvel at that, I advanced upon him so fast he had no time to do more than cry out in fear.

I heard the door fly open at my back and crash against the wall as I seized his desk and lifted it above my head. Without pausing, I flung the desk against the wall, smashing it to kindling. "Now you have your proof, Man! Bear my message to your master, and bid him await my master's pleasure."

And with that, the berserker strength that possessed me was gone—just in time for the truncheons wielded by the two guards to catch me in the head and side and hurl me to the ground, my vision dimming and bright sparks of pain lancing through broken ribs. I have no recollection of those next moments, for blows rained down and robbed me of any consciousness other than the agony of the beating. When I at last returned to my body, I was lying on my side in damp, stinking muck in a tiny, stone-walled cell. Faint light came from a torch outside my cell, weak and flickering through a barred slit at the top of the door. I tried moving, then thought the better of it as pain surged through my head and side, almost causing me to lose consciousness again.

I lay there, lost, my thoughts so confused I feared the guards had injured my mind when they'd struck me down. I lay there in misery, not even able to contemplate rising when the keeper entered my cell.

"So you're the one who attacked the chancellor, are you? You don't strike me as the sort." The man knelt behind me and began running his hands across me, as if seeking something. "Hmm... they didn't leave me much, did they? But wait—what's this?" His hands came to rest on my hand, where Orgrim's ring lay.

I found what remained of my voice, mumbling around a tongue gone thick and disobedient. "Leave it. It's not mine, and you'll regret taking it."

He laughed with obvious relish. "Think you I've never heard that before?" His fingers worked at the ring, but it clung to my finger. My arm was like a dead weight, and I couldn't resist.

"Don't go anywhere," he laughed. "I'll be back."

I lay there, unmoving, until the light in the room brightened. He'd returned, bearing a torch and a large knife. "Last chance, friend. Will you surrender the ring, or must I resort to persuasion?"

My mind was too dull to perceive his meaning, and I watched, uncomprehending, as he set the torch into a crack in the floor and knelt beside me. He stretched out my arm, and held the knife against my hand, where the finger joined it. I could feel a dull sense of alarm rising in me, but couldn't muster the energy to do anything about it. Even as I tried, the keeper leaned his weight hard on the knife and a searing pain shot down my arm. Blood spurted, and my finger and the ring it bore separated from my hand.

He laughed. "Bide a moment, friend. I'll fix that for you." The pain did little to clear the heaviness in my head, but was no less real for all that. I would have shrieked, but my voice had deserted me again and all I managed was a whimper. Then I did shriek, for while I was contemplating what he'd done, he freed the torch from the floor and thrust my wounded hand into it. The pain was blinding, and I lost consciousness; I recall finding my voice long enough to shriek with what scant air I'd drawn into my lungs after my mutilation, but the heaviness in my head was such that I couldn't testify even to that.

An indefinite time later, I regained consciousness to the taste of bitter liquid in my throat and the stench of burnt flesh in my nostrils. I lay there, uncomprehending, and listened to the conversation that was going on.

"I'd urge you in future to take better care of what I've given into your possession."

"How is that my concern? You know it's not the husk that interests me."

"Be that as it may, that husk serves *my* purposes, and you forget that at your peril. Need you a reminder?" That was greeted by sullen silence. "Good. Now get him up."

I rose to my feet, and it hadn't been me who made that decision. My head was still heavy and my thoughts confused, but things soon improved.

"Morley? Can you hear me?" There was concern in that voice, and still numb, I nodded. "Good. Now listen: I'm going to reattach your finger. You could serve me without it, but I don't want your effectiveness impaired in any way. This will hurt, so prepare yourself."

He wasn't exaggerating. The pain that seared through my hand and up my arm made the half-remembered pain of the knife and torch seem nothing by comparison. I screamed, making my throat raw with the force of that scream, and then, all at once, the pain was gone. I looked down in wonder at my hand, which was whole again save for a thin scar and a dull throbbing ache beneath the ring. The pain in my ribs was gone, though I felt twinges as I drew a deep, shuddering breath.

"Don't worry," Orgrim spoke with evident amusement. "It's not as if your cries will bring any attention; they're to be expected in this place."

"And the keeper?"

"...is in no condition to worry about your cries."

Orgrim pushed me ahead of him through the open door, a hand upon my shoulder both to guide me and to keep me erect now that there was only me to command my abused body. In the corridor ahead, the keeper's corpse lay against the wall, horror frozen on his face. I looked away, shuddering, for though I'd wanted nothing more than to kill the man for what he'd done to me, his had not been an easy death.

Orgrim sensed the direction of my thoughts. "I came when he began playing with the ring, as I would have come had you done the same," he scolded. "Did you deliver your message to the King?"

Without thinking, I shook my head, wincing in anticipation then discovering the pain had vanished. "No. I delivered it to his chancellor, though."

"That will suffice. Now we must bear the message elsewhere. Enter within my cloak."

The old mage spread wide his cloak, and within lay that same darkness I'd seen before. I passed within for the second time, reluctant. There came a moment of disorientation and a cold shock like plunging into a spring lake, then I was back in the open air again. As my eyes adapted to the fading light around me, I recognized the facade of the library where

I'd performed my first task for Orgrim. I was home in Ankur, and with a feeling of growing dread, I realized where he meant me to bring the next message.

Chapter 13: Ankur

Ankur's Court had become a home of sorts, and one I'd made for myself. Even so, I often wondered whether it was worth enduring the Osrics and other frustrations in exchange for what satisfaction could be gained from living among people who most often detested or, at best, ignored me. Sometimes, in weaker moments, it seemed I was indulging in stubbornness for its own sake, with no other benefit than to test my strength of will. Other times, I felt true security. Indeed, now that Bram and his family had entered my life, there was an elusive promise of more than just the traditional protection afforded a King's fool.

But it was promise conferred by someone else, not earned by my own effort. Akin, in that way to the acceptance I'd earned among the foresters: a quiet voice I could never silence insisted I was fooling myself, and that they accepted me solely because of the respect they held for my father.

So I'd left the forest and tried to make a new home in Ankur, to find a role earned entirely by my own wits and worth. But no matter how well I played my role, there was always a sense that I never truly belonged and that my place was guaranteed only by another's influence—now, the King rather than my father. Though it was reassuring to be bypassed when the languid currents of intrigue swept through the Court, being ignored wasn't what I sought... nor what I needed.

So I returned to Ankur with mixed feelings: grateful to be home, but bearing the burden of knowing I was about to jeopardize what little security I'd found.

I felt a hand on my shoulder, interrupting my musings. That hand turned me to face my companion like a child being forced to pay attention to an adult. "I have little time, for things are moving faster than I'd anticipated. Listen closely: first thing in the morning, you must bear the same message to King John that you brought to Volonor, then hide so you cannot be found. I'll contact you in perhaps a week to prepare you for your final task when I return. Is that clear?"

Enough of the fog had lifted from my head that the word *final* struck me as more ominous than hopeful. But I nodded, not trusting to words. "Good. There's no time to retrieve any of your lost gear, so replace what you feel's essential. But only that—you have scant time for shopping." He thrust a heavy purse into my hand, met my eyes, and scowled. "In the meantime, get off the street. I've restored you to a semblance of physical health, but there are limits even to my magic. You've paid a heavy toll for what you've endured, and you'll be unable to stay on your feet much longer."

I watched, numb, as he gathered his cloak about him and faded into the twilight, growing transparent as the mist that dances atop a lake's still surface on autumn mornings. Whatever medicine he'd given me earlier had put me back on my feet, but I could feel an overwhelming weariness hovering at the edges of my mind, and I knew Orgrim was right. I shuffled off in the direction of the Golden Kettle, where I'd stayed the last time I needed shelter here; I wasn't very steady on my feet, and I could tell from the stench that hung about me that I was grimed in a mixture of dungeon muck, blood, and my own rank sweat. I forced a rueful smile at my imagined appearance, and that lifted my mood: it would prove interesting trying to gain entry to the inn.

My refilled purse dissolved the expected obstacles with its mundane magic. I remember pressing one coin after another into the innkeeper's hand until he swallowed his concerns and let me enter, and I remember asking him to have new clothing ready by morning (more coins) and to send a messenger to fetch several medicines I was familiar with (still more coins); I have no clear recollection of the final sum, but it must have been enormous. My consciousness was fading too fast to do more than note this for future reference, and a curious fatalism gripped me. I remember being shown to my room, and I remember crisp linen sheets and a faint scent of lavender. Then, nothing.

***

I woke to a shaft of sunlight streaming past curtains opened by a gentle breeze. That same stir of air wafted me the scent of baking bread, awakening my stomach. The quiet noises of a smoothly functioning establishment drifted up through the floor, and heavy snores penetrated the wall of the room to my left. The heaviness in my head felt more odd than unpleasant, more sleepy than hung-over. However, the odor that emanated from beneath the sheets was sufficiently unpleasant I'd have to do something about it. I pushed into a sitting position, bracing against expected pain, but apart from a few twinges, there was nothing. Dim images of yesterday's events began coming into focus in my fogged mind, and I glanced with trepidation at my ring finger. For a moment, I was afraid I'd be unable to remove the ring, as the jailer had been unable to remove it, but that proved not to be the case. Beneath the ring, there was an obvious seam where the flesh had been knitted together. I contemplated hurling the ring from me, but a wiser part prevailed; I felt sure that nothing so simple would free me from Orgrim, and the ring might yet prove useful, as it had been in Volonor's dungeon. I shuddered, and replaced the ring.

At the foot of the bed lay a table heaped with towels, a pile of clean clothing, a small leather shoulder bag, and a large basin of water. The steam rising from the water was evidence someone had been in my room while I slept, and worry over my money cleared the remaining fuzziness from my head. I rose, naked, and found my old clothing washed, dried, and piled neatly on the floor by the bed. Pushing it aside, I reached under the thick mattress and found my purse where I'd been sure I'd left it. It would have been difficult to lift my weight off the mattress enough for a thief to remove the purse, but not impossible; its continued presence meant I'd chosen my refuge well. I glanced over at the water, wrinkling my nose at the smell that wafted from me every time I moved my arms away from my sides, and began pondering how to feel—and smell—alive once again. But the water awoke more urgent thoughts, and I sought and used the chamber pot instead.

Afterwards, I laid towels on the floor by the basin and scrubbed with the coarse sponge and perfumed soap they'd left me. As I scrubbed at the accumulated grime, watching the filth and old blood sluicing down onto the towels, I contemplated the day ahead. Somehow, I'd have to enter the palace and make my way into the King's presence. My fate in Volonor suggested that this time, a measure of discretion would be wise. I thought back to my last exit from the palace. The odds were good I could enter the same way I'd escaped. What I'd do after I delivered my message was a problem for later; Orgrim had told me to go to ground, but other than suggesting this was possible, he'd provided no clues as to how. I shrugged, consoled that Orgrim's ring could summon help, one way or another.

I gathered my scant belongings. Casting a last glance over my shoulder at the fouled water in the basin, missing the lute that had accompanied me since long before I left the forest, I headed downstairs. It was long enough after sunrise, the common room was empty, most customers having long since risen and set about their duties. My stomach, having recovered from its discomfort at my aroma, was stirring with increasing vigor, and I realized I couldn't remember the last time I'd eaten. A heavy brass bell hung from an iron bar over the counter, and I rang it to summon the staff. A young boy appeared from the kitchen, smiling uncertainly.

"Sir?"

"Breakfast, and quick. Let's start with that wonderful bread I can smell baking, a wedge of cheese, a slab of ham, and as many eggs as you can spare."

The boy disappeared behind the bar and I sat by an open window. It was early enough to be cool, and I enjoyed the gentle breeze as I watched the street traffic beginning to pick up. The breeze was pleasant, though no doubt it would become less so as the summer sun began coaxing the city's odors from the streets. It wasn't long before the boy returned, bearing a tray laden with an abundant breakfast. The food was excellent, but I fear I ate too fast to do it justice. It was gone all too soon, and when the boy came back to clear the table, I caught him by the arm.

Fear flared in his eyes, and abashed, remembering my own experiences at the hands of larger men, I released him. His eyes remained wary, but he realized that I bore him no ill will, and stood a little straighter.

"Sir?"

I pushed back the cutlery. "I need a good knife, lad—not this fine silverware, but rather a fighting man's knife. And I need to find a carpenter." I laid enough coins on the table to cover my fare and a few extra for him.

"There's a carpenter just down the street and past the market, about a quarter-mile past the tanner's. I think there's also a weaponer's place thereabouts."

"Yes, I know the place. Thanks." I belatedly remembered the shop. It wasn't one I'd visited, but I'd walked past it before. It alarmed me that I'd had to ask. By the evidence, even a sound night's sleep hadn't fully restored me. I pushed back from the table, and rose, not looking back as I left the inn.

I'd mulled over my plan as I ate, and decided it would get me into the palace. I'd need a ladder and rope; the dagger was only a tool, as I'd had enough of combat to last me a lifetime. As I walked, I forced my sluggish mind to focus on my memories of the palace's kitchen window; it wouldn't do to buy a ladder that was too short.

The carpenter's door was open when I arrived, and he was at his workbench, crouched over his project with a drawknife, curls of wood cascading to the unswept floor at his feet. I repressed a smile, for he was a small man, not much larger than I'd been, though it was hard to tell for sure given my altered perspective. I cleared my throat, and he raised his head, unalarmed, the knife coming to a swift halt. I watched his face harden as he took in my size, and wondered whether my own emotions had ever been that transparent.

"I need a ladder."

He nodded. "You've come to the right place. I make the best in town." A well-worn mask of politeness replaced the momentary hostility.

"So I hear," I lied. "But I'll need it this morning."

He frowned. "Impossible. I've none in stock, and with my current backlog, it'll be at least a week before I can help you."

"I can't afford a week," I replied, pulling my purse from beneath my cloak. "I can afford an hour."

"An hour?" He snorted in disbelief, but the purse drew his eyes, as it remained large enough to impress. "Still impossible, but let's talk details." He laid aside the drawknife, composed himself, and turned his attention from my money to my face.

"Not so impossible as you might expect. I don't need anything that will last me years, just a simple climbing device that will last me one or two uses."

His gaze sharpened. "I see. Perhaps you'd prefer a grappling iron?"

I repressed my smile and feigned anger. "If you're not prepared to be serious, I suppose I'll go elsewhere."

His face fell. "Forgive me, Sir. A ladder, you say..."

"Sturdy enough to bear my weight, even if only briefly, and 10 feet tall. Something temporary will suffice."

"And something easy to dispose of afterwards," he muttered under his voice, not realizing he was speaking aloud; his eyes had gone distant with concentration. He pulled a slate and a stick of chalk from beneath his work table. "Something like this perhaps?" He sketched a single piece of lumber, pierced by dowels at intervals. If properly braced, the ladder would support a strong, nimble man able to climb it in a hurry.

I smiled. "That should do."

He nodded. "*That* I can do in an hour." He named a price, trying to look casual. It was extortionate, but I had money enough there was no need to haggle.

I laid the coins on his workbench, then added more for good measure. As it seemed likely I'd soon have no use for any money, there was no need to conserve funds. "Agreed. I'll return in an hour. See that the ladder is ready."

He turned away even as I finished, pulling an auger from his toolbox and slapping it on the table and rummaging for his drill bits. I smiled, pleased at my own cleverness and at having done a good turn for someone I could sympathize with. I vowed to return here when everything was over and determine whether he needed a friend as badly as I'd once needed one. Then I left so I could stretch my legs until the ladder was ready. With luck, the gentle exercise would help restore clarity.

I had an hour to pass before I could begin Orgrim's next task, and much to think of during that time. Something in me had changed as I stood beside the ocean. Until then, I'd believed I knew what was amiss, and that I was my own agent, not under Orgrim's control. That proved to be only partially correct. The demon had forced my hand in Volonor, convincing me that any sense of control I'd nurtured was a delusion; I had precisely as much self-control as the demon permitted, and that freedom was, in turn, circumscribed by such freedom as Orgrim permitted the demon. This situation couldn't be allowed to endure, even if I ignored the implications of today marking my next-to-last task. Despite the demon's incomprehensible threats and its overheard conversation with Orgrim, I still had no grasp of what fate awaited me. As near as I could figure, Orgrim had promised me to the demon when he no longer had any use for me. Given what I'd seen of demon behavior thus far, that wasn't a pleasant prospect, though still a better fate than many; either I'd be slain and devoured, like the Goblin, or my consciousness would be extinguished and the demon would go its way among men in my body, slaying and taking its pleasure until it was itself caught and slain. Either way, my problems would soon be over.

That argument satisfied my rational part, but that was by no means the larger part. The stubborn *me* that held this inner dialog had kept me alive through many dire circumstances and feared an ending, railed against this fate and demanded an alternative. Under that prodding, I came up with a solution: I'd surrender to King John, warn him what was happening, and beg his mercy. I knew the kind of man he was, and the resources at his command, and if anyone could stand against Orgrim, it was him. At worst, he'd clap me in the dungeon and thereby see me safe; at best, perhaps I could betray Orgrim and see his plans confounded. Doubt still haunted me, particularly given that the demon must be listening to this inner debate and smiling to itself, but I felt sure I could retain my self-control long enough to deliver my message and await the consequences of my action.

I'd been so lost in thought that I missed the first time when the palace clock tolled the hour, and forgot my desire to purchase a weapon. When the half hour rang through the streets, I'd grown eager to see an end to things, so I returned at a jog to the carpenter's shop. When I entered, breathless despite the distances I'd traveled and my newfound endurance, he was eyeing the door impatiently, as if expecting me.

"You're late. I was beginning to wonder if you'd forgotten me or been caught."

I ignored his innuendo. "It's ready?"

"Of course. Here you are." He handed me three long, straight pieces of near-identical lumber.

I turned the wood over and noted that each piece had several holes bored in it, each filled with what appeared to be wooden plugs. Crude brass fixtures topped one end of two of the pieces; this puzzled me until

I noticed how the remaining piece would fit into those bands. But as a ladder, it lacked a certain something. "That's it?"

"Of course not. You'll need these too." He handed me a leather bag that made a wooden clicking noise as its contents rolled about. I opened the bag and saw a dozen six-inch dowels. "When you're ready to climb, remove the plugs and insert the dowels in the holes. It'll be a tight fit, but with muscles like those, you should have no trouble."

I was taken aback, and angry at having been taken advantage of; moreover, I could tolerate no delay now that my plan was settled, not even the delay required to assemble the ladder. "Didn't I leave you enough time to assemble it?"

He smiled. "You're new at this, aren't you? No," he continued, catching the look in my eyes, "let me finish. Surely you don't think you'd get far carrying a ladder through the streets to wherever you're going? The watch would spot you in an instant and take you in for questioning. You'll have to assemble it at your destination."

All at once, my anger vanished, and I could feel my cheeks coloring. "I take your point. I'm in your debt." I removed a few more coins from my purse, hesitated, then gave him the whole purse. One way or another, I'd have no further need of it.

The carpenter's eyes widened, then filled with concern. "I apologize for any offense I may have given. At a guess, I'd venture that you have no expectation of returning from wherever you're going, and if that's so, I regret having added to whatever burden you bear."

"I doubt that would be possible. But I thank you nonetheless. Use the money better than I would have. Perhaps we'll meet again some day and I'll tell you more."

"But you don't believe that or wish me to believe it either. You've the look of a man going to his doom. I'd wish you luck, but I doubt that luck's what you need." His eyes were sober and sympathetic, and I turned from him and left the shop before I could further delay what I must do.

It was swift work to make my way through the streets to the palace. As the carpenter had predicted, nobody gave a second glance to a burly, unarmed man carrying what appeared to be nothing more than building supplies. It was simple to find my way to the alley behind the palace and position myself beneath the open kitchen window. Once there, I removed the wooden plugs from the lumber and forced the dowels into the holes. The fit was as tight as the carpenter promised, but posed no challenge for my newfound strength. To finish off, I joined the two brass-bound pieces to the centerpiece. They made a surprisingly sturdy ladder.

As it turned out, I'd neglected one small fact: though the window was less than 10 feet above the street, the ladder would have to be braced at an angle during use, and that left it short of the mark. This distressed me, until I realized that with luck, I'd prove tall enough to stand at the top and grasp the window ledge. I set about examining the ground, then fitted the butt of my ladder as best I could into a crack in the pavement. When I was done, I leaned the ladder's top against the wall, relieved to note that it fell only a few feet short of the window. I tested its balance, then once I was sure it would hold, I began climbing, resting my weight after each step before taking the next. The ladder creaked and bowed beneath my weight, but held until I could grasp the window ledge. I pulled up and peered over the edge, listening with dismay as the ladder fell away beneath me. It landed with an alarming clatter, and I realized I might have little time before someone came to investigate.

The storeroom was empty, and my arms were beginning to feel the strain of holding such a large weight suspended above the street, so I hauled up far enough to reach across the ledge and grasp its inner rim. My other hand slipped then, and I almost fell. But I'd caught that inner rim, and was able to hang swaying from the ledge, the muscles of that one arm straining with the effort and my forearm compressed against the stone of the opening. I flung up my other arm and caught the rim again, then followed the arm with a leg. In another few heartbeats, I'd pulled onto the ledge, panting with the effort.

I was fortunate in arriving between meals, for the few kitchen workers who remained were dozing; the kitchen staff woke early and worked late, and sleep was a precious commodity, to be taken whenever possible. Nonetheless, it would be wise to have an excuse for being here, so I sought around me for an appropriate prop. That prop came in the form of a small cask of ale, which I lifted to my shoulder and held tight against my neck, partially concealing my face. That got me through the kitchen and the first few halls without a question, as I had the look of a minor servant who belonged here. Once I'd reached a safe distance from the kitchen, I lowered the cask to the floor and left it resting against the wall. Thereafter, I walked as if I belonged there, which indeed, I once had. This was aided by the fact that I moved in parts of the palace I could never have reached without the tacit or express approval of several teams of guards, so there was no reason anyone should think to question me. Moreover, with my clean new clothes and the lack of any supplies that marked me as a traveler, what reason would any have to suspect me?

A few questions told me where I could find the King, and I set off in that direction, moving slowly enough not to appear suspicious, but fast enough that I'd delay this encounter no longer than necessary; in addition to the fear of discovery before I could deliver my message, I was impatient to reach a resolution. After a time, I came near the workroom where the King was said to be, and I made my final preparations. From within my medical pouch, I withdrew the bag of coffee beans, then changed my mind; despite its ability to sharpen one's thoughts, its side-effects argued against its use. I replaced it in the bag and instead found a certain small vial and took a sip; then, thinking of the battle I would soon be waging, I downed its entire contents and hoped I'd survive such a strong dose. The bitter taste of the herb known as headstrong washed my tongue and throat, and immediately began its work. My mind cleared, my vision sharpened to a razor's edge, and I was free of all doubt; indeed, in that moment I knew I could challenge Orgrim himself and win. I'd pay for this courage when the drug wore off, but for now, I was the true King here.

I strode, confidence personified, towards the guards who leaned against the wall outside the workroom. They straightened as I drew near, but remained diffident; I had the look of someone who belonged, and it was a time of peace. I recognized neither one, and they didn't recognize me. Having prepared my lies in advance, I introduced myself.

"I bid you good morning, gentlemen. My name's Modred, and I bear our King a message from Lord Bram. Is he within?"

The guards, recognizing the source of the message if not the messenger, knocked twice, then opened the door and let me pass without so much as checking for concealed weapons. I smiled in what they took to be courtesy, but was actually contempt at how easily I'd fooled them. Even so, my keen mind noted, with uncommon insight, their sloppy behavior. I made a point to discuss it with the King, along with several other criticisms I'd been nursing for months, should the opportunity present itself. The door closed at my back, and I faced a table with the King and several counselors seated around it, faces grim.

The chancellor rose, a stern look on his face, as I went to one knee.

"You have business with us?"

I bowed my head. "Sire, gentlesirs, I bear ill news for the King."

The King rose too. "More bad news from Volonor?"

I remained kneeling, feeling the first stirring of the demon within me. "Sire, far worse than that. If you speak of what I suspect, then I bring the same news to you."

"Your name, Sir."

"Modred, Sire, but you once knew me as Morley." Sensing something was wrong, the demon surged against me, but I was ready for him, and the drug gave me strength. I felt the demon's surprise and rage as he reached for control—and I held him back.

"Morley? I know one Morley, and he's a dwarf less than half your size and long since gone missing. You speak riddles."

"Nonetheless, Sire, it's me, your former fool, and my current condition is proof of the ill news I bear. I've been transformed by an ill magic, and bound to the service of one who means you no good. And the message I bear is this: that my slavemaster, a sorcerer named Orgrim, has come to wrest control of our lands from us. I throw myself on your mercy and beg your protection. But first, you must bind me to protect yourselves, for I fear he'll compel me to harm someone before I leave." The demon surged again, and I clenched my jaw, fighting it with all my strength and understanding, disbelieving, that despite the drug, I was losing ground.

As I'd named the sorcerer, there came a sharp collective intake of breath, and several paled, but my thoughts focused inward in a last attempt to keep the demon at bay. As I did this, two things happened, and had it not been for the artificial clarity of my thoughts, I'd have missed them. First, the chancellor seized upon a bell pull and rang it, summoning the guards; second, an older man who'd been watching all this time rose to his feet, keenly appraising me.

The door opened, as loud in the silence as the scraping of wood on stone when those at the table pushed back their chairs and rose, grasping for weapons. I was seized from behind, but my mind focused on my inner struggle within with an intensity I've never known before or since. The demon began to master me despite my best efforts, for wrestling him was perilous as walking on the slick, algae-grown rocks beneath the surface of a stream. I felt my shoulder muscles bunch, and despite my waning efforts at control, I threw off the two guards who held me, that other voice issuing from my mouth.

"The dwarf speaks truth. We are Orgrim's messenger, and we come to inform you that you must surrender to our master when he returns to your city." I felt an impact as the flat of a sword slammed into my head, but it didn't even stagger me. I lashed out with a fist and sent the guard reeling; I'd felt ribs break beneath the force of that blow, and a predatory grin spread across my face.

The King blanched in horror, but it wasn't him who spoke. The old councilor moved around the table to stand between us. "We knew of your coming, demon, and you won't find us unprepared." He drew a slim wooden wand from one sleeve and held it between us like a fencer's blade.

We laughed, mocking them. "Old bones contain the sweetest marrow, fool. As the dwarf feared, I shall feast upon yours before I return to my business with your betters." We made to advance upon him, but as we did, he released his grip on the wand and spat a command. That slim piece of wood interposed itself between us and hung in the air, emitting a deep thrumming like the bass string on my lute. All at once, we struck a barrier, and though the wand bent almost double as we pushed against that barrier, we progressed no further. Worse yet, the wand set itself before us no matter which direction we turned.

"You'll not be feasting on anyone's marrow again, demon." The old man withdrew a drawstring pouch from his pocket and dipped his hand within. When it emerged, bearing a small pile of metallic powder, he spoke a few quiet words and flung the powder in our direction. The powder flew apart into a shimmering cloud that surrounded us, passing through the barrier as if it didn't exist and filling the air with the sharp tang of silver. The wand fell to the floor, but it had done its work; we remained rooted in place.

"Silver, the sovereign remedy against all things mystical," the mage whispered, a bead of sweat rolling down his forehead and belying his outer calm. Despite that calm, his eyes held an intensity that would have made us step back had that been possible. He spoke another unfamiliar word, and the cloud of dust collapsed inward, clutching our skin in a tingling grasp. "And now, demon, I command you to return whence you came." His calm vanished, replaced by concentration that increased to match the intensity of his gaze, the change as startling as the feeling that came over me—yes, *me*, for the demon had retreated deep within, leaving my body once more my own.

For a moment, it felt as if my entire body had been draped in cobweb and someone had removed that nauseating stuff all at once. But as the mage chanted, that feeling moved deeper inside me, passing through my skin like the warmth of a sauna after a cold winter's hunt. The warmth spread through the depths of my body until I felt it kindling within my bones. Deep within, I felt the demon's rage surging, and my own answering surge of elation as the demon fought the magic that permeated me, leaving me ever more control. But that elation was short-lived, for another change clutched at me, something that drew and tore at my essence as if trying to pull my bones from my flesh. I felt the demon's ravening hunger, and knew on an instinctive level he was trying to take me with him.

Then all at once, that pressure was gone, and the silvery cloud that had clung to me stood apart, large as two men, its silvered face contorted in rage. From within that shape, a voice boomed. "You shall pay for this effrontery, mage. Orgrim shall flay your skin from your bones and hang you still living in his workroom to watch as he brings me back to feast on your—" The demon concluded with an unknown word.

The mage's sweaty face tightened with concentration, and he spoke another word, clenching his fist before him as he did. The silver contracted inward upon itself so fast I nearly missed it, and that fast, the demon was gone.

"That may well be," the mage whispered, staggering as the cloud of silver dust collapsed to the floor, "but not today. Nor shall it be as easy as you hope. And perhaps we may yet surprise you."

My elation at the demon's departure vanished, for a nausea grew within me. All eyes turned to me, and I felt the second soldier's sword pressing against my back. But though that familiar presence in my mind had departed, something else took its place: pain. That night when I'd undergone my transformation into the giant I now was, the pain had been as intense as I imagined being broken on the rack would be. This time, when that pain surged, my instinctive knowledge of what was happening made it worse; this time, I both knew what I'd endure and understood what I'd be losing. For a moment, I hoped that what I'd been through had taught me to endure such pain; instead, it seemed I'd learned to appreciate it more keenly. The agony shot through me, searing through every part of my body and mind. I lost all track of time, and at some point in my screaming, I lost consciousness.

***

I awoke to silence, the taste of old blood and bitter medicine in my mouth, and a dull ache that throbbed in my head and echoed throughout my body. Atop this lay a weakness and lethargy that smothered me like a heavy blanket, until I could only lie there, scarcely breathing, and stare with fuzzy vision at the dim-lit beams of the ceiling far above my head. It was a long time before I recognized that I lay once again in the infirmary.

It was an effort of will to look around, for my head wouldn't move and I could make that survey with my eyes alone; even then, I moaned. Each motion of my eyes awoke a new wave of pain in my head. I lay there alone, and listened, which was all I could do without gritting my teeth to hold in the screams. From the character of the noises around me, it was evening. That meant most of a day, or perhaps several days, had passed; from the fullness of my bladder, I expected the former. I felt no urgency to move, but that lethargy itself raised a faint alarm. Though it was likely the aftereffects of the headstrong I'd consumed, I feared that having the demon torn from me had caused more serious damage. Then another fear cut through my lethargy and made me force myself up to inspect my condition.

With considerable effort, I rose to a sitting position. Pain shot through me with each movement, but it was the bearable pain that comes the day after great exertion rather than the agony that savaged me earlier that day. I sat, my legs dangling over the edge of the cot, the chill air of the palace raising goosebumps on my naked flesh as I strained to touch the floor with my toes. Had my thoughts been clearer, I'd not have squandered my energy that way, but the dullness clutching at my mind kept me reaching for the floor, too scared to look down. And when I failed, the realization that I'd returned to my former stature crashed down upon me like a falling wall and I fell back among the blankets. Then I wept, long and loud, great racking sobs that echoed in the dimness of that great hall.

The catharsis of that weeping exhausted me, but at the same time, restored a curious vigor. I'd lived my whole life this way, and old defensive reflexes that had kept me alive through times of great despair awoke and helped me shake off that self-pity. And the first act I performed to reassert myself was to slide off the cot and use the chamber pot. Pitiful though that small affirmation was, it was also a first step towards reclaiming my dignity. When I returned to the cot, shaking with the chill and drained by the effort of rising, the fuzziness and despair still lay heavy on my mind, but I'd once more reasserted ownership of my body and mind. It was not much to cheer me, but it was a start.

I lay there beneath the covers, staring with unfocused eyes at the ceiling, and concentrated. The mental fog began easing. Though my demon had been driven forth, Orgrim still awaited, and when he returned, I'd best be ready. I raised my hand to stare at the ring, and was shocked to discover it gone. Fuzzy though my mind was, I knew I was seeing the correct finger, for the white seam of scar tissue where Orgrim had reattached my finger was plain, even in the poor light, and throbbed when I focused on it. Remembering what had happened to the last person who'd removed that ring, I shuddered.

So I had no way of summoning Orgrim? Very well. Then that meant he had no easy way of finding me either, or so I hoped. This provided more time than I might otherwise have had. It also meant that his power over me might be gone, or at least weakened, for I was certain he'd not left me the ring for my own benefit. Perhaps I could remain beyond his grasp if I fled to the woods as soon as my strength returned; after all, I'd delivered his messages, and without the demon in me, I'd no longer be so useful a tool.

Approaching footsteps interrupted my musings. I turned my head to meet the gaze of the approaching surgeon. Without a word, he sat beside me on the cot and held his hand to my forehead; when he'd done, he pressed a finger into the angle of my jaw and I watched his lips moving as he counted. Then he took my hand in his.

"Grip my hand," he commanded. I complied. "Harder!" I exerted myself until at last he relaxed, satisfied. "You'll live. You may not enjoy it, but you'll live."

"Thank you."

"Don't thank me. You're tough and stubborn, else you'd have died in the King's presence. Indeed, there were those who insisted on slaying you where you lay. But one of the councilors argued so hard in your favor that they spared you."

"Bram?"

He frowned. "No, the old fellow. Raphael."

The name awoke memories, but in hindsight, I didn't remember him at the meeting I'd interrupted, so he must have arrived afterwards. "Please thank him."

"Thank him yourself. He'll visit you in the morning. In the meantime, sleep and regain your strength. If even one part in twenty of the rumors flying about the palace are true, you'll be needing your strength." He withdrew a flask from his pocket, and measured me with his eyes. "Take one mouthful—and mind you, not a drop more."

"What is it?"

"A sleeping draught. An infusion of sleepbalm and honey that will help you rest."

I nodded. I'd used the same medicine before. Through sheer willpower, I forced an arm up from beneath the sheets to take the flask and hold it to my lips. My arm shook, but I managed a single mouthful without spilling any and returned the flask. There was a cloying taste of honey and a bitter aftertaste, but nothing intolerable. He nodded approval, laid his hand on my forehead a last time, then left the room. I closed my eyes, and sank into a vast, dark pit.

***

I awoke to the smell of steaming porridge and fresh bread from the stool beside my bed. Whoever had left it hadn't bothered to await my return to consciousness—or had chosen to leave me in peace. I shrugged off the haze in my head, and found my thoughts far clearer than they'd been the previous night. My muscles, though still aching, cooperated better than during my previous waking. I propped myself against the cold stone behind the bed, shielded from that chill by a pillow that was too large for me. I didn't dwell on that, but forced my attention instead to breakfast.

The porridge, thick and lumpy, bore a load of honey and swam in cream; the bread was so fresh it was still hot enough inside to melt butter, and I smeared it with the fresh butter that had hidden behind the bowl of porridge. My appetite was slow to awaken, but fierce once aroused, and I ate every last morsel and looked around for more.

There was no one in sight, so I seized the opportunity to use the chamber pot—which some kind person had emptied during the night— then ducked beneath the covers again. Soon afterwards, the surgeon returned to examine me. He repeated last night's inspection, sniffed the chamber pot, and nodded approval. "You heal fast. Good. There are visitors waiting. I'll send them in one at a time."

Visitors?

The door opened to admit a familiar figure: Bram, who'd treated me so nobly. I turned away, suddenly ashamed by what I'd done. After a time, a gentle hand fell upon my shoulder.

"Are you well, Morley?"

Without turning, I nodded.

"Look at me, friend. You've naught to be ashamed of."

That startled me enough that I faced him. "How could that be?"

Bram's smile was slow, but warm and genuine. "How could it *not* be? Raphael told us what you've been through. Revealing yourself to the King as you did was an act of great courage. I don't know the whole story, but—"

"If you did, you'd not be so charitable." Tears of shame welled up in my eyes, and I fought them back, burning away shame with anger.

"Then tell me, that I may understand and find a way to forgive a friend who won't forgive himself."

I complied, the words coming slowly and painfully at first, then increasingly easily, pouring from me like water overflowing a boiling kettle. Bram listened without interrupting, compassion growing on his face. When I finally ran out of words, he nodded. "I can see how you might be ashamed of what you did; there are many things not to be proud of. But you've left much unsaid, and from that, I see evidence of considerable courage."

"Courage? Say blindness and greed, rather."

Bram bit his lower lip. "Perhaps blindness, but greed's too strong a word. Like you, I've always been an outsider here, so I can understand the strength of the desire to be treated like everyone else." As he said it, I recalled the words of his former countrymen and knew he spoke the truth. "No, even the blindness I find hard to credit. Did you know aught of magic when you accepted Orgrim's offer? Did he tell you the price would be more than your obedience? Did he not perhaps use his magic to seduce you into accepting his offer without thinking it through? Is it not obvious that much of what happened after you were captive of the demon was not your fault?"

The silence stretched. "That's one way of looking at it," I admitted.

His voice hardened. "Any other way would be self-flagellation, not honesty. What's done is done, and you can't change it. Accept that—and accept a chance to begin anew so you can atone for what you did in a way that will let you live with yourself."

"I'll try," I replied, chastened but wanting to believe what he was saying.

"See that you do." His voice softened again. "Believe me, Morley, when I say that I too have experienced a magical compulsion. Like you, I was controlled by forces beyond my knowledge, yet I survived. And won a great victory." I stared at him, surprised, for the sudden lack of conviction in his voice made me wonder what he'd left unsaid. But his eyes looked past me. "None of us can escape our fate, but we can at least fight to divert its course."

"And now it's my time to do so."

"So it would seem."

"And how did you turn aside your fate?"

His gaze returned, trying to read me. "That's a longer story than I have time to recount, for another visitor awaits you and the King awaits me. When we reach an ending, I'll tell what I can of my story. In the meantime, our problem is how to turn aside *your* fate."

"*Our* problem?"

He smiled, and it warmed me. "To the extent that you'll accept my assistance, and in all ways save those paths you must walk yourself. But I must leave now, for as I said, our King has need of me. Your part in this may be over, but mine is just beginning, I fear." He squeezed my shoulder and started to rise.

"Bram?" He paused. "Thanks."

My friend—for such he was—nodded and left. The door half-closed behind him, then opened again to admit the counselor who'd argued to spare my life in the council chamber. Blinking away the dampness that filled my eyes, I had a moment of confusion; at first, I saw the familiar, unprepossessing face of Raphael, one of the King's counselors—yet at the same time, I saw the old mage who'd banished my demon. That image vanished, leaving Raphael. He moved towards me with a grace that belied his age. But when he sat beside my bed, I saw the shadows beneath his eyes and the lines graven deep in his face. He studied me a moment, then let out his breath in a long, weary sigh.

"Have you recovered enough to talk?"

"How could I deny such a little thing to the man who saved my life? You're Raphael?"

He bowed his head and answered softly. "I am." Then his voice strengthened, and there was surprising fervor in it. "But I repudiate the debt you'd thrust upon yourself. Whatever you may believe, my actions were first and foremost to save our King and my own poor life. If I saved your life too, so be it. You owe me no debt."

"Nonetheless—"

"*Nonetheless!*" His voice echoed in the room, and abashed, he lowered it before continuing. "If you feel a need to repay your debt, start by telling me your story. Some I can infer from the ending, but there's much I need to know about what set you on this course."

I nodded, and told my story for the second time that day, and the telling was easier. When the words ran out, I met his calm gaze and steeled myself for his judgment. "Where does this leave me?"

Raphael frowned. "Only Orgrim knows that for sure. Your role may be ended, for you're no longer his tool. But should he choose to reclaim that tool, your part may begin again. One thing may make that decision for you." He opened his cloak to reveal Orgrim's bone ring hanging from a silver chain about his neck.

"The ring!" I watched it with horrified fascination.

A smile played on his lips. "Fear not. For now, I've severed the connection with its owner."

Orgrim's image rose before my mind's eye, and I scrutinized the counselor. The resemblance was slight, but I hadn't imagined it. "You too are more than you seem."

He smiled wearily. "You look more deeply than most."

I pondered a moment, then chose to leave it be. "Your words suggest you've left another thing unspoken."

"You're perceptive too. Our foe chose his tool well." There was a certain harshness in his tone, but it wasn't directed at me. "You're right, of course. There will come a time when we must confront Orgrim, and I'd far rather do so on my own terms."

"I can understand that."

"No, you cannot. For all you've experienced, you know nothing of the ways of sorcerers. My reading of the situation is that your former master is too busy right now to investigate what happened to you, but from the instant I pulled his ring from your finger, he's been aware that something's gone astray. When he finishes dealing with whatever holds his attention, he'll return his attention to this ring. Then, you must decide."

"Decide?"

"Whether to flee, to stand with us against him—or to once more accept his bargain." The horror of his last suggestion struck me like a blow, for I felt a sudden yearning for what I'd had. I shuddered, and met his eyes again. He nodded approval, and went on. "It's hard to tell which would be most risky." He took the chain and ring from around his neck and placed it around my own. The chain lay cool against my flesh, but the ring warmed against me. Raphael continued, ignorant of what I was feeling. "So long as the ring remains on that chain and Orgrim's attention lies elsewhere, you'll be safe. Should you free the ring of its chain and place it once more on your finger, his attention will return to you."

"And if I don't?"

"Then his attention will return to you anyway, for you bear his mark, and ring or not, he can find you wherever you run. The ring makes it easier, that's all. This is why I'll leave the ring with you rather than bearing it."

"You fear him that much?"

Raphael's smile hardened. "I'd be foolish to fear him less. I took many precautions, so there's a chance he remains ignorant of who I am. Oh, I haven't fooled myself; he knows for certain he's been forestalled by another mage. Yet if I'm fortunate, he doesn't yet know who. I'd like to keep it that way."

"Until you can meet him on your own terms."

"Yes. And that will require preparation, which I must be about. There may be little time, and there's one more curious thing I must investigate."

"That being?"

"You spoke of a cat that accompanied you, and what the Elf said of it. I must learn where that piece of the puzzle fits, for it strikes me as something best understood, and soon. I'm not enamored of mysteries where sorcery is concerned, for their solutions oft prove fatal to the unprepared." He rose. "Be well, Morley, and heal fast. Your part hasn't yet been decided, by you or your former master, and I mislike that uncertainty. Though you've done well to survive this long, I've a suspicion we'll need you a while longer."

He rose and left. I felt guilty for lying abed, but for the moment, there was naught I could do. Without even clothing to my name, I had little choice. In any event, the catharsis of telling my tale twice, combined with the apprehension Raphael's predictions raised, tired me more than I'd expected. Still thinking on what he'd said, I slipped into a light sleep.

***

I woke to a warm hand on my forehead. Opening my eyes, I gazed up at Margrethe, concern in her voice but distraction in her eyes. "Morley, wake up. We must talk."

I smiled up at her, trying to force the cobwebs from my mind. "What time is it?"

"Not long before dinner."

"And you didn't want me to miss my dinner?"

She laughed, the distraction leaving her briefly. Then she sobered again. "No, it's rather that my husband bids you leave the palace and stay with us this night." My shock must have showed. "Nay, fear not. It will be no imposition."

"Imposition? Hardly that. You endanger your family by taking me in. Did Bram tell you nothing of what happened?"

"He did, and I was the one who insisted you stay with us, though he put up no more than a token fight." She frowned, as if wondering at her victory, then the distraction left her eyes. "Do you think so little of us that we'd not come to the aid of a friend?"

"And do you think so little of me that you believe I'd endanger a friend?" I lifted the ring by its chain, not daring to touch the smooth ivory, even though it had lain next to my skin for at least a day, and on my finger, unnoticed, for weeks before that. "I cannot accept."

Margrethe lifted a bundle of clothing from the floor by her feet. "On the contrary. You cannot refuse. Consider Bram's offer a command from a higher authority."

I was incredulous. "The King's intervened?"

She held the frown a moment, then laughed, unable to stay mad for long. "No, not *that* higher authority. I meant *me*."

I was flabbergasted, and it showed. "Lady, how can you command such a thing? How can you imperil your children?"

The frown returned, this time with no mirth behind it. "Think you I would do so, even for a friend? Then you don't know me."

"No, I don't. Neither do you know me."

"I know all I need to know. I know that without you, I might have been widowed, and without the comfort of the man I love. Did you pause to question your own danger or our worthiness when you intervened to save him from the boar's wound?" I began a reply, but the look in her eyes forestalled me. "Could I do any less? No, fear not for my children. I've sent them to stay with friends in Volonor. They'll be as safe there as they would be anywhere, and safer than had they stayed here. Whatever happens next, it will center around the Court and those who serve it."

The fight went out of me. "As you know more of these things than I do, I must perforce accept your decision."

The smile hadn't returned, but the edge had gone off her anger. "Yes, you must. There's much we know, but did Bram tell you *why*?"

"He didn't, though he hinted the two of you were no strangers to sorcery."

She sighed. "My husband, for all his virtues, has the bad habit of concealing dangerous knowledge. There are times when I want to wipe away that concerned, overprotective smile with a mace." The unmistakable affection in her voice belied her words. The remaining anger drained away, leaving an echo of that former intensity in her voice. "Morley, know you aught of what came to pass here during our war with Amelior?"

I pondered the question. "I know what everyone knows."

She nodded. "Then you know nothing important. The war itself was a small thing, though it didn't seem so at the time. What was truly important were the deeds of a sorcerer named Dariel, who travelled in the semblance of a bard."

"Dariel? Whose namesake was the pre-Exodus minstrel whose name remains to us when so much else from that age is lost to memory?"

"More than a namesake; it was Dariel himself." She watched the shock growing in my eyes with a certain malicious satisfaction. "There's much I don't understand, for some things Bram and his oathbrother Gareth never told me. But this much I do understand: Dariel set out to accomplish what this Orgrim even now sets out to accomplish. Bram and Gareth defeated him, though it was a near thing and required a measure of witchcraft, but that sorcerer is gone from our lives. Had they lost, we wouldn't be worrying about this Orgrim; Dariel would have resolved the problem for such of us as survived."

"How is it I heard none of this? That no one did?"

"Few knew of Dariel's role in events; most of those who came too close have been dead these eight years. Even those of us nearer the center of things than most still don't understand everything, not even how we survived him." Frustration freighted her voice, but I saw fear in the set of her eyes and the tightness of her lips.

"Yet you survived," I prodded.

"Yes, we did. And whatever may happen in the near future, my husband and I know we survived worse in the past—and will do so again this time. Foolish confidence, you may think, and I can't deny that accusation. Yet I know what I feel, and I have faith in my husband and those who are loyal to him."

I felt a rush of emotion, but managed to keep it off my face; I was tired of being read like a scroll. "You've convinced me. I'll stay with you for so long as I believe I'm not endangering you. Should that change, no argument or force you can muster will keep me there."

She measured me for a moment with her gaze. "Agreed." She thrust the clothes towards me. "Now get dressed. I've taken these from your room and had them cleaned, for they'd grown moldy during your absence." She rose and headed for the door. "I'll wait for you."

I dressed as fast as my abused body permitted and followed her, limping, out into the streets.

Chapter 14: Home's where they take you in

Home—my true home—was an oakwood far from Ankur, in a small half-timbered one-room shack that was damp and moldy in the spring and summer, and cold and worse in fall, when the winds that foretold of winter penetrated the halfhearted defenses afforded by the walls. It was where my father and I lived most of the year, and where I learned my woodland skills while I recovered from the deep wounds inflicted by my childhood. Home was also a large longhouse, maintained in far better shape, that my father and I shared with the King's other foresters and their families during the winter. That building, crudely but lovingly furnished, was proof against the worst winter could offer. It was hung with so much male paraphernalia there was scarce room for the wind to penetrate—hunting trophies, wood carvings, fishing rods, dartboards, kits for cleaning and maintaining weapons, and old, musty wineskins of dubious origin. That place never grew truly cold, for our collective efforts stocked enough firewood each summer to keep a fire burning throughout the winter, and the warmth of all those bodies added to our comfort. It was also full of the unpleasant scents of many unwashed people packed together, gamy meat hung to ripen or to cure over the hearth, and furs and skins being prepared for subsequent use. Though most who lived there never fully accepted me, it was nonetheless my home and offered another warmth: that of companionship.

Ankur had been my residence now for the past few years, but had never become a home. Yet despite that, walking the streets with a beautiful woman and watching with her as the sun set over the far west where I'd seen Elvish magic and the slaughter of Goblins, a comfortable feeling stole upon me. I'd walked these streets often enough they'd become familiar, and the welcoming light of Bram and Margrethe's house ahead in the distance promised a comparable warmth in my heart, uncomfortable as that promise felt for one so unused to the feeling. The door opened before we had a chance to knock, and James stood there, a sword prominent on his hip and his eyes roving past us to scan the street even as he welcomed his lady home.

"Milady, Morley, welcome home." Relief was plain in his voice as he shut and bolted the door.

"Thank you, James. Is Milord Husband home yet?"

Young eyes lit on hers, concern evident. "No. Should he be?"

Margrethe's laugh warmed us both, easing James' tension. "Lad, you're worse than he is. No, I have no idea when he'll be home. He may even spend the night at the palace if the King is as concerned as our absent Lord claimed. Relax. If it's sorcery we're up against, that sword of yours will do us little good."

James, nonplussed, appeared uncertain how to take those words, and struggled for a safe reply and an appropriate expression. In the end, embarrassment won out. "Nay, Milady, 'tis just that the streets are no place for a woman at this time of day."

"I was hardly unescorted, James." She laughed again, and though James cast me a dubious look, the sound warmed me.

We left James behind at the door, peering outward one last time through the viewing slot, and I trailed behind my hostess, examining the details this time. The rooms, sparsely furnished, held a few homely decorations, various bits of antique bric-a-brac, and the dry smell of summer-warmed stone. The floor was stone, covered with thick woolen rugs, and we walked in muffled silence. Margrethe led me to a small kitchen and began rummaging through the pantry.

"You must be half starved."

As she said it, I realized I was; I'd eaten little as I recovered from my ordeal, but I'd not asked how long I'd been asleep. "Yes, Milady, I am."

"It's *Margrethe*, Morley. This isn't the Court, and we're not formal here."

"Thank you. Please forgive me if it takes time; I've never been so familiar with anyone of the Court, and there are years of habits to overcome... Margrethe."

She cast a warm smile over her shoulder, then returned to her rummaging. I climbed onto the stool she'd used to reach the higher shelves so I could watch. During our brief conversation, she'd turned up several ceramic plates, a heavy ceramic bowl with a close-fitting wooden cover, a loaf of bread, pewter mugs, a bowl of nuts and dried fruit, a heavy wheel of cheese, several covered crocks, a surprising variety of fresh vegetables, and a pitcher. She smiled again and set about preparations. Slices of bread appeared as if by magic upon one plate, then a large, partially eaten roast chicken emerged as if by its own volition from the covered earthenware bowl; slices of the chicken joined the bread upon one plate, followed by piled tomato, onion, cucumber, horseradish, bell pepper, and carrot slices. Her slim, graceful hands were swift and sure, and it was a pleasure to watch them.

So I watched, bemused and feeling the saliva spring up in my mouth, until she broke the silence. "You can earn your keep by putting together sandwiches. Four of them, if you would."

I gave her a guilty smile she pretended not to notice, and turned to the work. One of the crocks held thick mayonnaise, and the other held strong mustard. "Does anyone have a particular preference?"

"Mustard for me; mayonnaise for the men." Thick slabs of cheese had appeared beside the vegetables. "We all eat a good selection of vegetables, but James takes no cheese on his sandwich."

I spread the mustard and mayonnaise as directed, taking care to follow the directions, then heaped the various ingredients upon the bread to finish the sandwiches. They were thick and hearty. By the time I was done, Margrethe had poured drinks, and the aroma of cider permeated the small room. My stomach growled.

Margrethe laughed. "I thought you'd be hungry. Go fetch James." I was spared that necessity by the arrival of another servant, one I'd not met before.

"Milady, our Lord sends his regrets; he'll be spending the night with the King, for they have much planning remaining. He sent this."

Margrethe took the folded parchment, which had been closed with sealing wax, and broke the seal. Ignoring the two of us, she read it, and her face softened. A touch of color rose in her cheeks, and she turned away to hide it. James and I exchanged envious grins that turned into broad smiles as we recognized our shared thoughts, and I found myself liking the young man. Nonetheless, we composed ourselves, and managed to display suitably neutral expressions by the time Margrethe turned back to us, a large wooden tray in her hands.

"James, fetch the blanket; Morley, load the tray and take it to the garden. I'll get the door." She removed Bram's sandwich and placed it in the covered bowl, in case he should return.

She brushed past me, a faint aroma of rosewater and clean sweat touching my nose, and it was a moment before I could comply. James, more inured to her presence, had already set about his task. I composed myself, and set about loading the tray. I followed in the direction Margrethe had taken, watching where I placed my feet lest I trip. The tray was heavy and awkward now, and I regretted the lost strength of my giant frame, though I proved capable of managing the task. I followed the faint scent of rosewater that preceded me, and coming to the back door, where Margrethe and James awaited me. James made a hesitant motion towards me, then stopped as Margrethe's hand fell upon his arm. I pretended not to notice, and strode past them and into the garden.

The sun had finished setting, and there was a faint orange and aquamarine cast to the western sky. We made our way by that uncertain light and the dim illumination cast by oil lamps in the house to the patch where we'd sat when first I visited. The sky had darkened enough overhead that the first faint stars could be seen, and the air was filled with the scent of night-blooming flowers that came close to concealing the city's stench. We ate in silence, enjoying the air and the sharp stars. There was no moon, and the garden walls rose high enough to block much of the city light, so the stars were about as bright as they could be in a city.

When the last crusts had been devoured, the last crumbs swept to the ground, and the last drop of cider swallowed, we sat upon the blanket, side by side, and watched the stars.

An old song, one of the few I'd written, came to me as I lay there. I mourned my lost lute, but the song suited my voice, and it felt right enough that I began singing quietly, so as not to disturb the mood.

"Every twilight is a special time, as daylight slowly fades

The setting sun's a painting done in swirling pastel shades.

But the magic of the twilight's in the softness of the light

For the harshest outlines soften, every shape awaits the night..."

The rest of the song spoke of the beauty of the fading sun, of the children playing, and other homely things.

Margrethe rose up on one elbow. "That's beautiful, Morley."

"I call it *Twilight*. I wrote it many years ago for my father. The real one, the one who raised me."

Sensing what lay behind those words, Margrethe changed topics. "Don't you ever wonder by what magic those lights have been placed in the sky?" Her hushed voice came from just the other side of James, who'd sat between us without seeming to have given it any thought. I smiled. From the corner of my eyes, I saw him scanning around us; I wondered if he remained on guard even while he slept.

"It's no magic known to man, of that I'm sure," I replied. "But I'll wager the Elves know of it."

"The Elves? Bram told me you'd spent time with them, that they were real." I could see Margrethe resting on an elbow now, past the quiet bulk of James, who'd continued his surveillance as if we were talking of things no more extraordinary than the dinner we'd just consumed.

"I did, though there's little to tell; they're hostile to all of us, and for good reason. I have my own notions of the stars, though, if you'd hear them."

"I would."

"I spent considerable time learning of the days before and after the Exodus when I was a youth, for in winter, there was little to do in the woods but read and share stories, and those who lived with us spent much time memorizing and retelling the old tales. One of the oldest tales from before the Exodus tells of a wizard with a thousand magical eyes who spied on everyone; when he made the mistake of spying on a young warrior and his lover, the tale says, the enraged warrior hacked each of those eyes from the wizard's skull and cast them high in the air, where the wizard would never use them again to spy on his fellow men."

James laughed and swept his arm across the sky. "His strategy would seem ill-considered."

Margrethe and I shared his laughter. "Worse, for the sages claim there are thousands of thousands of stars in the sky, all looking down upon us, which would suggest those original eyes settled down and raised families. But I don't much like that tale. There's another one more interesting."

"Do tell," said James, amusement still in his voice.

"This one is a newer story, and involves a human thief and the Dwarves who live in Stormhold. Back when men were new to these lands, and hadn't yet alienated the Dwarves and the Elves, it's said a thief penetrated to the very heart of Stormhold, where the Dwarves keep the magnificent treasures they hew from the depths of the world. There, the thief filled the largest sack he could carry with rubies, diamonds, sapphires, emeralds, topazes, amethysts, and many more hues of crystal and gem than I can name. Hoisting the sack on his shoulder, he slipped from Stormhold and fled into the night. But when the Dwarves discovered what he'd done, they set out in pursuit, bearing razor-keen, double-headed axes as wide as the Dwarves were tall. Over the mountains they raced, drawing ever closer to the fleeing thief, until at last they trapped him upon the tallest mountain peak that lies south of Ankur."

"And what happened next?" Margrethe exclaimed.

"Standing at the edge of the precipice, the thief threatened the Dwarves that unless they swore to spare his life, he'd cast their treasures into the abyss, where they'd never again be found. The Dwarves agreed to his terms, but imposed their own on the thief by means of a terrible spell. Having regained their gems, they chose to impress upon our race that such simple, replaceable things had far less importance to the Dwarves than the message that none might so offend the mountain folk and escape unscathed. The strongest of the Dwarves seized the sack of gems, and whirling it about his head, flung it high into the night sky. The sack struck the crescent moon and tore open, spilling the gems across the length and breadth of the sky. Then, with the rough humor they're famed for, they told the thief he could have his life, but only if he could recover all the gems. The same Dwarf who'd cast the gems into the sky seized the thief and flung him upwards too, and he seeks until this day, striving to gather the scattered gems and return them to the Dwarves."

James laughed again. "A fitting fate. But you sound skeptical, friend Morley."

I smiled in the dark. "Those are old tales, and pleasant to tell, but they're just tales."

Margrethe spoke. "And you have your own notions."

"Yes." I thought back to what I'd read in the library before Orgrim sent me to the Elves, and the silence stretched a long moment as I gathered my thoughts. "All I've read of the Exodus tells me there was an unimaginable magical cataclysm, and that our race sacrificed something important in exchange for surviving that disaster." I licked my lips, which had gone dry. "I sometimes think the stars are reflections of the fires that still burn in the land that gave birth to our race, and that we see them every night to remind us what once happened, that we might never forget."

"Yet as is our wont, we've forgotten, and see in them only beauty," Margrethe whispered. Then she changed her tone. "This is far too dark, Morley. Sing to us again, this time something lighter."

My last tale had cast a pall, for it erased the calm I'd known; that same ancient magic lay waiting for us, and playing at domestic games was fooling myself. But I did my best, seeking songs I'd long practiced for the ladies of the Court and trying to do justice to them without my lute. It took time, but the discipline I imposed on my voice and the concentration it required freed me to accept the calm that always came when I lost myself in music. Margrethe and James joined in where they knew the words, and we passed a pleasant time until my voice roughened from fatigue and Margrethe, sensing I was fading, faked a loud yawn and retired to her bed, leaving James and me to clean up.

"Sleep, Morley. Your room is nearest this door, beside the painting of the stag. I'll clean up."

"Let me help," I protested.

"No, friend, for you're a guest here, and have already done your share of the work. Moreover, I heard some of what happened to you, and know that you need rest. There will be time to work here later. For now, rest."

I reached out and clasped his hand. "Thanks." His grip was tentative at first, then strengthened when he realized that despite my childish stature, I possessed a man's strength. "You're a good man, James, and they're lucky to have you."

His smile was obvious in the reflected light of the oil lamps. "No, Morley, it's I who am lucky."

I recognized the justice in his remark, and that I now shared his fortune. I bade him good night and headed to my room. There was a lush bed, of a comfort I'd rarely experienced, and enough blankets to bury a much larger man. I used the chamber pot, set it beside my door, and paused only long enough to undress. When I hit the bed, I sank into those blankets like a stone into a lake. My consciousness sank as fast, despite the foreboding that lurked around the edge of my thoughts.

***

In the morning, I woke early, feeling better than I'd felt for many days despite a few remaining twinges in my muscles. I used the new chamber pot that had appeared by the door, then dressed quickly. During the night, whatever my forgotten dreams, my mind had seized upon what I must do, and the longer I delayed, the harder the doing would be. Taking the chamber pot, I made my way to the back of the house, where I'd seen the telltale signs of a honey hole. After emptying the pot, I rinsed it with water from the rain barrel provided for that purpose, and returned it to my room. My stomach was now awake, and I made for the kitchen. I'd planned to make a light snack to keep life in my body until the rest of the household arose, but James had risen before me and was already there. There was also a large covered bundle on the floor beside the hearth.

James' attention was on a large black frypan in which eggs and a thick slab of ham were just beginning to sizzle. Without taking his eyes off his cooking, he cast a greeting back over his shoulder. "Good morning."

"And to you, James." I crossed over behind him to stand by the bundle on the floor. "Is there aught I can do to help?"

He laughed and turned to smile at me. "Nay, not a thing; if Milady or Milord found out you'd helped me, I'd never hear the end of it. As you know, my master was once a knight of Amelior, and though he no longer lives that life, he retains certain unfortunate notions about the discipline that goes into the making of a squire."

I returned his smile, enjoying comradeship without questioning it. Leaving James to his work, I squatted by the bundle, a large oilcloth, and opened it to reveal a cloak, a shoulder pack, a hatchet, a dagger, a water skin, and a floppy-brimmed hat. The half-open pack revealed several bundles from which various savory scents emerged. Someone was going on a journey?

"Milord sent us a message last night, after you were abed," James commented without looking back. The smells of eggs and ham had begun to permeate the kitchen.

I replaced the oilcloth. "Oh?"

"He warned us you'd be wanting to leave, and that we should ready certain supplies for you."

I stood dumbfounded. Until this morning, I hadn't thought of leaving, not since Margrethe had commanded me to join her small family. But leaving had indeed been on my mind from the moment I'd regained consciousness in the infirmary, and I'd only admitted it this morning. Bram had been perceptive, and had foreseen that no matter how much I'd enjoy my stay here, I would have to leave, and soon. "Your master sees more than he lets on."

"He does indeed." James rose from the hearth and moved to the counter. With a practiced flip, he transferred the ham and eggs to a plate, and poured me a mug of skimmed milk; fresh butter lay upon a small, covered earthenware plate, and bread soon made its appearance from the pantry. "Toast?"

I nodded, and James sliced bread and set it to warm in bacon grease. "Eat, Morley."

I climbed back atop the tall stool that had been my perch last night. "Won't you join me?"

He laughed again, a broad smile growing. "Nay, I've already eaten enough to hold me till Milady rises."

"That doesn't sound imminent."

"No, that it is not. She was a lady in waiting for many a year, and had her fill of that life. She never rises with the sun, as we poor men must do."

We exchanged smiles at his irreverence, and I needed no more urging. I set about my meal. As I ate, James elaborated on Bram's message. "He said you'd want to leave, and that I should tell you we had no plans to stop you, but that you were welcome should you choose to stay. He told me to expect you to leave anyway."

I licked egg yolk from my lips. "He was right. I shouldn't be here even now, and I do you all a disservice by endangering you. I was weak and easily overborne by your Lady, else I'd never have come here."

James laughed again, a sound I was growing to enjoy. "There's no weakness in that, friend. Milady isn't one to gainsay once she's made up her mind; even Milord has been known to yield the field rather than trying to defeat her in open combat. But you must understand, Morley, that our lives are yours should it come to that; my master and mistress would expect no less from me."

"And that's why I can't stay. Such loyalty deserves better."

James was still holding the frypan, and the muscles on his forearm bunched and knotted. "Would that I could come with and offer my sword in your defense."

I put a hand on his shoulder. "Should it become necessary to defend me, a sword will be of no use. It's magic I flee, not mortal man. I've given it some thought, and I feel sure I'd be safest in the woods for a time, as Bram guessed. You're a townsman, and you'd be little help there."

James snorted. "Perhaps, and perhaps not. I learn fast. But more to the point, I can't leave Milady here alone, even with Bram in town. That makes my decision."

"Nonetheless, I thank you. When this is over, I can take you and teach what I know of woodcraft. To prepare you for the next time." I finished my meal, and knelt to remove the oilcloth from the equipment Bram had prepared. There was no reason to delay my departure, so I gathered the gear about me without delay, folded the oilcloth and tied it about my waist, my pack rubbing against it, then rose, fully but not uncomfortably laden. James showed me to the back door, gripped my free hand with a concerned look, then let me go.

I took no more than a few steps before turning back to find him waiting. "Tell Margrethe and Bram—"

"They know. Return soon, Morley."

I turned without another word, hiding the dampness in my eyes.

At that early hour, the streets were deserted. I made my way without incident to the south gate, nearest the direction I was headed, and found it already open. It was a time of peace, and the King's soldiers kept bandits and brigands far from these walls, so sealing the gates at night was a rare thing these days. I tipped my new hat to the guards as I passed, and they nodded in return. Then I was out on the open road.

Walking was a very different thing from what it had been. It hadn't taken me long to grow accustomed to my giant's legs, and I was disappointed by how little progress I now made. Still, I'd walked far enough these past weeks that my muscles were firm, and the aches soon faded as my muscles warmed. I moved ever farther from the city, and as I walked, I let my mind turn to the one thing that was uppermost in my thoughts: what would I do about Orgrim? It was clear that running to the woods to hide offered no permanent solution, for he'd find me there as he'd done once before. Yet staying in town offered little benefit, for it was doubtful anyone there could aid me, with the possible exception of Raphael— and he wasn't yet ready to risk his life, though that would change once Orgrim learned of his new foe and set about eliminating him. No, I'd have to return to the city, find a place to summon Orgrim and try, once and for all, to be free of him.

I'd been walking along a road that passed through lush farm fields as I thought this through, and I was enjoying the mist rising from the grass and the freshness of growing things. Ankur's walls fell farther behind me, and after a time, as I turned to glance back at the city, I spotted a covered wagon catching up. I'd been walking long enough it had grown warm, and with the dew now risen from the road and the grass, it would soon grow dusty too. If the cart was traveling far enough, perhaps I could ease my journey. I found a patch of rock by the side of the road, dropped my sack, sat down, and washed the dust from my throat while I waited for the cart to reach me.

As the cart drew closer, its contents became obvious despite the heavy canvas frame sheltering them from the sun: barrels, lashed down with thick ropes. I smiled; the brewery was shipping its produce to the estates that lay south of the city, near the King's hunting preserve. Perhaps I'd have an easier trip than I'd expected after all. When I could see the driver's eyes, I called out to attract his attention.

"Ho, the cart!"

"Ho, yourself, and a good day to you," the teamster replied, cheerful enough to belie the suspicion in his eyes and the way they swept the fields around him.

"Would I be right in assuming you're making a delivery to the forest estates?"

The cart drew to a stop, the four horses watchful from behind the shade of their blinders. Their driver's suspicion vanished, swept away by a broad grin. "Yes, that'd be the place. And you'd be the King's fool, unless I miss my guess."

I swept a deep bow, brushing my hat through the dust. "Morley, Court Jester at your service. And as I'm heading for the same destination, I'd sorely appreciate a ride."

The teamster chortled. "Aye, with those bandy little legs, I imagine you would." He pondered a moment. "Climb aboard, Morley. You'll pay for your passage with those fine songs I've heard it said you sing, and I'll pay for those songs with a mug or two of my cargo. Have we a deal?"

I was already moving as he spoke, and I slung my pack up onto the seat beside him before hauling myself up. The wagon was moving before I'd even settled on the hard wooden bench. We shook hands; his was dry and callused from moving barrels and gripping reins. "We have a deal. And you are?"

"Karl, teamster by trade and glad of it. Welcome to my workplace, Morley. And what lures you out from the comforts of the palace on this fine summer day, off to the rough life of the woods?"

A wicked impulse urged me to tell him the truth and watch his look of shock, but I repressed it. It was uncomfortable being reminded of the less pleasant parts of me that remained even in the demon's absence. "Not so rough as all that," I replied instead. "I spent my youth with my father, one of our King's foresters. So in many ways, I find the wood-lands more comfortable than Ankur itself, for all its luxuries."

He was watching me in puzzlement. "Aye, I'd heard of that. Yet I think, though you call yourself jester, *fool* is the better word for anyone who'd live beneath the trees without being outlawed first. But don't be taking that amiss, friend. I speak as a townsman, and one who prefers the comforts of stone walls to those of an open wood roof."

I smiled back at him to show I'd taken no offense, for indeed I'd not; Karl's open and honest callousness was a refreshing change from the calculated cruelties I'd grown accustomed to at Court. "Let me begin to pay my way, Karl. You'll have to excuse me, for I've my voice alone to entertain you today."

He nodded. "Aye. I imagine you'd not want to haul one of those great lutes upon your back over the distance you'll be going. Sing on, Fool, something that a simple man like me can appreciate."

I paused a moment in thought. Neither a love song nor a song of war would be right for this man, and those were most of my stock in trade. Then I had a notion of what might do.

"There's a different kind of feel outside the city
In the country when you leave the stone behind
With the tallest things in sight the ancient oak trees
That gently nourish cleaner states of mind..."

I sang of the things that had touched my heart, and the sense I'd had long ago after my initiation into the mysteries of the foresters, a sense of becoming part of something larger.

"A tad overdelicate," he observed, "but pretty enough. Still, I'll take Ankur any day. Though I'll grant you, when the summer's heat hits the city and gets to cooking the stink from the sewers, I'm happier out here than in there. Give me another one, if you're up to it."

I pondered a moment, then found a song appropriate to what I'd spent my morning doing.

"There's a rhythm when I'm walking
All alone, by day or night
With no settled destination
And a mood that's always light..."

I sang of the joy of walking, of putting miles behind me, and my recent excursions made the words heartfelt and strong.

"Hmph," he snorted. "You've got a good voice, all right, but that song's too fancy and the words too tricksy for my taste. Can't you find one fitter for a simple man?"

I smiled, and tried him on a few drinking songs I thought he might know. After a time, he joined in. He had a strong, clear voice, but didn't know how to use it. That didn't matter, because the exercise was more important than the art. We paused for a drink now and then, and after time and practice had put a few more miles behind us, his skill had grown remarkably until he seemed the finest singer I'd known. We passed the hours in a companionable manner, singing every now and then or just appreciating the scenery in silence. By late afternoon, we were within sight of the forest, and the cart was turning into the yard of one of the estates I'd visited with the King in days past.

My companion sighed. "Morley, if size were all, then I'd never have thought to enjoy my time with such a small man, but you've been a companion all out of proportion to your size." He took my hand and shook it hard. "If you're ever in need of a ride to and from the town, I'd be honored to share a bench with you."

I smiled right back at him. "And I you, Karl. Enjoy your stay here tonight."

He frowned. "Won't you be spending a last night indoors before you enter the forest? With a voice like yours, you'd be welcome here."

I'd spent a night here before, and knew he spoke truth, but I'd not come this distance to sing for my keep. There was much I needed to think about, and the distractions of human company would prevent that. "Thanks, Karl, but I can't. I still have many miles to go."

He shook his head, uncomprehending, but he let me go. My legs had stiffened from sitting for so long, but that soon faded as I left the road and set out across a field for a place I knew from previous visits. Though a heavy burden still lay upon me, I felt my spirits lifting and my stride lengthening as I entered familiar land. Long before the redness in the sky faded, I found the sheltered spot by a small spring where I'd planned to spend the night.

There were sufficient downed branches that I soon had a fire burning, and I opened my pack to see what Bram had prepared. It was a small measure of my distraction that I'd let a townsman pack for me, and it was with considerable trepidation that I began the task of sorting through the packages. My fears proved groundless, though, for Bram knew his business. When I returned—if I returned—I'd have to ask where he'd learned those skills. Or perhaps not—remembering my stay with the Goblins and their foes, it was all too clear where Bram had learned to pack for the road.

I shook off those memories and set about selecting various ingredients and preparing my meal. I don't recall what I ate, but it was filling and tasty, for my thoughts were pulled hither and yon by memories of the past few weeks and fears of what lay ahead. Afterwards, as the fire burned down and I lay wrapped in my bedroll, I stared up at the night sky, full of stars that had been invisible through the city's funk.

All the colors of the rainbow danced there, and the light was bright enough to cast faint shadows, even in the absence of the moon. You could lose yourself in that sight, as I'd done on many previous nights, but tonight I was reminded of my explanations for their presence in the sky. As a child, I'd always preferred the tale of the thief that explained their origin, but this night, I couldn't chase the darker explanation from my mind. After all, I now had clear evidence that my last explanation might be the correct one. At some point while I gazed up at the sky, marveling at the sight yet chilled by its implications, I fell asleep.

This time, though, I dreamed. In the dream, I was again in the woods on that night when I'd first made my decision to leave for Ankur and seek employment at Court. I'd camped beneath the stars, then, and held debate with myself on whether to cling to the safety of the woods and spend my days shunning the company of men other than the foresters we shared our winter quarters with. There was safety there, and comfort, but also the fear that my acceptance would only endure as long as my father. On top of that lay a fear that this safety and comfort came at the expense of an end to my progress and ever more restricted horizons. In the end, it was the fear of that stagnation and the sure knowledge that the growth I'd attained thus far had come from risking my security that made up my mind and led me to Ankur. My father had acquiesced, grudgingly, but ever after, there'd been a certain distance between us.

I awoke with the memory of that dream clear in my head, and the rarity of remembering what I'd dreamed was what convinced me. I'd half believed I was fleeing to the woods for their safety and to gain time to think, but now I knew why I'd really come. There was someone I had to see before I made any decisions about where I'd go and what I'd do in the days ahead and the events that would shape the rest of my life, however short a span that might be. I had a cold breakfast, ensured that the fire was thoroughly drowned, and set off along familiar trails that led me deep into the woods.

Towards the end of the day, I came within sight of the sturdy log house in which I'd spent many winters. Though each of the King's foresters had his own part of the forest to tend, and had a small shack from which to do it, the winters in this part of the country were harsh enough that those huts proved inadequate; as well, a wound sustained in winter, when travel was next to impossible, could prove fatal with no other man near to help. So at the first snows, each forester packed up his gear and returned to this place to spend the winter with his fellows, sharing new tales and old songs, honing skills with the aid of others more experienced, and enjoying that brief season of camaraderie before we resumed our solitary existence. I paused at the foot of the small rise that led to the house, feeling the urge to leave again warring with the need to seek what awaited me within. The urge to leave was winning.

As I followed those thoughts to their end, delaying that decision, a sharp blow between my shoulders propelled me face down into the leaf mould, and a heavy boot pinned me to the ground. Then all at once that pressure eased, and strong hands pulled me to my feet.

"You've grown soft in your city, Morley."

I smiled up at the familiar face and voice, dark eyes smiling out from amidst a mane of equally dark hair and reflecting the even brighter smile nestling within his thick beard. Mixed memories surfaced. "Not so soft I didn't hear your oafish footsteps long ago, Teren. I figured I owed you at least one victory."

Teren had been an opponent of my youth, and later, as I'd matured, an occasional companion. Like all the foresters, he'd grown to respect my ability and accept my presence, but never easily, nor without having to work at it constantly; he'd been raised with the prejudices of the country folk towards changelings and had feared me enough to withhold any true measure of friendship until we were both much older. Had it not been for my father, I doubt he and the others would have let me stay long enough to earn his trust.

The smile broadened. "So you say, and I thank you. Still... it was a rare pleasure to make you eat muck." He brushed a few leaves from my chest.

I brushed at the leaves in my hair, and asked the question that had brought me here. "Is he here?"

Teren's smile vanished, and a deep sadness replaced it in his eyes. "Yes, Morley. He's grown frail these past months, but he's still a vigorous man and a wonder to us all. You know I'd have sent word had there been any fear of us losing him."

I felt the tightness that had grown, unnoticed, in my chest relax. "Thank you." I meant it, and the look in his eyes told me he knew how deeply I meant it.

Having lost the opportunity to leave, I turned without another word and made my way to the house. I swung the heavy door open, the renewed leather wind barrier dragging across the smooth wooden floor as I did, and I stepped onto the floor, feeling apprehension rising again. At the far side of the room, in front of a stone fireplace, a large man lay slumped in an armchair, asleep before the fire. Though I'd said this place was for the winter, it was also a refuge for those too old to continue on their own through the summer, and the other foresters took turns tending to the needs of their failing fellows. I made my way to the sleeping man and knelt at his side, putting my hand on his arm and squeezing.

"Georges?"

My father woke with a start, comprehension growing slowly in still-piercing green eyes above a nose that had grown more aquiline with time. Those eyes were all that remained of youth about him. Though still the giant he'd been as a young man, age lay heavily upon him. My father hadn't been young even when he took me in, and many years had passed since then. Now that he could no longer fend for himself, the others kept him here at the winter quarters, where they could take their turns keeping an eye on him throughout the year, and could bring him food and other supplies. I felt tears growing in my eyes, and forced them back, not wanting to impose that burden on him.

"Morley! It's good to see you again, son."

"Father!" And despite my resolve, I laid my head upon his knee and wept quietly, enjoying the comfort of his strong fingers caressing my hair and his deep voice telling me all would be well, as he'd done so many times in my youth. After a time, my tears ceased and I dabbed at my eyes.

"You look well," he added, a hand still caressing my hair.

"Father, looks can be deceiving." I poured out my story, for the third time in as many days, and once again, it eased my burden. When I'd done, he cleared his throat and spat into the fire.

"So you've come to share your fate, have you? Though I'm not yet ready to occupy that bed beneath the forest floor our friends have prepared, I nonetheless thank you—I think." His smile was gentle as always, but his eyes had narrowed.

"Father, that was the least of my intentions. The one thing you've taught me above all else is to stand on my own against my troubles, and it's served me well."

I saw pride grow in his eyes, and it warmed me and reinvigorated me. "Then if not for protection, why have you come?"

I saw he'd already answered that question, and felt the same answer growing in me. "For advice, Father, not protection. I feel sure that if I flee far enough from the city, Orgrim might not seek me; he has little need for me and his work lies in those cities, not here, far from anything of importance in the larger scheme of things. All the main players now know of his presence, so perhaps my work is done. Yet I fear he's not the kind to leave ends dangling for others to tangle."

"And flight sits poorly with you."

"It does. Not because he might still seek me out, mind, for that too would resolve matters; I won't serve him again."

"It was not well you did so in the first place." The words stung, but there was honesty in his voice, not condemnation. "If you no longer fear him, then what's your dilemma?"

I paused, unsure. "Could it be simply that I fear bringing his wrath upon my new friends?"

He was silent a moment. "Put another log on the fire." I complied, then returned to his side and took his cold, callused hand in mine. "That seems improbable. Though I always taught you to stand alone, I also taught you to know your limits and to accept help from those who offer it freely should you find yourself beyond those limits. Even here, we've heard of this Bram and his deeds during the war, and he strikes me as a good man to have at your side. And if you're not just spinning tales to entertain an old man," his hand clenched on my shoulder, "this Raphael represents your best hope."

"What, then?"

The smile left him. "You fear that once in the presence of Orgrim, you'll accept his gift again, despite the consequences."

I nodded, though reluctantly. "Perhaps that's indeed what troubles me."

"There's no *perhaps*, and you knew that before you came. You just wanted someone to confirm it." He squeezed my shoulder.

"Father..."

"There's no need. Morley, I'm pleased you came. My time's not yet done, but it must come, and sooner rather than later."

"I should stay the night..."

"Why? Has your stay in the city made you fear the forests? Staying would only be delaying what you must do, and I never taught my son to hesitate over the inevitable. Go do what you must, then return once again before my ending."

"More than once, Father. I swear it!"

His smile was gentle, and I threw my arms about him as best I could and hugged him close. His answering hug was firm enough to squeeze the breath from me, and again, I marveled at the man's vitality. We'd communicated all that needed to be said, and I left him gazing into the fire without looking back, vowing that whatever chanced, I would return at least that one last time. When the door closed behind me, Teren rose from where he'd been squatting, back against the wall.

"He's a good man, your father. We'll all miss him when he's gone."

His eyes were sober and for the first time since I'd known him, I saw not so much as a flicker of mistrust there. Sheepish, I wondered how long it had been absent, unnoticed.

"He's all that you say, and more." I turned and made to go, but his heavy hand fell on my shoulder.

"Morley... It speaks well of you that he accepted you and brought you among us. Never forget that; I shall not."

I clasped his arm, then turned and strode back into the forest. My stay at the longhouse had lasted little longer than it takes to recount it, yet in that brief time, my resolve had solidified, and I had something in my spirit which made me unvanquishable. If that strength lasted until I reached the city, and was no more a delusion than the strength I'd taken from the headstrong, I'd live to honor my vow to my father.

Chapter 15: The cat came back

Two days later, I was back in Ankur, standing outside Bram's townhouse, stained with the dust and sweat of the road and feeling the sweet fatigue of long exertion. The door opened before I could knock, and James stood there with a welcoming smile.

"Morley! Welcome, friend. Did you find what you sought?" I nodded wearily. "Enter, then, and clean yourself. You have visitors, but they instructed me to give you time to recover from your voyage."

I nodded. *Visitors*? There'd been a strangeness in his eyes when he said that, and it awoke a sense of apprehension. James took my pack and my filthy cloak, then led me to my room, where a steaming basin of water and a heap of soft towels awaited me. The water was so hot it must have been boiled recently, and that foresight hinted at the identity of one of my visitors. I washed slowly, organizing my thoughts and letting a brisk rub with the towels reinvigorate me and reawaken my mind. When I'd done, I donned the fresh clothing that had been prepared, and headed for Bram's study.

As I'd expected, Bram, Margrethe, James, and Raphael awaited me, sitting in a companionable silence and sipping warm drinks, failing to disguise looks of anticipation. James filled a mug and pressed it into my hand even as I sat. James had said "visitors", and I scanned the room for the other guest or guests. It was when I sat down that I saw the other visitor. A small, furry body shot across the room from where it had lain dozing by the fire and vaulted into my lap, spilling hot wine across my hands. Grey settled himself and set up a loud purring that brought smiles to everyone.

For a moment, I was speechless, despite the sting of the hot liquid on my fingers. "How can this be? I left him so far to the west that he should have been dead of old age before he returned."

Bram's eyes fixed on the cat as he spoke. "Unless I miss my guess, this is the selfsame witch's cat that haunted me from our stay in Belfalas through the siege of Ankur, though I knew it as 'Precious', the name its witch mistress had given it. I would have sworn the cat was at least ten years old when I first met it, and it has been eight years since."

"The cat is older by far than that, Bram." A touch of humor crinkled the corners of Raphael's eyes. "Morley, this is no ordinary cat, as you surely suspected. If my divinations are accurate, he's nothing less than a contemporary of our friend Orgrim."

"But that would make him hundreds of years old!"

"If not older. As I said, no ordinary cat. And that's why I sought him out and returned him to you."

"You sought him out across that distance? How?"

Raphael smiled broadly. "Suffice it to say that I learned of this humble beast's importance in determining our fates, and was motivated to bring him here." His wrinkled brow knit together. "That alone would have prompted me to seek him, but I was unable to scry anything else about him. It was as if he didn't exist to my magic, and I couldn't resist that challenge."

"You couldn't find him by magic, and yet you found him by magic?"

Raphael's smile turned smug. "Sometimes a thing's absence is as revealing as its presence. Now I've brought the two of you together again, for it wasn't chance that brought you together in the first place, and I'm curious to see what will happen. A small gamble, if you will, but an informed one."

"What happens next?" I asked the question to buy time, though I already knew the answer.

Margrethe spoke, disapproving, from where she sat beside Bram, studiously not holding the hand that rested in her lap. "They've already decided that. You'll summon Orgrim and confront him."

Bram captured her hand, but had something of a struggle to retain it. He made to speak, but I cut him off. "Forgive them, Milady. Though they made the decision without consulting me, I'd already come to the same conclusion. 'Twas I who started much of this, and I can't evade responsibility for ending it."

Margrethe showed concern now, but she'd stopped struggling and let Bram hold her hand. "It's as I told you, beloved," he spoke only to her. "Though we made the decision, Morley must carry it through to the end, and not unwillingly." Margrethe's hand rested more comfortably in her husband's, though her face remained tight with concern.

"When will this happen?" I asked, turning my gaze towards Raphael.

"Tomorrow, during the day, for we can't give Orgrim more time to plan for my presence, and day is always more auspicious than night for confronting dark magic."

The others nodded, and I mastered my fear long enough to commit to this course, for there was still a part of me that urged flight. "Agreed. First thing in the morning. And where shall we confront him?"

"In the crypt beneath the palace, where everything began. There's a symmetry to that arrangement that favors our plans." Raphael's voice turned musing. "There's a spell that should hold him helpless long enough to slay him. I don't much like that, yet I see no alternative for one so dangerous."

"Nor could the King's council, despite more than a day of deliberation," added Bram, regret plain in his voice.

"And your part in this?"

"He'll be the fool wielding the sword," Margrethe whispered, concern plain in her voice. Bram gathered her to him, heedless of the others in the room, and held her close, whispering something into her ears that clearly failed to reassure her.

"I urge you all to seek your rooms," Raphael spoke into the silence. "You'll need a good night's sleep to arm you for what lies ahead. There's little you need to know, and that can all be told in the morning."

Everyone rose, and with a few sympathetic backwards glances in my direction, departed; all save Raphael, who took my arm. "Morley, I sense unease in your heart. Are you certain you're ready for this?"

I met his gaze steadfastly. "No, I'm not. Yet I know this: that if I hesitate and delay, I will either flee Orgrim and leave you to your fate, or I'll embrace what he offered me. I couldn't live with myself if I accept either alternative, hence I must act."

Raphael nodded. "So it seemed to me." He pressed a small crystal vial into my hand, and squeezed my hand in reassurance. "Drink this when you seek your bed; it will grant a deep, dreamless sleep so you can awake, refreshed, tomorrow."

I thanked him and returned to my room, Grey padding along behind me. As I lay in bed, Orgrim's ring heavy upon my chest and the cat's warm weight heavy upon my legs, the magnitude of what awaited me on the morrow grew painful, and it was without the slightest reluctance that I unstoppered Raphael's vial and swallowed its sweet, cloying contents.

Chapter 16: Redemption

In the morning, I awoke, refreshed, hungry, and as eager to be about my business as if it were just another day. There was a warm spot on my legs where Grey nestled, not having moved during the night, and I shifted my legs with an effort before chasing my companion off the bed so I could rise. The cat accompanied me to the kitchen, a silent shadow. The kitchen was already full when I entered, and there was considerable commotion until Margrethe, exasperated, chased everyone out but James. We took refuge in the sitting room, filling the silence with small talk of the least consequential kind. Breakfast, when it arrived, followed the same pattern, but by the time we were done, only Bram had eaten heartily, the mood had grown very different, and silence fell. It was Raphael who broke that silence.

"It's time to begin." There was much uncomfortable clearing of throats and shuffling of feet, and the old mage looked grim.

"Tell us your plan. You *do* have a plan?" I wondered aloud.

"How could I not? Is this not too important and risky a venture to leave to chance?" Raphael licked his lips and continued. "Three things must happen for us to succeed: First, Morley must summon Orgrim and occupy his attention while we prepare; second, I must immobilize our foe while he's distracted; third, Bram and any companions he requires must slay him.

"The specific details are as follows: First, Morley shall go to the crypt, and remove the ring from the silver chain that now binds it. After slipping on the ring, you must concentrate on your former master, as you were instructed; that should bring him to you. When he arrives, you must explain what happened, and why you are as you now are, keeping as much to the truth as possible so you regain his confidence; he'll be suspicious, of course, but if you assert that you've returned to once more serve him, that should allay his suspicions long enough for me to snare him. Finally, when Bram hears our shouts, he must enter and slay the mage before he can free himself from my spell. Does that make sense?"

"All save one aspect," Bram replied. "What role is the cat to play?"

All the while, Grey had been lying at my feet, occasionally swiping at a leg of my pants with extended claws, for all the world an ordinary housecat having forgiven his master's absence and grown pleased at his return. Now, with every eye in the room upon him, he became diffident, and set about grooming himself. I reached down and picked him up, turning him to me. "Yes, what role are you to play in this, Cat?" Grey met my gaze for an instant, inscrutable as always, as if he knew full well his role but had no intention of sharing that knowledge. As I set him down again, he turned away, unperturbed, and resumed grooming himself.

Raphael looked uncomfortable. "That's the one part of my plan that bothers me. I feel certain the cat's essential, yet I don't know why or what its actual role shall be."

I had an unpleasant thought. "Always before, he disappeared before Orgrim arrived, as if he knew the mage were coming and chose to flee. How can I keep him close this time?"

Raphael's frown deepened. "We could bind him, whether by leash or by spell, but my instincts warn against this." He sighed, his tension relaxing. "I fear we shall simply have to trust that the cat knows his role and that if I'm wrong, we shall ourselves be adequate to the task."

"Not a comforting thought," Margrethe muttered. "And little to hang our hopes upon."

Bram put an arm around her again, and she snuggled against him, eyes downcast. "We've hung our hopes on less in the past, Beloved." Her nod was barely noticeable.

"It's agreed, then." Raphael rose from his chair, smoothing the folds of his robe. "Morley, you shall leave at once, bringing the cat with you. Bram and I shall make the necessary arrangements at the palace, then hasten to take up our positions. I'll know when Orgrim arrives, and shall do my best to surprise him. All you must do is tell your tale without haste, and do your best to convince him you're eager to once again enter his service. Take as long as you can without being suspicious, so we can move into position; stall him as long as necessary."

I nodded, speechless and terrified now the event was upon me. Together, we left the house, Bram pausing to embrace his wife and whisper a few words in James' ear; the young squire looked displeased and rebellious, but settled down at a sharp look from Bram and moved to stand beside Margrethe, his jaw clenching and unclenching. A short while later, we found ourselves in the palace, and what happened along the way, I cannot recount; somewhere along the way, Bram had acquired men armed with axes and a crossbow. My thoughts were elsewhere, and it was all I could do to rein them in. In short order, I stood on the brink of cold stone steps that led downwards into darkness, lantern in hand. Bram squeezed one shoulder, patted the cat who crouched on the other, and turned away without a word, grim and distracted. That left Raphael.

"I'd offer magical aid, Morley, save that he'd sense it and avoid our trap."

"Just as well. I'd rather do this without magic if we can. I've not liked my few encounters with your art."

Raphael smiled. "Then console yourself that this should be the last time you're forced to deal with it. Best of luck, Morley. We'll follow, close as we dare."

I turned and descended into darkness, walking cautiously in the lamp's faint illumination. It was easy to find the crypt, for my previous journey to that place was etched in my mind. When I arrived, Grey jumped down and set to prowling about the room. I sat upon the slab, staring at the faint traces that remained on the floor from the spell that had summoned the demon to inhabit me, and the chill I felt was more than the crypt's damp cold. I lifted the ring from about my neck and held it in my hand, staring at the dull, white object nestled amidst the coils of silver chain. Then, knowing that Raphael had concealed himself in the dark beyond the open door, and that Bram and his men awaited Raphael's signal, I seized the ring with trembling hand and removed it from the chain before I could think better of it.

As I slid the ring onto my finger, Grey yowled and disappeared at a run. Too late, I wondered whether I should have closed the door to lock him in, but remembered Raphael's words: if the cat were truly important, we'd have to trust that he knew his role. I closed my eyes and concentrated on the ring, sinking into it as I'd done once before, and my heart leaped as a voice intruded on my consciousness.

"What has happened to *you*, my servant?" I forced my eyes open, heart pounding in my breast, to see Orgrim standing before me. "Someone has interfered with my plans, and shall be punished for their temerity; I shall send a clear message to those who league against me."

I took a deep breath, forcing calmness as I'd done before countless performances, and bowed my head so Orgrim couldn't see my eyes. "Master, I beg your forgiveness. All went well until my mission to Ankur. There, I met one who was your equal in sorcery, and he did this." I swept my hands across my body, emphasizing the change that had come over me. Then I recounted what had happened when I bore my message to the King, omitting only details that would have revealed my rebellion. Anxiety swelled as I awaited my rescue—and none came. Licking dry lips, I focused inward on how I'd felt upon first meeting Orgrim, and I felt tears rising to my eyes. I lifted my gaze to meet the wizard's cold stare, and spoke with trembling voice.

"If you can restore me to normalcy, I'll gladly endure that pain again that I might serve you." In that instant, I felt within me a burst of desire that gave that statement the ring of truth, and though it strengthened my voice, it weakened my resolve. Before that strength failed altogether, I went on. "But first you must answer my questions."

Orgrim's appraisal turned coldly amused. "Must I? Very well. You've served me loyally thus far, and so long as it suits me, I'll answer your questions."

I pursed my lips, then asked the safest of the many questions I'd wanted to ask since our first meeting. "Why steal those scrolls from the library? Surely they were of no use to one so powerful as you?"

Orgrim's eyes narrowed, and I felt his gaze like a physical force. "The scrolls you stole speak of me, and contain information that would give my foes a valuable edge, perhaps enough for them to defeat me. By helping me steal the scrolls, you ensured that cannot happen." His smile grew colder, self-satisfied.

I swallowed, not daring to look around me for any sign of rescue. I asked a more dangerous question. "Tell me of the demon that hid within me."

Orgrim's gaze hardened further. "*That*, I cannot explain, for a great magic blocks any such knowledge from your people. Believe only this: that the demon means you no harm. You have my word on that."

I felt a chill take root in my heart, for I knew he was lying, and though I struggled, I'm sure I wasn't able to keep that knowledge from my face.

At that moment, there came a motion at the door, and out of the corner of my eye, I saw Raphael enter the room. But no sooner had he crossed the threshold then he froze with a look of horror. Orgrim turned towards the door and smiled coldly. "Welcome, Rafe. It's been long indeed." Though Raphael's body was frozen, his eyes widened.

The door closed with a dull thud, sealing us into the chamber. Before I could breathe twice, there came a pounding on the door, quickly replaced by the sound of axes. My other rescuers had arrived, but too late to be of any use. If I'd believed I had no distance left to fall at that moment, Orgrim returned his gaze to me, triumph glowing in his eyes, and I felt my spirits sink even lower.

"And that is that, Morley. I shall now take you up on your offer to return to my service; I realize your heart wasn't in that offer, but a starving man will eat the dish he's been given, and there's more I need you to do." From the door, I heard curses, and the axemen redoubled their efforts, to no apparent effect.

Orgrim turned away and began laying his tools upon the slab. I couldn't speak, and sank to my knees, all strength gone and blackness gathering around the edges of my vision. I almost missed the movement in the shadows that resolved into the cat. As I watched, numb, Grey stalked across the room as if he were hunting a mouse, unseen by the mage, and it struck me like a blow how extraordinary the cat must be. I'd understood this intellectually for some time, but this was the first time I knew it in my heart. All at once, Orgrim spun on his heel, a look of hatred transforming his face, and he flung his arm out to strike down the cat. But he was too slow; Grey had sensed the movement, and sprang for Orgrim even as the mage's hand lashed out. The cat caught that arm in midair and dug in with teeth and claws, and Orgrim shrieked in pain; then, skin and cloth tore, and he hurled the cat from him. It struck the wall with an unpleasant *thud*, and slid down to lie unmoving on the floor.

In that moment, while Orgrim's attention lay elsewhere, I rose to my feet, lantern still swinging from my numb hand, and all the anger and humiliation at what he'd done to me rose within. Fast as I'd ever moved before, I lunged towards him, and with all my strength, swung the lantern in a whirring arc that ended against the side of his head. The lantern shattered, spewing burning oil across the room, and Orgrim dropped like a deer I'd once taken through the heart with an arrow. Flaming oil guttered in shallow puddles, but somehow didn't set the mage's robes alight.

In what remained of the light, I looked around, and saw that Grey wasn't yet dead; indeed, those small, fierce eyes caught my own, imploring and commanding, and without further thought, I carried the dying cat to Orgrim. With the last of its failing strength, the cat bit the mage on his cheek and held that pose for several breaths before collapsing beside him. Numbly, I fell to my knees, at the end of my resources, awaiting my fate. What happened next wasn't at all what I'd expected.

Orgrim began twitching, as if experiencing a seizure, blood welling from his wounded cheek and clotting in his beard. The seizure increased in intensity, and a sense of foreboding rose in me, as if I were a mouse and I'd just noticed a hawk stooping; I'd felt that feeling once before, and knew what it foretold, but I had nowhere to flee, and could only await the outcome. As I did, a darkness gathered above the fallen mage, coalescing into a humanoid form. Another demon hovered there, a deeper black amidst the natural shadows of the room.

The demon solidified in the air above the body as the last of the oil began to sputter and its light to fade. It examined the room, turning at last to me. Its voice, deep and cold as the grave, filled the room. "For what you've done, I should slay you now, little man, and take all of value from your dying body, but it amuses me to leave you to live on, in ignorance. A gateway once opened remains always open, and some day I shall return to claim you; then, you shall learn of your race's creators, and curse them as your forefathers did for forsaking you." With a laugh that beat me to the floor, the demon faded from the gloom, leaving a foul stench and the chill of its presence. The fruitless pounding at the door continued in the background.

Though the threat they carried was clear, the words themselves were meaningless. But I had no time to ponder them, for Orgrim had regained consciousness and managed to prop himself up against the slab while my attention lay elsewhere. Frantic, I sought about me for anything I could use as a weapon, but there was nothing; the dagger from my belt was gone, as if it had never existed, and I'd never noticed its loss. I looked back to Orgrim, realizing that I must kill him with my bare hands and steeling myself to do so. But he read my intentions.

The mage winced and dabbed at the blood on his cheek, then probed the wound on his temple. "You'd be justified in killing me now, Morley, and if you insist on doing so, I won't stop you. But I beg that you forbear a moment." His voice had changed, and after a moment, I understood how. His arrogance was gone with the demon who'd been responsible for it, along with that instinctual power over others, and in its place lay deep sorrow. In the dwindling light from the last of the oil, I could see tears trickling down his cheeks.

I paused, irresolute. The sorcerer had earned his death, but with the demon gone, I understood that this man was no longer my nemesis, any more than I was the same giant who'd assaulted the chancellor of Volonor. It took me two tries before I could speak. I knew the answer, but it felt necessary to ask. "Tell me why I should spare you."

Some of the old energy returned to the mage's voice. "I didn't say you *should* spare me, only that you should not kill me before I've had time to explain. Will you grant me that boon?"

I nodded, and Orgrim sat upright. He gestured with his free hand, and a dim, sourceless light sprang up in the room. "I know that you've learned more than your contemporaries of the cataclysm that destroyed our old world, yet you lack crucial details. Let me explain, and when I'm done, I'll leave myself at your mercy."

Curiosity, combined with a certainty this was no longer the man who'd enslaved me, stayed my hand. "I'll grant you that time."

Orgrim nodded, then winced at his head wound. "I won't describe the source of the cataclysm that destroyed our old world, for only Raphael would understand me, and I'd not have that knowledge loosed again for other ears; once was enough. My part in this began, for the most part, once we knew our doom was upon us. The forces of destruction we'd unleashed gathered round, and it became clear they could be delayed, but not halted. I knew there might be a way to turn those forces against themselves and buy us the time we needed to flee; I was confident the ocean would prove a barrier against what we'd unleashed, but to buy time, I'd have to risk my—" he used a word I didn't recognize. He saw my incomprehension. "Something more important than my life. For if I failed, I knew I'd be turned against our people. But I had no choice other than to take that risk."

His voice enthralled me as it strengthened, and even though I knew he might be enchanting me, I couldn't bring myself to stop him. "I've heard the word"—I tried to pronounce what he'd said, and failed—"whatever you said, the thing you claimed to be risking. If my suspicions are right, it's something I came across in one of those scrolls I stole for you, but couldn't understand."

"It's knowledge our people forswore before the Exodus, and breaking the powerful magic that prevents you from understanding that word and others is beyond even me." Pride returned to his voice for a moment. "That's not strictly true. Perhaps I *could* overcome that spell, so our race could learn such things again, but I've meddled too much already and shall soon reap the consequences. Too many things hinge upon that spell, and I wouldn't tempt the attention of"—he used another unfamiliar word—"by interfering. And no, I can't explain that word either. Those explanations are not for this time."

I felt that same frustrating sense of being close to understanding, yet separated from that understanding by an impenetrable barrier that made my skull ache when I pushed against it. "Yet you claimed you were risking something more important than your life in what you did."

"More important, yes. But it occurred to me I might save both that thing and our race if I could preserve it in a vessel where it would be safe from corruption while I strove to turn the forces of destruction against themselves. So I transferred that something somewhere safe for the duration of my striving." His eyes sought out the motionless cat, tears welling in his eyes as he returned to his story.

"I protected myself, and my spell succeeded; I bought our race time to cross the ocean, time to visit the Elves, and the Dwarves, and the Goblins, and time to barter for safe passage. Then I returned to make right what I'd set wrong. But I was a fool, for my efforts had weakened me—or perhaps the thing I'd taken within me was always stronger and had just been biding its time for a chance to corrupt me. My first sign that I'd gone too far came when I destroyed my cat." The tears overflowed his eyes and ran down his cheeks, washing the blood from his wound into his beard. "Or tried to, for my old friend was more robust than I'd considered, even if not robust enough in the end to survive our final encounter. But he served his ultimate purpose today, and returned to me what he'd carried safely for so many long years." His voice shook, and he took several deep breaths until he'd composed himself.

"I have no memory of what happened for some time after that demon claimed my body. I know only that I was caught up in the destruction that overwhelmed those lands, and that it has been less than a year since I regained my physical form and came here. Would that I hadn't done so, for I brought great wrongness upon us. That's why I won't resist should you choose to kill me now."

Orgrim closed his eyes and mumbled a few words, then clutched the back of his head and spoke a commanding word. Light flared between his fingers, and when he opened his eyes, they were no longer so haggard and the blood had ceased trickling down his cheek. Hesitantly, he rose to his feet and stood, back braced against the wall.

I shook my head, trying to take it all in. "And you're telling me you did all this selflessly, for the sake of our people? How can you expect me to believe that given how you've behaved since returning to these lands?" Despite my angry words, I already half believed him.

"Having grappled with your own demon, you should understand how one's actions don't always follow one's desire. Though my intentions were good, I acted as much to prove to the world I could do it as I did to save our people. *That* I can never atone for."

Orgrim crossed to Raphael, and spoke in an unfamiliar language. A moment passed, then he nodded and brushed his hands across the other mage's eyes. Raphael staggered and fell into Orgrim's arms, then gathered his feet under him and moved to stand beside me.

"A demon left your body, or was cast out, while you were unconscious. It made threats we couldn't understand, and promised to return and take Morley with it. It also said something about us cursing—" He used that same unfamiliar word, but it was evident from his eyes that he understood it no better than I did.

"Is it so? Then my work isn't yet over." He swept us with his gaze, visibly bracing himself for what lay ahead. "That being the case, I beg your mercy for longer than I'd intended. I don't dispute your right to vengeance, but I have further damage to repair. I can tell you no more about what the demon said, for that understanding is denied to you. Let me say only that I long ago opened a door I must now close. I may fail in that task, in which case Raphael will know, and must take my place."

Raphael nodded. "I may need the Elves to help us. They'll demand a price I'm loath to pay, but it's a necessary price."

"And if you succeed?" I asked Orgrim.

"Then my fate is out of your hands. I'm not untainted by what I did, despite being absent from my body during those deeds. But that cannot absolve me of guilt. If you spare me, I shall go to my death, and perhaps I'll be shown mercy."

Raphael and I shook our heads in unison, baffled by what he was saying. I spoke first. "By whom? I still don't understand."

"And you never shall, so long as the great spell remains. All that remains is for you to decide whether I go to that judgment on my own, or whether you'll send me there yourself and take upon yourselves the burden of my final task."

Orgrim composed himself, and waited for us to pronounce his fate. Raphael put a hand on my shoulder, forestalling my reply. "The door must be closed, as you say, and I doubt that anyone but you can do it unaided. I grant you our mercy on the condition that you mean what you said, and swear to close that door." I gasped at his words, but his grip on my shoulder tightened.

"Convince yourself, then." Orgrim's voice was so compliant that I gazed at him, dumbfounded, noticing only then how Raphael had locked eyes with the other mage, and stood as if reading his thoughts. After a long silence, broken by the ringing of steel upon the door, Raphael relaxed, and pity replaced his wariness.

"I'm convinced. I wish you luck in the task you've set yourself, and mercy from those who can grant it should you succeed."

Orgrim bowed his head, and knelt to gather the cat's broken body in his arms. From his kneeling position, he looked up, and there was a terrible sadness in his eyes. "I can't ask you to forgive me for what I've done to you, Morley, but I can ask you to believe that I shall soon atone more fully than any vengeance you could inflict. Can you accept that?"

I'd already done so, but a small, unworthy part of me wasn't yet ready to release him. "Before you leave, could you restore what you once gave me? That would go a long way to helping me forgive."

Anger flared. "Haven't you had your fill of magic?" Then his expression eased, replaced by compassion. "To my knowledge, there's nothing wrong with you that magic can heal. There are spells of transformation that would accomplish what you ask, but they'd require me to remain here to renew the spells, and I cannot remain."

The brief hope I'd allowed to grow died, and left a gaping emptiness. "No, you can't." I looked to Raphael, who nodded approval. That was more comforting than it had any right to be.

Orgrim bowed his head, and began to fade from our sight. As I watched, fascinated, he vanished like frost in the sun. But just as I began to look away, something caught my eye. In the mage's arms, a shadow among shadows, the form of a cat watched me with all too human eyes. Then the cat winked and faded, leaving me floundering.

"Did you see that?" I whispered.

"See what?" Raphael replied, puzzled.

I shook my head. "Never mind."

Raphael shrugged, and crossed to the door. "Cease!" he called in a commanding voice. "It's over. I'll open the door."

The pounding on the door ceased, and when Raphael hauled the door open, Bram rushed through, sword drawn, followed by two burly men with axes and a fourth man with a heavy crossbow leveled. The four swept the room with their eyes, then turned to us.

"What happened? Something kept us from opening the door. We couldn't so much as carve a splinter from it." Bram's eyes were cautious, and the guards didn't relax for an instant.

I removed the bone ring from my finger and handed it to Raphael. The old mage held it out before him, palm upwards, so all could see, then curled his fingers over the ring while rotating his palm downwards again. When he opened his fingers again, his hand was empty, and the release of tension in the room was palpable. "We vanquished Orgrim. Once and for all. It's over."

Bram looked to me. "Truth?"

I felt drained by what had happened. "Truth, at least as much as I understand of it."

Bram shook his head. "It sounds like you two have a story to tell, but this isn't the place for it." He dismissed the guards, and we followed them out of the crypt and upwards, towards the light of day.

Chapter 17: Endings and beginnings

The consequences of far too many days of fear and exertion finally caught me. I had just enough energy left to describe what happened to Bram's small family, and to hear Raphael's commentary, before the world spun around me. Margrethe was first to notice, and guided me to my room, where I passed into oblivion for a time. In the end, I spent more than a week confined to my room, drained of all energy and emotion. Bram, Margrethe, and James left food, but I had little appetite.

It's not that I was sick; rather, it was the kind of malaise that drags you down and leaves you with no energy for anything save sleep. Also, I had much to ponder concerning who I'd been and who I'd become. On the one hand, it distressed me how important it had been to be seen as normal and accepted, and disappointed me at having so easily fooled myself into believing I could achieve that with no cost. On the other hand, every time Bram or Margrethe entered my room, I remembered what they had and what I could never have.

What finally brought me out of my self-pity was the battered old lute that Margrethe propped against my bed one day. It was out of tune, and the fingering was too wide, but it gave my mind and hands something to do beyond lashing myself with remorse or sinking into self-pity. That first day, I did nothing but tune the instrument and teach my fingers the new positions of the strings and the chords they offered. It was therapeutic, and within a few days, I was playing old songs and savoring memories of the first time I'd learned them, at my father's knee. Playing those songs was like a journey through the same past that had shaped me and given me strength to stand against whatever insults life offered.

At the end of that time, I emerged from my room and cast off the cloak of darkness that had covered me. Bram's household was all smiles, until I informed them of my plans. James shook his head, Margrethe looked sad, and Bram repeated his offer of employment and protection, but some time during my withdrawal, I'd decided. First and foremost, I'd honor my vow and return to my father, for perhaps the last time. I'm sure he understood what he meant to me, but sometimes you have to speak the words aloud to reassure yourself of that understanding. I'd spend time with him—days at least, and perhaps as much as a month—then I'd set out on my own journey from which I might never return.

Well, perhaps that's too melodramatic; if I succeeded at what I intended, just perhaps I would return to these lands some day.

My first stop would be the forest of the Elves, where my mischief had begun. I had serious doubts that I'd ever again see one of the fair folk given the note on which we'd parted, but I had new songs to write and sing about what I'd learned of our past, and I was certain they'd hear my words. Whatever turmoil I'd precipitated among the Elves, perhaps recounting the end of my tale would lay it to rest. Some day, there might even be a chance to restore a dialogue between their race and mine. If nothing else, their woodlands had been beautiful in their own strange way, and I could live there for a time while I gathered strength to fortify me for the rest of my plan.

The part of my plan that still scared me, despite my resolve, involved returning to Amelior. Despite my inward focus these past weeks, I'd not forgotten the hatred and bitterness of the Goblins and their resignation in the face of Amelior's war upon them. It would never be possible for the two sides to like each other, but I could hope I could at least convert Amelior from active warfare to a more defensive strategy. Bram expressed open skepticism, and made no effort to hide his disbelief, but he agreed to ask our King for a letter of introduction to Amelior's Court, granting me minor ambassadorial powers. If I could persuade Amelior to cease its assaults, however briefly, I'd have a chance to act as an apologist for mankind, to explain what had happened, and to try forging a better understanding between the two races. There was a solution, and if I could stop the warfare for long enough to seek it, perhaps we could find it together.

Opposing me, there was the weight of centuries of hatred and mis-understanding, and a deep, abiding mistrust, each side certain that the fault lay with their foe. For my part, I counted among my assets the knowledge of languages that Orgrim had gifted me with at the start of my travels, and that hadn't departed with my size—that and the certainty the Goblins would accept *me* sooner than they'd accept any other of my kind, for I was sufficiently like them now that they wouldn't fear me. Having been rejected by mankind, having been the object of fear and hatred for more years than I wanted to count, I knew better than any living man how they felt. There was no guarantee I could make them understand that, but success would perhaps be enough to atone for what I'd done.

It was a hope worth striving for.

Author's notes: Morley and being a dwarf

Part of the fun of writing fiction is the dialogue that arises with readers if you're lucky enough to have any. Since I've always enjoyed learning about an author's thought processes and how it shaped what they wrote, I've provided this postscript to describe what I was thinking while I wrote this book and some of my goals. The result is a kind of FAQ that I'll expand on request.

Morley is what we moderns would call an achondroplastic (https://en.wikipedia.org/wiki/Achondroplasia) dwarf (https://en.wikipedia.org/wiki/Dwarfism). I'm told the term of art these days is "Little Person", but I've chosen the older wording because it fits better with the pseudo-medieval tone of the story world. Morley's mostly blessed with freedom from pain and gross physical deformity. That allows him to function more or less normally, which is a prerequisite for him to lead an active life with the King's foresters, which is in turn an essential part of his background. There are many problems that can accompany achondroplasia as a medical condition, and I chose not to dwell on them; like all fictional heroes, Morley should represent the best of what we are, whatever our body size and shape, not the worst, and frankly, I already felt bad enough about what I was putting him through.

In making that choice, I recognize that I'm risking cultural appropriation: I'm not a dwarf, and thus have no experience of being one other than what I can achieve through empathy. If you, ungentle reader, are offended by my choices or feel that I didn't do an adequate job of dealing with the issues raised by living as a dwarf, I apologize: *mea maxima culpa*. Please communicate via my blog (see the last page of this manuscript for details) to inform me of what I did wrong, and how I can fix it. (A note to friends and colleagues: Please don't defend me against any criticisms raised by this story: typically, this degenerates rapidly into unproductive name-calling and overly defensive behavior. In particular, please don't try to defend me against legitimate complaints that come from people who know better than we do. My intentions were good, but that doesn't justify getting important details wrong.)

On one level, I chose to make Morley a dwarf because I wanted to remind readers of the prejudices we moderns try not to acknowledge, and because I wanted a character who would be an outsider and have to deal with the consequences of being different. To a pseudo-medieval culture such as that in the story, particularly one with many superstitions still haunting them after a disastrous experience during the vanished age of magic, the diminutive stature and "subtly wrong" facial and body appearance of a dwarf would be truly scary and disturbing. I'd like to think such biases are gone from modern life, but a little Googling suggests it would be naïve to make any such claim. It's also true that I wanted to provide a plausible reason for Morley to sympathize with the Goblins, and a literary parallel that I hope was clear without being too blunt.

As a survival mechanism, Morley has been in a severe state of denial about many things for most of his life: he's had a nasty past, and it's left scars that still bedevil him. This is a large part of why so many things that seem obvious to the reader appear obscure to him. There are definitely better coping mechanisms than denial, some of which he'll learn by the end of *Jester*. Others will await discovery in a future book. During the course of creating this story, I grew to like Morley a lot, and to admire his courage, and I hope to have him star in a future book when I have time to write it.

The world of the story

The world of *Jester* is what might be described as "high medieval" or perhaps even "early Renaissance", but let's be clear about one thing: it's a pastiche of many different and potentially incompatible things that I chose for the sake of creating a flavorful stew rather than an attempt at historical verisimilitude. As is revealed in the novel, and as is revealed somewhat more cryptically in the prequel, *Chords* (http://geoff-hart. com/fiction/novels/chords/index.htm), human civilization was quite advanced before the magical catastrophe that led to the Exodus and arrival of humans in the new world—at least as advanced as early European Renaissance civilization, and more advanced in some ways because of the possibilities opened up by the use of magic. This explains the relatively sophisticated language and level of education of most urbanites, and why there are actually such things as public libraries (and other things such as public schools or their equivalent that don't intersect the story arc). It also explains some of the modern-ish gender politics in the story, not that we really need an excuse in a fantasy world.

Footnote on gender politics in the world of *Jester*: Yes, this is a male-focused society and told from an almost exclusively male perspective. This is because I explicitly set out to critique that perspective in *Chords*, the prequel to *Jester*. There, you'll learn much more about Margrethe's history and the untold part of the traditional male-centric story. Let's be clear that her much richer story in *Chords* is probably far more historically accurate than the narrower perspective of *Jester*.

Many old technologies were preserved at high levels after the Exodus, particularly those that would have helped the early colonists survive. These include things such as weapons manufacture, the construction of extremely strong fortifications such as the fortress of Volonor, and basic Renaissance-level medicine and medical skills. Other technologies may have been preserved, but were not deemed sufficiently important for survival to be actively practiced; this is why bound books are only now, more than two centuries after the Exodus, beginning to replace scrolls.

The complete absence of anything resembling religion from the book's human society is not an accident. Morley's reading of the scrolls in the library provides some hints, but his frustrating dialogues with the Elves and Goblins should be all you need to infer the answer. If you're saying to yourself "this is one whopping great anomaly", and that it's unreasonable for such a huge level of mystical censorship of human thought to exist, you're not wrong. Remember, this is fantasy, not alternate history, and that "the absence of evidence is not evidence of absence". That leaves only one possible explanation, and when you eliminate the impossible, the explanation that remains should be clear, even if the details aren't. I'll resolve the mystery in a planned third book set in this world.

There are many deliberate anomalies, such as why detailed accounts of certain aspects of the Exodus were preserved when all such records were described as having been destroyed, and how a ragtag band of refugees in overcrowded boats built a colossal fortress such as Volonor. Then there's the question about the existence of (at least two!) wizards when all such were said to have been destroyed before the Exodus. The answer is the same in each case: the preserved stories of the Exodus are severely flawed, and the reality must have been something very different indeed. It was, and the planned third book will explain some of these mysteries.

Although I undoubtedly had thoughts of the conflict between Western (European) culture and Islam on my mind when I began describing and characterizing the Goblins, I want to make it perfectly clear that there is no allegorical intention here. The Goblins are ***NOT*** standing in for Muslims. Similarly, although the invasion of a new continent by people who more closely resemble Europeans than any other culture, who traveled from the east to a western continent, and who largely destroyed the native cultures is a strong part of my cultural consciousness, this too is not a deliberately allegorical comment. I am specifically ***NOT*** equating the Elves or Goblins with native Americans. My explicit goal for including both races in this story was to make it clear that colonizers rarely make an effort to understand the native peoples they displace, nor any effort to find peaceful ways to coexist. Furthermore, I wanted to make it clear that although it's convenient to demonize cultures such as the Goblins, they deserve more understanding than they receive in most stories. *That* allegory is one that I will confess to perpetrating, and if you want to apply it to the treatment of Muslims and native Americans by European-derived cultures, that would be a limiting but reasonable interpretation.

A word on language

Language choice is always an issue when you're writing something ostensibly "medieval" or set in a foreign culture. Since linguistic games weren't my goal, I didn't adopt the Tolkein approach and try to create my own languages or even a subset thereof. Neither did I want to painfully salt the book with *thee*s and *thou*s or made-up words that sounded foreign but were really pulled out of (to be polite) my hat. Instead, I opted for a somewhat stilted and ornate style that would suggest formality rather than modern informality, and evocative words such as Amelior to suggest a concept (amelioration, because its founders saw it as an improvement over the society they were leaving) rather than as clumsy symbols.

Speaking of clumsy symbols, Ankur isn't one of them: I didn't choose that name as a clumsy symbol for "anchor", an interpretation that could be justified by reading *Chords* in a certain way. If memory serves, I chose it long ago (how long I won't reveal) because I was reading about Turkey, and liked the Turkish city name Ankara. Ankur is here not because of any resemblance to Turkish culture, past or present, but rather because of the city's long history and importance as a crossroads. That made the name seem appropriate.

You may have noted that with the exception of those times Morley spends with the Elves and Goblins, certain words are missing from his vocabulary, and for the most part, only appear during conversations with these races. That's not an inconsistency; that's the magical gift of tongues bestowed upon him by Orgrim. For historical reasons that you should be able to infer, Orgrim is also the only human who is able to use these words, even if nobody else can understand him.

Come join me online at <http://icanhascoffee.livejournal.com/4715. html> to provide your comments and discuss the book.

About Geoff

Startled by an aggressive dictionary during the 9ᵗʰ month of her pregnancy, Geoff's mother was shortly delivered of a child who showed a precocious antipathy towards words. Over time, he transformed this antipathy into a more functional, if equally passive-aggressive, career as an editor. After more than 30 years of editing, the verbal flame still burns as brightly, leading to an errant, semi-evangelical career ranting against the evils of words from pulpits at any editing or technical writing conference that will have him, tirelessly seeking new recruits for his cause. In his spare time, he roams the globe, entertaining and enlightening locals with his creative and unrestrained interpretations of their linguistic conventions. He also commits occasional fictions.

If you liked this book

Visit Geoff online at http://www.geoff-hart.com
His non-fiction books can be found here: http://geoff-hart.com/books/index.htm
His fiction can be found here: http://geoff-hart.com/fiction/index.htm